Trip of A Deathtime

Sol Gatos

Dedicated to Reclamation
Of the
Sacred Mind

Chapter 1

Thirty days in a person's life passes by like hours. That is, until you find out you only have thirty days to live. Then, these valued days will be like a blink. All the loose ends to tie up and goodbyes to say. All the knowledge to pass down and a life to recollect. All of this while fighting for the last vestiges of an existence.

Time would be anything but dragging.

Some humans don't place the value on time that it aptly deserves. Wasting or killing time is a favorite pastime of the homo sapiens. Most never realize just how fragile the time we are given truly is. Each person has the choice to do with their gift as they please. Most are complacent while a few are adamant. Those who see the truth are the productive. Those who don't see can try again in the next life.

Sue tried to convince her husband to go to the doctor for a long time, but he was stubborn. She could see, for more than a year, his health was failing. He had one excuse after the other for not going. She reassured him, repeatedly, that he could trust their physician: Dr. Benjamin had been their doctor for over twenty years. Try as she might, her husband simply refused.

Everything changed when Jack had a couple episodes of blacking out. Twice in one week he lost consciousness. Once was when he was brushing his teeth, the other when he was cooking dinner. It wasn't like him to pass out, especially doing routine acts without exertion. He knew, for quite a while, this day would come; he just wasn't sure when. Eventually his health got so poor he was forced to go to the doctor.

When he finally agreed to see Dr. Benjamin, Sue knew he was in bad shape. In their long years together, she only saw him go to the doctor when he was bleeding profusely or had a compound fracture.

When the doctor told Jack, he had an advanced stage of cancer, the patient laughed out loud. The physician looked puzzled and asked the man if he understood what he said. He had to shout to be heard over the madness. In his thirty-three years of practice, he'd never seen anyone react like this when they were told they had terminal cancer. He literally didn't know what to think.

Jack saw the bewilderment in the older man's face. He stopped with his maniacal laugh and regained his composure. "Yeah, Doc, I understood you," he calmly said. "I'm sorry, please don't mistake my laughter as madness. I'm not insane. My laughter has nothing to do with comedy. I wasn't surprised by your words. I've known for a while I was going to die. I could feel the invader taking over my flesh pod. I knew it was a matter of time. I'm relieved to hear your diagnosis."

The doctor looked carefully at his patient. He only met the man once a year; it was the extent of their relationship. He realized, during those office visits, that Jack was a different kind of person. He remembered some of the things the man said over the years as being odd, but profoundly true. The doctor realized Jack saw things the way they were. Not only did the patient see things, he voiced his opinion too. While many of Doctor Benjamins patients were afraid to be honest with him, Jack was the opposite.

"Why didn't you come in earlier?" the doctor asked. "We may have been able to save you. Now you only have, at most, thirty days to live. There's no chance of saving you. You say you're not insane, but these aren't actions of a rational man. Think about your family and your friends; how are they going to feel about this? Death hits all families hard; yours' will be no exception."

There was irritation in the doctor's voice. He could have saved this patient. These were the worst clients for him. When he cared more about a life than the person, it was very frustrating. The thoughts would weigh heavy on him for many years after. He graduated from medical school at the top of his class. He'd gone into family practice because he wanted to help people. He abandoned the riches of a specialist for a humble life filled with empathy. His patients truly mattered to him. If they didn't do their part, he felt betrayed.

"It's okay Doc. I've been ready for death since I was born. It isn't something that gives me fear. I knew it was coming since an early age. I'm happy I made it to fifty-eight years old. I never thought I'd make it to this age, when I was young. I've had a great life and did everything I wanted to do. Adventure was always there for me; as it will be for the next thirty days."

"My job is to help people, Jack. If you don't do your part, it's hard for me to do mine. I care about my patients and want to make them better. Now, along with your wife and kids, I will also have to live with your decision."

"Well Doctor Benjamin, I apologize if I created any heartache for you. It certainly was not my intention. You've been our family's doctor for over twenty years. We first came to you with aches and pains and you gave us a prescription for medical marijuana. You also told me about the inversion table to help with my back pain. I thank you for that and everything you've always done. You've truly been a trusted professional in a field that normally lacks confidence from people like me. I refused your tests, every year, because I have a theory about it all. If I feel fine, get tests and then find out something is wrong with me, it's going to create a domino effect."

Jack flicked a finger to emphasize each of his points: "First, I will be stressed out about my malady which will make it worse. Then, I will spend all my money to heal myself. I will be forced to sell my house just to get better. Since the insurance I pay dearly for doesn't cover but a fraction of my bills, I will forever be in debt, without a home. All this so I can live an extra ten years or maybe twenty. Then, I can die in a retirement home where everyone forgets about you. A place you spend your last days where nobody has any respect for you. No thanks, I chose not to have the tests because if I didn't know, I wouldn't worry about it and would probably get better. If I did know, my family would have been fucked." All of Jack's fingers on one hand were sticking straight up in a visual fortitude of his words. He looked at the older man with confidence and strength the doctor seldom saw in people.

"Nobody ever said it like that to me," Doctor Benjamin said. "But you said you knew you were sick. I don't understand why you didn't come in."

"Because I didn't want to leave my wife homeless and poor. We just paid off our house three years ago and have saved up a good little amount for retirement. It's not a lot, but that, with social security, would've gotten us through our elder years. Now, that money will get

Sue through her golden era. I would rather have her live alone, comfortably in our home, than both of us struggling for the rest of our lives. My death will be hard on her, no doubt about that. Living in a fight with cancer and having her take care of me, without any guarantees of recovery, would be harder. It's not something I would do to my wife."

"That's honorable, I suppose. I'm not so sure she'll feel the same, however. There are things you could've done. Your insurance is good; but you're right. I've always been honest with you Jack, I'm going to continue to be now. They would have sucked every bit of money from you. When your cancer is advanced, it gets expensive. If you got tested all along, we could have fixed you right up and your insurance would have paid for it all."

Jack lied to get the doctor off his back. He'd known his pod was failing for a very long time. The last time he was at this office, for his yearly medical marijuana prescription, he already knew he was sick. "Yeah Doc, I know. I only realized I was sick in the last six months. By then, I knew it was well advanced. I was just going through some hard times after my sister died. Things really wore on me for the last year. Our lives were just starting to return to normal. When I thought things would be okay, this happens."

"I would like to go over these test results with you. There is much to discuss. Many plans are going to have to be made. Would you like for me to talk to Sue?" The doctor rattled his words as if on auto-pilot. He was more in shock than his patient.

"No Doctor Benjamin, I'll tell her. It's my responsibility. We've been married a long time. I know this is going to crush her. As for the test results, there's no need. They don't concern me in the least. I'm going to die either way. Just more time I could spend with my family." Jack stood and made his way toward the door. He'd never been claustrophobic, but now, the walls seemed to be closing in on him.

"You'll have a lot to take care of in a short time. My secretary will give you information on hospice. There is equipment you'll need. I'll want to see you every three days at first and later, every day. I'll come to your house if you can't leave. I'll give you some prescriptions of pain killers. It's all I can do at this stage. I'll give you drugs as strong as you like."

"Well Doc, I'm surprised you're trying to give me drugs. You were always so against them. It's one of the reasons I came to you. You're not a drug dealer like so many other doctors. You know I was

4

never one to take drugs of this nature. I stick with the marijuana. Your words make it sound like I'm going to be bedridden, very soon, and in a lot of pain."

"Yeah Jack, you are going to be bedridden and in a lot of pain. You have terminal cancer which has spread to every major organ in your body. You can get the prescription filled and have them if you need them. I only prescribe these sorts of drugs to people who really need them."

"I would prefer to wait. If I'm going to be seeing you every couple of days, it will be no problem to get some drugs from you. In the meantime, I'd rather go out with a clear head; with my brain working at full capacity. Opiates just cloud the experience. They make me feel terrible."

The doctor looked at Jack with a sense of pride. It wasn't something he often felt for his patients. This was the first terminally ill patient he ever treated who refused drugs.

"You are a different individual, Jack. I can give you some mild samples if you'd like."

"You doctors are all the same," Jack said jovially. "Always trying to get the patients hooked on your drugs. No thanks." His tone again became serious, "Thanks again Doc. I apologize for the stress I've caused you. I understand your position and respect you for it. Please, respect my position, too. It's my life, after all." Jack reached for the doorknob as the doctor closed the distance. Their hands met in the middle and the embrace was firm and long-standing.

Both men experienced a moment of unity with the other during the brief handshake. The healer could feel the disease riddling the other man's body. Above that feeling, he could sense a calmness in the man.

Jack could feel the honesty and sincerity in the older man. Above all else, he could sense strong certainty in his family doctor.

Both men held a strong respect for the other. The thought occurred to both: they could have been friends under other circumstances. Unfortunately, it was only a thought.

When Jack left the exam room, the doctor walked him to the counter. The desk ladies had sincere empathy in their faces as they fumbled to get the hospice information together. Another patient came in and, to Jack's relief, distracted the doctor. He needed to be alone and collect his thoughts.

This was a lot to comprehend in a short time. Many things were racing through his mind. The office was full of energy. Everyone seemed to be watching him to see his reaction to the news. Like the exam room, these walls were beginning to close in, making it hard to breath. He wanted to get away from it. All these distractions were frustrating him, clouding his mind even more.

His main concern was how he was going to tell his wife. He wasn't worried about his life or death, or his feelings. He was worried about how his wife would handle this news. Their partnership was ending; she would be running their small ranch without him. At the moment, there was nothing else on his mind.

A clap on his shoulder broke him from his thoughts. Doctor Benjamin was there as the receptionist appeared with book and pen in hand. He told her which days he wanted to see the patient and Jack conferred the times. The other office lady appeared from the back with a manila envelope overflowing with pamphlets and papers. Jack normally liked packages like this, but suspected he wasn't going to feel the same about this one.

As she handed it to him, Doctor Benjamin said, "Let me go through some of this stuff with you Jack. This information might come in handy in the next few weeks. I really feel it would be in your best interest to go over your test results, too. Otherwise, you'll be blind to what is happening to you."

"I'll go over it at home with Sue. See what she says about it all. In the meantime, I've got to get going. Time's a ticking." Jack ended with a crazy laugh. The entire office, including the patients waiting, looked to the man who seemed out of his mind. Every one of them could see death lurking around Jack's being.

Then, just like that, he was normal again. The laughter was replaced by his usual calm. The two men shook hands, once again, while the physician looked quizzically at his patient. After telling him he had cancer, Jack wanted no other details. It seemed like he wanted to get away from it all. He didn't even care to wait around and talk about pain therapy or hospice. There was something very odd about his patient's behavior. Troubling would be the way the doctor described it. He felt obligated to try and engage his patient further.

Doctor Benjamin opened his mouth to ask Jack back into his office. At the same moment, the patient turned abruptly, opened the side office door, and swiftly made his way out the office. Everybody in the room stared blankly as the door silently shut behind him.

The moment he got outside, Jack took a deep breath. It felt good to be away from all the madness going on inside the doctor's office. He needed to gather his thoughts. He would only be able to do that away from other humans. Jack was always more comfortable amongst nature than with people. He went straight to his car and threw the papers in the back seat. He closed the door and looked around for his next action.

Jack spotted a smoke shop across the street and headed in its direction. His first thought was to get away from the front of this office building. He quit smoking cigars a few years before, but somehow, one sounded good right now. He figured what the hell, it wasn't going to kill him. He chuckled at his own joke as he walked across the street to the strip-mall.

The selection for cigars was extensive. He was happy they had one of his favorite brands of Rare Corojo. It would help take his mind off his miseries before getting back to reality.

Jack was a strange guy. For his own reasons, he told the store employee about his cancer diagnosis. The heavily tattooed girl behind the counter was full of piercings. She looked at the customer and said nothing for a moment. She chewed her gum and looked at Jack with no care in her gaze. As she gave back his coins, she said plainly, "then maybe you shouldn't smoke." Jack took his change and said nothing more as he made his exit.

He lit the stogie outside the store with some matches the cashier gave him. He walked around the block for some time smoking his prize. There seemed to be many people out and about for a Tuesday. The office was on the corner of a busy street, but the cross street was a residential neighborhood. The amount of people in this area today surprised Jack. Everything seemed surreal to him. It felt like, since leaving the doctor's office, he was part of a movie.

As he walked along, he became slightly light-headed from the tobacco. It was a feeling he liked from this plant. It put his mind in a different frame. It helped him see things clearer and to come up with good solutions. He'd always been one to alter his brain for spiritual gain. Anything that created sensation was welcomed in his world.

Halfway through the cigar, Jack became dizzy and thirsty. He headed to a nearby convenience store and got the largest water possible. He was sweating and green when he paid for the water. Again, he felt compelled to tell the girl behind the counter his story. This girl, also, was tattooed and pierced, as was Jack. She was about the same age as the other cashier, but her reaction was much different. She looked intently at the customer with familiarity in her gaze.

"I know," she said as she pushed his money back. "The water is on the house. Go home Jack. Be with your family. Be safe."

Jack looked at the woman with puzzlement. She didn't look familiar to him, but she knew his name. He began to speak but the younger woman turned and walked into the back room. Her long black hair seemed to wisp with an unseen wind as she walked. The smell of roses permeated Jack's senses. He shrugged his shoulders and left. Strange things always happened to him. It was part of his daily ritual. Some days, like this one, were filled with bizarre occurrences. He figured the numbers must have lined up today and were creating mayhem.

On this day, however, not only did the numbers align; the planets did as well.

His cigar was strategically waiting for him on top of the ice machine, sitting outside the door. It was still burning slightly, so he took a monstrous puff off it. A huge cloud of smoke expelled from his lungs. He fumbled with the water bottle as a large crow flew threw his exhalation. It looked like the bird materialized out of the smoke. Its loud cawing rippled through Jack's thoughts.

The water refreshed his being. He wandered around back to finish his cigar and drink. His head was spinning from the tobacco. He leaned against the building for support but refused to quit puffing the Corojo. The alleyway was void of people or cars. He finally found his small spot away from the rest of the world.

He was thinking about all the things he should be doing instead of being here. He knew he had limited time, but smoking this cigar was time well spent. As a matter of fact, there was nothing Jack would rather be doing now then enjoying this smoke.

The crow was perched on top of a brick wall, just fifteen feet away. Its loud cawing was incessant. The two made a bond as their eyes connected.

Jack's mind was beginning to clear from the dizziness as he spoke with his new friend. The two shared a mutual language of clicks and caws with a mellifluous sound. Jack had always related to crows. Since he was young, he had befriended many of these feathered creatures. Meeting this one, at this moment, seemed like destiny for the both.

Jack was looking to the bird when a group of four big guys came around the corner. They all looked like they were trying to be tough guys. He hoped they would just pass on by but knew it wouldn't be the case. His friend, the crow, also read the coming shit-storm and elevated his perch to the top of a telephone pole. His being the best view of what was about to go down.

The thugs were of mixed ethnicity and wore similar clothes. Two of them had tattoos on their faces while they all had them on their neck and hands. They all wore long sleeves. The bills of their brown hats were flipped up. Jack presumed they were all in their early twenties. With the way they carried themselves, they all seemed comfortable bullying people.

He'd met guys like this his whole life. In the last years, with social media, they were even worse and more plentiful. Jack could read these guys like a bad B-movie. They wore long sleeves because they only had tattoos on their visible spots. They also had small tattoos only. Jack had a full body suit. He'd been involved in tattooing in some form for over forty years. He read the gang like a children's book. These guys were pussies. They couldn't take the pain, so they got only visible, miniscule tattoos. They thought the markings would make them cool, but it was the opposite. They were only tough when they were with their buddies. These were the kind of guys Jack laughed at, not feared.

The first one approached Jack with a side to side, ape-like walk. He said in his bad-ass street talk, "You got any change, man?" His voice was meant to be dominant sounding. It made Jack snicker to himself.

The other guys gathered around their victim in dog-pack formation. They had Jack cornered with his back against the bricks. These guys didn't scare him in the least. He was ready to say some smart-ass shit, as usual, but held back. He didn't need any more problems today. He really didn't care much about anything, now, except getting home and telling his wife the news.

He'd been analyzing the situation since it began. These guys had him surrounded and were feeling brave, because of their number. Jack already had his angle planned. He was going to punch the head dick-weed in the solar plexus, step beyond him and fight the rest if need be. In his many years, he knew when the head guy was done, most likely the others would be too. These guys had the mentality of wild animals. It's why they robbed people instead of working. Their tattoos and clothes made them think they were tough until they got home and looked in the mirror: they and their families knew the truth. Without their trendy armor and buddies, they were weenies.

Jack reached into his pocket with lightning speed. He thought of himself as a gunslinger and gave a slight chuckle. His action made the perps jump back about a foot. Now, there was no doubt in his mind about the courage of these thugs. As he pulled out his wallet with the same speed, he saw fear in the leader's face. Jack didn't once take his eyes off this kid. He opened his wallet and took two hundred dollar bills out. He then, calmly, handed them to the head bully.

"I'm dying of cancer. I just found out," Jack said without emotion. "I don't need this money and I sure don't need problems with you guys. You can even have my credit cards if you want. I'm cancelling them as soon as I get home, either way."

"What else you got, cancer boy?" barked the aggressor. The lack of confidence didn't go unnoticed by Jack. He was never one to be bullied and wasn't going to begin now. He wasn't one to fight but didn't back down when it was necessary. The training he'd gone through in the Navy wouldn't let him back down even if he wanted to.

"I've got some swollen balls you can suck," Jack said as he burst into his crazy laughter. He folded his wallet with the money inside and slipped it back into his pocket. His next move was going to take out this punk. Through his burst of laughter, he got out the words, "now you're not going to get shit, bitch-boy."

The guy to the left of Jack made a slow, clumsy movement of attack. Jack was ready and ducked aside just as the man's fist flew by and hit his buddy square in the jaw. The blow rocked the big man and made him sway back. As Jack was standing back upright, he saw a gun in the belt of the man who'd just been struck. He'd always been fast and now was no exception. What did he have to lose, he thought. The notion brought that crazy ass laugh that was becoming oh so common.

Jack's adrenaline was rushing like crazy. Time seemed to slow down to a fraction of reality. He could clearly see every move the others made. He even had time to think he was like a fly, buzzing around while everything else was slow.

The man's gun became exposed upon the impact of his buddy's fist. Jack could clearly see that it was a Smith and Wesson 9mm. A gun Jack was very familiar with. He reached for it and had it in his lightning grip. He ducked to the side of the offended man, pushing him with his shoulder. A spin move to the other side and the victim was now the aggressor. Jack had the drop on the four low-life's in front of him. He chambered a bullet, clicked off the safety, and had both hands firmly on the gun.

The look on the faces of the thugs was the funniest thing Jack had ever seen. They were shocked, pissed, and scared all at the same time. The wall they formerly pinned their victim against was now reversed. "I got the drop on you, assholes. On your knees." Jack's laughter did not diminish. If anything, it got crazier.

To his surprise, the others reached for their guns. It was too late and a useless act. By the time the first had his gun in hand, he was shot dead in the middle of the chest. His long red hair seemed to fan out against the wall as his body slammed into it. His white shirt was instantly soaked in red.

The second dropped his pistol just before Jack's bullet hit him in the forehead. He tried to play gunslinger and failed. His brains splattered on the wall behind him as his corpse crumbled to the pavement.

The smell of blood and gunpowder hung heavy in the air. Jack could barely hear. It felt like he was in a warzone. His ears were just solid ringing. He felt more alive than he had in a very long time.

The leader came closest with his gun getting aimed at Jack. If that's what you want to call holding a gun on its side with your arm outstretched. Jack almost felt pity for the youngster: his hand was shaking so bad he'd never hit his target. He hadn't even chambered a bullet as Jack shot him in his throat.

The other brute decided to go for it and picked up the gun his friend dropped. Since Jack had his gun, it was the criminals only option. It was a bad decision on his part. Jack shot him right between his eyes. His brains mixed with those of his buddy on the wall behind them. All four fell in a crumpled pile of human waste.

The leader was taking his last gurgling breaths as Jack surveyed the scene. He saw his cigar laying a few feet away. Miraculously, no blood was on it. He puffed it a couple times and got smoke. Three of the robbers were obviously dead. The leader was holding on to a life that was over. Jack stepped to the dying man and leaned closer. "A little advice," he said, "next lifetime, learn to shoot if you're going to rob people with guns."

"Fuck you," the dying man mouthed through a flow of blood. His close-cropped hair was well groomed. It looked to Jack like he may have gone to the barber on his way to the robbery.

"No thanks, you already tried that once," Jack said. He rolled the lit part of his cigar in the other man's bullet wound, coating it in its sticky redness. The sizzling sound was accompanied by the smell of burning blood and a moan from the thug. The dying man was looking on with horror as his killer took a long drag off that cigar. The smoke billowed around him, looking like he had wings. He realized they fucked with the wrong dude.

They tried to rob death and death killed them.

Jack's mind worked smoothly after what just happened. It seemed like it was all happening in a movie. Everything was scripted, and he just had to go along with it. He wiped his prints off the gun and put it in the hand of the guy he'd taken it from. He used the other guys hand and pulled off one quick round into the ringleader, three feet away, ending the fourth life of the day.

Jack dropped the perp's hand, turned and walked away. The cigar never left his lips; he took a big puff and faded into the alleyway. His heart was beating faster than ever in his life as he got as far away as possible. Less than fifty feet, he found another alley, and then another. After the fourth or fifth one, the sound of sirens became deafening.

He wasn't worried at all. It had all been self-defense. He didn't even have a gun on him. If the store had cameras, they would prove it. If there were no cameras, all the better. He didn't need this hassle in the last days of his life. There was plenty of other stuff to take care of.

His adrenaline was rushing as he got to his car. The sirens became piercing wails, but it was further away. He was surprised; after the amount of people earlier, he hadn't seen anyone in the alleyways or the parking lot. If he hadn't seen anybody, then nobody saw him.

He put out the last stub of cigar on the curb and threw it in the bushes. He wiped his mouth and hands with a disinfecting hand wipe from the glove box. These went into a garbage conveniently located next to his car.

Jack calmly got in his car, checked himself in the mirror and left the parking lot. He went in the opposite direction of the shooting. The police were surely putting up roadblocks already. He didn't care. He just wanted to get home.

The situation that just happened rattled him. He just killed not only one, but four humans. This, just after finding out he was going to die himself. The entire day was shaking his being. This was already the weirdest day of his life and it was barely noon.

He was ready for some adventure, though. If the next month was going to be like this, he would need death just to rest. He only had thirty days and he wanted them to be awesome.

Unfortunately, home today wasn't going to be his sanctuary. There was going to be no rest on this day nor adventure. He was going to have to tell his wife and it wasn't going to be easy. This thought consumed his mind as he drove onto the main avenue and faded in with the rest of the cars.

He didn't even pay any mind to all the cops going the other way. All he could think about was telling his wife and family how he let them down.

Chapter 2

The drive home was the hardest thing Jack ever did. The paperwork from the doctor, in the back seat, was lurking like a heavy shadow. He tried to forget about hospice and pain, for now. These were things he could deal with when the time came. His thoughts, now, were with Sue and their clan. He was a pillar to their family: The Patriarch of three grown children and six grandchildren: married for thirty years.

Things hadn't always been so good for the family. As with all families, there were trials and tribulations that tested the strength of each member.

Twenty-five years before, their eldest son was abducted. He was murdered by a serial killer. Tommy was Jack's son from his first marriage. Jack raised his son after his wife was killed in an auto accident, when the child was five years old. The boy was fifteen when he vanished. His body wasn't found for eight years after his disappearance. It devastated the family, especially Jack. He and his son were very close. They'd gone through so much together and always remained a team. Jack's high hopes, for the kid who excelled at everything, were ripped away by a lunatic.

Sue and Jack had been married five years when it happened. They were friends for a few years before. Sue had two children from her previous marriage. Her husband committed suicide around the same time Jack's wife died. The devastation on the three children was evident. Each of them lost a parent in horrible situations. It was one of many bonds the family would share.

The couple met by chance at a baseball game. Their seats were next to each other. Both adults were with their children. It's what single parents do. The friendship they formed that day between the two of them and their children would last the rest of their lives.

The next two years were spent enjoying friendship from a family in the same situation. At first, Jack and Sue would see each other about once a month. Both were still in a grieving process of their own. The other family were the only people who understood what they were going through. Their friendship grew out of respect, understanding, and empathy.

The adults began to feel more than friendship. Their love grew naturally but they had to keep it under control. Neither wanted to feel the self-imposed guilt of cheating on their dead spouse: no matter how silly that would seem later.

The visits became more frequent until the five were spending almost every weekend together. Camping was a popular choice. Neither family were well off. They, like most others, were the working class of America. True slaves in the land of the free. Their camping trips took them all over California. They explored all twenty-eight micro-climates of their awesome home state. Their friendship grew stronger.

After they'd been friends for two years, Jack got shipped out to sea for six months. About a month before, the two decided it would be best for Tommy to stay with Sue. He was ten years old and got along great with Ronnie and Becky. Otherwise, the boy would be sent to live with his grandparents, in Idaho. The decision was easy for Jack with full input from Tommy. The boy wanted to stay with his adopted family; his true friends.

Sue wrote to Jack every day while he was out at sea. He, in turn, wrote back with the same intensity. He made drawings and paintings for the woman, and kids, he was falling in love with. While floating, a small battle erupted with an Arab country. The event was bombarded in the news. The entire time, Sue couldn't take her eyes off the television. She was so worried about Jack, she couldn't even eat.

When the skirmish ended after three days, the news said Jack's ship was untouched. Sue felt relief like no other time in her life. It was then she realized she'd fallen in love with a sailor.

Marriage happened thirty days after Jack returned home. It was the same day he got out of the Navy. Sue quit her job at the bank one week before. The married couple opened a tattoo shop that would afford them enough money to build their current house in the mountains. It would be the beginning of their creative lives together.

Their child together was born after a couple of years. Jack Junior was going to be their only baby added to this family. Jack's son and Sue's oldest were the same age. Sue's daughter was two years younger. The family was getting along nicely. The business was opened when tattooing just became popular. Jack, being former military, saw the advantage of opening next to a Navy base. It was a decision that put the family in financial security for the rest of their lives.

When Jack's son, Tommy, came up missing, they'd been married five years. It devastated the lives of their happy family. It was the hardest thing any of them ever went through. Losing a loved one is terrible; having one missing is the worst.

The police accused the parents of wrongdoing. They were sure there was abuse, forcing the child to flee for safety. The children went through hours of interrogation. The cops were sure something was amiss in the house. They could just look at the parents and tell they were no good. They both were heavily tattooed like a lot of the criminals they encountered. This kind of behavior by the cops took days off the initial investigation. By the time they realized Tommy wasn't from a broken home, the trail was cold.

Jack and Sue held the clan together for the next years. They realized being strong and getting through this, as a couple, would also help their children through it. As usually is the case in tragedy, the children helped the adults just as much as they received help. The family, together, kept harmony amongst themselves. When one would lose strength and break down, another would be there to lend support.

With this tragedy, the family bonded with the unity of catastrophe. Whenever there is mayhem, the family who remains together will realize this bond, which will last forever.

It was eight years later when the authorities found Tommy's body. He was buried next to an isolated lake along with the remains of eleven other boys. There were many clues, but the police were never able to pinpoint the perpetrator. "Another serial killer gets away with it!" the headlines said. They called for the resignation of the Sheriff and his entire crew. In the long run, politics and greed reigned supreme, like always. Nothing ever came from any of the murders except for some episodes on 'whodunit' television a few years later.

After they put Tommy to rest, the family truly began to heal their wounds. The eight years before was in limbo. There was really no way to go forward until you could put the past to rest. The kids all excelled at school and their activities; while the parents did well, creating their art. They did their best to carry on with life but there was always something different in their ways. None of them felt as if they fit in with others, only their family. The rest of their lives would be filled with distrust for people.

They'd gone through terrible things: it gave them an inner strength most would never know.

Just after Little Jack's graduation from high school, tragedy struck the family, once again. It had been seven years of happy times and rebirth for the clan. The tranquility was shattered during the course of a year.

A torrent of death struck Jack and Sue's family. Both sets of parents and six siblings between the families passed. It was a tough time for the family dealing with the heartache of death and, in a few cases, getting the affairs of the deceased in order. Jack and Sue kept the family together, once again. Unity and love were strong in this family besieged by tragedy. Their spirituality of the Wisdom was inspiring.

The family was acclimated to death, but this new wave took a terrible toll on their minds. It was hard losing your people. It took years for them to get their spirits back to the light. In the meantime, dark clouds were around every corner. Ominous forces followed the family. No matter how good things got, something bad was always lurking in the shadows.

All these thoughts were flowing through his mind as he drove. They just recently got over the deaths that plagued them. He counted himself lucky that a decade passed since they lost anyone. His children and their kids were healthy, as was Sue. He really had no worries for his family: except how they would deal with this situation, regarding him.

The garage door was open when Jack pulled up. His heart sunk a bit as the realization was upon him. Sue was home, there would be no way around it. He drove up to the front door as quiet as possible and closed the door gingerly behind him.

As he walked to the door of his house, the solution was bluntly in his mind. He would simply walk in and tell Sue right away. There was no reason to prolong it. The deed must be done. It was his second visit to the doctor this week, she knew where he went and for what reason: To go over his test results.

So much happened since he left this door earlier. The phone call from the doctor came this morning. It was three days after his initial visit. He said it was important, come as soon as possible. Of course, he hadn't told Sue about the urgency, although now he wished he would have.

Now, as he turned the knob, his heart was heavy. He knew Sue and the kids would miss him. They were a team and one of their players was getting traded to the other side.

They paid off their house in Mountain Ranch three years before. After the house was paid, they walked away from their business of twenty-five years. They both felt as if complete creativity could only come with solitude. Of course, they liked people; they just didn't want to be around them all the time. Sue and Jack were both creatures who made things out of anything they could find. They built this house and made a humble living from using their imagination and hard work.

As Jack walked into the house, Sue was sitting at the breakfast nook paying bills.

She wasn't concerned because Jack had given her no reason to be. She asked her husband how it went and then looked in his face. He tried to remain calm, but Sue could see right through the façade.

She'd seen the look of death before. Sue held the hands of both her parents when they passed. Both left an indelible mark on their daughter's soul. The look in their eyes in their last days was exactly what she saw in Jack's now.

"What did they say?" Sue asked her husband. Her voice quivered a bit. She had a bad feeling about this. A knot swiftly formed in the pit of her stomach, making her feel light-headed. The tone of her voice was one Jack hadn't heard come from her mouth in a very long time. It was the sound he heard every time catastrophe struck. Jack knew it; Sue was in shock.

"It wasn't very good," Jack answered as he approached his wife for a hug. His bride of thirty years was shivering like she'd been dunked in ice water. "Calm down, it's all going to be okay," he said to help calm the situation. "Let's go sit on the sofa and talk about it."

The few steps into the living room seemed to take an eternity for Sue. It seemed like she was walking to the gallows. Dark shadows permeated the space. Unseen forces seemed to dampen their progression. She knew these shadows. They were all too familiar. They accompanied bad times.

She felt dread like never before.

When they sat, Sue asked, "so, you going to tell me or am I going to have to drag it out of you?"

"Well," he answered plainly, "I have cancer." The words just came out and Jack felt relieved from it. A huge burden was lifted off his shoulders with the utterance of his statement.

Sue didn't burst into hysterics. Her eyes simply filled with tears and she fell into the embrace of her husband. The energy between them was strong. Even after thirty years of marriage, they were still there for each other.

Minutes passed before she worked up the courage to ask the next question. "How bad is it?" she choked out without lifting her head from her husband's chest.

"It's definitely not good," replied Jack in a shaky whisper. "I'm in advanced stages of bone cancer. It's spread to the rest of my body. They said I've had a recessive gene, BCRA2 or something, since I was born. I'm lucky to have made it this long. It's the same thing Lisa got. It's in our genetics. They said it's too late to be cured."

"How long have you known you were sick?" Sue blurted out. She knew her husband and his stubborn ways oh so well. She pushed herself from Jack as she angrily spoke the words. She was filled with fear mixed in with every other emotion she ever felt. Her world was crushed. This was the only love she knew and the only one she wanted. Losing her husband would be like losing half of herself.

Anxiety had her in its deadly grasp. She knew her husband had a passion for life; she also knew all about his fascination with death.

"I guess I've known for some time now that I wasn't well. I didn't think it was going to be something like this though. I thought maybe I had a virus or something."

"How long do you have?" Sue's voice changed to one of resolve. Getting angry at her husband now wouldn't help the situation. Right now, they needed one another like never-before. All the heartache they went through in the past was a warm-up for this final event.

"He said I have thirty days, but you know how doctors are. I'm strong. I think I will go on for a long time." Jack's voice betrayed his words. Sue read through it all and sobbed deeply. She wasn't one to lose control, but her sanity was swiftly ebbing away. Her life, once again, changed in an instant. Her comfortable existence they worked so hard to achieve was shattered. She didn't know why it always happened, but it did.

"What are we going to do Jack? I need you. Our family needs you. Why didn't you go to the doctor earlier? They may have been able to help you."

"I didn't want to go earlier, Sue. I don't trust doctors and I'm not going to leave you behind with nothing. There wouldn't have been any guarantees except the one with us giving all our life savings to the medical 'industry'. I would never even consider doing that to you. I guess it's my time to hang out with Tommy again."

Sue looked strangely at her husband. She knew he never got over the death of his son; nor did she blame him. The father and son went through a lot after losing a wife and mother. That tragedy formed a bond with the two that Sue recognized. She knew it was always in Jack's mind to be with Tommy, once again. "What about those of us here Jack, we don't matter?"

"Of course, you matter Sue. You know I'm still deeply in love with you and care about our family with all my heart. I'm just also ready to see Tommy again. His death has always worn on me. If I would have done a few things different, he'd still be here with us. Instead, my negligence lost me my boy."

"I've told you thousands of times, Jack, you've got to stop beating yourself up over this. It wasn't your fault. He walked home from that football game on his own accord. Whatever happened in between there, and our house will forever be a mystery."

"If I hadn't been drinking, I could've picked him up."

"You haven't had a single drop of alcohol since that night Jack. You just need to let it go. You were a great father to Tommy and to our other children also. Now, we need to talk about the present."

The ringing phone broke their conversation. Jack said not to get it, but Sue thought the doctor might be calling about something. She answered the phone and said it wasn't a good time to talk. After an uh-huh and oh-really, she gently hung up the receiver. Instead of going back to the couch, Sue took a detour and turned on the television.

"Who was that?" Jack asked. "Why did you turn on the television in the middle of the day?"

"It was my friend Nancy. Something happened over by your doctor's office and I wanted to see it. Did you see anything happening over there?"

Jack's face was pale as his wife approached the sofa. The memories of the convenience store came flooding back into his memory. How he forgot he just killed four people, he did not know. His mind was so wrapped up in his own dialogue, he blocked the event completely from his memory. He looked instinctively at his pants. Sue was switching the channels and didn't notice the panic her husband went into for a moment. Miraculously, there was no blood, dirt or anything else amiss on Jack. By the time Sue found the news, he was composed once again.

With the T.V. showing the scene, it came rushing back to him. They kept going from the back lot where the killings took place to the front of the store where the cashier was getting her fifteen minutes of fame. She said to the camera as her long black hair fluttered around: "a man came in, bought some water, and said he was death. He was covered in tattoos and looked how I imagine death looks. He said nothing as he walked out the store. Minutes later, these four big guys come in waving guns in the air. Out of fear, I gave them all the money from the register. One of the guys broke into the back office and destroyed all the surveillance equipment and tapes. The leader hit me in the side of the head with his gun, but it glanced off. I played like it knocked me out and I fell to the ground. They left the store and minutes later I heard the gunshots. I called the cops. Someone shot those dirty robbers like the dogs they were."

Jack's mouth went dry. It was the same exact feeling that brought him to that store in the first place. Sue looked to him trying to see his reaction. Her husband was pale and very agitated. "You know something about this, Jack?"

"I saw the cops flashing by on my way home, but I didn't see anything else. Why do you ask?"

"I noticed you smelled like tobacco when you came in. You get that at a convenience store. The clerk said a heavily tattooed guy came in. I was just wondering."

"Well, I stopped at the cigarette store next to the office and got a cigar. I smoked it in the parking lot. The convenience-store they're talking about is a few blocks away. What, do you think I'm some kind of badass now that I have cancer. I'm dying but have superhuman strength. I go around using my powers to fight crime."

Sue laughed at her husband's remarks. She was happy to see he had some of his humor left. She knew this was a traumatic thing and wanted to support her husband in any way possible. "I don't think smoking is going to help your cancer Jack."

"I don't think it's going to kill me at this stage Sue."

Jack got to his feet with a moan and headed toward their shared bedroom. The house only had two rooms. A living room, which was also the kitchen, and the bedroom. Each of them was seven hundred square feet. The open floor plan embodied the creativity of the pair. Now, it would be Jack's final resting spot.

"I'm going to go lay down for a bit," he turned back and said to his wife. "It's been a long day and I need a rest. My brain feels like it was hit by a truck. Please, Sue, don't let me sleep too long. There's a lot we need to talk about and many plans to make. Please don't tell anyone else just yet either. I think it best if we discuss our options and come up with a good plan, together."

"Anything you want, Jack," Sue replied. "I'll be right here when you get up, so we can talk about it. I love you Sweetheart!"

"I love you too, Babe," Jack answered over his shoulder. When he got to the bedroom, he closed the door behind him and rolled a fat joint. This years' harvest was recently completed so the quality was fresh and good. Jack prided himself on his growing abilities. He thought it foolish to buy substandard medicine from the greed when you could grow your own kick-ass strains.

As he lay in bed, puffing his doobie, his mind couldn't let go of the images from earlier. He never killed a man before, let alone four. He was never a badass, nor a vigilante. He knew the thugs would have killed him, but it still didn't alleviate the strangeness of the situation. It felt like he watched it all in a movie starring him in the lead role.

He never fully drifted off to sleep. Mostly, he lay there and rested his body. There was no rest for his brain. There were too many things to think about. A list, he started in his mind, got longer with every passing moment.

He finally controlled his breathing and shut down the worries. All thoughts of plans went away. Meditation was upon him. His body could take a break while his mind went to the semi-subconscious.

Death was the only thought in the room. It came knocking on the door of Jack's life this morning and wasn't going away before collecting its prize.

Chapter 3

Sue didn't hear Jack emerge from their bedroom. Her thoughts were consumed with so many things; she couldn't focus on one. Her life, once again, got turned upside down. She knew this day was the beginning of another round of hardships for her. Losing Jack was going to be the worst thing that ever happened to her. They were a team. They relied on one another.

It saddened Jack to see his wife sitting at the breakfast counter, staring into space. He could imagine what she was thinking but didn't know for sure. He wasn't one to tell people that he understood what they were going through in their time of misery. Hundreds of people told him that when his son went missing. Then there was another wave of pity after they found the body. Every time someone said that to him, Jack lost respect for that individual. There was no way they understood what he was going through. Unless the same exact thing happened to them, they had not a clue.

Jack came up behind Sue and wrapped his arms around her. Her arms melted into his as they languished in the tight embrace. When it broke, the husband took a seat on the opposite corner of the counter. Sitting this way, the couple was face to face.

It was obvious that Sue was in shock. He'd seen this look on her face many years before. It was a look Jack never forgot. Her expressionless face and distant gaze told her husband what he needed to know. He could have a conversation with his wife right now, but it would be repeated soon. Sue was in no state of mind to deal with this situation now.

Jack retrieved a notebook he used for writing and keeping tabs on things. He figured there was going to be so much to take care of in the next weeks, it would be best to start a list. This wasn't the time of his life that he could afford to miss even the smallest of details. This time, there would be no going back to tie up loose ends.

He started the list with basics: Telling the kids and Grandkids. Telling the family friends. Getting Sue on the right path. As he progressed, the list became more and more extensive: From paying bills: working out the hospice: getting the paperwork for the house in order, and so many other things. The more Jack wrote, the more he realized how short a time he truly had.

Sue took notice to this list and added a few of her own to it: Spend time with your wife: travel together: try to have some fun. As the list went more in this direction, Sue seemed to come out of her shell. The two even laughed when they both said, in unison, that they wanted to go to the Vermillion Cliffs.

The list began to take on a whimsical tone as it got longer. Dancing in the moonlight appeared. Throw a stone at a window. It started to take on the undertones of a bucket list. That was the moment Jack put down the pen and was done with the agenda. He felt like he already did everything he wanted in his life. Writing down more was a waste of his time. The original purpose of the list had become convoluted in their fantasies.

Sue wanted to continue the schedule, but her husband refused. She saw the therapy it created not only for herself, but for Jack also. For the briefest of moments, the writing enabled them to forget about the impending doom. During that moment, Sue felt her sanity seeping back into her being. Everything almost seemed normal, like yesterday.

"I guess I'll go call the kids. I'll invite them over tonight and tell them all at once," Jack said. "I think it will be best to break the news in person." He paused for a moment to look for Sue's reaction. "I think it will be proper if they're all together."

"Whatever you want, Dear," Sue said flatly. Her husband's words were mere sounds to her fragile mind. He could see the list was helpful to his wife, but only a temporary fix. It wasn't something good for his mind now. It made him have regrets. Jack wasn't going to start doing that now, on his deathbed. He lived a life without regrets; his death would be the same.

He worried for Sue but knew, in the long run, she was going to figure it out on her own. It was what we all had to do. When something happened, it helped to have support, but it was up to you to heal yourself.

The two released the grasp their hands formed. Sue barely looked at Jack as he made his way out the patio door. He looked back to his wife before opening the slider. "Are you going to be okay Sue? I'm going to call the kids."

"Yeah, I'm alright," she answered. She looked up briefly and met the gaze of her husband. The look tore her heart out. All she could see was the death permeating around the man she loved. She immediately returned her focus to blankness.

Jack went into his garage to make the calls. Being mid-afternoon, he knew his kids would be at work. Normally, he'd never call his children at their job; but this situation wasn't normal. If he wanted them to be there tonight, he needed to contact them now. He knew his call would get them worried, but there was no option. Jack felt like he couldn't even wait one day to tell his kids; every day mattered too much.

Ronnie was the first he called. Being the oldest, he felt it was the right sequence of things. This son was a successful architect in Lodi. He was shocked his father called him during the day. It was the first time his dad ever called him at work. "Is everything okay Dad?" he asked with worry.

"Yeah, Ron, I just need to talk to you and your siblings. Something has happened, and we need to talk about it as a family. Please, no more questions until you arrive. It's really important."

"When are you thinking, Dad? We're going to be out of town this weekend. Can it wait until next weekend?"

"Tonight, seems like a good time. You can come after work. I'll make dinner for you guys if you like. Bring the kids if you can't get a sitter."

"Now you have me worried, Dad. Your first call ever to my work and you tell me to come over after I get off. Something is going on. Can't you just give me a hint?"

"No Ronnie, I can't do that. Just be here tonight. I'll have dinner ready at eight. It'll still be hot whenever you get here. I love you son. See you tonight."

Before Ronnie could answer, there was just a dial tone. His father hung up before getting any more questions thrown his way. The architect looked at the phone with a strange expression and hung up. It was probably the oddest phone call he ever received.

The next two calls were almost identical. Becky was a writer in Stockton for the local newspaper. She just published her first novel, making her parents very proud. She, too, thought it odd her father was calling in the middle of the day with a cryptic tone. She didn't try to dig for information; she readily agreed to meet the family that night.

Little Jack was not so easy to get ahold of. A tattooer who worked in Modesto, the youngest sibling wasn't always easy to contact. Jack left a message at the Tattoo Shop and they promised to get the message to his son. It wasn't more than five minutes before Jack returned the call to his father. "Is everything okay, Dad?" were the first words out of his mouth.

"I just want to see you all together, tonight," Jack told his son. "There's something important I need to tell you."

The younger man could hear the weariness in his father's voice. He was close with his dad and could tell when something was wrong. That, and the fact he called him at work, just didn't add up. "Just tell me now Dad. What's going on?"

"I would prefer to tell you, your brother and sister all at once. Please, Jack, I don't need any more stress right now. Just be here at eight."

"All right Dad. As always, I respect your wishes. Love you Man."

"Love you too, Son."

It was with regret that Little Jack hung up the phone. He promised to be there this evening but knew he could never wait that long. He just finished an outline on his client and was getting ready to shade. With apologies, Jack told the lady they would have to call it quits for the day. There was a family emergency and he needed to go.

With hugs and best wishes from his client and co-workers, Jack raced out the door. When he got to his car, his senses began to kick in. He was one who kept a cool head when dealing with an ordeal. Every catastrophe had a set of steps to be taken care of. He analyzed what needed to be done and took care of business. He learned this from his father and practiced it since an early age.

A call to Ronnie would be his first step. His older brother would surely know what was going on. He sat in his idle car, took a couple deep breaths, and made the call. His brother answered on the first ring. "I just got off the phone with Becky," Ronnie said without even a hello. "Dad just called you too, right?"

"Yeah, man, what's going on? Did he tell you anything?"

"No Jack, he just said to be there at eight. I'm leaving work right now. So is Becky. I can't wait a few hours in anticipation. I'm on my way there."

"Me too Ron. I'm in my car now. See you there, bro." Jack hung up without a goodbye and tossed his phone into the passenger seat. He took a deep breath, started the car, and casually pulled away. He didn't even consider going home or anywhere else. All he could think of was being there for his family. They meant the world to him.

The distance for each was almost the same. All three siblings lived in the San Joaquin Valley in central California. Sue and Jack lived in the foothills to the East; in the Gold Country. It was exactly one hour and fifteen minutes away for each of the siblings. Although living over a forty-five-mile-long stretch spanning highway 99, the three had the same exact amount of driving.

All three siblings pulled up to the house at the same time. Their clocks, as siblings, were wound the same.

Living on five acres with rural neighbors, you could see someone coming from a very long distance. Jack saw the cars of his children as they drove onto the access road. Normally they would drive slowly to keep the dust down, but today they sped in.

When the three came to a stop at the front of the house, they saw the disheveled appearance of their father. Each of them was thinking about the worst-case scenario on the trip up to the foothills. Normally, the journey would be filled with excitement and anticipation of seeing their elders. All three came up often with their children. The grandkids loved to come and explore this little gem in Calaveras County. It was a place that called to the entire family. On this day, though, the drive was filled with dread in each of the three cars.

"Where's Mom? Is she okay?" was the first thing Becky said as she got out of her vehicle. All three raced to the side of their father. Becky hugged her dad and went right inside in search of her mother. The two had always been very close. They were always there to support each other. Becky had been Sue's support after Tommy came up missing, and vice versa. They were close before the incident, but the tragedy made their bond solid.

"How did you guys all arrive at the same time? I told you to be here at eight. I'd say you were a few hours early." Jack said with mock scorn.

The brothers looked oddly at one another and shrugged their shoulders. "We were just worried about you Dad," Ronnie said. "I guess it was a coincidence we arrived at the same time."

"There are no coincidences, only pre-destined situations," Little Jack said.

"Whatever it was, it's weird. Come on guys, let's go inside," Jack told his boys. "It's much nicer in the house."

Becky had her arm around her mother's shoulders when the men entered the house. Sue had a shocked look on her face, like there was a death in the family.

"Let's go in the living room where we'll be more comfortable. You guys want some coffee or tea? Something to eat maybe?" Jack asked.

"Why don't you just get it over with and tell them?" Sue said to her husband. Tears began to well up in her eyes. All three of her kid's eyes were on her face when she said the words; they shifted to that of their father's after.

Jack looked flushed, like he might pass out. "Here Dad, sit down," Becky said. She cradled her father's arm and helped him to the chair opposite his wife. His back was to the counter and his kids were in front of him. He felt like he was in a vaudeville comedy for the briefest of thoughts. If only he had a ventriloquist's dummy to do the talking for him.

"I have cancer!" Jack blurted out to the shocked look of his kids. "It's terminal," he said dejectedly.

Ronnie burst into tears and was the first to get to his dad. Little Jack was close behind with tears filling his eyes. Becky exclaimed, "Oh No!" and threw herself into the mix. Sue joined in and the entire family shared a tight embrace.

Memories came rushing into the minds of each of the members. Countless times, they had embraced like this in the face of calamity. Many years passed since the heartaches, but some memories never go away. The ones that did, were now remembered with vivid intensity.

When something terrible happens to a family, one good thing does come from the ashes. It's the phoenix. The cycle of the end to the beginning, the beginning to the end. The healing process involves a closeness among the survivors which is an energy which will never go away. Each of the members might put it in the back of their minds to get over things. Then, one day, tragedy will strike again, and the close bond will be reborn. It's the force that keeps true families together.

The family sensed the agony in each of the others. Their bond put them in touch with the other's emotions and thoughts. They were all connected as one. Their family, in this capacity, could get through anything. The problem was, one of their members was no longer going to be. The circle would no longer be complete.

"What's the diagnosis?" Becky asked. Her eyes were watered over but no tears streamed down her face. Jack looked proudly at his daughter. Emotionally, she'd always been the toughest of the three.

"It's in my entire body," Jack said solemnly. The others could sense the weakness in their Patriarch. It was something none of them had ever seen before.

"And...." Becky stated while rolling her hand. She was always the one to goad anything out of her parents.

"I only have a month to live," Jack said. Ronnie and Little Jack cried aloud when they heard the prognosis. Tears even began to stream down Becky's face. The family hugged tightly and shared their energy. This would be a time they would all have to be strong. Stronger than ever, for that matter. It wasn't going to be easy watching their beloved slowly die.

When calm returned, the family broke apart and meandered into the living room. Becky again helped her father the short distance. She, above all the others, could sense the lack of strength in her elder's body.

The five sat and talked about plans. Sue got the to-do list, to the chagrin of Jack, and showed her offspring. They all laughed at a few, toward the end. Jack said, "I told you not to show them, now they think I'm an idiot."

"We don't think you're an idiot, Pops," Little Jack said. "It's just that some of these at the end are pretty funny. Like do a line of coke off a stripper's tit."

The whole room erupted in laughter that is only found in close families. Jack said, through his outbreak, that some of them were just jokes.

"Yeah right," was the reply from Little Jack. The pun brought another round of laughter.

When they settled down, Jack said, "This is how I want to see you for the next month: Joyous and happy: Filled with laughter. If I get too sick where you can't be with this positive attitude, please just stay away. I won't hold it against you. I want you guys to remember me for the good times; not for my last days. It's my wishes."

The other four agreed and set in motion a schedule that would consume the last weeks of Jack's life. A couple of times, he put his foot down to stop an idea or plan. He tried to get his family to reason that maybe he didn't want to be busy non-stop until he died. He, too, had things he wanted to get done. A novel he started earlier in the year needed the last edit. A couple of oil paintings, near completion, and other art projects were sure to fill his time.

The others understood; they just wanted to spend as much time possible with Jack. In the end, they came up with a plan where each of them would visit almost every day. It would be a lot of driving for the three, but it would be well worth the effort. They each knew the time they spent in the next month would be the last with their father.

Becky knew it was the beginning of making this drive more and more often. She knew her mother was going to need her more, after her husband wasn't around. She didn't dread the thought. Her mother had always been there for her, and she was always there for her mother. She would do whatever it took to make her mom happy; now and in the future.

For now, though, her main concern was the welfare of her father.

The kids had arrived at three in the afternoon. It didn't give Jack time to prepare a nice dinner. Instead, they just made sandwiches from some leftover tri-tip he barbecued the night before. They didn't need much: none of the family had much of an appetite.

It was eight when the siblings left. The sunset this time of year created shadows through the forest, obscuring the road. Sometimes, it was like driving blind. Jack and Sue made sure their offspring left when it was safe, well after dark. They needed their children safe and strong in this time of mayhem.

All three siblings had a worrisome drive. None of them were expecting to hear this kind of news. It saddened them knowing their father was going to go through so much anguish. It also weighed heavy on their hearts thinking about their mother and how she would get along.

They also worried about how they were going to tell their spouses and children. It would be late when they got home, but all the grandchildren would be awake waiting to hear what was wrong. The three called their spouses earlier in the afternoon explaining where they were going. They hadn't phoned since. Their families were unaware of the bomb about to hit when the news was told.

After the others left, Sue cooked up a quick dinner. She and her husband shared the food on the porch. The moon cast a purplish, orange hue across the sparse clouds in the night sky. A couple of bats passed by, getting a meal of their own.

Jack barely ate any of his food. Sue was the same. She said she shouldn't have even cooked but her husband put her thoughts at ease. "We still need nourishment. Even though we aren't that hungry, we ate some. I have a feeling there is going to be a lot of days like this in the next month."

"Me too," Sue said. "I'll be here with you until the end. You know that. You are my husband and I love you dearly. I'm going to miss you so much. It's going to be hard on us without you. We'll be strong though; getting by with the strength you have bred in each of us."

"Thanks Sue, I know you'll be there for me. I don't want to be a burden on you. I care about you way too much to cause you any inconvenience."

"You won't inconvenience me Jack. Now, get up and get the dishes done." Sue finished her words with a swat of the napkin. The couple both laughed as they cleared the small patio table of the dinner dishes. They dropped them in the kitchen and Sue headed for the bathroom.

Jack took the opportunity to turn on the ten o'clock news. As he suspected, the robbery and murder were all over the television. The police said the killer was wanted only for questioning. He wasn't in trouble, like he may be thinking.

They only had a couple of clues; the man was heavily tattooed and was smoking a cigar. Surveillance tapes from a local tobacco store showed a heavily tattooed man buying a cigar, but there was something wrong with the video and the man's face was not discernible. The police had nothing else to go on. There were absolutely no witnesses nor surveillance cameras that caught the man's face.

Jack heard Sue approaching and swiftly turned off the television. He didn't want her to hear any of it; especially the only two clues they had. She'd changed into a see-through chiffon negligee, nineteen-fifties era. It was one of Jack's favorites. "You ready for bed, Big Boy?" she asked with a sultry voice.

Her husband was up in a flash. He didn't need to be invited twice. After thirty years of marriage, he was still deeply in love with his wife. He wanted to spend as much time as possible together.

Sue was sprawled out on the bed when he entered. He went into the bathroom, brushed, flossed and took a shower. He felt as if he was washing away the stress from the day.

He was excited to get back to Sue. Having sex with his hot ass wife was the best thing to get rid of his worries.

He entered the bedroom naked; then he entered Sue.

Chapter 4

Like so many times in life, their plans didn't go as envisioned. They joked a couple of times, saying they shouldn't have made any plans at all. The list turned out to be a curse. All it did was cause a lot more stress and anxiety. The agenda did serve one purpose: It reminded the couple that Jack's time was very short.

The next two weeks were spent going through the house and finances. Jack was adamant about making sure everything was in order. He insisted on doing all the handyman work around the house. Sue didn't like the idea of her dying husband up on the roof, cleaning gutters, but it was useless to argue with him. Somehow, she sensed it was therapeutic for Jack to be doing all the chores. She could tell the tasks wore him out. His already tired body was devastated every day at the end of his projects. It was difficult for Sue to see her husband like this, but she knew it was his way of forgetting his worries.

Their children were at the house daily with their children. Jack nor Sue complained about this. They loved their family and never looked at them as being a burden. They respected their children and grandchildren for wanting to spend the last days with their elder. Never once did any of them ask Jack for one of his possessions. Any question directed his way was about his family history. Each of the family knew, when Jack was gone, so was his heritage.

It was one of the grandchildren who really bonded with her Papa in these weeks. Paige was ten years old; the middle child in Becky's family. After her second visit, she insisted on staying for a few days. It was Friday evening so there were no problems. When she tried to stay Sunday, when her parents were leaving, there was little debate about what would happen. This family was close. It was important for all of them to bond, even the little ones.

School took a second seat to a child who wanted to spend the last days of her grandfather's life with him. The girl was a spiritual companion to her Papa for the entire visit. She reminded Jack of his sister when they were young. Lisa had been a strong girl, always ready to help her family spiritually and physically.

Paige was the best assistant any grandpa could ever have. She followed her elder around the yard and house for eight days straight. She wasn't one to shy away from the hard work. Fear wasn't an emotion present in the girl. At night, she would read one of her Papa's stories aloud to her grandparents. They thought it special the youngster would read a story written by her own grandpa when there was an entire library to choose from.

Most things Paige did were special to her grandparents. She cooked for her elders and cleaned the dishes. When she wasn't outside with her Papa, she was inside with her Grandma. Either place, the child worked like an adult. She knew things about the stars, herbs and nature, impressing her kinfolk. "The child is an old soul," they would say around dinner. The title made Paige proud. She didn't understand what it meant, but she could tell by the way her grandparents spoke, it was good.

The grandchild painted and made things with her people. She, Jack and Sue made a collaboration painting almost every night of the visit. The girl wrote poetry and even a couple of short stories during her stay. The creative spark was evident in the youngster. It made Jack happy to see some of his offspring were taking his and Sue's ways. They gave him hope their family would carry on the tradition which started so long before.

After the first week ended, the child tried to stay longer, but her parents didn't want troubles with the school. She begged repeatedly, but in the end, she knew what her responsibilities were. When her grandpa told her, she had to get going, she reluctantly agreed.

When Becky came to pick up Paige on Saturday, it was a solemn time. Jack and Sue got used to having a little one around again. They stayed up until midnight every night watching scary movies together. Their routine changed with the input of the youthful energy. She breathed a new spark into the shadowed house.

As she was leaving, Paige hugged her papa's neck as tight as she could. She comprehended it might be the last time she saw him and wasn't going to ruin it with tears. She understood so much after the days with her elders. They taught her about life and death and gave her knowledge; all because she was the one to listen.

"I love you Papa," she said, cheerfully, on the way out the door. "I'll see you next time." Paige winked at her grandpa and skirted out the door. Jack didn't need to say anything in return. His face told Paige all she needed to know. It lit up so brightly there were colors all around her grandpa. For the youngster, it was the closest moment she ever shared with another human.

When she was gone, the house seemed empty. All the grandchildren would come with their respective parents daily, but the visits were short. Jack understood, it was a long drive. Especially after working all day. He wasn't stressed out about the short visits. He cherished his time alone and felt like it was needed in the next weeks. There were a lot of things to get done. Nothing would get accomplished if there were people around, all the time.

The couple made a trip to Reno to visit the spot they were married. Two weeks passed since 'the news' and it was their first trip. The list they made was long ago forgotten. It seemed like years since they made that nonsense. Few of the things were achieved; mostly important stuff with the house and finances. The others became meaningless.

It was a beautiful rose garden in Idyllwild Park, near downtown Reno. The couple were married in this spot with their children, siblings and parents by their sides. They loved the tranquility of the park and chose it for their wedding. Now, thirty years later, it looked the same. There were an abundance of roses covering the hundreds of bushes. The smell of flowers and fresh cut grass floated heavy in the afternoon sun.

Jack and Sue walked through the rose garden for almost four hours. They talked about their economy wedding and everything that happened since. Their whole existence was recollected with mutual banter. Once, an ice-cream truck went by and the two danced to the melody being played on the speaker. They each chuckled a hearty laugh and held hands as they strolled around the path.

After the park, they went to one of their favorite restaurants in the city and had a seafood grub-down. A walk downtown, after, gave them a chance to hit up some pawn shops. The memories of these pawn shops were joyous ones of when they were younger and just met. Jack bought Sue's wedding ring in one of these stores, on this very street.

The thought of a gift was way heavier than the weight of it, Sue felt. This night would be no different. Jack bought her a white gold ring with small diamonds. She always had simple tastes and chose this one like others before. When he ceremoniously put it on her finger, in the middle of Virginia Avenue, she hugged her husband and sobbed with the love she felt. By the time they got in the car, they were both exhausted.

The drive home began just after dark. They didn't mind taking turns driving; it's how they always did it. "I sure had a good day," Jack said. He reached over and held Sue's right hand while she drove.

"Me too. Thanks again for the ring. I'll cherish it forever."

"I would have gotten you a more expensive one."

"I know, but I like this one the best. It was the same when you got me my wedding ring. Then, you got me this ring when we first moved to Mountain Ranch." Sue waved her hand in front of her husband's face. Jack felt exhausted after the long day of travel and walking. He felt like he could sleep for days.

"It's one of the many things I love about you, dear," Jack said with respect. His wife meant a lot to him. He liked seeing her happy.

Moments passed with silence in the car. The radio stations at this altitude were intermittent at best. It was better to have silence than static. Sue broke it with a question Jack was waiting on for the last two weeks. "Are you scared, Jack?"

He didn't speak for a few minutes. It felt to him like the air in the car was humid. Sue thought he was asleep when her husband's voice came out of the dark. "No Babe, I'm not scared. I've been dead since I was born. I told you before. I have no regrets for my life either. However, I do regret leaving you and I'm sad for that. The last thing I ever wanted was to hurt you."

"I'll be alright. I'm just going to be so alone without you. You've been my soulmate for more than half my life. We've gotten each other through times most people couldn't dream of going through. I'll have to get through this one without you."

"You'll have the kids and the grandkids. They'll be there for you."

"Maybe at first they'll be there for me. After a while, though, their visits will become less frequent."

"At first they'll be coming around a lot. They know you need them. Trust me Sue, our kids will be there for you. They'll taper off their visits when they see you're healing and getting on with your life."

"I don't think I'm going to be healing any time soon, Jack. Getting on with my life is just a phrase to me that I can't relate to right now."

"You know you will. Remember when Tommy disappeared, we thought it would be something we never got over. It was terrible. Every day we woke up not wanting to wake up. In the long-run, we did get over it. It took a lot of family support but, in truth, each one of us did it on our own. Sure, we were there for each other, but we were also dealing with it on our own. When we laid down at night and thought of the anguish, we were alone with our thoughts. It will be the same for you. You are strong Sue; the family needs you. Mostly though, you need you."

"What if I fail them?"

"Come on Sue, there is no way you'll fail them. You're the strongest woman I ever met. How many other women do these things together: Raise their kids: work full time: get their bachelor's degree: have a great career: get a full body-suit? You're strong, and you are special."

"I'm glad you've always shown confidence in me. You've been my anchor for a long time." Sue grasped her husband's hand. Jack said something, but it came out as a mumble. The more they drove, the less his words came. By the time they were halfway home, Jack was sound asleep. He would always lay his seat back and use a pillow made by Sue to nap when he wasn't driving. Usually his sleep was fitful, but this night, he slept silently.

Sue drove the entire way home. She didn't want to wake Jack. If he was this deeply asleep, she figured, it was needed. She also knew that he'd been working his ass off around the house; the relaxation would be good for him.

Jack didn't wake up when they pulled up to the gate. Sue got out, unlocked the steel enclosure, and swung it open on squeaky hinges. Jack still didn't wake up when she slammed the door and drove the one hundred yards to the house.

The trip home was a long drive for Sue. Her mind and body were worn out. She couldn't quite think straight.

She got a terrible feeling that her husband was dead. It wasn't normal for him to sleep on all those windy roads. When he didn't wake with the commotion of the car stopping, Sue knew there had to be something wrong.

She got out of the vehicle and unlocked the front door of the house. Their small dogs came running out, happy to see their people. They pounced on the door that concealed Jack, but he still didn't stir. When Sue opened the passenger door, he almost fell to the ground. If it weren't for her aptitude, he would have been eating the road-base.

His body was limp when she pushed him back into the car. She couldn't detect breathing. There wasn't movement in his facial features nor extremities. Sue shook him, but he didn't wake up. She felt for his pulse in the neck and became panicked when she didn't discover one. She checked his wrist and found the same situation: No pulse.

Sue dragged her husband out of the car and got him on the smooth concrete of the porch. His lifeless body was dead weight to the woman who was his same size. As soon as she had him flat, she began to give him CPR. She tried frantically for over four minutes before reasoning and fatigue took over.

She got to her feet, ran to the kitchen and snatched the phone off the wall. She called 911 and was immediately on with an operator. When the man asked the nature of the call, Sue said, through gasps, "my husband collapsed; he isn't breathing!"

"Calm down Ma'am. What happened?"

"We went to Reno and coming home I was driving," Sue had to take a couple of breaths. Her speech was frantic as would be anyone with a dead husband on the porch; especially after giving CPR for five minutes.

She just about had her composure when Jack walked in the door.

Sue turned white. She gasped out a few times and was on the edge of hysterics. She felt like she might faint but the voice from the phone brought her back to reality. "Ma'am are you okay? What's going on?" The questions seemed like they were being barked at her by a rabid dog.

"Uhhhhhhh," stammered Sue, "my husband is up and walking. I don't know how. I just gave him CPR and could have sworn he was dead. Hold on," Sue set the phone on the counter as she finished her words. She pressed herself into the body of her husband and felt he, indeed, was alive. He looked at her quizzically, like he didn't understand what was happening.

"Why was I laying on the porch? Who are you talking to? You seem to be in a panic. Is everything okay?"

"I thought you were dead," Sue blurted out amid tears. Jack gave a loud, insane laugh, and said he was just fine.

"Eating all that lobster and crab for dinner did me in. It put me in a coma. Who's on the phone?"

"911 operator," Sue said sheepishly. She was staring at her husband with disbelief.

Jack grabbed the phone and said into it, "I'm alive and well. I was just asleep in the car and my wife thought I was dead."

"It's okay sir, an ambulance is on the way right now and the sheriff. It is customary with any call we receive."

"It's okay if the sheriff comes and checks it out, but please cancel the ambulance. There is no need. I have terminal cancer and it would be a waste of our money. Sorry for the inconvenience."

"No problem sir, the ambulance Is canceled. The sheriff should be there any moment."

"Yeah, they're here right now. Have a good night."

"I'm so sorry," Sue said, "I feel like a fool."

"Please don't. I must have been out of it if you were giving me CPR and I didn't wake up. I would've done the same."

The two met the police on the front porch. The cops wanted to come in the house, but the couple didn't trust this. Once they came inside, they would perp around looking at everything: trying to gather any kind of evidence to put you away. These officers seemed like nice enough guys but experiences in the past made the couple weary. The cops were displeased, at first, but Jack reminded them that it was not a domestic violence call. It was a medical emergency and he was obviously fine. He explained his condition and his opinion. The police left with handshakes, and good-wishes, all around.

As they went to bed, Sue made Jack promise he would go to the doctor the next day. He already cancelled his appointment four times. Now it was important. Jack agreed. He would call Doctor Benjamin in the morning. It was a promise

Jack laughed at the situation earlier. He told Sue, just before sleep, it was ironic happening after their trip to Reno. "I think it's only appropriate that you thought I died tonight; after dancing in the rose garden earlier."

"I hope you never scare me like that again. I guess, in a weird way, it was like a dress rehearsal or something." There was sorrow in Sue's voice as she spoke.

Jack thanked her again for the great trip. He was so happy to get out of the house. "I love you Sue," he said. A light snoring was the reply. He understood, she just drove many miles after a day of adventure. Once again, she took care of business. This was why he bought her the ring in Reno. He had the utmost respect for his wife. She was the queen of TCB.

The clock said 11:11, a typical moment for Jack to look at the time. He thought about the day and was able to put everything else out of his mind. He felt happy for the first time all week.

As he drifted off to sleep, a new revelation came to him: The trip to Reno would be his last time to leave this property.

Chapter 5

The next morning was the first, of many days, where Jack was too weak to leave the house. Sue got up early, as usual, and made breakfast for the two of them. She decided to let her husband sleep in the extra hour it would take to get it prepared. After the day they had yesterday, she knew he must be exhausted.

Sue made a big spread which she brought to their marital bed on a large tray. Jack was barely waking up when she brought the second tray along with silverware. She made fresh squeezed orange juice which she poured for the two of them. Jack looked to his wife and asked what time it was. "It's ten already. I thought you might sleep all day."

Jack tried to get up, but his muscles wouldn't cooperate. He felt like they had been in a car accident the night before. The pain wracking his body was the worst he ever felt. It filled his mind like a blow-torch. He knew, in his heart, it was a precursor of things to come.

After struggling for a few minutes, he became frustrated. He felt helpless for the first time in his life.

Sue came in and out of the room at least three times during his ordeal, bustling about with breakfast. It wasn't until the last one when she recognized the condition her husband was in.

She raced to his side and asked if everything was okay. "No Honey," Jack answered with sarcasm, "I'm dying of cancer." His frustration had boiled over. He lashed out at the only other person around.

The words hurt Sue deeply. She began to weep at the dreadful thing Jack said. She just made this big breakfast and was in a great mood. Now, it was shattered.

"Come here Babe," Jack said, "I didn't mean it like that. It was supposed to be a joke. I know it didn't come out that way. I'm in a lot of pain today and can't seem to get the strength to get out of bed. I've got the red-ass going on. Sorry to take it out on you. Can you help me to the bathroom? It's kind of an emergency. Then, we can enjoy this bomb ass food."

Sue was a strong woman. The tears were dry in seconds and she was helping her husband to his feet. They'd been married a very long time. They both knew the other's way. When he had one arm around her shoulder, they both stood at the same time. Jack moaned loudly and stood in place. His body felt like it was throbbing to his heartbeat. He felt like he might even pass out from the pain.

"Where does it hurt?" Sue asked.

"Man, I'm fucked. I hurt all over. Even my feet feel like they have nails in the bottom of them. It feels like my head could explode and everything else would follow. My body feels like a powder keg next to a bon-fire."

"I'm making you a doctor's appointment as soon as we get done eating. I think you really need to see Doctor Benjamin today. You haven't seen him in almost two weeks."

"First, I've gotta be able to walk," Jack replied. He took the first small step on the journey to the bathroom. Every goal had to get started with the first step. Jack understood this since he was a boy. It was one of the things that made him successful. Coming up with ideas and making them happen was success.

It took a few minutes for the couple to cross the fifteen feet to the bathroom. Jack was winded the entire time and complained in between gasps and moans. When they got to the toilet, Sue helped ease his naked body onto the pot and let him be.

"Sorry to be such a baby," Jack said as he settled his aching body onto the wooden seat. "You probably think I'm a bitch."

"You have cancer Jack," Sue said with sarcasm. Her crack came out more as a joke and the two laughed at the pun. She hugged her husband and stated her love. "Holler when you're done," she told him as she left the room.

Sue wasn't ignorant to her husband's ways. She knew if she didn't make the appointment, then it would never get done. She grabbed the phone off the nightstand while looking up the number on her cell phone. Service hadn't come to this part of the planet yet; landlines were the only way.

The doctor got on the phone personally when he learned it was Sue. He asked her how her husband was doing, and she gave him the report. When she finished, the doctor said, "I've been worried about him. His tests were very bad, I'm sure he has shown you. Has he gone over the hospice information with you or the other literature I gave him?"

"I haven't seen any of it," Sue said. "He's stubborn, you know." She wasn't shocked by this revelation. Her husband wasn't one to call in outside help. He'd always been one to take care of his own business. He wouldn't want hospice, a nurse, or anything else that would drain their bank account. Even if it were to his benefit, she knew he would put his well- being last, after his family. "He says he can deal with it himself," Sue added.

"I hope he feels the same when the pain really comes on," the doctor said. "I'm surprised it hasn't started earlier. He's lucky it's waited until today."

Sue made the appointment for noon. Doctor Benjamin said he would skip his lunch break today. It was important for him to see Jack. He knew the patient needed to be examined and medicated. With the amount of pain, she described, Jack would surely want some relief. The doctor told Sue he would do anything possible to help Jack and their family. Mainly, he wanted to make Jack's last days as easy as possible. Time was of the essence for a man with less than three weeks to live.

Jack called out to Sue while the doctor was talking. She excused herself and said she had to go but the professional said he'd have none of it. He wanted to talk to Jack. Sue told him it might be a few minutes before she got him back to bed and ready to talk. The doctor said he would wait. "It's important for us to speak," he said.

Jack wasn't as stiff when Sue got to the bathroom. He was still in a lot of pain, but it wasn't the same intensity as a few minutes before. It took about three minutes for Sue to get him back to bed and the phone in his hand. Doctor Benjamin, true to his word, was still on the line. He was a true professional who cared deeply for each of his patients.

Their conversation was brief and courteous. All Sue heard were agreements from her husband mumbled into the transceiver. When he was done, he told the doctor goodbye; he'd see him in a couple hours. Sue took the phone from Jack and hung it up. She asked, "where's this paperwork the doctor gave you to give to me?"

"Oh yeah," Jack said sheepishly, "it's still in the back seat of my car. So many things happened that day. I threw them back there and forgot all about it. They are there, in an envelope, if you want to see them."

"Of course, I want to see them. I made you an appointment for noon. Do you think you'll be able to go?"

"I'll try. I'm starting to feel a little better now. Maybe after we eat, I'll have some strength. I guess you wore me out yesterday."

"You wore me out with that scare you gave me last night. I thought you were dead in the seat next to me. My heart could have stopped, and I would've been the one dead. Then you'd be on your own."

They both laughed lightly but knew it was not a jovial situation. It could come true at any moment. It made Jack realize he didn't want to go far from home. He wanted to die right here. This was the place he and his wife built together. This would be the place where his energy was left behind for the next generations. He knew his premonition from the night before was true. He was never going to leave this land again.

The breakfast was delicious and fulfilling. Jack mostly picked at his food while Sue barely did better. It broke her heart to see her husband picking at his bacon and pancakes when, in the past, he would have eaten multiple plates. He did talk a lot during breakfast, which was very unusual. It made the meal last over an hour. The two picked at their food as the conversation flowed like Koi fish.

"If I would've died last night," Jack said as Sue dug into her half grapefruit, "I would have gone out with a smile. Yesterday was great. All the memories. The great company." He playfully jabbed her in the ribs to punctuate his speech. She grabbed his hand and twisted him into an embrace. Some of the food fell onto the sheets, but it didn't matter. Trivial things that bothered them before were now seen for what they truly were: Minor distractions.

During breakfast, they talked about their history together. Jack spoke of things that happened when he was a child which were unknown to Sue. He never talked much about his family; only Jim and Lisa. His other brothers, sisters and parents were different than the three. Sue met his parents and other siblings only a few times over the years. When they passed away some years before, Jack wasn't interested in any of their possessions. Jim and Lisa were the same. They gave the money and things to homeless people throughout their travels. One item, their magic gong, gifted to them as children, was all that remained in their family after the death.

They talked about the kids, grandkids and great-grandkids to be. Sue was sad Jack wouldn't be able to experience any of it, but he put her mind at ease. He was moving on to the next level. He would be better off than the ones left behind.

Eating was done sporadically throughout the conversation. Sue took the dishes away, cleaned them a bit along with the kitchen, and went for the shower. When she was done, it was time to go.

San Andreas was about ten to fifteen minutes away and she didn't like to be late. In these California foothills, you never knew what you were going to encounter on the road. There were a lot of slow drivers and road construction, especially at this time of year.

Jack wasn't even close to being ready when Sue came out of the shower. He was still in the same position on the bed she'd left him ten minutes before. "Are you going to get up, or do you need my help?" she asked him.

"I don't know man. I'm very stiff and in a lot of pain. I find a sweet spot and it is the only one that will be pain free. If I move even a finger, my whole-body hurts. I'm sorry Babe, I'm not going to be able to go. I thought the breakfast might help, but it didn't."

"It's okay, Jack. I knew you'd say that. Doctor Benjamin said he'd come over here after work. His last appointment is at four, so he'll be here by five. You'll be well enough to visit with your doctor, right Jack?" Sue's voice was a little loud. Jack could hear the tone of her voice indicating she was getting irritated with him.

"I'll be fine to talk to him. I just can't go out. I don't feel like it. I'm sorry if I disappoint you. Doctor Benjamin told me, too, he'd come over after work. Trust me though, it's not the reason I don't want to go. I really feel like crap. I just want to rest. I think I really wore myself out yesterday."

"Alright then, Jack, I won't make you go. If you see the doctor, I'll be happy with that." She lifted the small brass cigarette case off the nightstand and pulled out a freshly rolled joint. Jack's eyes lit up as his naked wife lit the good green. Its smell was sweet to him. Its taste was euphoric.

Jack had been smoking pot for forty-four years. He started when he was fourteen, took a little hiatus during his military years, and never stopped since. Sue's, minus the military, was the same exact story. The two of them, since meeting, always enjoyed a good smoke together. They both understood the medicinal purposes of this herb. For the mind and the body, it had healing qualities. They didn't need the government, nor anyone else, to sway that opinion.

Sue took a couple of big puffs, to get it going, but didn't inhale. She handed her husband the smoke and set about getting dressed. Jack took a huge hit but didn't hold it. He learned long ago that holding the smoke was a myth. That would just deprive your brain of oxygen, making pot smoking bad for you. By the sixth or seventh puff, Jack was really feeling the weed. Its taste became even sweeter and savory. The smoke was like feathery oil exiting his mouth.

The herb sat heavy with Jack's senses this day. Normally he could smoke all day and barely feel the effects. This day, it was like he was a teenager puffing with his buddies. His mind went into a realm he hadn't felt since those early days of partaking. His thoughts became heavy and dreamy while reality around him was warped.

Jack knew from the first puff that it wasn't their home-grown weed. They just finished harvesting and were smoking up the bounty. This tasted way different and the effects were not like marijuana. "Where'd you get that shit?" Jack's words were slurred and almost incoherent. Sue understood, this was her husband. In their younger days, they partied very hard. She'd seen her husband fucked up many times in the past.

"Your brother Jim sent it. It was postmarked New Mexico. He sent a shit load of it and a bunch of mountain tobacco. He said these two herbs will be good for you. They will take away your pains."

"I could sure use some of it then. After this morning, I was a little worried about my mobility in the near future. Now, after smoking half that joint, I'm feeling no pain. I feel like I took Morphine or something, but I know Jim would never send me something like that. Whatever it is, I'm feeling great!" Jack fell to the side at the end of his words and was instantly asleep. His snores told Sue he was out for some time.

She didn't have an idea what was in those quart mason jars Jim sent. One was labeled daytime, one was nighttime. If the daytime herb did this, Sue wondered what the nighttime would do. Jack was mumbling something in his sleep. Her husband sounded like he was speaking in a forgotten tongue only he could decipher. She didn't care. He was relaxed and not in pain.

Sue went about the house cleaning for the visitor. She always kept the house tidy, but any kind of activity now would be welcome.

There was so much going on in her mind, she needed to occupy her thoughts on something else for a few hours. Cleaning house and baking would be that something else.

After finishing the chores, Sue went into town and bought a few groceries. She dreaded these trips. Everyone in this small community heard about her husband and all of them wanted to be up in their business. Sue didn't care for this kind of attention. She wasn't one to accept pity nor false condolences. Before this happened, the people at the store would barely acknowledge her or Jack. Now, they thought they were being helpful by inquiring about a dying man. All so they could have something to talk about later.

Sue arrived home as Jack was waking up. She put the groceries away and was sitting with her husband when the knock on the front door came.

Doctor Benjamin was impressed with the condition Jack was in. He'd gotten up and around just as the medic was arriving. He didn't seem to be in pain although Sue said he was in agony on the phone. "Are you feeling pain, anxiety or headaches, Jack?"

"Actually Doc, I'm feeling great, now. Earlier in the day, I smoked some herbs my brother sent from New Mexico. I figure he probably got it from some natives there. Whatever it was, it helped me tremendously. I couldn't even get out of bed this morning and now I can walk around."

"That's good to hear Jack. I know all about those herbs in the Southwest. I would say be careful but it's a silly thing to say to a man who's dying. I brought you a prescription for morphine, but I already know what you'll say." The doctor crumbled the paper and threw it in the garbage next to the bed. Again, the men shared a glance filled with mutual respect.

Blood tests were drawn, and a brief examination administered. The two talked the entire time about an obituary. They spoke about how the dates were your birth and your death. Then there was your life, the little dash mark in the middle. Jack offered the doctor some of his fresh grown herb but the professional declined. He said he didn't smoke much and many clients already gave it to him. It would just go to waste.

The doctor stayed over an hour. He personally gave Sue information on the hospice system and information for survivors. He spent most of the time with Jack alone in the bedroom, but the last ten minutes were with Sue. He asked her many questions about her family and her mental health. He knew all too well of the tragedy which struck this family. He thought it a cruel twist of fate they were besieged once more.

Doctor Benjamin could see Sue was frail but strong at the same time. She wasn't one to falter. He saw it was going to be a long hard road for the woman, but in the end, she would emerge. He also knew she'd stay strong for her children and grandchildren. He'd seen this family for more than twenty years and detected the closeness amongst them. When tragedy struck, they stuck together.

When he left, he covered everything he could think of to the soon-to-be-widow. Her mental health would be fragile for the next weeks, months, and then years. The doctor, having lost his own wife, knew the cycles of grief. At first, you think you're never going to get over your loss. Death Is a terrible thing to happen to a family. In the first weeks, you learn to adapt to your loss, but the grief is horrible. Then, the months pass in a fog of everlasting twilight as you grasp your way through reality. As years pass, the loss is still there but you've learned to accept it. It is what it is. We all have it waiting for us. Death is a friend to no one.

In this life, we only must die once but we have to endure many deaths.

A car was coming up as Sue walked Doctor Benjamin to his vehicle. It was Becky and her kids, coming for a visit. The doctor said hello to the family, who were also his patients. It was a swift exit for the older gentleman and a promise to come back in two days. Sue thanked the man she trusted all these years and told him of their gratitude. She walked him to his car as the others got out of theirs.

Sue hugged Doctor Benjamin as he was getting into his car. The act surprised the older gentleman, but he straightened and returned the embrace. "I just wanted to say thank you again, Doctor Benjamin. You've really helped us all along. I know we're going to need you a lot in the next weeks. I'm thankful to you, for that, in advance. I don't know what would happen if Jack didn't have you. He would just wither away on his own."

"He's got you Sue, it's all he needs." The doctor nodded his head to Sue, got in his car and drove off.

Sue turned toward the house and saw her grandchildren were no longer in sight. Becky was standing on the porch, waiting for her mom. Sue walked the twenty steps and embraced her daughter. The two looked in the other eyes and read the emotion. Both were confident their loved one was dealing with the situation. Each had their sanity still intact. Relief showed in the mother and daughter as they understood each other.

The sun was going down, creating long shadows in the driveway. Sue hoped the doctor would be careful. Currently of year, the shadows from the trees at sunset were blinding. Many accidents happened on Mountain Ranch road. Its curves mixed with the shadows and idiots added up to disaster.

The kids didn't need invitation. Like their mom, they were at home. They ran into the bedroom and jumped on the bed. Jack was happy to see his grandkids. He was bustling about with something in the closet. He dropped what he was doing and clumsily fell on the bed with the kids. All three let out shrieks as their Papa gingerly wrestled with them on the king size bed.

When Becky didn't come in right away, he wondered if everything was okay. Over five minutes passed before they came into the room. Jack knew the two women were close. As with all mother and daughters, there was a bond there that couldn't be replicated. He was sure both women had a lot to talk about, even though they'd seen each other two days before.

Jack was happy to see Becky. Although she was his stepdaughter, he always looked at her like his own. He loved her and her family. "Where's Brad?"

"He stayed home to get ready for work tomorrow. You know how we are Dad, dedicated."

"I do, and I respect it," Jack said. "I also respect you coming to see me so much. I appreciate it. I'm not very strong today, but I feel good. My thoughts are clear. I'm not taking any of the drugs from the doctor. They cloud your head."

"I know how you are, Dad."

Sirens began sounding in the distance. In this sleepy hollow, sirens weren't a good thing. They meant either fire or an accident. Over the next fifteen minutes, they got worse until the family became worried. Darkness arrived when the sirens ended. There was no road news in these parts. Like always, they would have to wait until the next day to see what happened.

The family spent the next couple hours making wind-chimes. Paige and her grandma cooked up a feast of spaghetti, salad and garlic bread. Paige cooked the spaghetti all by herself from a recipe she found online. The feast was incredible; the craft projects were rewarding. The time together brought a warmth to the adults and children alike.

It was a great time and the kids went home with some cool things they made with their grandparents. It would go with all the other things they made with their grandparents in the past. Jack and Sue were creative people, they wanted to instill the same in their kin. When they were old, the children would look at these creations with fond memories of their grandparents.

When Becky left at ten, her kids fell asleep immediately. They didn't even get to the end of the dirt road. Her drive home for the next hour and a half was in silence. Her thoughts were enough to keep her occupied. There was enough of them. She was surprised her stress wasn't so bad. The time with her parents and her kids together mended her broken heart. She knew this would be the key for the next few years: being together with her people.

She passed a spot, on Mountain Ranch Road, where there was evidence of a recent accident. Glass was strewn across the road and a fender was off in a ditch. She was happy it was cleaned up as the only detour would add an extra hour to her drive. She passed the spot with thoughts of her father in her head.

What Becky didn't realize was the accident did involve her. Doctor Benjamin was going westbound, when a texting driver crossed the yellow line in the Eastbound lane. The vehicles collided head-on. The other driver was in a pickup truck just arriving in the area for harvesting pot. He sustained a broken arm and a few cuts. Doctor Benjamin was killed instantly when the motor of his car broke through his dash and landed in his lap. It crushed the life from him.

Sue would find out the next day about the accident. When she told Jack about it, he was sad. He said he always liked the doctor. He also said it was all part of the cycle.

Sue asked her husband if there was another doctor he wanted to see from the office, but he just shrugged it off. She knew he wouldn't want any other doctor. He would be happy to just die here in peace. After seeing the effects of the medicine Jim sent, she didn't blame him.

"Speaking of that medicine," Jack said, "you got any rolled?"

Sue looked at her husband oddly. She didn't speak for a minute, then said, "I wasn't speaking about 'that medicine'. Not aloud at least."

Chapter 6

The next two weeks were spent in a flip flop of feelings for Jack. He would be in excruciating pain one minute, followed by euphoria the next. The herbs Jim sent were beneficial, but they put him to sleep every time he smoked it. The daytime would make him sleep for three to four hours. The nighttime would put him out for a solid nine. The medicine worked great to rid him of pain, but he didn't feel like he had all this time available for sleeping.

His body was decaying rapidly, riddled with its parasite. When the agony would become too intense, he would smoke some of his brother's medicine. It would alleviate the pain immediately. When it got to be terrible, Jack would smoke a whole joint to his head. The sleep would come rushing upon him like a freight train. The dreams would begin, and the torment would end. When he awoke, the misery wouldn't be present for hours. Whatever herb his brother sent him, it was truly a miracle.

Jack smoked pot all day in between. It made him relaxed and hungry. He smoked it like cigarettes; at times even chain-smoking his little hand-rolled doobies. He still hadn't taken any of the drugs the doctor prescribed, nor would he. He wanted to have a clear head in his last days. Prescription drugs were just man-made pollution people willingly ingested for the profit of the greed. The herb his brother sent, on the other hand, was from the Earth. It was harvested by true Shaman; the real doctors of the planet and its people.

Most of his days were spent in bed. His body wasn't making it easy on him. Sue would bring his paintings in, so he could work on them, but the hours were limited. The soreness would quickly turn to pain and the brushes would be forgotten. He wrote some letters and fiddled on his computer but all of it made him hurt. It was hard to be creative when your brain couldn't think of anything but pain.

He was happy when he finished his last will and testament; it seemed like a huge accomplishment. He remembered what death was like without a will and wasn't going to go out like that. He was going to be sure his family knew exactly what he wanted. There wasn't going to be fighting or outside forces trying to stick their fingers in his family's affairs. He knew how close his people were: he'd also seen, firsthand, the destruction death could bring to a family. Everyone had their own opinion about how to deal with things. The differences could be profound.

The few hours he managed to get up every day were spent visiting with his children and grandchildren. He didn't want them to see him weak and vulnerable in bed. He was the patriarch to his family, he would play the part.

Their children were still visiting religiously. Both Jack and Sue could see the stress it was causing on the family's sanity. It was a lot of activity to throw in to three already busy lives. One of the kids or more would visit every day. They made up a schedule amongst themselves but each of them came on their 'days off' to see their beloved father. Sometimes they would bring their kids, other times they would come alone.

Jack was happy to see his family every day. They were there to support him and Sue. The parents were proud of their children. All three turned out to be good humans. Times like this was when true family became evident. Both Jack and Sue, coming from large families, had seen both sides of family loyalty.

Jack wasn't one to have many friends, throughout his life. He doubted any of the few he retained would come see him in his last days. It was all the better, he thought. He didn't have many friends because he didn't want to give up his time to socialize when he could create. If he spent time with friends now, it would take time away from his family and the many projects he hoped to get done.

Many of Jack's friends, throughout his life, were older gentleman. He hung out with people of all ages, but somehow, the older dudes took a liking to him. Almost all these friends passed in the last few years. It had made him realize he wasn't far behind. He wasn't much younger than some of those fellows. Watching them go with the grace of age, made the cycle ever clearer in Jack's mind.

The only member of his family who hadn't arrived yet was Jim. It saddened Jack, he was very close to his younger brother. Jim lived twenty miles away in West Point. He'd been on the road tattooing for the last year. He came home a few times, but the visits were minimal.

Jim and Jack worked together for many years. Their creativity together left behind an indelible presence wherever they tattooed. Their reputation as people who cared about their clients was solid. While most tattoo guys were just into it for the money and fame, Jim and Jack were into it for the love of the tattoo. They traveled the world plying their craft and building their reputation. Their respect didn't come from self-promotion, it came from hard work and dedication.

The two still talked every day, as they had for over thirty years. Jack pleaded with his little brother to come and be by his side. Jim told him over and again: he was on his way back but there were stops on the road he must make first. Jack told him he would pay for his lost work, but his brother assured him, it was nothing about money. He even asked him if he was afraid to see his older brother dying but Jim laughed at the idea. "Your ideas about life and death are the same as mine," Jim said. "I'm not afraid of death, Bro; yours or mine."

Since the moment he was told the news about his brother, Jim packed up his tattoo equipment and headed back to California. The stops he made along the way were of a spiritual course plotted out long ago. The brothers made a pilgrimage when they were toddlers, with their true family, through these very lands. They met with medicine men and women and shared tales and secrets. They were initiated into a world which was scoffed at by science. They'd been accepted into another reality.

It came flooding back to Jim when he got the call from his brother. As soon as he hung up the phone, the memories of the trip, so long ago, returned. He remembered everything about it and everywhere they went. He understood: his mission was to retrace those footsteps and find the true path back to his brother. In doing so, he would be showing his brother the trail. Just as it was so many years before, the two would be making this trip together: this time, only in spirit. Jim knew they wouldn't be alone. Lisa and the rest of their clan would be by his side the entire adventure. This was a time of rebirth for the family.

The two brothers were close their entire lives. Just two years separated them. Their childhood found the two, inseparable. Their sister, Lisa, was usually by their sides. They grew up with the same hobby: Painting and drawing. Whenever they were creating, the three were happy. Throughout school, they always had the other sibling's back. When they were in high school, the three hung out in the same circle. They bought a beat up 1969 Chevelle when they were teens and worked for years turning it into a badass hotrod. When Jim turned eighteen, he and Jack enlisted in the Navy together.

When the mayhem struck Jack and Sue, it was Jim who was there to help put their lives back together. He always looked out for his brother and his family; just as they always looked out for him. Jim never married nor had children. He never settled for one woman. He could never sit still for long. He was always on the road or traveling somewhere. Whenever anyone asked him about not having a family, he'd say he was happy enjoying Jack's family. It was all he needed.

Jim moved to West Point fifteen years before. He saved his money and bought a modest house in the forest. With ten acres of land and no neighbors, it was the perfect spot for him to hone his artistic skills. When not traveling, he commuted to Stockton once a week and worked in a tattoo shop on the Miracle Mile. He purchased a boat on the delta and used it as his temporary home when he was in the city. He stopped drinking years before, after the tragedies in their family. He knew drinking and drugs were not the key to any form of healing. He steered clear of both: for himself and to set an example for his people.

After the death of their sister, Jim went on a mind-altering excursion throughout America. Not only did he need to find out who he truly was, he needed to know the history of his people. Without knowledge of their history, he could never look to the future.

When he spoke to Jack and learned his fate, he was in Fargo working at a small tattoo shop owned by his friend. He headed out after finishing the tattoo he was working on. He didn't get on the road until ten at night, but the desolate landscape of North Dakota doesn't matter what time of day. There were things to get done before getting on the road. His mind was racing with the visions of his route. It was like he was watching a movie in his mind, showing him the way, which was soon to become reality. He packed up his stuff at his buddy's house and plotted the route on a map. It wasn't difficult plotting the course, his mind already knew the path.

He drove all night and the next day. He only stopped to get gas or occasional food. A few early winter storms brewed up on the journey but, luckily, they didn't hamper his mission. He drove to Eastern Colorado before he knew it was time to stop.

Jim was in the middle of a high desert that was familiar to him. He drove with intent to a small homestead, some twenty miles away from nothing else. As he pulled up, he noticed there were no tire marks on the dirt road. He was the first person here in a very long time. On the porch was a guy who seemed to be ninety years old, or older. He was dressed in a fine, black suit like he was going to a funeral. This old man was the one who gave him the herbs he sent to help his brother.

Jim stayed with this shaman for two days. He was the first visitor in twenty years. The old man lived out here by himself creating his magic. His garden out back was his only nourishment. It is where he grew his food and medicine. He was an herbalist who could see the future and the past for which they truly were. Secluded as he was, this was one of the few people on the entire planet whose mind was not polluted by society and technology. This man was completely in-tune with Mother Earth.

They smoked herbs during the entire visit, but it wasn't the same as Jack received. The elder told Jim that he mixed those herbs just for Jack. As they smoked the yellowish leaves, the shaman told Jim he knew many things. He said he knew Jim was coming. He also said they met before, but Jim had been very small. "I can see that you remember my face. Although so many years have passed, our scars prove it, you recognize me. Your family brought you here, to this very house when you were a small child. I never forgot your parents, nor you, your brothers or sister. Your family was very important to me."

"I do remember. I'm retracing their travels. I must make it back to California in the next week to spend the last days with my brother."

"I have something else for you, young warrior." The old man took a small pouch out of his pocket and handed it to Jim. "I made this for your brother. I told you, I know many things about you and your brother. I've been having visions for the last few weeks. Since the last full moon. Your brother's cycle ends on the next full moon. I have dreamed it repeatedly."

The smoke they inhaled put Jim into a trance. He seemed to be floating above his body. The words spoke below were heard from above. His sight was level with the roof. He could see outside and into the top of the tree, which was eye-level. He was amazed at the dual perspectives he was encountering. He was floating in the room but also floating above the small house. A large crow flew by, did a double-take, and came back to investigate. The creature came eye to eye with Jim and seemed to speak with its mind. Words weren't formed, Jim just knew what it was saying. The bird was telling him, "welcome back old friend. The adventure now continues. Come, I will show you the way."

He began to follow the bird in flight and was impressed with his flying skills. As soon as he got to the corner of the roof, he was yanked back to his flesh pod, sitting idly by inside. He fluttered his eyes open to see the shaman looking directly at him. He seemed to be studying his pupil. The old man laughed a cacophony of madness. "You saw your guide. Now, go, be with your brother. You have a long road ahead my friend," the old man said.

"Yes, and I thank you." Jim gathered up his few possessions and got in his car. He realized, as the old man again stood on the porch, that he hadn't even learned his name. It was the way it was meant to be, Jim figured. Out here, you didn't need a title.

There was a thick layer of dust covering his truck. When he left, he turned on the radio to get some news. It was then Jim realized two days passed while he was here. It seemed like he'd been here for mere hours, but it was not the case. Something in those herbs made Jim go on a journey which took away his time. In the next days, on the road, those journeys would all come back to him, along with the wisdom from the shaman. When he was alone with his thoughts, the visions became coherent.

This old man passed on the wisdom of the plants to Jim. His way, raising a garden in the middle of a desert, was spiritual. His only friends were the plants and the few animals which passed by. His only companionship for twenty years was growing in his backyard; he listened to what they said and understood. He was like a scientist making experiments on himself, the lab rat.

The crow circled overhead and flew to the northwest. It looked over its shoulder once to make sure Jim was keeping up. He was following. This all seemed like a dream just days before, but after being here, he realized it wasn't a dream. It was his destiny and he'd seen it. He was part of it once and now he was bringing it all back around. The cycle was again going to be complete.

It was a destiny that began many years before, when they were children. Now, that destiny was going to be fulfilled. What was set in motion by their parents, was going to be completed by the children.

Getting to Jack's house was part of the destiny. So was every stop on the way. There would be six more. All of them would bring a little more solution to the puzzle. When he was done with his journey, Jim was going to help Jack more than any doctor ever could.

He wasn't going to heal Jack's flesh pod; he was going to ease his soul into the next cycle.

Jim was bringing spirituality to his family.

The awakening was near.

Chapter 7

Sue wept when Jim walked in the door. Knocking long ago ended with the closeness of family. She hugged her brother-in-law tightly. Relief washed through her soul.

"How is he?" Jim asked in a hushed voice. "Sorry it's taken me so long to get here."

"It's not looking good for your brother," Sue said. "He refuses to see a doctor, so we can only guess what his condition truly is. He is so weak Bro. I think he only has about a week left. He's lost almost all his strength. I think the only thing that's kept him going was waiting for you. Where have you been Knucklehead?" Sue pushed Jim away in mock anger. She crooked her finger his way as she spoke, "your Brother has been asking about you."

"I know, and I apologize. I've been talking to him every day, but I couldn't tell him why it was taking so long. I would just make up some bullshit every day when I called to answer his question about where I was. Fuck Sue, I've been on a mission to seek the truth. I've gathered so much knowledge in the last few weeks. The peregrinate I went on has completely enlightened me. I can really help Jack out. I have his cure. It is something we discussed when we were younger and now the theory has become reality," Jim said with confidence.

Sue could use any hope and help she could get, but this was ridiculous. "You haven't been around Jim. You don't know." Irritation filled her tone as she scolded her brother. "There is no cure for your brother. He's on his death-bed and there's nothing you can do about it. We've seen him withering away and now you're saying you have the cure. It's a bit late, Jim."

"I'm not talking about saving his flesh pod Sue," Jim said as he pushed into his brother's bedroom. He knew the importance of time and there was none to waste. The last thing he wanted to do was to argue with his sister-in-law when he could be chilling with his brother.

Jim was completely prepared for what he saw. He, too, didn't fear death. It was all a cycle to him and his brother. They talked about it many times throughout their lives. They began this discussion when they were small children. The theory of death, life and everything between those cycles was in their philosophy. What happened when you were living your life was up to you. What happened when you died and were reborn was up to destiny.

Jack awoke the moment Jim entered the room. Their energy was connected and had been for millennium. The dying man's wearied face instantly perked up when he saw his younger sibling. "I thought you were never going to show up," he said with a weak voice. Jim was by the side embracing his beloved brother. He missed being here the last few weeks but knew it was all part of the scheme. If he would've been here, the kids wouldn't have hung out with their father the same.

If he hadn't gone on his journey, there wouldn't be one now.

"I thought you were afraid to see me like this," Jack said as the hug ended.

"I don't think so motherfucker," Jim blurted out with respect. "I already told you how I feel about it all. I've been out fulfilling the destiny we set in motion so long ago. I've dreamed of you every night on my travels. I knew exactly how you would look. I spoke to the shamans and met with our ancestors. The ball is rolling Bro, and it's picking up speed. As your physical energy subsides, the enlightenment thrives." Jim was talking with so much animation, Jack knew he must be on something that took him to another level.

"What kind of madness you up to now, Jim?" Jack asked. There was no doubt in his voice; he had full confidence in his brother. "Whatever it is, you know I'm on board. Spending my last days in this small room with a progression of family saying goodbye wasn't how I envisioned going out. I thought my ending would be spectacular. I certainly didn't think I would burn out. I wanted to go down in flames. A fitting close to an adventurous life. I guess it wasn't meant to be."

"It's not over yet, Jack. It's not pity-party time. You have some time left here and I'm going to make sure it's a bang, not a fizzle. I'm going to be right here the entire time. I have the truth and I'm ready to share it with you. Wisdom awaits you at the end of this journey. The story began long ago. It was written many centuries before our births. This story guided our destinies throughout our lives. Now, I know the story. My last task as your brother, in this existence, is to spin this yarn to you. It will guide you to the next step. Our next phase of the cycle. The story and journey are long. Are you prepared?"

"I have nothing but limited time Bro," Jack said. "Just an hour ago, I was lying here thinking that my last days were going to be worthless. After this great life I've lived, the last of it would be meaningless. Funny how quickly things can change. I knew you'd come through. I knew you'd be by my side, sharing your energy. I'm so ready to be enlightened. Now, little Brother, show me the way." His voice seemed to Jim as almost normal. The dying man was already energized by his brother's presence in the first few moments of his arrival.

"Right on man, but first we must open our third eye," Jim said as he pulled a small leather pouch from his pocket. The object gave off an aura as Jack's gaze was fixed on it. When Jim opened the drawstring on top, light poured from the opening.

Jim dumped the contents of the pouch into his hand. It was a glass jar about an inch tall and three-eighths of an inch thick, with a cork on the top. It had a silver dragon ornately wrapped around its exterior which was hourglass shaped. The purple glow emanating from the glass gave the dragon a multi-colored hue. Jim uncorked the bottle but was interrupted by laughter.

"You're going to give us doses?" Jack asked with a chuckle. "Fuck man, you've only been here a few minutes. Did you tell Sue about this?"

"I didn't tell Sue; but she dropped acid with us in the past. She knows she can trust me. I've been to spiritual leaders across the lands in the last few weeks. Trust me Bro, I know what I'm doing. This LSD was formulated expressly for the two of us. I tested it more than once. It's very good. This is the first day, Jack. All week, I have new medicines to ingest with you to help guide us to our ancestors. They're waiting for you, Man."

"Just tell Sue so she isn't worried, okay? She's done so much for me in the last weeks and I know this death thing has stressed her out, big-time. Maybe she could even go visit her mom now that you're here with me. Out of respect though, please tell her. You know how I am; if I have stress during my trip it isn't as good. This would be something heavy on my brain."

Jim was already putting the small cap on the vile as he began to talk. "No problem Jack. I just now arrived anyhow. I'm excited to see you and get this adventure started. I'll try to calm my enthusiasm. It's just two o'clock and we have all night ahead of us. I've been on the road for weeks and haven't had a good shower, or meal, the whole time. My life has been primal at times. I'll tell you about it this week. For now, I'll shower and maybe Sue could make us some food. Then we'll have energy for the journey we're about to traverse. It's going to be a trip that really opens your eyes, Bro. It holds the answers to all the questions we used to ponder. Wisdom is what I've brought to you."

"Right on, Man, I'll be ready when you get back. I'll rest for a bit and get my thoughts prepared for this journey tonight. It's good to see you Jim. I hope you don't think I'm trying to back out of this. It's the farthest thing from the truth. I need to be on this flight."

They both laughed as Jim walked out the door. They saw the irony of the situation. Jim arrived barely ten minutes before and all they talked about was doing acid together. There was no mention of medical status or anything else. All that mattered, now that Jim was there, was the journey.

Sue was in the kitchen, already, preparing something that smelled delicious. Jim walked to the counter and said, "Sure is smelling good in here." The casualness of Jim's behavior spoke volumes of the relationship between the two.

"Yeah, Bro, I thought you might be hungry. You look like you haven't been home yet. As a matter-of-fact, you look homeless. You just rolled into town and came straight here, didn't you?"

"You know it Sue. There was no time to go home. I've been away long enough. This road trip was the most exhaustive I've ever been on. Now, I'll happily use your shower. I have clothes in the car. I'm going to stay here for the next week anyhow, if that's good with you. I want to be close to you guys for the last days. It's important to me."

"You know it's fine with me Bro. You're welcome any time. Even when you're bringing along hocus pocus. I don't know what you're up to, but I trust you. Go take a shower now and get refreshed. Please! Grub will be ready when you get out."

"Thanks Sue. I always appreciate being here and everything you do for me. Whatever you're cooking smells great. It'll be much better than anything I've eaten in the last weeks." Jim headed toward the bathroom but stopped in the doorway and turned back toward his sister. "One more thing, we're going to drop acid tonight. Do you mind?"

The woman stopped the cooking and looked at her brother-in-law without expression. She stared at him for half a minute, trying to see if he was joking. Jim returned the stare defiantly to his sister-in-law. "Are you serious or are you joking?" she asked.

"I'm completely serious. I've been to shaman and spiritual healers all the way across the west. This is very deep Sue. I know all you can focus on is your husband dying, but there is a much larger picture. Reality is not what we perceive it to be. I'm going to show Jack the truth. There's no question it's going to happen. It's our destiny. I now hold the axiom about that destiny. I have learned the truth. When Jack goes to the ancestors, he too will have the Wisdom."

"It sounds pretty crazy, but I trust you Jim. You two are adults, anyhow, and can do what you want. Is Jack good with this?"

"Yeah Sue, he is more than good with it. Think about it, die wallowing in your own misery; or die having the adventure of your lifetime. Which is it you think Jack would want? Or yourself for that matter."

"I think he would want to go down in flames. I've read about cancer patients being given hallucinogens to help ease the transition into the next phase. I was always intrigued but haven't once thought about it since, until now. So much other madness has been happening. His doctor died in a car crash on the way home from our house. Jack felt terrible. He refused to see another doctor. Now you have arrived with the solution to his misery. One of only a few people he trusts. You've brought something that might be called a true miracle."

"Exactly my feelings Sue. Me and Jack talked about this so many times over the years. You were there during some of those conversations. LSD is a miracle drug which has spiritual powers. It's not a party favor; it's a serious catalyst into other dimensions. It opens our minds, so we can see the fringes of these dimensions which exist all around us. I have tested this acid. It's good, beyond what words can describe. It came from the same old guy in Eastern Colorado that I got the herbs from." Jim got sidetracked from his dialogue by his own exuberance. "The herbs I sent to you, have they been helping?"

"Oh, hell yeah, they've been helping. It erases Jack's pain every time he smokes it. At night, he's in a coma for long hours and wakes up pain free. Thank you so much for sending it. That stuff helped us both out."

"This LSD is from the same guy. I drove to Eastern Colorado to meet with this dude and we hung out for two days. It was the first stop and the first shaman I would meet on my journey. I knew exactly where to go to meet this guy and everyone after. I met six more before arriving here. It was the same at each. I would stay anywhere from hours to four days. Each visit left me more enlightened. They would experiment on me to make the proper dose for Jack. Since we share the same DNA, it was easy for them to concoct the perfect batch."

"I can't wait to hear those stories," Sue said. "If the same guy made this dose that gave you those herbs, then I'm all for Jack doing it. If it helps him, I say thank you."

"You're going to hear about things you never knew possible in the next week. You're going to be part of this entire trip. The three of us have always been bonded together, now we're going to be cement. It's going to go on all week long. Enlightenment awaits us at the end of our journey. Tonight though, after we eat, I think it would be a good idea if you went to see your Mom for a bit. I need some time with Jack alone and I'm sure you need to get out of this house. I'm sure you haven't left your husband's side since this began."

"I haven't. I would love to go see my Mom. She isn't so well these days either. I'll go late afternoon and come back after midnight. Thanks Jim, for always being there for us. All those years ago, we bonded. I know you'll be here for me and the kids after this is all over." Sue walked around the counter and hugged her brother. She wished she could show Jim how much he meant to the family; somehow though, she knew she didn't need to.

"I'll always be here for you guys," Jim said with sincerity. "You're my family and mean everything to me. Family is not just a word to me. I feel the connection with you guys. Our energy, together, makes one."

Sue went back to her cooking. The menu was going to be scant this afternoon. She didn't have time to go for groceries or anything else. She'd been in the house for the last week. Jack's appetite was slight; their pantry fulfilled the needs. But now, things were running out. She found some eggs and frozen hamburger which she made into Salisbury steaks. Some expired tube biscuits and frozen hash-browns completed the put together meal.

Jim stood at the doorway and watched Sue from behind for a few moments. He had the utmost respect for her. He wasn't looking at her in any sort of inappropriate way. It was his sister and he cared for her as a person. He looked at her with admiration. He was happy to have a strong person to help him through this ordeal. Even though he wasn't afraid of death, he was going to miss his brother. The next months and years, without Jack, were going to be hard on him and their family. Jim knew, you lived through many deaths before you got to your own.

She felt him standing there, watching her. Her senses were strong like those of the brothers. When he stood there, she felt a sense of joy for the first time in ages. A small smile crept up on her face which soon became a large grin. In a matter of moments, Sue's demeanor completely changed. Her brother brought good energy. It was exactly what the family needed.

By the time Jim got out of the shower, Sue was singing while finishing up lunch. She felt better than she had in so long. Today, she knew everything was going to be okay.

The food was a big hit. Jim even got his brother to eat a decent amount. Sue ate more than normal; Jim ate what was left. He looked more like himself after showering and putting on fresh clothes. Sue could see his health hadn't waned in the least during the long miles traveled; nor his appetite.

The three talked about the kids and grandkids throughout the meal. It was consumed in the bedroom with Jack being the central point.

Sue took the dishes away when they were done. This hadn't been a fancy holiday meal or anything. There was no need to make it drawn-out. It was just nourishment. She stacked the dishes in the sink and got the notion to make a cake. It wouldn't take long and her mom would really appreciate it. She whipped it up and popped it in the oven, all within ten minutes.

As the cake was baking, Sue took her shower and got ready. It didn't take her long. She was more than ready to get out of this house for a bit. It wasn't her husband; it was being in one place, for much too long, that got to her.

When she was dressed and ready, the cake was done. From the kitchen, Sue could feel the change of energy in the house. She was waiting for the cake to finish cooling. It delayed her departure but would be well worth the time. Anything she could do to make her mom happy would make her happy. Modesto was over an hour away, she would still be there before too late.

When she heard the laughter coming from the bedroom the second time within the hour, she headed that way to investigate. She hesitated briefly with doorknob in hand. She hadn't heard her husband laugh in a long time. She stood silently and reveled in the sound that she knew might be the last time she heard it. The thought saddened her but made her happy at the same time. Sue would cherish this laughter she was hearing for the rest of her life. It brought up so many emotions in her, she had to lean on the door-jam for support.

By the time she opened the door, the laughter and energy built so much Sue could swear it burst through the opening. Both men had tears streaming down their faces. The previous joke was long forgotten as they progressed on to more silly humor. Sue could see, immediately, that her husband and brother were tripping. There was a look in the eye and an amplification of the aura that was the sure signs. She wasn't angry in the least. Jim showed her the respect and asked her permission. She thought how respectful the act had been: asking to save her husband's soul.

She knew of the bond each brother possessed for the other. She also knew both men well and knew their outlook on LSD and hallucinogens. She hoped this would ease the transition, and anguish, that gripped her family.

Sue stood silently in the doorway for over five minutes. Neither man ever saw her. It wasn't a problem to her; she was happy to watch. She eased her way out of the space and closed the door. She had a smile on her face as she headed to the kitchen and then the car. It was a nice evening for late October. She thought she could catch up on some writing that she'd been wanting to get done when she got home. She knew, from experience, that she wouldn't be able to sleep as soon as she got home, no matter what time. Writing always helped her unwind, and tonight, she had a lot to say.

Sue looked forward to seeing her mom. They'd always been very close. When her father died ten years before, Sue was the only one of her children who was there to help.

With the smell of the German chocolate cake in the backseat, she drove off. She thought to herself: she hadn't felt this good in a long time.

.

Chapter 8

The late afternoon sun fell upon Jack. Its rays fully engulfed the dying man but nothing else. His aura was illuminated with a golden glow. It was obvious to the brother what was happening. Each shaman told him about this coming miracle. Jack was being touched by the hand of god.

Jim reached into the light and gave his brother one drop before taking one himself. He felt the warmth of the sunbeam and smelled its pureness. Jim never felt connected to anything more in his life than with this energy. It enveloped the brothers in golden sunshine. All either of them could think of was goodness. These were the purest thoughts of their life. Unfortunately, the moment passed swiftly.

The sun set just enough to steal its warm beam from the dying man's body. The instant Jim reached into its holy domain, the light began to subside. These rays weren't meant for the living. He wasn't saddened, just happy he got to experience a bit of the magic. He was blessed in that brief exchange of light; a reward by the gods for the good he brought his brother.

"I tracked this acid down by following clues given to me in my dreams. They were messages from our people, man. They've been showing me the way. The path to this moment was guided by us. We had an equation to figure out and we've been working on it our entire lives. Now, exam time is here." As he spoke, Jim adeptly put the cap back on the vile before slipping the small object back into its leather pouch.

"This LSD was devised for us with the overall picture in mind. We're going to trip for the next seven days. Each dose was designed by a different shaman I met. Some of these shamans are related to us. They each devised the exact formula to merge into the trip from the previous day. By the seventh day, we'll achieve total enlightenment. Our God, Wisdom, will have visited us and given us the knowledge."

"I don't know about you, but God just visited me right now. You know I'm in Bro," Jack replied. "I fully trust you and am ready for anything. Since you got here, it's all I can think about. You're truly saving my death by healing my life. You are a great brother."

"I hope you say the same on the seventh day, Man. Each day this week will represent the visit I had to acquire the medicine. That moment and this will run parallel, like an alternate universe. They will be in the same order as I obtained them. I can say, from experience, they get much stronger as each day progresses. I only had a small sampling of what's coming, and it was fucking crazy. I went places and learned things hidden from humans a very long time."

"It's so cool you went through all this for me, Man," Jack interrupted. "It was in my thoughts you'd show up with some acid, but I couldn't even have dreamed of something like this."

"You don't even know Jack. On day seven, we're going to merge our beings for a moment and cross over to the other side together. You'll be staying there, but I'll be coming back. A piece of you will remain with me, as a piece of me will remain with you. It's how it has always been."

Jack interrupted his brother's words with a raised hand. "This is what we talked about when we were kids, Jim. It was just kids on drugs talking bullshit about things we didn't know anything about. I thought you understood that."

"Maybe to you Jack, it was bullshit. To me, it was the beginning of a path I've been on since. When I tell you this story, you'll have no doubt. You'll see what we talked about all those years ago wasn't fantasy. It was repressed memories that have been in our bloodline for thousands of years. I've learned a little on my journey. Together, we will learn a lot."

"I know all about your stories Jim. I'm sure you're going to spin a whopper of one today. Like I said, I'm ready for anything."

"Why do you think we always talked about the same thing?" Jim asked. "You think it was coincidence we were so passionate about it. No man, this is a game we play. It's not our first time playing. We keep playing, over and over, until we lose. Then, it's game over."

Jack raised three fingers and said, "I know two things Jim: I trusty you one hundred percent" a snicker and snort followed his pun on words. He calmed and said, "I'm beginning to feel that acid like a motherfucker." Jack's voice was higher than normal but strong. The expanded feeling of tone in his talk surprised even him. His funny use of words and miscount with his fingers didn't surprise Jim.

The brothers laughed at the joke and found themselves unable to stop. Their laughter got so loud, it would have disturbed the neighbors, if they had any close by.

As the doses were taking hold of the brother's conscious, the sun slowly set. Its lingering descent cast long shadows across the room which were enhanced by two active imaginations. When the light was completely twisted inside the small room, the LSD had full command of the travelers' consciousness.

Jack's mind opened like a flower in its prime. Suddenly, everything his brother told him earlier was true. His eyes opened wide as did his pupils. With his eyes open to reality, he was ready for the enlightenment. He looked to his brother and listened for the story he'd waited his entire life to hear.

Jim began his saga: "Our tale began long before we were born. Our ancestors were our beginning, as it is with all animals. We are small threads of their DNA mixed with other threads, creating who we are. All those threads sewed together is the patchwork of life on the planet. It is the code which controls everything living."

"I don't really need a biology lesson, Mr. Sagan," Jack said with amusement, which turned to laughter. "We've talked about this shit our entire lives. I understand about DNA. It's been showing its colorful twists to us since we were small children." He burst into laughter so hard, tears filled his eyes. Jim was looking at his brother and saw the transformation in his face. His features were twisted. His skin was waxy looking; his eyes were changing color. Jim couldn't hold back his own laughter at the sight and sound of his brother morphing in front of him. Jim let go and laughed hysterically for a good five minutes.

Out of exhaustion, the two slowly weened themselves away from the hysteria. It was another five minutes before they finally got it under control. After assurances from each other, the story telling resumed.

"Come on, Bro, you can't just jump into a story," Jim said. "Now shut up and listen, I'm building up." The two started to lose it again but they regained control; each reminded the other of their agreement.

"You've been telling me to listen, but you ain't saying anything I don't already know. If you're not going to say something good, then get the fuck out of here" Jack said with sarcasm. He would never speak like this to anyone but his brother. Their relationship had always been honest. They didn't offend each other. They knew when the other was joking and when they were serious. Either way, they wouldn't be mad at each other over words.

Jim mocked clearing his throat and continued: "Okay, enough about the ancient history of DNA. That will have to wait till you're tripping balls. Then, maybe, you'll be more interested in the beginning of the story. The end will be much better if you know the beginning; but have it your way."

The brother's voices were like music being played under water. They both had a rhythm that made their words flow like a tune, but the garbled sounds would have been indiscernible to anyone but them. In their minds, the other was speaking perfectly normal, if not mellifluously.

"Come on man, most of this story is stuff I told you anyway. I'm sure you'll be telling me what I already know." Jack was a spiritual person since childhood. Out of seven kids, Jack, Jim and their late sister, Lisa, were the ones connected. Their parents made them go to church when they were children, but they despised it. The three steered clear of that nonsense as soon as they had the option. They all knew God didn't live inside a building waiting for humans to give money to appease 'him'. That whole scenario of a man-God who wanted money for salvation was a complete joke to them all.

Jim began again: "Our parents weren't truly our birth givers. We come from a long line of Shamanic people whose ancestry I traced back thousands of years. Our true parents were murdered by the catholic church. The same exact church we were part of growing up in Stockton. They claimed our family's healing power was witchcraft. In truth, the church was losing parishioners rapidly. The people were becoming less trusting of an organization that took their riches and judged them for centuries."

"The people were beginning to go back to the way of the Earth and the Sun. The true Gods were once again being worshipped. The masses began looking up to the same folks the church condemned for eons; like our family. The people wanted clergy who could heal them with herbs and songs. They wanted to be able to do as they pleased without anyone judging or persecuting them. The church would have none of this. Without their followers, they would have no more treasure. They were the first corporation in the world. They knew how to keep their power. They pointed fingers and made accusations; it's how they do things. They turned the people against the true healers. The prophets of the true Gods, not man-made fairy tales, were branded as liars. They were discredited and murdered. The corporation spread fear to regain control. It was their cycle from the beginning."

Jim took a big swig from his glass of water and continued. "The Catholics burned our family alive, in the middle of the night. They made it look like it was a black man from down the street who they had issues with. He had spoken out about the local church and one of the priests. He accused the clergyman of molesting his child. The church resented it. They were thorough in their set-up; he's still in prison today for the murder of our family. The church sent in their minions, pretending to be someone passing by, to remove the three of us. I was only two months old. You were barely three. Lisa was a year and a half. We had two older brothers who were in their teens. They were burned alive in the fire. They weren't permitted to live. They were too old and would've been able to tell what really happened that night. A few 'eyewitnesses' sealed the fate of the neighbor while the true perpetrators continued on like usual."

"The people who raised us as our parents were part of the conspiracy. Their other kids, our older sisters and brother, were not our blood. They were part of it too. Remember how religious they were. They were deep in the church. They were so different than us but tried so hard to make us feel like we fit in. It was a cult, or something, where they traded children. Multiple families had the same thing happen to them in the fifties and sixties. The family would be deemed evil by the church; the children were taken as the parents perished. The children would live with their new families and become part of the flock. Our story is one of many clans persecuted by the greed. However, unlike most, we woke up."

"When Lisa died last year, she told me what happened. She took a DNA test and the ancestry didn't add up to the rest of our people. She started asking questions and doing research. With the internet and other resources, she realized the truth. We've been lied to our whole lives."

"Our family first came to this country in the early sixteen hundred's. Before that, they came from a small region in Latvia. They lived there over four thousand years. During this time, they spread their wealth of wisdom throughout Europe. Their ancestors came from the Tigris river area. They were part of the ancient city of Ur. They migrated to Northern Europe when it was inhabited by primitive man.

These ancestors had gifts that were valuable to the natives. They had healing powers, along with knowledge of the cosmos. The seeds they brought on their backs was the beginning of civilization on the continent. They brought language and arts which shaped humans into the creatures we now are. Without our people, Europe would have been a battle-field instead of a cultural icon."

"I already know all this stuff," Jack exclaimed. His voice sounded like a warped record playing with a bent needle. It made Jim laugh uncontrollably which was contagious. Both men's raucous laughter brought a healthy aura to the room. The shadows were alight with the energy of the two. Full light wasn't needed when you could truly see.

The story Jim told was projected on the ceiling by some unseen lens. In Jack's mind, it was clearer than any movie he ever saw at the cinema.

By now, the acid-trip was in full after-burners. Like every time they tripped, it took control of the craft. The brothers could sit back and enjoy the auto-pilot feature. They had nothing to do all evening and night but tell their story. By morning, they'd be ready to retake control of the cockpit. The landing would be manual as would be the next take-off, which would soon follow. There would be no long layovers on this trip.

The familiar expansion in the back of the throat signaled they were up to full speed. The journey was coming around the next bend. The feeling of cotton in the head was clearing the brain of its nonsense. All the senseless stress that built up from daily life was expelled with one little drop of liquid. Only true thoughts would happen on this trip.

The brothers looked at the other twisting face with wonder. Within two minutes, that wonder turned to laughter. This time, no pact was going to stop it soon. This was an all-out free-for-all of madness.

The laughter in the house continued for a long time. Both men's red faces were streaked with tears. Their eyes seemed to be glowing as did their auras. When they finally controlled their laughs, mere words or slight actions would begin the outbreak once again. It took all their willpower to get the laughter under control. They realized their task was going to take all their thoughts. They had no time for this foolish behavior.

When it was restrained, Jim's tone became more subdued and serious. His existence felt like a helium balloon being inflated. The inflation wouldn't stop until he burst with knowledge. He said to his brother, "okay, I know you were close to Lisa also, but I have learned so much more in the last year. My travels have truly opened my eyes. I told you I was on a tattooing road-trip, but it was only partially true. I was tattooing only enough to make money to keep on the road. You know how it is. There was a lot of research and a lot of people I needed to meet. I've met hundreds of people in the last year who were related to us by blood or related to us by friendship."

"Where all have you been?" Jack asked. His voice still sounded like he inhaled helium and was singing underwater, but the brothers were over the laughter. This talk had been waiting to come out for a very long time. Their minds were open from the doses, they didn't need to block them with laughter. The outbreak had purged their beings of the trivial monstrosity of everyday life.

"I was in every state in the Continental United States. It was the western states I spent the most time in. West of the Mississippi that is. I started traveling just after Lisa died. Of course, I've been here a few times, but I've mostly been on the road for a year. I've been searching. There were so many of our people out there. With the internet, I found a few. After meeting them, I was introduced to so many more. They were all spiritual people, just like us. They were all very interesting folks. Some of them taught me things that seem like they would be in a science fiction novel. All of them were very helpful. They all were in tune with your plight and said they were sending you energy. Some even remembered us from when we were very young, before the fire. I can see all their faces right now; it's like they're here with us."

Jack was staring out the window as his brother spoke. He loved this place. Something about Mountain Ranch called to him when he was young. When Sue's family came along, it was natural for them to move here. He loved the fact he was going to die right here in his own little paradise.

Jack was weak before, but now felt like he could go jogging. A new strength was sparked in his brain. He slowly got his legs out of bed, swung them to the side and got his feet on the floor. It was a few minutes before he dared even sit up. All the while, Jim's voice rattled on his story in the background. His voice sounded like it was in a different room but was still perfectly clear. It was like a megaphone at the sideshow, in Jack's mind. He pictured Jim wearing a top-hat and standing behind a podium.

When he got the strength to sit up, the momentum of his torso pulled him to a standing position. On shaky legs, Jack triumphantly stood tall.

Jim watched his brother try to get up the entire time he spoke. It would have been comical if not for the seriousness of the situation. He was proud of his older brother. He knew his voice was acting like a drum beat of sorts, motivating the sick man. When Jack took his first step, Jim wanted to applaud. Instead, he kept on with his story. It went on a very long time as Jack's snail-like progress to the window and back took all evening. Or so it seemed in their minds, where there was no need for time.

"It's no coincident that Lisa died one year ago. This weekend will be exactly one year. The day you are to die, Jack, will be the exact date, a year removed. It's also the day our parents died. The day the church gave us to our adopted family. This date, October 13 is not a coincident. Nothing is a coincident. Lisa got cancer just like you have now. It was rare in her and you have the same shit. She, too, only lived for one month after being diagnosed. Don't you feel like that's odd? After we were captured and given a new family, they did mind control experiments on us. The church, government or whoever else warped our young brains. For all we know, Man, we could be the next Manchurian candidate. Fucking scary. You won't be around to be manipulated, but I will be. Why did they leave me alive out of the three of us? They clicked a switch in you and Lisa and gave you cancer. I'm either going to get the same thing or they have plans for me. Whichever it is, I'm fucked."

Jack stopped in his steps. He was halfway back to the bed, but these words required a reply. He was listening carefully all day to his brother's dialogue. Now, he was going a little too far. "You're out of your mind, Manchurian candidate. Where would you get that notion? I don't feel like anyone had mind control over me."

"That's what you say, Jack, but remember how the three of us always talked about being abducted by aliens. Well it was true. Since we were children, we were abducted; our memories were manipulated. Our brains were washed of any memory of our real parents. These memories of alien abductions were just part of the experiment. They could control our minds and make us do and believe anything they want."

"Who is they?" Jack asked. He was only a couple of feet further in his journey, but he felt proud of his progress. The fresh air from the window he opened was the best trophy he ever received in his life. He earned that prize; the walk had been exhaustive. If not for the energy from the hallucinogen, he would have stopped long before getting back to bed.

"The same people in control since the beginning of civilization on this planet. The Greed. They control everything. I don't know exactly who they are, but my guess is they're from another planet. They brought technology and knowledge with them and they have slowly given it to the humans. In return, the humans are their slaves. We mine their minerals for them. We grow their food and prepare it for them. We build their houses, electronics and infrastructure. We are their servants. They are ones who control what they created just for more control. While the humans slave away, the greed wallow in our riches. All the while, they tell us what is good and evil. Without a doubt, they are the evil."

"When they first came, the humans thought they were gods. The Earthlings were hunters and gatherers. They had a crude written language that was universal. It was a language of symbols. That was as far as their evolution progressed until the visitors arrived. The humans worshipped the Gods from the sky and gave them food. With the technology from the newcomers, they built shelter and temples for their new idols. The aliens liked this new treatment and decided being in charge was the way when sharing a planet with an inferior species. In truth, the humans were not inferior at all. They were an earlier version of the visitors. DNA was spread throughout the cosmos. Where life could be supported, it manifested. It was different in every place, but occasional species would pop up throughout the universe. The human gene was one of them. Because of this, some of the newcomers disagreed with the new agenda. They went in search of life to enhance their beings as well as the planet they colonized. These beings saw the natives as equals. These simple Earthlings were in touch with the planet and its bounty. They knew of the stars and the seasons. On their home planet, the visitors knew mostly about war and technology. It's what drove this exploratory team to the neighboring solar system. These few alien rebels dispersed amongst the natives and shared their knowledge as one, bringing about peace and comfort for all. The rebels made it clear they were not gods. They saw the planet as a place where art and empathy could prevail. A place where everyone was equal. There would be no riches, so there would be none of the issues associated with the greed. Unfortunately, the rebels were few while the colonizers numbered many."

"The Greed was much stronger than the dissenters. Their power was derived from weak natives looking to join a side. With just a little fear, these beings knew how to control the masses. When the humans saw the greed being worshipped, they wanted to be on that side. The couple hundred alien individuals and couples who couldn't be a part of this control, moved to all corners of the Earth. They wanted no part in enslaving an entire planet for their own comfort. They built boats with the natives and took many with them as companions. The rebels befriended the few humans who had no interest in getting things from the greed. They wanted to continue a life living in harmony with the planet. They wanted to be happy and not have a lot of worries. The enlightened humans were happy as the rebels took them to their new homes. At first, they were safe. The long arm of the greed didn't yet stretch to other continents. There were plenty of riches where they were, in northern Africa. When the greed expanded their empire, bringing civilization with it, it was the beginning of the end. Manifest Destiny was a word created to destroy others in the name of spreading your own name. These guys never cared about wealth, only power and watching people suffer. If the people from the beginning could have figured it out, it would have prevented a lot of chaos around the globe for the next forty thousand years. As huge tribes perished, the greed was still cherished."

"Soon after the rebels departed, the greed were content with DNA experiments on the natural beings of the planet. Millions of species of animals and plants went extinct at this time as the aliens altered DNA to make things more to their liking. There was inner turmoil amongst the leaders. A fight for control of the group waged for twenty thousand years. Exactly what they left their planet for, they brought with them to this one. The humans were used in these battles like pawns. They painted petroglyphs in caves, hidden from the greed, recording the times. These petroglyphs tell the history of humans on Earth. When the battles were over, only two hundred of the original colonizers survived. Established as Gods, these beings were happy to sit back and enjoy the spoils of their war riches, without sharing. All the beings on the planet belonged to them and they would do with them as they pleased. They felt the same about the Earth. They treated their own planet the same and two other satellites in their solar system, before. Now, they did it to this planet."

"Around the fourteenth century, the greed amassed enough humans to carry out their ultimate plan. These bastards went after the defectors who abandoned their vision. To these elite, the others were traitors who had no place on this planet. With the powers they possessed, these rebels would be a danger to the Greed and their minions. A threat to the stability of chaos the greed created. They figured it would be best to erase all these families from the face of the Earth. All the bloodlines would be exterminated. Once they had one of them, all their identities would be known through DNA. Long before these invaders arrived here, they knew about DNA and its powers."

"Wars raged in Africa while the rest of the planet lived in harmony. The rebels taught a new way to the humans. Instead of enslaving them, these visitors taught them arts, astronomy and peace. Their architecture at this time was some of the most amazing ever created on Earth. Some of the humans became very smart while others grew angry. It was all about where you were born and whose DNA you received. The rebels also spread their DNA, but it was through mating with the humans. They didn't see themselves as Gods who were better than the natives. It was the opposite. They saw the primitives as loving, kind beings who worked well with their group. They looked at them as equals and found them attractive. After living with them for a couple of decades, it was only natural to mate with the native humans. All the while, the greed only mated amongst themselves. Their idea was to keep the pure race intact. If they were to mix with the commoners, they would be common themselves. They were more than happy to remain gods."

"It turned out not so easy to find all the dissidents. Some hid well, while others blatantly used their powers to help the humans. Some of the rebels became messiahs who began religions which remained strong for thousands of years. Each of these Shaman were found and murdered by the Greed. They didn't hide at all. Our ancestors, at the time, were in Northern Europe, out of the watchful eye of the Elite. It was safe there for them until the fifteenth century when England decided to overtake the Black Sea. The Greed found hundreds of our people scattered throughout Scandinavia and murdered them all. Our ancestors were some of the lucky ones who escaped. Some of our people moved on with their kin to Greenland and Iceland. The Americas had been explored extensively by others of our kind. Many even colonized this part of the planet, bringing their knowledge to the natives."

"Everywhere they went, the temples were built in tribute to their Sun and Moon, the planets and Earth; all the true Gods to the people. The greed found pleasure destroying every temple they encountered. As our kind became less in number, they learned to adapt at moving around; hiding in the mix with the rest of the humans. Their DNA would always pop up, though, and bring light upon their existence. Then, the greed would find the other members of the clan and systematically take them out. This is what happened to our parents. They found them through my birth. It was an emergency and the hospital got involved. After the tests, their secret was in the open. Because of this exposure we've been watched by the Greed our entire lives. They planted microchips in us. They knew if these devices were found, we would assume it was connected to the alien abductions we experienced. It was connected all right. Everything is connected"

"The death of Tommy was part of their grand scheme. So was the death of his mother. You see, Jack, they've been fucking with us for a very long time, just because they can. They're still chapped at our ancient ancestors who told them to fuck off. It hurt their shitty little egos so much, they still must persecute the offspring all these years later. Lisa was murdered by these fuckers, just like you. I'm sure, after all these years, you miraculously had another abduction within the past six months. It was the same as Lisa. It spanned years since it happened to any of us and then, Boom! Six months later, she was dead. Has this happened to you lately?"

"How can you say that about Tommy? He was taken by a serial killer. We have all the proof and evidence. I don't know how you can say it was the elite who killed our sister or my son. So, what if I had the dream again recently? It doesn't make any difference."

"It makes all the difference, Jack. They implanted you with a virus destroying your flesh pod. These bastards are thorough in their work. Their lies and deceptions make us believe whatever they choose. They want to exterminate us and all of those like us. Not only are they killing our pods, they're taking our souls. When they're done, our existence will be forever gone. That's why I'm here to help you. I'm going to save your soul and send you to our ancestors. Many of them have been saved. These talismanic rituals have been performed for a very long time. Our parents and many generations before them sacrificed their flesh pods to be whole in the other dimensions. The Greed never even knew it. In their smug celebratory back slap, they overlooked the fact that one of their weapons was thwarted by those who held the same intelligence."

"What about my kids then? Are they going to be taken in too? Did they steal Tommy's soul?"

"I don't know about Tommy yet. It's something we'll find out in the next days. Ronnie and Becky don't share your blood-line. They don't want to take out just anyone. Little Jack, on the other hand, will be in danger his entire life. Just as we have been in danger our entire lives. I would like to think that I could help him and his kids, but it would be a lie. I can't even help myself. I'm next. They got Lisa, you and I will be last. I don't care Jack. Our souls are safe if we have one of our kind nearby and ready to help. For you, that person is me. For me that person is Jack Junior. We all have someone."

"Who's going to help Little Jack?"

"There's no need for worries Bro. I'm sure you remember these talks we had when we were kids about all kinds of shamanic things. It was true what we were talking. We were just remembering from past lives. This knowledge has been in our clan for hundreds of thousands of years. It was natural for us to talk about them all those years ago. It was yet another preparation for now."

The talk abruptly came to an end. It was a lot to take in. Both men were having visions flashed into their conscious from a higher wisdom. For the next three hours, the brothers relived past events in their lives; silently in their own minds. As the sun set and darkness overtook the room, the acid went into the next phase and put both men into deep thought. Every memory they ever had flashed through their minds. Their breathing slowed as they both went into the trance of remembrance.

After hours passed, the silence of the dark room was interrupted by Jack's powerful voice. "Remember when we were kids and we would play tree darts?" Jack asked with a chuckle. "We would throw the darts to whoever climbed the tree and they would drop them to the board on the ground."

"Oh yeah, I remember. You threw one and it got stuck in the neighbor kid's head," Jim said. Both men began to laugh uncontrollably again. The acid controlled their senses and now it was time to break the silence. Their minds were a rollercoaster of deep thought interspersed with laughter. The two continued to recollect the stories that their thoughts dredged up. Their talk interspersed with the other throughout the entire conversation. Both men spoke at the same time but understood clearly what the other was saying.

It was a shit-talking fest of past events. The two opened their minds and brought up memories from as early as six months old. Most sentences started by one brother was finished by the other. They were in-tune with one another in thought, as in spirit.

The laughter returned along with the memories, but it wasn't like before. Now, it was a more controlled laugh that was focused on one thing, not everything. It was deep, insightful laughter. The stories seemed to go on for hours. They didn't end until the next phase of the trip began.

With the stories, the laughter ended. Now the spiritual phase of the adventure could begin. Both men's minds were on the same plane as the ancients. They were now open to the cosmos and all its beauty. The energy of the room, and its occupants, seemed to combine until it became one entity: The One.

Walls and every object in the room became animated. Colors appeared that weren't there before. Both men's skin tingled from the acceptance of the energy in the room. All their senses were awake. It felt like they were floating in this reality. The LSD awoke their beings. They could clearly see the DNA breakdown of every object in the room. Patterns in the carpets and bed spread held hidden messages they could decipher. Anything with the slightest organic material in it was alive. Even particles in the air which were normally invisible to the naked eye were in plain view as the creatures they really were.

The space became void of conversation for some time. It was far from being silent. The low hum of the electricity running through the walls set the rhythm for the rest of the symphony. The DNA showed itself to their wandering minds. Cosmic serpents, always around but seldom seen, were present throughout the room. At first, the brothers could see the serpents in the building blocks around them. After a while, they realized each individual serpent was part of the bigger, overall scheme. Together, with all the DNA combined, it made the two colorful deities' cascade through the room.

Both men listened to the sounds of the space while pondering the cogitation in their heads. Thoughts raced through their minds like a Los Angeles freeway. Answers to the questions of life were presented to the two. It was as if the cosmic serpents were emitting knowledge with each swoop through the room. Deep knowledge from the universe was theirs. Wisdom opened its door to the brothers and they came waltzing right in.

"Do you remember when we were really little, and we saw the cosmic serpents?" Jack asked. His voice broke the silence that engulfed the room. Instantly, both brother's minds went back to when they were very small children. The two colorful snakes that filled the room scared them when they were small. Although Jim was only months old at the time, the memories were there. They didn't understand what they were seeing, as children. It was the only recollection either had of their real parents. They would come to the rescue of their small, screaming children and put their minds at ease. They would tell them there was nothing to fear. These were not ghosts nor demons. "They are the building blocks of everything," their mother would say to soothe them. "Their intelligence controls all life. They are not monsters, they're Gods."

"I never knew what they meant when they said that," Jack said. "Until now. They're beautiful."

Jim said, "now, I understand it all. The cosmic serpents are the original DNA. It was spread here after having been seeded by a distant galaxy. Our planet was just a huge seed pod. The DNA colors and numbers mix with water, and organic material is born. Slight variations which have occurred for billions of years has created the diversity of animals and plants that we know on this planet."

The serpents were splashing throughout the room with intensity. The sight brought both brothers back to their childhood. Only now, they were in awe at the spectacle that was being presented to them. Their eyes, blind hours ago, were now seeing what was clearly there, all along. The serpents were the Gods. They were part of everything, making everything Gods. When this planet was void of all life forms, it would be DNA that would be extinct.

"Everything that existed was offspring to the first strands of DNA seeded on the planet. It didn't only come here. Millions of solar systems throughout the universe were impregnated with this DNA. All living creatures on Earth and throughout the universe are connected through this universal God. All our DNA is similar, but slightly different. The serpents liked the variety they created on this planet. Some planets were not as hospitable as others and their offspring evolved into nothing more than single cell creatures. Some planets evolved intelligent life way superior to humans while others would have monsters which destroyed. Whatever it was didn't matter to the cosmic serpents. If they brought life, they were doing their purpose," Jim finished.

"Yes, Brother, you're correct. DNA is our God; the seeds of Earth. Earth, the sun and cosmos are our Gods. DNA is a deity in itself. The DNA controls the living creatures of this planet and the universe. It is like a supervisor appointed by God. Its job is to control all life. This same God is prevalent in every other solar system throughout the universe. Not only is it the building blocks of all life, it's life, itself. It's the spark that animates us all. Its building blocks are inside every creature, like a mini-universe. Some call this a soul," Jack said.

The moon passed in the line of sight out the window. Its three-quarter wane was particularly bright this night. It appeared to have a rainbow around it changing the color of the sky. Both men looked out the window, fascinated. The sky was a rose color mixed with splashes of purple. It was an amazing moon to top off an amazing day. Both men looked out the window as the colors danced across the mountain tops. Long shadows were cast on the land.

The colors told a story as they crossed the room. It reminded Jim of when he was little: Sitting in his room, listening to the transistor radio as the sun went down. The lights from a crystal, hanging in the window, provided a rainbow of colors in his room every day at a certain time. He understood a child's mind produced its own chemicals which opened it. It was the only time of life there were no distractions; the conscious could be open to see reality. When you got older, you have so much shit on your mind, it takes hallucinogens to clear the brain.

As we get older, stress of life takes away the innocence of youth. We no longer see the things happening around us. The memories of these times were chalked up to fantasy. Adults would look at children like they had an overactive imagination when they were just seeing what was truly there. The distractions eventually take over our reality. Then, what we see with our eyes isn't even close to what's truly happening. Therefore, everyone perceives reality in their own way.

Jim and Jack long ago realized you could re-awaken that innocence and knowledge of youth with a little chemical alteration. This would put them in touch with life and God. The planet held many secrets whose answers were right in front of us. Unfortunately, these visions were blocked by an angry force that liked to spread fear and suffering. The control of the mind and creativity were essential in making every one of us slaves for the elite. If more than a few knew the truth, their evil ways would swiftly be over.

Jack also saw the story the colors were spelling out in front of them. They were creating symbols he'd seen on pictographs in the Southwest and other places on his travels. The patterns didn't duplicate themselves over and over because they were an alphabet. This was the first written language on this planet. Scientists for a couple thousand years were trying to figure it out but the truth was known by the elite all along. They would throw misinformation into any scientific discovery there was. Anyone who came forward and said they knew the truth would swiftly change their minds when branded a lunatic.

The brother's eyes were wide open and fully aware of everything in the room. It was alive with movement, even without light; the colors became more subdued and darker. The two were reading the story in front of them. It told of the DNA being seeded. It showed how it came to Earth when the planet was still full of volcanos. The serpents dug deep into the Earth, awaiting their turn to make their appearance through thermal vents. The DNA also went to every other planet in our solar system. Each planet was alive in its own way for millions of years; some still were. This God was something that formed in a star cluster in a distant galaxy. Its birth happened at the beginning of the universe. When there was a massive explosion of heavenly proportions, the DNA was blasted into space.

The heads of the serpents began intertwining. The symbols which its aura produced were still in full story mode. Jack and Jim couldn't take their eyes off the spectacle. The heads twisted together until they formed one large mass. It changed to a gray color which began to get black. When the heads began to separate, the brothers could see the cosmos in the space created. The black heads came apart and the cosmos was beyond. It was beautiful; a portal to cross when our pod expired on this plane. This was the passage to the next realm. The other side.

The brothers looked on with awe at what they were seeing. Both tried to figure out why they feared such a beautiful sight when they were younger. As the heads separated, more of the universe became visible. An extremely bright star was clearer than the rest. The humans understood. This was another place where DNA evolved into humans. It was a parallel world to Earth. Our lives, upon death, would be reborn there. When they would end there, another planet was a skip away on the cosmic path. A whole new existence awaited on the far-away realms. It was the cycle of the DNA. The end was always the beginning, as the beginning was always the end.

Death never came to a living creature's soul; only a new beginning.

The entire room filled with stars and the universe. It felt to the brothers as if they were standing on a rock in the middle of space. They felt connected with the other living creatures on each of the planets in their binary code. Each sun was a God and its solar system consisted of its Demi-Gods. The DNA was what spread the life among these Gods.

DNA and the cosmic serpents were the thread that tied it all together. They traveled the entire universe and worked with each God. Together, they brought life.

The stars in the room began to pass the brothers as they stood still. It was as if they were the cosmic serpents and it was they who were looking out over their creation. They both knew, in their hearts, all wisdom was about to come to them. Standing on this rock, in the sea of creation, they too were Gods.

Sue opened the door from the hallway just as the revelation was erupting. Light flooded into the room and the men's eyes. The cosmic serpents were instantly gone along with their colorful presentation. Both men sighed. It was a sigh of frustration but also one of exhaustion. They were on a trip like no other. The journey had zapped their beings.

When the serpents disappeared, so did all effects of the LSD. Both men were completely back to their normal brain waves when Sue turned on the light.

Jim and Jack had to cover their eyes to shield them from the intensity. The entire night, they sat in complete darkness. Their eyes could clearly see in the dark, but they were blind in the light. "Sure is a brutal way to come down," Jack said to his younger brother.

"Yeah, it is," Jim replied. "But don't worry, we're going to repeat this tomorrow, times two. Manana will be double dosage of some other shit. I will tell you that story then."

Both men felt the familiar relief to be back to reality, but also a regret of the experience ending. This, for both, had been the best trip of their life.

"I hope you guys are done playing for the night," Sue said with mock irritation. "You've been in here for twelve hours. It's four in the morning. I tried to sleep at my mom's place but her little room isn't cool to sleep in. I got home just a bit ago. I need my own bed. I'd like to spend some time with my husband, too, if you boys don't mind."

Jim said as he jumped to his feet, "I'm sorry Sue. I was just trying to help. I didn't mean to take up the entire day. I'm going to crash and leave you two alone."

"It's okay," Sue said. "I know what you're up to and I'm good with it. Anything that will make Jack feel better is a relief to me. I appreciate you Jim. I'm not mad at you in the least. I'm sorry for bursting into the room like that. I figured you guys were in some deep journey. There was a crazy racket coming from the room. It sounded like there was construction going on in here until I came inside, then it stopped. But enough of that for now; I'm tired. Go now, Jim, leave us some time alone. You can play again tomorrow."

Jack gave his brother a look of resignation. The shrugging of his shoulders told Jim that he was done for the night. It was a great day, but it was over. There was no way the younger brother was going to complain. He knew when to call it quits.

"Alright then," Jim said, "I'll see you both in the morning. Love you guys!" He didn't turn around as he walked out the bedroom. Even if he had, the lights would have prevented him from seeing. The twin serpents were completely wrapped around Jack's dying flesh pod. They were embracing him in the paternal grip only a loving God can provide.

It was the same in all deaths. The DNA Gods were right there with us ensuring a smooth transition to the next world.

This wasn't the end for Jack; it was the beginning.

Chapter 9

The thick smell of bacon permeated the house. Its sweet odor was the first thing Jim sensed when he woke up. He stumbled out of bed and into the bathroom. He felt revitalized. A huge boulder, which he'd been carrying for a long time, was fracturing. He knew, in days, it would disintegrate altogether.

When he emerged from the bedroom, his first destination was the wonderful smell accosting his stomach. He found Becky at the stove, spatula in hand. She was making a spread like days of old. When the kids were little, before Tommy disappeared, the family thing was to make a huge breakfast every Sunday morning. Jack and Sue would spend two hours preparing their feast. Jim was there every time to enjoy the family grub. This morning brought all those recollections back in a most pleasant way.

The memories were vivid in Jim's mind. The day before was spent recollecting all the moments of their lives. All day they watched movies of their existence, in their subconscious. If there was something they didn't remember yesterday, it didn't happen in this lifetime.

"Hey there, Uncle Jim," Becky spoke with genuine elation. "It's about time you woke up. I thought you might sleep all day." This had always been her favorite uncle. Since the first time she met her dad's brother, when she was about five years old, he meant the world to her. Her kids felt the exact same way about their great uncle; the feelings were reciprocated by Jim.

"Hey Becky, sure does smell good in here." Jim moved across the room and gave his niece a huge hug. A year had passed since the two saw each other last but the time seemed like days. Jim felt the concern in his niece. She could be strong on the outside, but she couldn't hide the tense muscles as the two hugged. It was always one of the things he liked about Becky the most. She was a strong person since the moment they met. Jim's confidence in his niece was unmeasurable.

The two separated so Becky could get back to the task. "I figured you and my Dad might be hungry after the journey you went on yesterday. I'm sure your energy needs to be replenished for today's excursion." She spoke but didn't look at her Uncle. Her attention was on the four pans of goodness cooking in front of her.

Jim sounded a little embarrassed as he answered; "your mom told you about that?"

"No way, my Dad told me. It was the first time he's been happy all month. I knew something was up, I could see it in his eyes. I pried the information out of him. Just a few days ago, he told me and my brothers not to come around anymore. He said he didn't want us seeing him in his last days. None of us obeyed those wishes. Today, not only was he happy, I saw hope in his eyes. Thank you for helping him Uncle Jim. You mean everything to my Dad and our family." Becky turned and looked to her elder, momentarily, to exclaim the importance of her words.

"He means everything to me too. I just want to help out my brother," Jim said. Becky turned back to the stove as he exited the room. He wanted to talk to his niece some more, but there wasn't time for that now. His mind was awake, and he was ready for the adventures to begin. This was going to be the second day of the journey. This escapade, like all the others, was important for the overall energy created. In the end, the journey would be accomplished by each trip, combined.

After taking a shower and getting a change of clothes, Jim was ready to embark on the madness. First stop, though, would be to get some delicious smelling grub.

Becky cooked it up right. Bacon, eggs, hash-browns, pancakes, biscuits and gravy, sausage, and fruit filled the counter. Five pitchers of different colored juice dotted the few empty spots. It smelled like heaven to Jim.

The cook was no longer present. All that remained was the feast of her efforts and Sue sitting silently enjoying it all. "Hey there sleepy-head," she said. "I thought you might sleep all day. Jack's been asking about you all morning. I don't think he slept last night. He's excited about your endeavor. He said it's making the transition better.

I don't know what happened yesterday, but he seems like a new person today."

"That's what I'm here for," Jim said. "My Brother means a lot to me. This isn't just helping him, it's helping me too. It's helping you and your whole family. We spoke of this same journey many years ago. The trip on the back of the cosmic serpent was in our visions. They showed us when we were children. Now, we're here. We literally predicted our future."

"You guys have always done trippy shit," Sue said. "I haven't always understood it, but I respect you Bro. I'm very happy you're here." She stood as her words ended and hugged her brother-in-law. Her embrace lasted. Jim could feel the uneasiness and stress in his sister. He was worried about his friend.

"What happened to Becky?" Jim asked as he broke the hug and took a seat at the breakfast bar. He continued to face Sue as she spoke.

"She had to go to work. She said to tell you goodbye. This has been hard on her. Mostly because of me. She's dealing with things fine like she always does. I just worry about the kids, the grandkids and everything else I could possibly worry about. I feel like I'm full of stress and there's no way out."

"It's okay, Sue. I think you would be abnormal not to have stress at a time like this in your life. I think you're dealing with the pressure just fine."

Sue respected her brother and hugged him again. He'd always been a good friend who knew just what to say. Jim understood his brother's wife. He knew she was going through a very difficult time. Her partner of more than thirty years was leaving her. If it weren't for the strength of the woman, Jim would worry about her. Knowing she would get on with her life, by herself, liberated him. With the confidence in Sue, Jim could focus his thoughts on his brother. All these feelings were passed between the two in their embrace.

Energy is a strong voice that can be heard by those closest to you. Jim was connected to living creatures around him and Sue was connected to him.

When the embrace ended, Jim said, "come on Sue, I'm starving. I'll hug you all day after I eat. I've been on the road for a long time and this is the second home cooked meal the entire time. Yesterday was the first. I used every bit of that energy on the expedition last night. Now I'm fucking starving. Please, sit down, eat with me."

"I'm sorry Jim. I wasn't trying to stop you from your grub. I just need a lot of hugs right now." Sue was on the edge of tears as she spoke but told herself to be strong. She lived her whole life with strength over adversity and now would be no different. She made up a plate of minute proportions for Jack while Jim loaded his three plates to over-filling. No words were said. She could see the hunger in her brother's eyes. She slowly backed out of the room as Jim tore into the food.

Jim ate his breakfast alone. He was hoping to spend the meal with Becky, catching up on things. He wanted to pick her brain and see how she was dealing with the imminent death of her father. Unfortunately, it wasn't meant to be this morning. She said she had work but Jim suspected something else. Becky knew the importance of what her uncle and father were doing. As hard as it was not to be there, she let the two men do what was in their destiny.

Sue spent the time by her husband's side. His energy was shining like a light this morning and she wanted to absorb some of it. Jack devoured the food she brought. He said it was the best breakfast ever. Sue asked if he'd like seconds, but the answer was no. He didn't want to get ill from eating too much; he wasn't used to so many calories. They were both surprised he could eat as much as he did. It was a sure sign he had regained some of his strength.

When Jim was done with his feast, he set about doing the dishes. He didn't want to leave a mess for Sue. At the same time, he wanted to give the couple some quality alone time. When he entered the room, quiet time would be over. He wanted to give every gift possible to his brother and sister. Solitude was one of the best there was to give.

Many thoughts filled his head as he washed the dishes. He remembered so many things from his youth. His memory was always good, but after yesterday, it was impeccable. Today, his life history was like a book he read repeatedly.

Standing at the sink, his gaze focused into the forest. He thought about their family growing up in the city. He found adventure with his brother and sister in the industrial pit of a port city. When they got older, all they could speak about was getting away from the metropolis. It's what propelled them to Calaveras County.

After the brothers got out of the Navy, Jack's family spent every weekend with Jim or vice versa. When they moved into this house in Mountain Ranch, his brother saw it as a new beginning to their lives. It was where they would grow old together. Jack was persistent in getting him and Lisa within the county in a few years.

The three siblings often talked about what they would be doing in their golden years. It was always some kind of wild fantasy that was more serious, sometimes, than presented. The one thing they agreed on was they would be spending their elder years together. The thought brought a tear to Jim's eye. His future had been drastically changed with the demise of his sister, first, and now his brother.

Jim quickly put the thoughts out of his head. It was selfish to think of himself while his brother was laying in the other room dying. He was there to support his family and that's what he intended to do. There would be plenty of time for grieving later. For now, there was a mission to go on.

Jim threw the dish towel onto the counter and scuffled off to his brother's bedroom. A short stopover in his own room to acquire the days dosage brought a slight pause. Jim knew today's trip was more of a two-part situation. First, they would take the dose, then, they would smoke a very fine marijuana grown to go specifically with this dose of peyote. He started rolling joints of the greenish purple gack.

This herb he got from an old woman in the northern part of Idaho. She lived in a small cabin only accessible by four-wheel drive, then a long hike. She was self-sufficient and completely lived off the grid. She lived where people didn't go.

When he drove through the dense forest for hours, Jim noticed the seclusion he was entering. The last thirty miles took the longest. The washboard road was painstakingly slow and bouncy to drive down. After driving all night, he finally arrived at his spot. It was nothing fancy, a small clearing off the gravel. He parked the car but didn't bother locking it. He hadn't passed a single car all night. He was literally in the middle of nowhere.

Jim hiked into her homestead, guided by a third eye which was lately present in his mind. There was never a doubt as he hiked an entire day and night through dense forest to wind up at the woman's place by early morning. He didn't have a flashlight or weapon but knew the path was safe for his travels. By the time he got there, it looked like he just walked around the corner. He wasn't dirty, sweaty or disheveled in the slightest.

Something in Jim's mind knew it was important to show up right at sunrise. It was the time of day that made his visit safe. He didn't understand these thoughts but didn't doubt them either. When he emerged from the forest into the small clearing, he thought of the fairy tales of old. The witches house in the middle of the forest was portrayed exactly as it looked in person. With the small trail of smoke from the stone chimney, disheveled shutters, and crooked roof, every detail was represented.

The old woman sat on the porch in a chair made of tree branches. As Jim breached the tree-line, she didn't move. He surveyed the darkness of the forest and the abnormally bright light in the clearing. When he was inside the illumination, the witch stood and raised a youthful hand in greeting. The entire scene felt like he walked into a fairy tale. Everything was abnormal.

When the light in the clearing hit him, he felt like he could keep on his travel for another two days without the slightest rest. His weary mind was filled with exuberant energy.

His thoughts told him to go to the stone house. Without even moving, he was standing at the porch-steps.

"Come in, I've been waiting for you," the witch said in the voice of a young woman. "I'm sorry, I'm not a very good host. I have nothing for you to eat."

"I didn't come here for food. I came here to meet you," Jim said. His visions foretold of the spells the woman was capable of. He knew better than to drink or eat anything she offered.

"I know why you came. I, also, have had visions about your visit for weeks. Now, I have what you came for." The woman brought her arm out of the loose-fitting clothes. The once youthful hand was now twisted into a talon, like that of a crow. In its grip was a container that looked to be carved out of a tree burl. It was about five inches across and three inches tall.

"I'm ninety years old. I've had this potion since I was a little girl." Her body showed no signs of her proclaimed age. The rags she wore for clothes concealed her true shape. Her face looked like that of a fifty-year-old. Her hair was solid black and straight. It was so black, the rising sun cast a blue tint off her locks. Even the tone of her voice betrayed the statement.

The woman reached her hand toward Jim with the object. He instinctively reached out to retrieve the burl. The crow-like hand retracted immediately. "Not so fast young one. What do you have for me in return?"

"I have nothing. I didn't bring anything for you. It wasn't spoken of in my vision."

"But you do have something I want. I know you saw it in your dreams. I'm sure I made you wake up with a boner. Now, take off your clothes. I will make this very pleasant for you Jimmy-Boy. If you do me right, then you will get what you came for."

The old woman swooped her wrist and the object was gone along with the twisted hand. The youthful hand of before was there as the replacement. When she swooped her arm again, the clothes she was wearing were swept away by an unseen breeze. Jim was impressed by what he saw. This woman who purported to be ninety sported the body of a thirty-five-year-old. There was no sag to any part of her anatomy. Her long black hair looked combed and enticing as it flowed across her naked body. Her hairless vagina and ample breasts swiftly aroused Jim.

The witch was right about one thing, Jim's visions did foretell this scenario. That, mixed with the sexuality of the situation, made it only natural for him to react the way he did. Even if he wanted to resist, he wouldn't have.

The love-making lasted for six hours. Jim thought, many times, that it was the best sex he ever had. When it was over, the lovers rested. When the woman began to snore, it swiftly built to a crescendo that was unearthly. Jim rolled on his side to tell her to quiet down; it was then that he saw. This woman was indeed ninety years old or older. Her skin looked like dried leather and he could see the outline of her bones through it. Her pubic hair was indeed not there but more like it was singed off by the sun. Her saggy breasts were topped by two dried raisins for nipples. The few strands of hair on her head were of a dirty gray tone Jim had never seen.

As the old woman slept, Jim found the box in her discarded clothes. He figured he paid well for this medicine. It was rightfully his.

He dressed hurriedly and made a swift path to the forest. The shadows were getting long already, but it was important to make sure he got what he came for.

When at a safe distance, he opened the small box and looked inside. Energy struck him in the face as it escaped the enclosure. It was exactly what he came for. Tucked in a nest of forest grown marijuana, were two peyote nodes. They looked like two large eyes staring back at him. They seemed to say "hello". When he closed the box, deep in the forest, he swore to have heard the witches scream in the darkness. His path back to his truck took half the time as the trip to the clearing, as did the drive to civilization.

When the last joint was rolled, Jim thought he heard a moan come from somewhere in the room. He looked around but knew what he would find. It was a familiar moan after all. He heard it ever since sleeping with the old woman. The moaning was from the owner of the box. She was a succubus who stole the souls of men through sexual enticement. In her youth, Jim would never have been able to get away from her. For many decades, she used her sexual charms to take the souls of men and women. In her old age, she was slipping in her ability to control and dominate. She was tired. It was prophesized a stranger would come seeking the box of power. It was in her destiny to pass her last vestiges of this existence to this shaman for the purpose of healing. A little piece of her soul resided in its wooden recesses. She held it so many times over her life, her hands created a natural polish on its surface; while her energy created an aura within the object.

He put all the doobies in the container and put the peyote on top. The arrangement wasn't pretty like when he first opened the box, but now it was more practical. After they ate the hallucinogen, there was no way they would be able to roll joints.

He strolled down the short hallway, box in hand, and almost whistled a tune. He thought this may be disrespectful to his brother and decided against it.

Jim didn't think twice as he grabbed the knob to his brother's room. He flung open the door and got a huge surprise.

Sue was naked and riding Jack. Her large breasts bounced slightly as she fucked her husband. His hands were on her hips. Both were sweating.

The couple turned to look at the sound of the door opening. They were too far gone to stop what they were doing. They had no intention of stopping anyway. Sue stopped bouncing at the same pace but didn't try to cover up as she saw the comedy in front of her.

They both saw the redness of Jim's face as he stammered out an apology. He backed out of the room and quietly shut the door. Then, the rutting couple burst out in laughter. It was a laughter only two lovers could share. An inside joke that's only present with closeness.

Jim stopped in the living room when he heard the laughing. He too chuckled and then called out, "I'll be outside when you two get done. Just come get me." After all the years they hung out, Jim never saw Sue naked. They lived together but never had an incident happen until today. A small laughing moan escaped the box. Jim looked to the object and understood. The witch's reach was strong. Her entire existence was based on sex. This was why Jim acquired today's gift. It was why he fucked a ninety-year-old woman. It was all for his family.

He didn't wait for a reply. It made him happy to see what he just saw. To see his brother and sister-in-law still in love after all these years was amazing. He wanted to give them as much time as they wanted. Hopefully, he thought, they would fuck all day. Then, the brothers would trip all night. The thought brought a small smile to his lips.

Jim smoked at least three joints while he waited on the front porch. The fresh air got his mind straight for the day's events. He didn't smoke the special joints in the box he rolled earlier. That was special pot made specifically to interact with the peyote. Now, he was smoking from Jack and Sue's harvest.

Sue came out about an hour later. Jim was high for this early in the morning; he didn't hear Sue approach. She said, when standing right beside him, "so, you like to watch, huh Bro?" She mussed up his hair while mocking him.

Jim began to stammer out an apology, but it sounded lame. Both adults broke out in laughter. When it quieted, Sue said, "we needed that. Thanks for being understanding. Whatever you did yesterday has given Jack a new hunger for life. I wanted to thank you. Now, however, your brother awaits you and your next journey. Go to him. Do what you're best at. Healing."

Jim stood silently and entered the house. He made the crossing to his brother's door and began to turn the knob. Something in his mind told him to wait. Instead, he softly knocked on the wood. Both men laughed loudly as Jim entered the room. The smell of sex lingered as did the smile on Jack's face.

"What did you give me yesterday?" Jack exclaimed. "That shit awakened my spirit! I'm remembering shit I forgot long ago. My mind feels more open today than it ever has. I feel like I'm ready to conquer the world."

"I told you, Man. I searched out the best shaman in the world. That acid was specially formulated for our DNA. If you think yesterday's trip was good, wait until today. Our journey today is going in a whole different direction."

Jack sat silently while his brother spoke. He knew in his heart this trip was necessary; he embraced it with jubilance. Just two days ago, he was burnt out. Now, he was on fire.

As he approached the bed, Jim noticed Jack ate his entire breakfast. He also saw his brother's grayish skin was now a more tranquil hue. The aura of the room seemed dark when he first entered the day before. Now, there was a brightness that was welcoming.

The day prior, they purged the lurking darkness. They brought about the ancestors and the light they possessed. By sitting in the dark, they created light. In the light, resides the Wisdom. Together, they became one.

As Jim pulled the small burlwood box from the folds of his clothes, both men heard a distant laughter.

When he opened the tight-fitting lid, moaning filled the room.

Chapter 10

When the two were younger, they tried many kinds of hallucinogenic drugs. Peyote hadn't been one of them. Always on their to-do list, the fungus always seemed to elude them. Now they both understood why. Today was to be a trip neither brother ever experienced before.

Jack was excited when he looked upon the open box in his brother's hand. The container seemed to have an aura of its own, calling attention to its contents. The two eyes looking out of a bed of joints was engaging to the senses. Both men felt if they stood still, the peyote caps would jump into their mouths.

Jim lit one of the joints from the box and handed it to his brother. He made a quick retreat from the room only to reappear moments later. Jack looked at him quizzically as he handed the joint back. His brother was already up to his antics.

After only four hits, Jack knew this was not your ordinary marijuana. The taste and effects were similar but much stronger. He felt like he was floating as he watched his brother hit off the smoke.

The brothers passed the joint until there was barely a roach. At the same time the doobie was finished, Sue walked into the room with two hot cups of water. She put them on the nightstand, looked to both men and gave a warm smile. She turned and left the room after taking care of the duty Jim asked her to perform. Not a single word was spoke while she was present.

Jim was in his own world. He felt like he was trying to fly away from this place, but something was holding him back. He barely even looked at Sue when she entered the room and was oblivious when she left. He was having a conversation in his head, while staring off into space. His eyes were wide as he shifted his gaze to the box in his hand. Jim carefully plucked the two peyote buttons out of the box and deftly dropped one into each cup of water. He didn't even look at the water when he dropped the caps. His mind knew it was there and his body followed its instinct.

"This day, Bro, we're going into the future. Yesterday, we recollected the past and brought up all those old memories. Today, we'll see what will be happening in the years to come. It will be like reliving memories that haven't happened yet." Jim spoke but his eyes were on the ceiling. He knew where he was supposed to be. He needed to break these bonds that were tying him down.

"I'm ready, Jim. Let's get this party started." Jack was so entranced by the prospect of their journey, he didn't realize it already began. His mind could only think of what was to come. This moment was used as a step to the next. The purpose of the present was only for getting to the future.

Jim told his brother it would take time to steep before the tea was ready to drink. In the meantime, he said they should get their minds ready for what was coming.

"My mind is ready for whatever is coming. You're killing me here with this anticipation." Jack was talking much faster than usual. Jim thought his voice almost sounded like one of their favorite cartoons.

"I'm serious, Man. This is going to be a trip like no other. The old woman I got this from was trippy. I'm sure her shit will be trippy too. You can already see how good her herb is. She was a shape-shifter or something. There's no doubt this witch was legitimate."

"Did you fuck her?" Jack asked blankly. It had always been a joke between the brothers. If one of them spoke a lot about a woman, the question was asked.

Jim blushed slightly and looked away. It was the answer Jack needed. He laughed and said, "I hope she was good looking at least."

"I wouldn't say that at all. Fuck man, I took one for the team. I never would have done it, but I knew this was an important part of the puzzle. Sometimes we just have to do things that we don't want to."

Jack laughed and said thank you. "I know you did it for me and I appreciate it. It wouldn't be fun though if I didn't bust your balls some. I find it hard to believe you wouldn't have done it otherwise; unless she was hideous."

"Like I said, she was a shape-shifter. She was hot as fuck, but I knew in my heart what she really was. I had visions of the entire scenario and I went anyway. I'm not complaining; it was some of the best sex of my life. I had to sneak out of there when she slept. I was worried she wouldn't let me go."

"Yeah, because you're some Casanova to the witches," Jack said with a chuckle.

"I'm really going to miss that about you, breaking my balls and all." Both men started laughing together. When it was over, Jim stirred both cups with his fingers and looked at the strength of the tea. He'd never seen anything like these buttons. They dissolved like pressed pieces of poop. It reminded him of those small pods that came with a seed starter kit. All that remained of the caps were the fibers floating in the brackish water.

The smell was terrible when the men put the cups to their lips. They each put their cup down once, brought it back into a Saluda, then drank the contents in one large swallow. The taste made each man want to vomit. It was like eating a chunk of shit. If they wouldn't have finished the entire drink in one gulp, it wouldn't have been fully consumed.

The next ten minutes were spent trying to keep the hallucinogen in the stomach. The brothers felt cramping in their intestines like they never felt before. There were seconds of less pain followed by minutes of stabbing agony. After ten minutes, neither man could take it any longer. Both Jim and Jack projectile puked. Jim, being mobile, could get the window open before his puke shot out into the countryside. Jack, however, was bed-ridden and lost his all over the bedspread.

As soon as the buttons were clear of the pod, the mind kicked in the trip. Jim, already seeing colors he didn't know existed, was quick to wrap Jack's blanket into a ball and toss it into the corner. He didn't want his brother to be stuck in his own puke all day.

The look on Jack's face told the entire story. He was tripping heavy and already on his own plane. Jim knew the look well. He was feeling the exact same way.

Knocking on the window brought the men's attention out of the room. Floating outside the window, as if it were standing on an invisible tree branch, was a large black crow. Blue tinted its wings as the sun glistened off the ebony feathers. Its yellow eyes cast a slight aura, making it look like the bird was magical.

The creature looked familiar to Jim. He saw this friend many times on his journeys. The bird was his companion throughout life.

Whenever good or bad happened, this raven was right there by Jim's side. When he traveled, the crow was there. Even in his dreams, he walked with this other being.

Jim stepped closer and considered the eyes of his friend. He saw a truth there making him feel at home. The bird was saying something to Jim, but only in his mind. He wanted them to follow. There was a journey to go on tonight, and he was going to be their guide. All they had to do was take the first step.

Jim turned to see Jack staring out the window. His face was fixed on the large bird which now perched on the open window sill. It cawed once, and Jack returned the sound perfectly. The crow took flight and, with purpose, flew around the room. When it landed on the blanket Jim had tossed in the corner, it kicked its talons and pecked the fabric. It seemed like the crow wanted some of what Jack left behind.

Jim came to the assistance of the bird and slightly unwrapped the blanket. A strong smell of oldness came wafting into the room. It smelled like an old, used book store. The bird peered into the recess created by Jim and, headfirst, jumped right in. The bird was no longer in sight as it vanished into the folds of the blanket. There was no movement nor was there a lump where the body should be. It was just an empty blanket. The crow vanished, like a magic trick.

Jack was there, on the floor, by his brother's side. Jim looked to the bed but indeed, Jack was no longer in it. He somehow got out of bed and crawled to this adventure that was unwinding in his marital bedroom. In their minds, the two were in a shadow box. The diorama was created by them to house their madness. Everything going on in the world, was all made up in their minds. The only existence was in their shadow box.

Jim looked back to the blanket; there was nothing but fabric. A soft whistle came from somewhere that sounded like under the house. When the sound became stronger, Jack peered into the blanket from only inches away. He suddenly fell head first into the recess of the fabric. The comforter seemed to swallow him and his being. It happened so fast; then there was no more Jack. Jim could barely believe what he was seeing. He always heard good things about peyote, but this was out of control. With all the drugs he took in his life, he never saw anyone disappear into the floor.

Jim thought, "why not!" Without a worry, he leaned into the blanket. The smell of old things consumed his thoughts as he felt like he was floating through a sea of moldy oil. His movements were restricted;

the only sense working was his smell and touch. Everything else was blank.

Jim had no sense of time as he was mired in the black inkiness. It seemed like he was in limbo for a very long time. Days seemed to pass while he was trapped in the confines of his subconscious. Even his thoughts seemed to be repressed by the darkness that enveloped his being.

When his mind opened, and the visions began, the first thing he saw was prison bars. There was nobody else around; Jim felt stifled. He had a terrible feeling about this place. He felt like it was a situation where he could be trapped forever. When he turned his head to look around, the black void returned.

It seemed like an eternity before the next vision took place. He was walking his great-niece, Mary, down the aisle of her wedding. Jim knew better this time to not turn his head, but he couldn't help himself. He had to see who else was present at the wedding. The moment his head turned from straight forward, the vision was gone, and the void returned.

The next vision seemed to take longer than the two before. In it, Jim was at a podium giving a speech for Becky. She just won a major award for her most recent novel. Jim was presenting the award to her. This time, Jim didn't turn his head. The vision once again faded out, but this time was swiftly replaced by another premonition. In this one, Jim was sitting by his brother's head-stone. The next vision was of him painting a large mural. Then there was the trip to Bolivia. When his vision showed him Sue, laying in a pool of her own blood, he couldn't help himself. In his vision, he saw a figure standing to the right. He turned his head in the direction to see who murdered his sister-in law. His vision came to a swift halt and the inkiness returned.

Jim's mind was full of turbulence as he settled into his familiar inky void. The last vision shook him up a bit. It was unsettling to see Sue dead like that. He was almost hoping the intuitions would end when they hit him like a freight train. The first premonition was replaced by the second and then they came in a line of madness.

Jim saw every moment from the second his brother died to the time he died. It was all on a super sped-up motion picture featuring Jim and his life. As he watched, every minute aspect of what was going to occur was presented to the man. If his mind could remember even a fraction of what he foresaw, he would have wealth beyond belief.

Jim and Jack were never ones who schemed to get rich. They felt like they were rich already just by having a place over their heads and food on the table. Having it all was never in their cards, they left that to the greed.

The visions didn't stop until Jim thought he was going to pass out. It was too much for him to see the things coming his way. He didn't really want to know the future; now there were no secrets to his destiny. His future, like his past, was going to be a roller-coaster ride of turmoil.

After what seemed like days passed, the visions slowed like the end of a long movie reel. As they slowed to a stop, Jim realized it hadn't gone to the end. His death was not shown. Everything else was there, but it seemed to end when Jim was seventy-two. He shook his head a couple of times, but the last picture was frozen in his head. In it, he was by the bedside of Becky. She was dying. He figured maybe this was all he was going to see. He wasn't supposed to see his own end.

This vision was locked and wouldn't go away. It saddened his heart to see his niece like that. He wished more visions would come to block the horrible things he just saw. He concentrated hard to bring on another premonition, but the future perceptions were no more.

He had a recollection of something long ago. His memories of the past seemed to be vague. Almost like he had no past at all. All he could think about was what he saw in the future. The recollection became something more like a hunch. Jim turned his head to the side and the vision vanished. His empty void of an existence returned. There was no longer a past or a future. Now, there was only this moment.

This time, he was happy to be in the inky void. It was quiet here and he didn't have visions. He truly felt like this was a place his mind and body regained their strength. It was the place where his conscious went when his subconscious was fully awake. It was the void in the middle of Jim's mind. Normally he wasn't aware of this place, but the peyote delivered him to the far reaches of his being.

When the bleakness of existence wore off, Jim knew exactly where he was. He was back in his brother's bedroom, sitting in a recliner in the corner. His head was cloudy for a moment as he regained his senses. Thinking it was another vision, he dared not move his head at first. He didn't want to go back into that void.

The room was lit by a single lamp in the corner. Its incandescent bulb cast a yellowish glow across the walls and everything in between. Mumbling from the bed brought Jim's attention to that area. He was happy he could once again turn his head. He was still doubtful of any sudden movement, but he needed to see what was going on around him.

Jack was lying in his bed, propped up by pillows. He was staring at the ceiling and speaking in tongue familiar to Jim. To anyone else, it would have sounded like gibberish. To Jim, it sounded like a language long used by their ancestors. While Jim was stuck in his own subconscious, Jack was hanging out with the kin folk.

Jim stood on wobbly legs. His mind was one hundred percent. All effects from the peyote had completely worn off. He looked to the clock on the nightstand and saw it was four in the morning. They'd been in here for fourteen hours. No wonder it seemed like such a long time. Jim was stuck in that damn void all day and night long. One thing was for certain, he felt more rested than he had in a very long time.

"What was it like for you, Man?" Jim asked. "It was pretty trippy for me."

"It was great man. I saw the future just like you said I would. Everything was so vivid. It felt like I was in a rainbow. I'm going home, Bro. Our ancestors are at the big white house in the middle of the forest, and I'll soon be joining them. It's beautiful, Jim. I look forward to going there. It's the place for our people. I'll be there waiting for you, Sue, and the kids. It's a place for all of us." Jack's voice was animated as he spoke. The change in attitude didn't go unnoticed by his brother.

"I'm so happy you saw the beauty you're going to. Unfortunately, I'm staying here, and you know how life on Earth goes. There will be good times and plenty of bad ones. I so wish I was going with you, Jack, but our family really needs me. Without you, I'm going to be the only one. I swear to you Bro, I will take that responsibility seriously."

"What happens in your future that's so bad?" Jack asked.

"Well, first, some jail time awaits me after this is all done. You did something you didn't tell anyone about. When you die, they're going to think it was me. Luckily, I was out of state and have legitimate alibis to attest to that. I'll be out in a short time. Unfortunately, the few years I'm incarcerated, the government is going to try and use me. I saw their whole plan and it isn't kind. I'll be ready for it and have my contingency plan in place. I saw a lot of things that I'll be prepared for in the future. I don't know why you didn't tell me about what you did, Jack. Now, I have to deal with it."

Jack's face lost color when he heard Jim's words. He didn't think anyone would ever find out about that, at least while he was alive. "What all do you know?"

"Just a little that I learned from the future. You're quite the badass. How many guys did you kill and where did you get the gun?"

Jack told the story from the time he left the doctor's office to the time he arrived home. The story was nagging at him; he was happy to get it off his chest. By the time he finished, he was animated like Jim never saw before. From his bed, Jack relived the entire shooting.

Jim on the other hand, could take no more. He was exhausted from the visions he saw earlier. Even when his brother was talking, all he could think about was what he saw for the future. He pondered if he could do something about it and change destiny. He figured it would be like when he turned his head in the visions and only got the void. He felt it was a warning of sorts to leave things the way they were. There was no way he would ever let the government use him, though. They already used his brother and sister and weren't going to get to him.

He told his brother goodnight. He couldn't believe the energy in the dying man. He seemed like a new person. Jack told Jim to send Sue in when he saw her. "I've got something special for her tonight," the older sibling said with flirtatious sarcasm.

Jim mocked holding his hands over his ears. "I don't want to hear any more, but I will get her for you." He glanced at the blanket on the floor as he passed by. He could swear he saw an inky blackness in the folds of the fabric. The sight made his stomach feel queasy. He reached down to touch what he sensed all night long. The void came alive. Its blackness became animated, turning to feathers and a crow which took flight and flew out the open window. Jim and Jack looked at each other and smiled a knowing smile.

One black feather fell from the bird as it made its exit. Jim picked it up and left the room. Sue was asleep on the couch when he went to her. He tickled her nose with the black feather three times before his sister woke up. She was a bit irritated with Jim but calmed quickly. When she was fully awake, she asked in a slurred voice "is everything okay?"

"Everything is great," Jim replied. He handed the feather to his sister and told her about Jack's wishes. "Is everything okay with you?"

She said in her sleepy-voice that everything was fine. When she got up to go to the room, Jim thought she was sleep-walking. He knew his sister didn't drink nor do prescription pills. She was totally out of it.

He didn't care. He couldn't think about anything else at the moment. He needed to lay down and wrap his thoughts around these visions that were swimming around his head.

Chapter 11

The sleep, this morning, for Jim was wonderful. He laid in bed for about an hour thinking and deciphering the day's events. When he finally succumbed to the subconscious, the dreams rivaled the visions from earlier. Every aspect of his reverie would be vividly remembered when he woke. They consisted of the last two days visions combined. The past and the future were mingled up in his subconscious. Together, in his dreams, they created the present.

So many things happened in this subconscious sleep. The house burning down was one of the first to happen. Jack's death, Sue's sorrow, and the pain associated with death were all in his visions. The incident with the gangsters at the store was relived in Jim's mind as if it were he who killed the perps. Most of the dreams were outside the room. They were in a place where Jim wasn't going to be. He dreamt about the scenarios involving his niece and nephews from an observation standpoint. His dreams helped him fully understand everything each member of his family was going through. It opened their strengths and weaknesses. After this night of precognitions, he would know his family better than ever before. With the help of his subconscious, he could now truly help his people.

The only time he awoke was around noon; refreshed and ready to go. After the exhaustion from the day before, he got solid hours of sleep. It was the deep sleep only dreams can provide.

Jack, on the other hand, didn't sleep at all. His visions, the day before, were completely different than his brother's. Both men's insight was about their future. Jack's future held a kind of paradise, while his brother's held suffering. He saw time on Earth was a test. A coming of age of sorts. When you got being a human correct, you could move on to the next level. Unfortunately, most humans took hundreds of lives before they got it right. Some never did and were destined to spend an eternity as a flesh pod, or worse.

The test, after all, was not easy. Suffering and dilemmas were the questions posted every day. How you dealt with those trials and tribulations was the purpose of the exam.

Jack also saw in his vision: the humans weren't even close to being the most intelligent species on this planet. There were many species much more intelligent. Some couldn't be seen because they were in another dimension, parallel to our reality. Some were there all along but, in their arrogance, the humans couldn't see the intellect in other animals. Then, there were the animals who chose not to be seen by the humans. These creatures spent their lifetimes in the shadows, observing a world out of control because of one species: Homo Sapiens.

In the afterlife, there were no species. All creatures were equal. There was no need for nourishment nor food. Creatures didn't walk around with a flesh pod. The intellect was the fuel that made everything work in the thereafter. Creativity was the glue that held it all together. There were no rulers and no wars. There was no prosperity, resulting in no greed. Everything was in harmony. Everything, combined, was God.

Jack's visions were spent with several ancestors. One by one they greeted him and introduced themselves. Some, he was familiar with through dreams or remembering them from his years in this pod. Many of these relatives crossed paths with Jack through his years. Some even became good friends with the brothers, not even knowing they shared the same DNA.

Others looked so familiar to him, but the knowledge of their former encounter was absent. Then, there were some who looked like complete strangers to Jack. In all, the kin-folk showed him who his friends would be in the next level. He felt a connection to every one of his clan. It was the same routine every cycle. You always went back to your kin-folk. You were tied together for eternity by that magic thread. Even in the afterlife, DNA was still who you were.

Jack and Sue talked all through the early morning hours. At first, Sue could barely carry on a conversation. She was out of it. Jack asked if she was alright and she told him she smoked one of the doobies Jim rolled for the peyote. She came in earlier, around midnight. She saw there was only one of the joints left sitting on top of the box, looking inviting. She figured since the boys smoked all of them, they wouldn't mind if she took the last one. When Jim woke her up four hours later, she felt like she was drunk and on opiates. It took over an hour and a half for her to get her head straight enough to carry on a conversation with her husband.

Their talk was broad and encompassed many aspects of time. The past, present, and future were all discussed in detail. Plans for Sue's future were solidified and put into motion. It was this morning Jack signed all the remaining papers he needed to sign. The mortgage, insurance, auto, utilities and anything else they could think of were signed by the pen that he carried for over thirty years. Its solid silver barrel was the pen used for anything important he needed to sign. This day, its use was the most substantial yet.

Jack kept thinking he was forgetting something. The feeling nagged at him like when you go on a long trip and can't remember if you turned off the water in your yard or not. As much as he tried, he couldn't conjure up what it was.

At one point, after sunrise, Sue dragged a large sea chest out of the closet. The box contained things from Jack's life she wanted him to go through. She didn't want to dig through his private things when he wasn't there, she told him. She pulled a chair next to the bed and dragged the large crate on top, within Jack's reach.

The box contained many memories for Jack; both good and bad. There were things from when he was a very small child, through his entire life. Some of these things, especially the ones dealing with Tommy, would be heart wrenching. He'd come to terms with most of it; time did soften old wounds. He realized long ago: his life went the way it was supposed to go. He had no regrets, only losses. It no longer mattered anyway, he'd soon be with his people again.

This was the morning he told Sue he was adopted. She asked him how long he'd known. He said his sister told him a year before. He said he simply didn't know how to tell her and it wasn't a big deal, anyway. Sue scolded her man for keeping such a large secret from her. She wasn't angry, she just didn't understand the way of her husband. Some of the things he kept secret boggled her mind. She knew, after thirty years of marriage, there was a lot she didn't know about Jack.

They noticed there were no baby pictures of Jack. All the pictures were of him at three or older. Some of the pictures present included Jim, but only around six months of age. Jack told Sue there was a conspiracy of some sorts. "Something bad happened to our parents. We were sent to live with our adopted parents and they never told us the truth. Even in their deaths, they hid their dirty little secret. Even our adopted brothers and sisters didn't tell us. They were older. Surely, they knew too. Their deception was complete. I think it was some bad shit. I think I'm about to find out about it all."

"I still don't know why you didn't tell me before, but I'm beginning to understand. It seems like a strange thing to put your three kids up for adoption when they're toddlers. Did Jim or Lisa ever search out your real parents?"

"Lisa did," Jack said. "Our family was from Latvia. Gypsy or witch doctors or something. She was very vague when she told me what she found. It was just the start of her investigation. She died one month later. She didn't know she had cancer until one month before she died, just like me. We have the same kind of rare cancer. Do you think it's a coincident?"

"I think you may be reading into this a little too much. You guys had the same DNA, so you have the same cancer. Sounds like Jim's been feeding you his theories again. Do you really believe any of this?"

"Yeah, I believe it Sue," Jack said with annoyance in his voice. "It's important for me to find out what really happened. Maybe Tommy's disappearance is tied into it all. It's all so weird. I don't doubt anything at this point. I think even our military careers were part of it. It's way deeper than what you're thinking. I just hope it ends when my life in this flesh pod ends. I don't want you to have to go through any of this experiment that's been perpetrated on my family."

"I'm sorry Jack, I didn't mean to doubt you. It sounds crazy, you gotta admit. I would like to see and hear the details of what you know. I've always trusted you and believe what you tell me. It does sound crazy, but we've been through some crazy ass shit together."

Jack was already digging through the rest of the box. His medals from the Navy, his dad's Navy medals, souvenirs, knives and keepsakes were all present. They flicked through the photo albums and talked about the old times. Some picture books, like the ones when they first got married, were looked at for the first time in thirty years. None of the books, nor the contents of the box, had seen the light of day in fifteen years. After the tragedies, souvenirs were much less meaningful.

When the box was empty, Jack and Sue surveyed the contents strewn across their bed. They spoke about the memories laid out in front of them with a mix of emotion. Everybody's memories included good and bad times; Jacks were no different.

Sue wiped out the inside of the box to get it ready for refilling. She noticed a small part of the chest was ripped on the inside corner; the paper was loose. Jack reached into the sea chest and tampered with the paper, trying to get it to lay flat. Instead, the small chunk of covering ripped free. "Dang it, my Mom gave me this chest to keep all my stuff in. Now I ripped the lining."

"I'm sure it doesn't matter, Jack. I'm sure some glue will fix it right on up." She looked in the box to see the damage and spotted something more. Tucked behind the ripped paper, hidden in its own compartment, was a small black and white photo. Sue could tell it was from the early nineteen-sixties by the style of photography. This one looked like it never saw the sun or anything else. It looked like it had been in the box since the day it was taken.

Sue carefully pulled the photo from the crevice and held it up like a trophy. Jack's eyes widened when he saw her prize. She handed it immediately to her husband, who was looking at the paper with hungry eyes. He instantly held it under the light and looked as close as he could at the seven figures in the picture.

"Where was this photo?" he asked Sue. His eyes didn't leave the object in his hand, once.

"It was in your trunk, in the corner that was ripped. It was behind the paper."

"I've had this sea chest since I was little. I dug through it so many times when I was younger. I never once saw this picture." Jack looked at Sue and waved the photo to her. "You know what this is?"

"I didn't look at it yet silly. How could I know what it is?"

"It's a picture of me, Jack, Lisa, our real parents, and our two older brothers. Look, I was only about three in this picture. Look at Jim, he's a little baby. Maybe one or two months old. This is the first picture I have ever seen of our parents or our brothers. We were never told about them, so we didn't even know they existed, until last year. The developing date says 1965. That would be exactly right."

Sue sat next to her husband and looked at the picture with him. It was a beautiful family who were very well dressed. The men wore black suits with gold filigree trim while the woman wore an elegant dress. Even the three, small children were dressed nicely in fine tailored clothes. It didn't look like people who would give their kids up for adoption, Sue thought. The family sat on a large sofa that looked to be very old and fancy. The surroundings were of fine paintings and other quality knick-knacks. It was obviously the home of the family in the picture.

"How do you know this is you and your family?" Sue asked.

"Because I've seen them in my dreams since I was a small child. My visions the last twenty-four hours were guided by everyone in that picture except for Jim. I've been hanging out with them all night. Trust me, those are my people."

Jack couldn't believe what he was seeing. It amazed him; he was gazing into the face of his parents and his brothers.

He saw an object in his father's right hand he couldn't discern. He asked Sue to go get his magnifying glass out of the desk. On her way out, he asked if she would make them some tea, also.

Sue returned about five minutes later with the requested items. Jack was still looking at the photo like it was the most interesting thing he'd ever seen. Sue thought about it and realized it was, indeed, the coolest photo her husband ever witnessed. Carrying a picture of this magnitude your entire life and finding it on your death bed was spiritual. This all seemed so pre-ordained to Sue; scripted right out of a Hallmark movie.

Jack noticed a couple of other anomalies in the photo. His older brothers were standing very close and awkwardly. Around his mother's neck was a pendant with some sort of symbol. The 10x eye loupe was just the tool Jack needed. Sue handed it to her husband and put the tea on the nightstand. Jack wasted no time.

He studied the object in his father's hand first and saw it was a seed-pod. It was dried tightly and gripped the same. He moved the glass to his brothers and had to study this part closely. Where the two met, there seemed to be a continuation of fabric. It looked like they were very close together, but, they were connected. Jack now saw why his family was persecuted. His brothers were conjoined twins.

He looked to the symbol on his mother's neck and saw it was a symbol he wasn't sure about. It seemed familiar somewhat, but at the same time vague. He studied the symbol for a few moments and the rest of the picture. An amber lamp adorned the end table while a large book was on the coffee table. The symbol on this book was easy to read but the lettering was in a dialect Jack didn't know. The symbol was a large pinnacle of white on the background of black. The oversized book looked to be about fourteen inches by twenty inches. Its thickness seemed to be dense, but the angle made it hard to tell.

On one of his own fingers, he saw a small ring. It also had a symbol but was much too small to see. He scanned the photo closer and saw Lisa had a necklace with the same symbol as their mother. Hers, however, was almost camouflaged against her pure white dress. On the finger of his father and the only hand he could see of his brothers, was the same ring. He knew these symbols were the same as his. They were also the same as the females. This was their family crest.

"What do you want me to do with all this stuff?" Sue finally asked. An eternity passed while Jack studied his photo. She waved her hand across the bed when her husband finally looked up to the sound of her voice.

"Just put it all back in the box. You can do whatever you want with it. It's just stuff to me anyway. This was the treasure we needed to find." He waved the picture once to prove what he was saying.

"What picture would that be?" It was Jim, standing in the open doorway of the bedroom. "You guys sure make a lot of noise. You woke me up early."

"You knucklehead," Jack said with lightness. "It's already afternoon. Me and Sue have done so much already. We went through all this shit and signed a shit-ton of papers. We've worked all day while you were sleeping your life away."

"I see you made a huge mess." They all laughed at Jim's joke. "I made breakfast. Not like Becky made yesterday, but I think you'll like it. I'll bring it in when you guys are ready, after this mess is cleaned up. If you're not hungry, that's alright too."

"We're starving, Bro," Jack exclaimed. "We never slept. We've been taking care of shit and going through stuff all morning. It works up an appetite, let me tell you. First, though, come here. I have something real cool I want to show you."

Jim went to the bed as Jack outstretched his hand with the photo. Jim thought Jack had much more strength today. Two days ago, he could barely lift his arm. Now, he was holding it out with a photo in it. Jim took the small paper and looked at it. He looked up at his brother who looked back and nodded with a strange grin. Jim looked again and didn't look away for some time. When he handed the photo back to his brother, Jack could see tears welled up in his eyes. The photo touched his younger brother just as it touched him.

"Where did you get that?" Jim asked.

"I found it in Jack's old trunk," Sue said proudly.

"Do you know what this means?" Jim asked.

"Yes, I do," Jack answered with confidence.

"Then, let's get 'er done," Jim said with a fake Texan drawl.

Chapter 12

Their family was reunited the moment each brother found out they were adopted. The dreams and visions were realized as the memories they were. Since the time Lisa told them the truth, they strived to find out as much as possible. Finding the picture opened a vault of knowledge to the two.

Growing up, they never felt the connection to their adopted family. At home, church and school, the three were outcasts. They were always in trouble. At an early age, they realized they weren't like other kids. The siblings spoke about growing up and going their own way. Their dream was to leave the madness behind and find their paradise. Unfortunately, as they got older, they realized that place didn't exist.

Jim dashed out of the room and returned moments later with a tray containing two plates. Jack was getting used to his brother swiftly departing only to return within moments.

On each platter was a glop of white stuff that looked like boiled turnips. "What's this?" Sue asked. "I would have made a proper breakfast if you would've asked. You're going to make us eat mush?"

"This is the proper breakfast for the journey we have ahead of us. I only made enough for two. Sorry Sue, you won't be going on this trip. Your journey will be with us tomorrow. Today, we must eat this boiled mandioca to keep our systems free of toxins. If we were to eat fatty foods now, the hallucinogen we're going to take will make us very sick."

"Where did you get mandioca in America?" Jack asked, incredulously. He knew, as his brother did; this vegetable was from South America. He'd never seen it in North America before.

"I got it from the same lady I got today's medicine from. I met her on a small beach in Washington. I drove up a peninsula to the very tip. Not many people were in this seaside area. The lady was cool as fuck. We ate oysters together for two days. She showed me so many things about the ocean. We ate mushrooms she picked out of her garden. It fucking put us on another planet, let me tell you. She grew the mandioca in the same garden."

"Did you fuck her?" Jack asked with a broad grin.

"Jack," Sue scolded. "Why would you ask something like that?" Their inside joke had been kept from the woman for many years. They both knew it would be offensive to the lady of the house. For this reason, it was their private joke. Of course, Ronnie, and Little Jack were privy to the joke at times.

"It's okay, Sue," Jim said in defense of his brother. "It's just a joke we say to each other. It's not meant to offend anyone. This lady was exceptional in her spirituality. To answer your question, Bro, no I did not fuck our cousin."

"How'd you find this lady and how did you know it was your cousin?" Sue asked.

"I just knew where to go," Jim replied. "I was called to these shamans by unseen forces. Each of them told me they knew of my arrival. When I met them, each seemed like distant family or long-lost friends to me. Some were kind while others were lunatics. I managed to get along with most of them except that lady in Idaho. She wasn't family, just disgusting. At least in the morning." Both brothers chuckled at the joke. Sue looked to each of them as Jim continued. "For the most part, I was introduced to a whole different realm of existence in my journeys."

The two brothers again giggled at the joke about the lady from Idaho. "Who da ho?" Jack asked with laughter. He normally wouldn't speak like this about a person in front of Sue, but he needed to cut loose. His mind was liberated; he had no more worries. He knew, anyhow, his wife would be happy to see him laughing.

"She was da ho," Jim said through his own laughter. The two of them were contagious as Sue joined in the revelry. It was a long time since they all laughed together about something so meaningless. It felt good to her; it put her soul at ease.

The brothers ate the mandioca in silence. The taste, without salt or pepper, was very bland. It took all Jack's willpower to get the slop down. Jim, on the other hand, seemed to relish the taste. He told the others he ate this vegetable every day he was in Washington. He said the first day he ate it, he felt the same as Jack did now. That night, however, he began to crave the taste. By morning, he was happy it would be what they ate that day with their pseudocellus mushrooms.

When they were done with the mush, Jim again skirted out the room only to reappear moments later. Jack wasn't sure if his eyes were playing tricks on him or if it was some residual from the weeks jubilation. Whatever it was, it seemed like Jim turned into a cartoon flash on the way out the door.

Upon his return, there was a leather bag in his hand. The entire sack was eight inches wide and tied at the top with a leather strap. The leather looked very old. It didn't look like it was made from cows. It was obvious by the well-worn patina; this satchel had been used for a very long time.

Jim sauntered his way to the bed and untied the sack. Jack marveled in the difference of the exit as opposed to the return of his brother. When he left, it was like lightning; when he returned, it was like a tortoise. As the leather fell away, Jack couldn't help but look into the bag. Inside, was nestled two solid gold singing bowls stacked on top of one another. A cloth made of animal skin buffered the two metals. Their polished hue cast an aura out of the opening.

The brothers knew all about singing bowls and the spiritual effects they could have. They played them many times in the past. It always created a tranquility that was difficult to equal. When they played the bowls under hallucinogenic influences, the sounds would open portals to other dimensions hidden among our world.

Jack reached in and grabbed one of the bowls. These were not like the ones they owned before. This bowl, although thin, still weighed over ten pounds. He saw there were intricate patterns etched into the gold. These objects were highly polished to the point of being mirrors. The patterns etched around the inner and outer surfaces was filled with a black paint. They were some ancient symbol Jack recognized; he'd seen the same symbols in the recently discovered photograph. These symbols and his family's jewelry were identical.

"Where did you get these beauties?" asked Jack. "I've never seen any this nice before."

"I got them from the same lady in Washington. The one whose mandioca you just ate." Jim had pride in his voice as he talked. "I knew you'd like them. They belonged to our true people. They've been in our family for generations. When we were small children, we used these singing bowls. Mom and Dad would play them for us to help us sleep. The first time I heard them play there in Washington, the truth came flooding back into my mind. My blocked memories were released. Of course, you already know this. Our memories were given back to us two days ago."

"I thank you again for that, Bro. If the bowls belonged to our biological parents, then how'd you get them?" Jack asked.

"Because I had visions of them and then tracked down some of our relatives. These were the shaman I've been visiting with for the last few weeks. The same ones I can't quit talking about. My energy was called to them and I couldn't resist the pull. I still feel the connection although many miles separate us. Our parents meditated with each of these people and created. The connection was passed to us because we were there along with our family. Through these shamans, I've learned our truth. At the end of the day, you too will hold the knowledge of our family history."

Jim took the other singing bowl out of the bag. They were heavier than any other singing bowl he ever held. Those other ones were made for mass production. These were hand-crafted by the family, for the family. They were made by their ancestors in Latvia and passed on for more than seven centuries.

The two were mesmerized by the gold artifacts in their hands. Jim continued his story: "Our Washington cousin, Rebecca, never met our parents. Her father was the brother of our mother. So, we are first cousins. Her parents were also taken and murdered, but much more recently. Just ten years ago, when Rebecca was thirty years old, the church came to her parent's house with their police puppets and took them away. It was the last she ever saw of them in person

Her visions of them ended years ago, which confirms their time on Earth has been ended. Growing up, they told her many stories about our parents and us. She had a few pictures, but most were destroyed by the church; just as ours were. That is why I was so happy to see that picture you found this morning."

"It's pretty cool! Sue found it," Jack said. "How come the church didn't come for our cousin after they killed aunt and uncle?"

"After our parents were killed, they had to be extra careful. The church throttled down their policy of extermination on families for a decade or two after our family's debacle. It didn't diminish the fears in our kin; they still had to be careful. Rebecca's birth certificate was forged, as she was born at home. When she went to school, it was under the disguise as a good catholic girl from a strict family. The ruse worked well. Nobody was ever the wiser. The preparation and foresight so many years before saved her life when she was older."

Jim reached into the bag, once again, and pulled out the two sticks that would play the instruments. Jack was in awe. They each were about six inches long and maybe an inch and a half in diameter. What made them special, though, was they were made of solid amber. In the middle of each wand, an ancient lizard resided for eternity. These strikers were just as impressive as the bowls. Certainly, the amber came from Latvia, the kingdom of amber.

"I can't believe the craftsmanship in these," Jack said in awe. "The bowls are bad-ass; but this amber. I have truthfully never seen anything like them. How old did you say these are?"

"I don't know, Man. When I got them from Rebecca, all she could tell me is they've been in our family for over seven hundred years. She told me their history was vague, coming from her parents. They told her when the time was right, she would know the truth of the singing bowls. Rebecca told me the few times she played them, she felt as if they were much older than seven centuries. She also said it put her in touch with her people, specifically her parents. She told me she would ring it every day to be with her parents, but there was a flipside to everything. 'The yin to the yang' she said. Every minute of playing was matched by an hour of sickness; keeping her experiences with the singing bowls to a minimum."

Jack listened closely to the words of his brother. He was interested in this part of their family, stolen so long before. All the while he listened, he stared at the beauty in his hands.

It took all his will, but he knew, in his heart, it would be best to wait and play the bowl. The object was giving off an energy like nothing he ever touched. The entire bowl gave off a warmth that spread through Jack's body. He felt a connection to it like they were one. It gave him a sense of being with his ancestors; people he just recently found out even existed.

The bowls began to glow a golden hue from the inside that soon spread across the room. The colors changed from golden to a warm blue. Its intensity was calming as it radiated through everything in the space. Jim looked to Sue and said, "Maybe you should leave now. This day is going to be very strange. Some things are going to happen you may not want to see. You know we love you, Sue, but today we really have to get this done."

Sue got up and went to the door. "I understand boys. Some things you just gotta do. If it means getting my husband to look like he has in the last couple days, I'll do whatever it takes. Tell me to leave, anytime, I won't take offense. Love you guys."

When the door was fully closed, Jim dropped three hard little buttons into each singing bowl. Both men looked to the other with insight. The amber wands almost jumped into action as they encountered the gold. The brothers began to play their respective instrument at the exact moment. The blue aura from inside the bowl penetrated the amber, giving it a soft glow, which was ephemeral. The lizards inside the objects became animated for the briefest of moments as they were recharged by the strong energy.

These singing bowls were the easiest to play of any they ever had. The instruments almost played themselves along with the rhythms of the room. The amber wands floated effortlessly around the golden rim. The sound they made was the most beautiful either brother ever heard. It sounded like what an angel singing would sound like.

Jim told his brother, "You're going to love this, Man. When our cousin gave me these bowls, she said they belonged to the both of us. She said they were passed down to the first daughter in every family. That was our mother. If there was no daughter, they would go to the son to be passed to his daughter. She picked these mushrooms from her garden while I was there, just for us. These doses are crazy, Bro. Look at them, close. I mean really close. It doesn't get any better than this."

Both men investigated their respective bowl as their hand swept the wand around the outer surface. The other hand, resting on their leg, was used to hold the heavy bowl in position. With each passing swirl, the intensity grew bolder. Soon, the melody and the light filled the room. It sounded like waves of sound permeated the space as the color followed suit.

The nodes Jim dropped into the bowls were about the size of marbles. Its flesh was fluorescent green. As the tones grew louder, smoke began to come from the pods. Their solid forms became a thick greed liquid. The mist wafted slowly out of the bowl, hovering just above the rim. Soon, the green smoke took on an odd shape, like that of a dancer.

When the wispy creatures were at full form, so was the rhythm. The mist was dancing to the beat of the music being produced. Its lethargic movements twisted in a sensual manner. The bowls themselves filled with an oily green substance which was the same color as the smoke. It too danced to the melody. The fungi were completely dissolved, leaving behind another realm.

Both men took a long breath, the longest of their lives. The green smoke slowly filled the brother's beings as it was drawn into their mouth and nose. It seemed like they were inhaling for hours. When the intake of breath ended, the green smoke was gone. They had ingested their spiritual guides for the day.

The smoke seemed to drain every bit of moisture from their bodies. It felt like they were becoming mummies in a matter of seconds. Out of instinct, both men raised their singing bowls to their lips. They tilted the heavy metal back and let the thick, green liquid pour into their bodies.

It was the best thing either brother ever tasted. It was like they just drank sunshine.

The harmony never ended as the brothers drank. Even without strumming their instrument, the music continued.

The two felt the vibration from the melody in the gold. When the liquid hit their stomachs, they felt the overture playing inside them.

Chapter 13

Sue felt the change in the house as soon as she heard the music coming from the bedroom. At first, its rhapsody was mellow and rich. It permeated throughout the house, giving Sue a feeling of security. Then the music got louder. It built in crescendo until it encompassed the woman's being. The sounds grew so loud, the walls began to vibrate. Sue felt as if the entire house was the singing bowl and she was in the middle of it.

She worked hard to get her thoughts under control. She was holding both hands over her ears. Not only was the house vibrating, so was the woman's being. The tone became a weight on her body, pressing her to the ground. Thinking she couldn't take anymore, everything went blank.

The effects of the mushrooms began as soon as the brothers inhaled the smoke from the singing bowls. Their minds and eyes were open to the truth at the moment the green dancer entered them. After drinking its contents, both men were fully tripping. The moment the liquid entered their soul, the beings completely transformed. They were no longer flesh pods; now they were pure energy.

The singing bowls never stopped playing, even as the adventure began. The melody didn't diminish, it just carried on with its mellifluous notes. The room was filled with the sounds and aura of the golden bowls. The brothers felt every particle of energy in the small space, which quickly became open space. Walls weren't in this dimension. They both realized at the same time: they were no longer in the same reality.

They were thrust into a parallel universe which was familiar to them but alien at the same time. The brothers were side by side. Next to them was Lisa, their sister.

They shared the same thoughts. Their minds and their auras were connected as one. They no longer had the weight of their flesh pods. Instead, they were blobs of energy, floating in this existence. Now, they were at their maximum potential. Sickness and doubt didn't exist in this world. All that existed in this realm was the mutual respect for everything else. This place was true harmony.

The three were in an ancient forest. Ferns fifty feet tall were only a small part of the green. Trees, thirty feet across at the trunks, dotted the landscape. Large insects and small animals were all around in the greenery. These creatures weren't afraid of the siblings nor were they a menace to them. The energy of the three existed in this place long ago. Their memory lived on in the creatures of the forest. They were all welcome here. Every creature in this dimension had respect for the new arrivals.

The plants, too, had an affinity for the newcomers. They spoke to the siblings in the wind. Their message was clear and welcoming. This was their family. They were part of everything, just as everything was part of them.

Jack, Lisa and Jim knew what they were seeing. This was their past. Their beginning on this planet. This was the beginning of their cycle of life on Earth. Each cycle before ended in destruction, making way for the new beginning. The planet re-seeded itself, from its inner DNA, countless times in its history.

The virgin forests were beautiful and plentiful. Trees hundreds of feet tall blocked out the sun in places. Fruit as big as a cow hung from low lying branches on some of the larger trees. Water was everywhere in streams and ponds. The smallest puddle held millions of tiny creatures. This was truly paradise. This was where life was born and nurtured for millions of years. This was Earth's incubator.

When they first came, there was only one species of bipedal creature in the area. The siblings mated with this inferior species for generations, until their species became more and more like modern human. Many other off-shoots of humanoid creatures evolved over the span of time. Almost all these would eventually self-destruct or become extinct through their inability to adapt to a changing planet. Over time, the human gene over-ruled the inferior genes, becoming the dominant species on the planet.

The three were humans who came from an ancient race. Their planet was struck with nuclear war. Technology blew up too fast on the utopia. The people couldn't keep up and it overtook them. When the artificial intelligence took control of the government, everything crumbled.

The technology became a power struggle to control. The greed had no mercy. They built underground bunkers thinking they would come out in a few years to a planet ready to rebuild. What they came out to was an atmosphere which was depleted by ninety percent; making it uninhabitable to any life. The greed went back to their bunkers, but after a couple hundred years, it became their coffins.

One group of scientists saw the madness their leaders were perpetrating, early on. These scholars built escape pods that could possibly extend their race. They launched them towards fifty planets they deemed habitable. Some were many light years away while others were in their solar system. It was literally rolling dice and trying to hit twelve every time. They knew the odds were scant but had no option. Even if one pod survived, the species would have a chance.

The scholars, artists, and scientists who escaped went out blindly on their own. Jack, Jim and Lisa ended up on Earth with over a thousand of their fellow refugees. Their craft was little more than a rocket ship. It was a one-way ride. They landed on the blue planet with no fuel to take off again and no provisions. Even if they wanted to take off, there was no place to go. Their planet was not life friendly anymore. There was no choice but to make Earth their new home.

The memories were pleasant to the three. Jack and Jim's energy was birthed as twins on Etranocias. Lisa was their sister. All three were philosophers and artists. They dabbled in the sciences and astronomy as well. The colony was extremely happy when they arrived at the blue planet. They knew, through their observations, Earth was habitable. Their purpose was to mate with indigenous creatures upon arrival to their new planet. Their mission was to seed a new world with their DNA. If there were no animals on the new home, they were to mate with each other and create animals. It would be a last effort to recreate the Etranocian race that already destroyed itself. Their function was not to create their own species again as it had been before. It was a destructive greed they had left behind. Instead, they would give the species of the new planet a shot of evolution and see what would happen.

The siblings quickly saw a power struggle going on amongst the colony. They observed the leaders taking advantage of the native inhabitants. They abused the bipedal creatures like they were slaves. When they saw a group of humans worshipping the colony, they knew it was time to go.

They had befriended a few indigenous people during this time. Three men and two women would accompany the three. These beings would continue through time with the family.

This group moved to Antarctica while other, like-minded settlers, moved to far reaches of the planet. Anywhere they could go was suitable if it was far from the controllers. Twenty percent of the original colony moved away. They held meetings and agreed to not change evolution, by altering DNA, among the native species of the planet. They would breed with the natives to spread their DNA; fulfilling the original mission. They would not, however, show this planet any of the technology which brought down theirs.

After many millennia, the planet was becoming populated with more species of bipedal creatures. At least ten new species of human developed during this era. The three were proud. The ones which perished were understood as the natural way of things. The siblings saw all aspects of nature and its beauty.

They, and their colony, brought life as they knew it to this planet. The three also knew they weren't gods. They were merely travelers spreading their seed throughout the cosmos.

Now, the siblings walked through their old home. Their flesh pods materialized as they progressed into their past and the forest. Clothes were not needed. The tropical forest provided ample warmth and naked was how they'd always been. The land they strolled on was before the ice age. Antarctica was a beautiful, lush home to countless creatures. It is where they ended up on their travels. It took the siblings over a century to find this secluded spot teeming with so much life. When they did find it, they settled in.

Many changes in the Earth's geography kept their home buried for thousands of years. At first, they made their home in a deep cave. With the global changes that occurred over the history of the planet, their original home was buried in dense ice.

The three saw the entrance to the cave they called home for thirty thousand years. It was a natural cave, over a mile deep. They had used their knowledge to tunnel the cave until it resembled a home. It took time, but there had been plenty of that. They also held knowledge, making things easier. Electromagnetism, long before, was harnessed by their people and these three had full knowledge of its properties. Each of them had their own professionalism that came in handy for the colonization; electromagnetism was one they all shared.

They dug their caverns into bedrooms, dens, living rooms, even recreational rooms. A large swimming pool was put in one chamber, filled with rainwater. It wasn't always so safe to swim in the water of a lake or a pond. There were some creatures considerably larger than the humans. They all lived in harmony but there was still the food chain. The pool provided year-round bathing and exercise. There was no need to drink this water, there were other chambers dug just for that purpose.

When they weren't digging, they were creating. Metals and other minerals were abundant in their mine. A soft metal they called gold was everywhere. It was used to craft anything from jewelry, machines and musical instruments. There was an abundance of minerals they used for forging while others were used for tools. Their offspring would mimic them and began their own tool making processes.

They also found minerals for paint and stains. They made paper and wood panels. Their time in the cave was spent well. They wrote thousands of books on their philosophy and the history of their people. They created non-stop and made millions of paintings, sculptures, music and other madness.

They were vegetarians. The plants provided everything the creatures needed. It was all part of the cycle. Food, medicine and hallucinogens were plentiful in this forest. There was no need for them to grow food. The forest provided all the nutrition they needed. It also provided any medicine that might be necessary. They used this medicine for anything from cuts to the anti-aging herbs which prolonged their lives as long as they ingested them.

Without the task of hunting and gathering, they could focus their minds more on creating. Imagination was the spark needed for a new species on a new planet. When beings were creating, they weren't even thinking about destruction. It was exactly what the fleeing refugees had envisioned.

The three never once assisted their offspring in evolution. Everything was left up to them to figure out and decide. If they observed the three making something, it was acceptable. Anything that would push technology, too swiftly, would be accomplished away from their watchful eye. Being part of their children's lives, as loving parents, made it difficult to keep their secrets hidden.

The only thing the new species of human picked up from these three were their symbols, tool-making, and fire building. The siblings used these symbols to mark spots in the forest for their future reference. The natives, over time, learned to understand these symbols and use them in their own daily existence. Over time, they spread across the entire planet, creating the first universal written language. As the humans traveled more, there was a greater need to create these 'roadmaps' with their markings.

Tool making completely changed the humans. They already had a sophisticated tool system, but it grew exponentially after observing the siblings. The natives knew about fire before contact but didn't realize what they could use it for. When they harnessed this element, it made the species progress faster than any other time in their existence. This is when they learned to cook.

The animals were their companions and teachers of the new realm. The three observed everything and learned from it all. Their quest was for wisdom. They didn't want to transform this planet, they wanted to become part of it.

The siblings made keen observations and noted the creatures were progressing well. Greed, in this region of Earth, didn't exist yet. The Earth was plentiful; there was no need to fight over its riches. Unfortunately, like on their planet, this would come later; it held hands with civilization. Sadly, it would be their own fellow settlers who spread destruction on this planet; just like theirs.

The cave was just beyond the husk of a giant fossilized tree. Its trunk was over twenty-five feet diameter and its height over a hundred. There was no door leading into their home as there were no predators, on land, to these humans. The siblings held wisdom; including knowledge of every creature on the continent. They were respected. They were the first modern human; the first shaman.

Just before entering the cave, the three picked a large red fig from an overhanging tree. It was the size of a softball. Both men were eating the sweet, purple flesh treats as they entered the cave. Lisa nibbled on the tasty fruit. She looked at her hands and saw they looked like they were covered in blood. The sweet taste of the fig and the intense red from its skin brought back fond memories of this food. It was one of the favorites for the three since the day they arrived.

This species of plant was extinct for so very long. Like many other species, they came and went. Some stayed longer, while others disappeared quickly. Some you were happy to see go while others saddened you. The strong species survived while the weak ones didn't.

Being the architects and builders, the siblings knew their way around the many entrances and corridors to the cave. They chose a portal to the left. After following the level passageway, they came to a room with a green glow. It permeated the walls of the tunnel as they approached. Its dim light provided all that was needed in their familiar minds. They knew their way around their former home like they left it yesterday. After being outside and now inside, they realized: yesterday was when they were here last. All the years since the last visit spanned just one day, in their home.

The green room didn't hold any surprises. They knew what they'd find. Having the same thoughts, and the same memories, all three knew.

In the center of the chamber was a stone altar draped in fern leaves. Laying atop the leaves was Jack. Jim and Lisa were standing by the altar holding their brother's hand. The time was near. They could see it in their faces.

The siblings walked closer to their spirits of another dimension. As they neared, the scene in front of them turned slowly to a smoky dust which hung in the air. The dust took on the green glow and amplified it. The light density and brightness increased exponentially until the three could no longer see.

Silence was thick as the air. It became deafening as the oxygen slowly went away. The three became light headed from asphyxia and were on the brink of passing out. Not being able to see or hear made things much worse. All they sensed was the bright-ass green light and that dreadful silence. It took all their will, but none of the three panicked.

Both men lost consciousness at the same moment. Lisa, reaching out to take hold of them, couldn't fully grasp the hands of her brothers. She too succumbed to the lack of oxygen. The green stifled their brains and their senses. It robbed them of consciousness and thrust them into its green subconscious. As soon as the three blacked out, the green haze faded and released its grip.

A loud banging sound brought them back to their senses. It jolted the men out of their green vision into darkness. Their eyes slowly accustomed to the change and they both looked over to see the sliver of light coming from under the door.

Jim got up and walked to the portal. He swiftly opened it to find a stressed-out Sue pacing in the hallway.

As soon as the door opened, Sue rushed into the darkness. She fumbled for the light switch and blinded her husband when she found it. "What the fuck have you guys been doing in here?" she blurted out. "It's four in the morning! You've been in here for sixteen hours! Why did you have the door locked?"

"Easy Sue," Jack said. "Everything is fine. Where have you been?" His head was clear of the journey. He was back in this dimension and knew his brother was too. He didn't remember being gone more than an hour or so; certainly not sixteen. It seemed like they were in the forest for a short time and then the cave; it didn't seem like sixteen hours.

Jim felt great. Never had he come down from tripping so swiftly and completely; until the last few days. The visions stuck in his head but were almost comical to him. He really needed to talk to his brother some while the story was fresh in his memory. This was a crazy journey, he needed to know some things.

"Are you listening to me?" Sue said loudly. Jack was staring at the wall the entire time she was talking. Jack thought the room was silent. He was thinking about what just happened, trying to figure it out.

"I'm listening, sorry. Please tell me once more."

"All the clocks stopped in the house and none of the electronics were working. I don't know what happened. I guess I laid down to take a nap after I left you two alone. I remember some crazy ass music or something. I woke up ten minutes ago on the couch. The lights and clocks came back on when I started beating on the door. Probably when I woke you Fuckers up."

Jack interrupted his wife and said with the sweetest voice he could muster: "Sue, I'm sorry to ask you for something but will you please get me some water?" The man was thirstier than he ever remembered. It felt like he had paper instead of flesh on the inside of his mouth. His main reason for asking the favor had nothing to do with thirst, though. He really needed to talk to his brother about what just happened.

Sue stood and stared at her husband for half a minute before answering. "No problem, Jack. I'll be right back." There was irritation in the woman's voice.

The minute she walked out, Jack said, "what the hell just happened, Man. Was that some real shit or were we just really tripping?"

Jim sat on the edge of the bed and said, "it was in your mind, Bro. It's up to you to decipher what happened. I know what I saw; I will be picking it apart for a very long time. You just need to turn your third eye inward and study who you really are."

"Enough with the Zen master bullshit. I'm being serious here man. I just had a vision that you, me and Lisa were some kind of weird Adam and Eve or something. It's hard for me to believe that. We left Etranocias and colonized this planet? We lived for millennium in Antarctica? Come on, Man, this shit is hard to believe."

"That's what you saw? I saw something totally different," Jim said. "I was on the road trip with our real family right after I was born. In my vision, I was a little baby, but I could speak like an adult. Everywhere we went, the people we met were amazed at the three children who were unlike any other. Many of these people I saw in this vision, I met on the road in the last few weeks. My vision just confirmed what I've been telling you all along about our family."

Sue re-entered the room and said, "what have you been telling him about his family?"

"That we're a bunch of weirdos. Some lunatics who were dropped off here by a race of intelligent beings that wanted to get rid of our people."

Jim stood to leave and laughed loudly. Jack, too, broke out in laughter. As Jim passed through the doorway, Jack said to him, "see you tomorrow, Bro." Jack knew they would be talking about this much more when they were alone. What just happened to him was really tripping him out.

Sue laid down with her husband as soon as Jim left the room. Her mind was clear, but she didn't know what happened to her for the past sixteen hours. Her memory of the previous day was a complete blank. She knew her body was exhausted, but she'd never slept this long at one time before.

"Jim's got you going on some crazy ass Juju, doesn't he?" she asked Jack.

"It's pretty damn amazing," he said with enthusiasm in his voice. Sue snuggled up with her husband and instantly felt the increase in his strength. His weak body, riddled with cancer, was now stronger. He almost felt like the old Jack.

It felt good for Jack to have his woman by his side. After the long journeys they were going on, his mind and body needed the comfort of his soul-mate. The exchange of energy created a new strength in the dying man. The bond with his wife completed his being.

Sue was amazed. She didn't expect to find her husband in this condition. He was so fragile in the last weeks and now he seemed like a new person. She knew the next days were going to be the same routine. Jim would be filling the days with his crazy adventures; Sue would have the rest for husband time.

She didn't care about the lack of time she was allotted. If it helped her husband out, she was all for it.

Jack told Sue about the ancient forest he visited. He described in detail how it was once their home, thousands of years ago. He told her how he, Jim, and Lisa seeded that part of the planet with their DNA. "Many humans now are descendants of ours," he exclaimed proudly.

"Must have been really good shit," Sue jested.

Jack shot back with tickles to her ribs. It turned into a wrestle match with both participants laughing like kids. The laughter turned to moans as the wrestling switched to groping. Soon, all clothes were scattered around the room.

The couple had rested all day. Sue slept for many hours while Jack only had hours left. Their energy was built to a crescendo; their balloons fully inflated.

Wild sex consumed the lovers throughout the early morning hours.

Chapter 14

It was noon when Jim stood at his brother's door. This day, he was all the wiser and knocked before entering. After no response, he entered anyway. He looked around, perplexed. There was nobody in the room. The bed was mussed up and the lamp on the nightstand was overturned. The room looked like a crime scene. The privacy blinds were pulled bathing the entire space in a cold blue light.

Jim thought this odd, but not at the same time. He saw the spark in Jack's eyes in the past couple of days. That look intensified every day of the week. As their journey progressed, so did Jack's spirits. Jim was happy he could help his brother, spiritually. There was always a connection between the brothers and would be until the end. Jim's brother and sister had always been the closest people in his life. It would be the same in death.

After a bit of searching, Jim found the family behind the house. Ronnie, Becky and Little Jack were present along with their parents. They were relaxing in the shade smoking a very large joint. Jack was in his wheel-chair while Sue sat on a picnic bench next to him. The other kids were sitting in their respective spots.

The brothers built this picnic table and chairs when Jack first bought the land. With the addition of three to their family, they knew a family size table was appropriate. With the help of Tommy and Ronnie, the table was made in an afternoon. Sue and Becky stained it the next day. The following weekend, the family used it for the first time. It was one of those meals none of them would ever forget.

As they sat around the table, they all shared their own fond memories of the family heirloom. The joint flowed freely along with the conversation.

129

"Hey Guys," Jim said as he approached. "Mind if I join you?"

Spread out on the picnic table was a meal big enough for a large family. Jim's stomach growled at the sight of the feast before him. He looked to his sister-in-law and got his reply without even asking. "I didn't need sleep after all the rest I got yesterday," Sue said. "So, I decided to put together a nice brunch as a way of thanking you for what you've done. We all appreciate you being here, Jim. You've always been here for us. Thank you"

Sue stood and hugged her brother-in-law. Her gratitude for what he did for her husband could never be properly re-paid. As Sue stepped aside, Jack's hand was there to replace the embrace. Jim took it instinctively. His older brother pulled him into a bear hug from the handshake. "I love you, Bro," Jack said with sincerity. "What Sue said echoes my beliefs. My body is decaying but my mind feels alive. You have rejuvenated my soul. Thank you."

Jim was groped by three other sets of arms. He stood slightly and fell into the embrace of his nephews and niece. There were no words needed from them. The uncle easily felt the connection and gratitude from the youngers. He held the same respect for them as they did for him.

"It's been my pleasure to help, and my honor to be here. We two brothers have been close since the beginning; it's only natural that we're together at the end. Especially when we both know the end is truly the beginning."

"Oh yeah, I know," Jack replied. "I've never once feared death because I know it's the gateway to the next phase."

"That's right Jack. We're there, Man. As for the rest of you, I've always been there for you and I'll continue to do just that. You're my family. It's not just a word to me. It's a way of life," Jim said.

"We know how you feel about us Bro," Jack said. "We're a family who understands the importance of each other. Right now, though, all I can think about is what you've planned for us today. The last three days have been fantastic. So, now what, Man?"

"Well guys," Jim said, "today is going to be much different. Sue will be going on this journey with us. It's going to take place right here in your backyard. This time, we will be dropping four doses since it's the fourth day."

"What if I don't want to go on this journey today, Jim?" Sue asked defiantly. "My mind is already fragile; my heart is broken. My husband is dying, and you want me to take acid with you. I feel like I'm going insane; this isn't helping the situation. The cliff is right there; you trying to push me off it, or what?"

"Well Sue," Jim answered, "feeling down on yourself right now isn't going to help your husband. He wants to see you happy and enlightened. Dying is a hard thing to do. Don't make it harder on him. There will be plenty of time for us to grieve when he's gone. For now, we need to celebrate his transition."

Jack was holding his wife's hand through the entire conversation. At the end of Jim's dialogue, she looked to her husband to gauge his reaction. She asked him, "is it true? Would you rather see me celebrate your death or mourn?"

The husband wiped the tears from his wife's face. The grip of their hands never broke. "You know Sue, I love you so very much. I don't want to see you suffer; especially my last few days. These last weeks have been awesome with you, but it could be even better. All you must do is let go. We're all going to die, we know it at birth. I'm not the least bit afraid for myself. My only fears are about you and if you'll be okay."

"I'll be fine," Sue said as she dried up her tears. "I'll have Jim and the kids. They'll help me along. I'm going to miss you fiercely. I'll just have to deal with it when the time comes. Today, I'll celebrate life, and death; with you and your brother. Today, I'll let go of my anguish. I do understand we're already dead. You've been pounding it into my head for years. 'How can you kill what's already dead' is what you always said."

"Exactly Babe. This death is one of many my being has gone through. Maybe it is the last one but somehow that isn't how it seems to work. Whatever it is, we're all on the same cycle. Our DNA connects us through eternity. We've lived our lives together before and we'll live them together again in the future. Or the past, whichever the case may be."

"Okay then, I'll go on the journey with you and Jim. I think I'm ready for just about anything right now. Maybe it will heal my spirituality some."

"It's going to help you like you don't even know, Sue," Jim said. "Let me get some of this good grub first," he said while grabbing a plate. "I'm going to need all the energy I can get today. You guys too. It's like when we were little. Better eat before the long trip cause we're not stopping. Use the toilet too you little fuckers." The entire family laughed at the joke Jim made. They were all familiar with road-trips. "Have you guys already eaten?"

"We were waiting for you, Bro," Sue said. She went about uncovering the food. She made fresh passion fruit juice which impressed the brothers. It was Jack's favorite; but not easily found in this part of California. Sue went through a painstaking ordeal to get the fresh fruit delivered to their door. She knew this would be one of the last meals for her husband and she wanted to make it wonderful.

She gave Jim, Jack and her kids a walk-around tour of the food spread she prepared. Jim said it was so perfect, along with her presentation; it seemed as if Sue was a television cooking show host. All six laughed at the joke. The connotation made the whole family picture Sue in a professional way.

The men were impressed with the items on the menu. She made bagels and lox, imported sausage from Germany, fresh crab omelets, julienne potatoes, cherry stuffed pastries, and of course, the passion fruit juice.

The brothers asked in unison if Sue would dish up their plates for them. She happily agreed as Jim volunteered to pour the juice. There was just enough for six large glasses. The smell brought Jim back to a place in Peru the three of them frequented in the past. It was a Cevicheria called El Villainos. Their ceviche and other foods were exquisite as was the fresh juice. This is where they were introduced to the delicious passion fruit. The owner of the place, Javier, befriended the trio and took pride in introducing them to his awesome cuisine. It was, easily, the favorite restaurant in the world for Jack, Sue and Jim.

The food was fantastic. Jack ate a large plate full of his favorites. The talk was of a good-hearted tone. Jim told the others how the LSD for today came from an old man who lived outside Klamath, California. "He was a cousin of ours on our father's side. He made this dose with the intent to bring us close to our ancestors. He said it was time we met our parents; this would help bring about that meeting."

"How long did you stay with this guy?" Jack asked.

"I was there for three nights. He dropped some doses in my water the second night there and we went on a magical journey. A Sasquatch came for a visit and guided us through the forest, all night long. He showed us the secrets of the woods which were hidden from the humans. He took us to his village where we met the others of his kind. We ate with these beasts and danced a strange ritual. When we awoke in the morning, I couldn't discern if it had all been a dream.

When I got up, my feet were torn up and my clothes were shredded. It was obvious; I'd been on a trip through the forest the night before."

"Sounds like you must have been really tripping to be seeing Bigfoot," Sue said mockingly.

"I know it sounds crazy, but I know what I saw. Either way, you'll see. This acid is going to open your third eye like nothing before."

"Mom and Dad were telling us about the journeys you've tripped on in the last days, Uncle Jim," Ronnie said. "It sounds like you guys are having some crazy ass journeys." This was their only child who didn't take hallucinogens. He didn't smoke pot nor drink. After Tommy's death, Ronnie became a loner. He was in drafting classes and his passion for that became his focus to block the pain. The boy, with drafting, grew up with a solid hobby. He never had time, nor desire, for drugs or alcohol. Hanging out with other people only took away from his true passion: creating.

"Yeah, Man, maybe there will be some of that for the entire family one day," Little Jack said. The group all laughed at the youngest sibling's joke. He was the opposite of his brother. He loved to party with friends and experiment with all sorts of drugs. As an artist from an early age, Little Jack was always looking to expand his mind. He understood the difference between use and abuse and never got in trouble with drugs.

"You might not want to go where they're going, Little Brother," Becky said with mockery. She understood the journeys her parents and uncle were going on. She had gone on a few of these journeys with her elders. After the spat of death a few years before, the family had dark times around them. Their stress and anguish were almost too much for some of them. Jim devised the idea to trip together. It would heal their souls, he told them. All participated except Ronnie. After the first time, Becky and Little Jack came back for more journeys. The trips made them bond like never before. It eased the pain of death and put them on the road to recovery.

"Are we going to talk about it all day, or are we going to take some acid?" Jack asked with sarcasm. He took the last swig of his fresh juice and set the glass on the table.

"You just drank the last bit of it," Jim said laughing. "I put it in yours and Sue's glass after I poured the juice. Buckle up Brother, it's gonna be a wild one."

"I guess it's as good a way as any," Sue said. She listened to what her husband said to her earlier. She wanted to make this transition as easy as possible for him. She was trying her best not to be stressed about things. In truth, Sue was being stronger than most people would be in her situation. She felt like she was dealing with it damn well.

She and the kids cleared the table and took the dishes in the house. There were minimal leftovers, even with the large amount of food she made. With six hungry mouths and the quality of food, it was a huge success.

She was impressed and pleased with the amount Jack ate. It made her feel good knowing she could bring some comfort to her dying husband. With food, comfort and the closeness they felt in the last days, Sue felt as if they were both healing their souls, together.

The leftovers went quickly into the fridge. The plates were bare of scraps, so the cleanup took only minutes. The kids were nice and did the dishes. They said their goodbyes outside first, then inside to their mother. They each apologized for leaving after eating. In unison, they said they weren't meant to be here today. They hugged Sue with love, respect and an inseparable bond. The siblings departed in their separate cars. On this day, driving home, all three would be singing in their vehicles. While self-performing, each tried to think of the last time they sung out loud and why they were doing it now.

The moment Sue opened the sliding door to the patio, two things happened: First, she noticed the other two travelers were just beginning to trip. Second, she realized she too was beginning to trip. That familiar feeling in the back of her throat and the cramping of the stomach were a sure sign the effects of the LSD were taking over. The tightening of her muscles signaled the moment she was giving over control of her pod. She would now be controlled by the subconscious with little mixes of conscious.

The hallucinogen hit her like a freight train. Instantly, she was in a better place. Her stress ceased immediately, and she saw things for what they truly were.

As in the past, when she took this drug, it completely opened her eyes to reality. The blocks and stress put in place by our society were gone. Now, Sue could see the truth.

Now, things would genuinely be okay.

Chapter 15

The weather at the end of October, in the gold country, is awesome. The colors of the leaves mixed with the sky and hills was spiritual. This place always held a special connection for the family. They, long ago, felt the energy which drew them here like a magnet. Even when bad neighbors came and went, they dealt with it. Mountain Ranch was a magical place.

A few years after Jack and Sue built this house, they went on an acid trip in the forest with Jim and Lisa. A small seasonal stream held a trickle of water, but it was enough to keep everything green. The four could feel the magic from the rocks and plants. This place, and everything in it, held an aura that was warm and welcoming. It was a place to meditate and see what was there. Sitting there that day, the three met the spirits of the trees and stones. They became one with the forest and its inhabitants. The plants and soil showed them knowledge in their freed minds. Nature welcomed the family, making this place home.

"Come, sit down," Jack said in a voice that seemed to be a few octaves lower than normal. Jim had helped him into a patio lounge chair under the maple tree they planted their first year here. He now turned to see Sue meandering toward them. She looked like a spirit to Jim. Her white sun-dress billowed in the soft breeze, along with her flowing grey hair.

Two more chairs were aligned next to Jack's. Jim jumped into one of them and called out to Sue: "Come on, this is the cockpit. Sit at your station. We're getting ready for take-off. You almost missed the countdown." His voice sounded authentically frantic and professional at the same time.

Sue laughed as she hurried to her seat. She awkwardly sat in the lounge chair which, in her mind, was the cockpit of a rocket ship. Its angle put her looking to the heavens and beyond. She was in the perfect position for take-off.

Jim began his count-down when Sue was seated. When she first entered the cockpit, he gave her instruction. "You'd better buckle up. It's going to be a crazy-ass ride." He was at seven when Sue got buckled in her seat. He was at five when she got settled. At three, she could swear she heard engines and felt vibration. At one, the entire backyard was shaking. Smoke seemed to be everywhere. The vibration was so bad, Sue could barely think straight.

When Jim said, "lift off," everything went blank. The light of day ceased for a moment. The three were in complete darkness. The vibration around them was so intense, it rattled their rib cages. A loud tearing sound was all that could be heard. The sound and vibration were overwhelming. It felt like their entire beings were self-imploding.

Just when the three felt like they couldn't handle any more, the cacophony suddenly stopped. The only sound left was the heavy breathing of the occupants. Besides that, the sounds were as void as the light. They had launched into limbo.

The three sat, with senses deprived, for quite some time. They didn't need them. None of them spoke. Their brains were replaying memories from the planet. Like a motion picture, these images rolled out with vivid reality.

Most of these memories were foreign to them. It seemed like they were remembering other peoples' experiences. All were from drastically different times. Some were from the ancient past while others were from the near future. However, deep in the subconscious of the three, these visions were familiar.

Things long forgotten to humans came rushing into their thoughts. These memories spanned millions of years and countless places. It was not just good memories. This wasn't how things worked. Everything good had a bad attached to it. Memories of heartache, regrets and injuries were along those of celebrations, milestones and good times. Cataclysm and destruction were shown parallel to rebirth and creativity.

Everything had a positive and a negative. Every living creature, every planet, every sun, galaxy and universe. It was the inhale and exhale of existence.

The memories seemed to play on for hours. The three participants sat in the darkness unaware of time or reality. They were too engrossed with the visions in their minds to worry about reality. Even the presence of the others was forgotten in favor of the reckoning. They were learning secrets long lost to humans. Secrets of life, death, and the cycle. Knowledge they gained in their long existence, but forgot in this one, all came back to them.

Hours passed in this hypnotic state. The flashbacks faded slowly as their senses returned. As they slipped back to the conscious, light slowly enveloped them. The void they entered slowly dissipated until reality returned. Where there was darkness in their minds, light came flooding through.

"Wow, that was intense," Sue said. "Is this what you guys have been doing the last few days?"

"Something like that," Jack said. They all three laughed at the joke. None of them were looking at each other. They each stared off into the forest as if it were the first time they ever saw it with their eyes. To an outsider, it would look like they were examining mystical creature nobody else could see.

Each of them was fully reclined in their wooden lounge chairs. The backs were up just enough for them to see forward and straight up. In this position, they could see the magic of the colors around them. The forest and the sky were alive. Shadows danced through the branches and leaped from the hillside. All three thought they might see a gnome or some other mythical creature in the abyss before them.

They sat silently, staring off into space and contemplating what just happened. The few words earlier were an awkward interruption to the solitude of silence.

They noticed the colors seemed different. Everything in their surroundings appeared brighter. The color spectrum expanded in their freed minds. The LSD enabled them to see what was truly there. It wasn't only their sight. Smells of the forest were awakened in the three. Sounds of the most minute creatures were now audible. They could feel every particle in the sun-rays permeating their bodies.

They were alive.

The depravation of their senses had, in-turn, reset them. Their sensory ability was at the purest level since birth. Their senses began deteriorating every day since the first; but today, they were replenished to max capacity.

Having so many other-life memories come back to you was a complete rush for the three. Taking in so much at once and trying to process it was overwhelming. The group felt exhausted, like they ran a marathon.

The feeling of completeness permeated the group. They realized this entire life was lived for this one moment. True spirituality crept into their beings when their senses were deprived. What was blocked from their conscious, so long before, was now regained. Today, their spirits were once again whole.

Like every life before, the three entered a new level of existence.

The sun slowly crept through the sky. It seemed like it stayed in the same place for a very long time. The three had no sense of time. Their thoughts were consumed with their multiple life memories. They didn't even feel like the same people who came out in the yard a couple hours before. Their eyes were now opened. Their true existence was presented to them. Now, they had to figure out what it was all about.

Hours passed before any of them spoke. Each of their minds was more active than at any other time of their lives. Inside their skulls, their brains were working like a super-computer. Regressed memories filled the three beings with wonder. Wisdom encompassed their beings.

Finally, after an eternity, it was Jim who broke the silence. The words were soft spoken but came out abruptly. "You guys ever think about that time when me and Jack sunk that boat on Walker Lake. If it wasn't for the fearless crew, we would have been lost."

Sue and Jack were staring into the sky when Jim spoke. A ridge of pressure here would put on a cloud display that would make a CGI guy jealous. The couple, seeing the truth in the sky, watched it like the magic it was.

As soon as Jim's words ended, laughter erupted from the three. It was the opening they were all waiting for. When the laughter ended, the talking began.

The trio talked about everything. In the hallucinogenic mindset, Wisdom expounded. The brothers were philosophers since they could speak. Their entire lives were spent spreading perceived truths. Their insight was unlike most others. Their dialogue would be life-changing, if only a few would listen. They would just as soon sit and talk all night instead of going out. Jack's garage was the everyday, spoken-word room.

Sue had listened to this talk for over thirty years. Sometimes, it would get late and she'd go to bed. Other times, the talk would be too important, and she'd be in for the long-haul. No matter which situation it was, the woman was always part of the conversation. The brothers never omitted Sue from anything.

On this day, in the backyard, the talk went into directions the woman never heard before. They spoke about the afterlife and the journey you took to get there. They also spoke of a major world event that was near. Jack told the others the time was upon them. They must be ready and prepared for what was coming. He apologized for not being there with them. It wasn't in his destiny, he told the others. They would have to go through the struggles without him.

The brothers spoke about things that happened thousands of years before. At first, Sue thought they lost their minds. Then, the memories began to sound familiar to the woman. She recollected some of the things the others were speaking of. Their memories and hers coincided, way before they should have. She thought the acid was creating crazy scenarios in her head. As she listened, she realized: they weren't hallucinations at all. She truly had been remembering her past lives and existences.

The sun slowly crept through the sky as the day lingered. All three revelers spoke about how it seemed to be standing still. Time was moving at a snail's pace. They were aware, and alert to it. Minutes seemed like hours or even days. "I hope time just stops like this for the next few days. If that's the case, I have years left to live," Jack said. Even as they spoke, their eyes never met; the three were too busy looking at the creator before them.

"Too bad it couldn't be like that," Sue said with regret. Her voice and attitude instantly changed with the thought.

"Come on Debbie Downer," Jim broke in. "We're here to have fun, not cry. There will be lots more coming your way that will be a surprise for all of us. Don't even think time can't stand still. The plane we're on now allows us to do so many things. Manipulating the fourth dimension is one of them. In this state of mind, you might say, we are magicians."

"Yeah," Jack said. "We've been manipulated with time for millennium. The way we perceive it is not the way it truly is. Humans at one point could slow down or speed up time. They manipulated it to their benefit. At one time, they were connected to time; as One."

"After the take-over of the human's minds," Jim put in, "time became a relative thing, controlling the masses. The roles were reversed. Humans lost all control, even of their own beings. This is when humans became slaves."

Sue was studying the forest as the men talked. She noticed the shadows in the forest weren't exactly corresponding to the rays of the sun. Her vision was twisted from the acid, she knew, but this was beyond that. Normal colors were now vibrant and alive. Objects, benign before, were now emitting an aura. The LSD completely opened road-blocks in their minds. They truly saw what was happening around them. What Jim always said was clear: everything was alive. God was everything, and everything was God.

At first, Sue thought her eyes were playing tricks on her. It looked like there were spirits in the forest. She could see some standing still, watching the living. Others danced to a rhythm only they could hear. She saw the rocks, trees and even ground were accompanied by spirits. Everything in the forest was emitting an aura. They were all connected by the same common bond: Earth, the Sun, and DNA.

Sue interrupted the banter of Jack and Jim. "Are you guys seeing this?" she asked incredulously while sweeping her hand in the direction of the forest. She took acid many times in the past, but she'd never seen anything like this. This one event confirmed in Sue's mind: The Earth was truly their God.

Jack said, "they've been there all along. They're always here. What you're seeing is the spirits of the rocks and trees. The forest is alive with the auras of our neighbors. This place is special. The Miwoks and the people before them knew it. It's why they settled here. They saw the wisdom of the land and learned from it. They lived in harmony with the forest because they realized everything was alive. Everything has a spirit. By destroying anything, they're destroying life and a piece of God.

These indigenous people were untouched by the control of the elite for thousands of years. Their minds and conscious hadn't been blocked. When the greed came, they fought the natives and controlled them. When they defeated them, they were fed alcohol and drugs to demoralize them. It doesn't work on all of them. The indigenous people of the planet, who are untouched by the greed, are the only ones who truly know what's going on. All the rest have been poisoned by technology, money and greed. The indigenous people are the only ones who ever lived in harmony with the planet. When the greed is gone, it will be the native peoples who will heal our beloved Earth."

Sue said, "but there are human spirits down there too. All along the stream are entities. They weren't there earlier."

Jim said, "yeah Sue, you know this used to be a mining area. Hundreds of thousands of men came to find the gold. It was a hard life for every one of them. A few struck it rich while most lived in squalor, barely making enough to eat. Their lives were filled with boredom and misery. They left energy behind like photographs recorded by the forest. You're seeing these visual memories. They're always there, but normally we can't see them. You have to open your inner-eye if you want to see spirits as clearly as this."

"It sure is cool," Sue replied. Her voice was distant. This sight really impressed her. She'd seen spirits before, but not a forest full of them. She knew she would never look at the forest the same again.

The day crept by as the talk continued. A pitcher of iced tea was enjoyed, but none of the trippers remembered going to get it. It was the sweetest tea either of them ever drank. No one wanted to go anywhere, not even to the house; they were afraid of missing something that was said or seen. The conversation this day flowed like a river. If you missed one little bit, you might be way downstream before you could catch up with the flow.

At times, the talk ended and the three would search in their own thoughts. These brief pauses allowed them to absorb a particularly interesting point somebody just said. At one of these moments of silence, a large crow came for a visit. The bird swooped down and landed in the middle of the humans. Its yellow eye shone with the intensity of the heavens. All three felt an instant kinship with the intruder. It was like a long-lost friend arrived to join in the conversation.

Jack rubbed his forefinger and thumb together to produce a strange sound. It sounded to the others like a clicking. The crow was intrigued by the noise. It couldn't take its yellow eye from Jack's fingers. The bird started to mimic the sound as if it were a lost code to its species. The two sounds merged, making a beautiful melody. Both sounds grew louder and more persistent as the creatures re-united.

The crow never ceased its racket. Even as it flew onto Jack's shoulder, it kept up its banter with the human. The wild creature seemed right at home on the man's being. They looked like old friends as they carried on in their wild conversation.

Jack looked to his brother. "It's time," he said in a cryptic tone. Their eyes locked for a moment as they read the thoughts of the other. The crow never ceased its clicking sound as the two brothers communicated. It was as if the bird was part of the plans.

Jim knew exactly what to do. He'd hung their family gong from a branch on the large maple before they started this journey. Now, he picked up the hand-made striker and walked with a stiffness to the bronze behemoth. He felt like one of those automatons on the old clocks that would robotically come out, ring a bell and go back into their closet.

He stiffly walked the few steps to the gong. This instrument had been in their family a very long time. The church, for whatever reason, allowed this instrument to remain with the children at adoption. This gong belonged to their birth parents, and many generations before. It was the sacred object for a clan of shaman. It was rung countless times by the brothers, in their lives, and by their ancestors before. Of course, they only found this out many years later. The gong was allowed in their lives with the belief it was from a distant family member.

Jim took the few steps but stopped robotically. He mechanically raised both arms. The striker was grasped tightly in both hands. He struck the gong like the automatons strike the bell. Jim used all his force and struck the metal directly in the center. The tone made was felt by all his senses. As soon as it struck the light of day, it was absorbed by everything. A golden ray burst from the center of the gong and shot into the cosmos. It shined its brilliance onto the hillside, illuminating everything in its gold hue.

On top of the hill, silhouetted by the intensity, stood a human figure. It seemed to be very large in proportion to the surroundings. The figure approached the group at a pace that seemed unreal. Jim held the striker in the same position. His arms were frozen in the intensity of the moment. His gaze locked on the scene in front of him as he took in the wonder the gong just opened.

As soon as the figure came into the circle of humans, the crow flew away and the golden light stopped. Only inky darkness remained. It was a dark that normally would have been impossible to see in. In their current condition, though, perception was clear.

The air was filled with a surreal silence. Even insects couldn't be heard. It was as if the darkness took away the sounds, along with the light.

The newcomer's face was camouflaged with black shadows. Its presence was comforting to the three. The stranger raised its arms and spoke. It was a female voice that said in a distant voice: "It's been so long."

Jim and Jack knew right away. DNA is a strong thing. They knew when they were amongst one of their own. This was their sister. The gong summoned her. Its echo rang-in the entrance of their kin. It had been more than a year since they were together, but reunited they were.

The four beings embraced one another in a joining of auras. It was familiar to each of them in their own way. Jack and Jim felt an instant connection with their sister. She, in turn, felt the connection with her brothers which had tied them together for millennium.

The four auras burst into the middle until they formed a star with their energy. Words weren't necessary as their thoughts intertwined. The four united, creating one entity of strength and unity.

A soft glow of blue lit up the darkness. A by-product of the combined energy, this light gave off warmth. Some yard art Jack placed nearby, years before, was magnetically drawn to the radiance. A group of bats flew in and out of the circle. They were propelled by a wave-length hypnotic to their beings. An unseen invitation they couldn't resist.

The creatures drew closer within this glow in their euphoric dance, as the metal objects did. They, like all things, were affected by magnetism and its mysticism.

The circle grew closer as the four beings tightened the embrace. When they were shoulder to shoulder, they stopped their movement. Their stance was odd. From above, they would look like strangers crammed into an elevator.

A quick shift of their feet and the three family members stood in a natural triangle. Sue was in the middle of the human pyramid; instantly consumed by the blue radiation. It encompassed her being and created a beautiful aura. She learned a lifetime of answers in the briefest of moments. Her mind floated on a cloud of wisdom that was finally in her grasp. All the memories, in the visions earlier, were now understood.

Jack, Jim, and their sister were the catalyst of this wisdom. Their family had ancient roots that held the knowledge of the universe. It was locked in each of the beings. Each possessed their own little piece of the puzzle. When they were together, the knowledge was free; open to all like a library.

The three, together, completed the box. The key to opening this box was Sue. She was chosen by the family, after choosing the family, long ago. She'd been re-incarnated hundreds of times to stand proudly by this clan.

These were her true people.

This was her family.

Chapter 16

Equations sometimes line up in a cosmic storm of synchronicity. Events align with the planets and histories are made. It's the way of the cosmos. Everything is an equation. Nothing is chance. If you deciphered the math, you figured it all out. Only a few humans ever scratched the surface of this wisdom. These people were seen as either lunatics, geniuses, or prophets. Whatever they were called, they were persecuted.

The great mathematicians, in the equation of life, were also the shaman. These were the ones who could see the way of the plants, animals and Earth. They healed the other humans with insight the planet and its beings provided. All because they could read the numbers and decipher their code. With this knowledge, they solved any equation thrown their way; with the digits of life.

The box was a calculator of sorts which equated these problems. It was a gift brought to this planet by the clan who controlled it. The brothers were the original keepers of the energy; they would be the controllers until the end. Even in death, their spirit lived on in the box. It was their existence. It brought their DNA to this planet so long before. It was all that was left of their ancient home.

When the box opened, the knowledge of the cosmos would be passed to the masses. When this happened, the elite would lose their foothold on control. Their greed and hunger would be replaced with fear. When the masses knew the truth, the elite were fucked.

The greed suspected the children had the same gifts as their parents. They made an experiment out of them by taking them away from their birth parents and giving them to an adopted family. If they weren't raised in their shamanic ways, they may not ever be aware of their gift. They decided to monitor the three siblings instead of exterminating them. This way, they could keep notes on the entire experiment.

The children were placed with a nice catholic family who were part of the system. They were controlled and watched ever since. The greed had a plan in place for these kinds of kids and families. It was called operation UFO; they were thorough in their deception. Whatever they wanted to know, it was just one small abduction away. The children weren't prisoners like their parents, but they were still lab rats.

When Lisa began to dig into their true history, she quickly became sick and died. It wasn't a coincident. Jack's cancer was identical because the same people administered it. He was building a device in his garage that was going to give the people an upper hand on the elite. It would be the first power change in thousands of years. They let him progress far enough but pulled his plug when it was time.

Jim's paranoia about the elite being involved in Tommy's death was correct. Tommy was a powerful being. His mother, mixed with Jack, created an entity destiny told of. He would be the one to open the box and make the energy flow. He would finish the device his father started and completely change the future.

Even the death of his first wife was all part of their conspiracy to control Jack's destiny. She would have pushed Jack into the direction of his device. She was his biggest advocate. Her husband spent many hours in the garage with their son. The boy was interested in everything his dad did and wanted to be part of it all. The greed would have none of this.

With their limited control of the numbers, the elite were masters of manipulating situations in their favor. The masses were oblivious of the equations fabricated every day by the main central computers. These equations controlled everything. Our past, present, and future were a bunch of numbers; just like DNA.

Whatever agenda they had, the elite would unleash the fear to get the job done.

Since 1947, during a UFO craze nationwide, the government devised a plan to spy on specific people and families who possessed certain gifts. It was simple. They would pump neuro-toxins into a home to put the people in a hallucinogenic state. Then, they would dress in silver suits with large heads and abduct whoever they wanted. Their awaiting science labs would get a field run of many different tests. It was like a blood bank but much more sophisticated. The genetic code of every one of these people was mapped. Some were given experimental drugs to see what would happen to them.

If the abductee awoke during one of these experiments, they'd think it was aliens who abducted them. The government, with their minions, would deny aliens existed and the people would be looked at like they were crazy. In this way, the government was in no way to blame for people being tested against their will. The elite would not only get their samples and tests, they would discredit those who posed a threat to their existence. It was a win-win situation for the greed and a losing one for everyone else. They completely covered their tracks while creating numerous people who were seen as insane by the rest.

The greed knew about the prophecy. An ancient tale told of an uprising in the beginning of the twenty-first century. It told of the masses taking control over the elite. It would gain momentum until the greed had no choice but to wage war against the people. They didn't want that to happen. They found it easier to control the special bloodline through spying, abduction, fear and control.

Jim, Jack and Lisa were recipients of this form of spying. Lucky for them, they never exhibited any powers out of the ordinary during these experiments. If they would have, they simply would have vanished or been murdered. Just like their parents. Thousands of people came up missing each year without any clues. Most of them were these people who were deemed 'special'. The elite could never allow anyone who might be a threat to them exist on the outside. It was easier to keep them deep in their laboratories until they died. Making people disappear was their specialty. If anyone got a little wise, they would say it was a conspiracy.

They also had special plans to create fear among the masses. Throughout their history, these elite were the kings of manipulation. Fear was always there, and they were the ones who could dispel it. In truth, they were the ones spreading fear among the people. Be it threat of attack, famine or gas shortages, there were always plenty of ways to make the humans scared.

They allowed enough disinformation to be put out about aliens; they were almost ready for their final show. They were going to use the fear they instilled toward aliens to destroy many humans. They were going to project alien craft arriving and taking over. It would really be secret craft they had been building for hundreds of years. Their underground bases were scattered across the planet, but the main bunker was in Antarctica. These craft flew for centuries, making the

Earthlings think they were extraterrestrials. It was the elite and their fucked-off games of control.

When the 'invasion' was complete, they'd idle their ships and let the humans self-destruct in their panic. The invaders wouldn't even have to fire one shot.

Their population had overgrown this planet. The humans were destroying the few resources that were left. The greed wasn't ready to let their way of existence be used up by the slaves. Nuclear war wasn't an option as it would affect them adversely. Disease wasn't an option because there was no guarantee it wouldn't mutate.

Their solution was the "war of the worlds" scenario. They knew it would create mass panic. People would fight over food and water if they thought there was going to be no more. The elite figured it would take about two years for the masses to be thinned by fifty percent. Then, they would send their ships back to their secret bases. They would pronounce the human victory over the aliens. "We sent them back to their galaxy!" chants would follow. A sense of triumph and human pride would envelope the survivors. Their confidence and power would be like no other time in history. They would be compelled to rebuild from the ashes while singing folk songs.

The greed would be sitting back watching it all. They stockpiled plenty of resources to last decades, or more, if need be. When the herd was thinned sufficiently, they would make heroes out of the survivors. Then it would be back to business as usual. Just on half the scale. There would still be farmers, builders and artists. They would still be there to create whatever the elite wanted. These survivors were the people who would feed the hunger of the controllers.

Those with the power would then, like always, take advantage of the people. They would suck up all the riches while the masses barely survived. They would again spread fear which would keep them in control.

Through subjugation and domination, the greed always got exactly what they wanted.

This time, however, it wasn't to work out like they envisioned. With their manipulation of the numbers, they thought they couldn't lose.

What they didn't realize was right in front of them all along. Those same people who were "abducted by aliens" over the years were wise to the game. When the greed projected the alien invasion, these people would awaken. The truth of their abduction would come to light as would the made-up scenario of the invasion.

The humans would revolt at the knowledge of being manipulated for so long. While still killing each other, many would turn their attention to the greed. They're the ones who brought hatred to this planet: Many folks would wake up and see the truth; their fellow man wasn't their enemy. Their only enemy was the greed. The ones that made the rules controlling humans and the planet.

When it was over, the planet would be in a beat-up state. Few species would survive. The remaining humans would have a serious choice to make, just like always. Would they go back to the way of the greed or would they go back to the way of nature. It would be an epic equation that would have to be solved. Its solution would determine the fate of the survivors and the remaining creatures on Earth for many generations to come.

The greed, and their computers, manipulated the numbers for millennium. It was just a small part, though. The elite tapped into the magic of this phenomenon, and DNA, but could never take complete control of the numerical grid. They were able to read the numbers and simulate, but not replicate, them. It's why the super-rich lived to be old as fuck; just a twist of the digits.

As much as they tried, however, they were never even close to controlling the equations created by the cosmos. The elite thought they could play god, but the true Gods grew tired of it. Their equations were created by the galactic computer. Nothing on this planet could override that capacity, especially an arrogant race of being.

Just like every scenario, it was all an equation. How that problem was solved would dictate the next equation and every one of them after that. It was all a ripple from this day's problem into that of the next.

Each solution would affect the later equation and its solution. If you always made the wrong decision, your existence would be a jumbled mess. If you made the right decisions, your existence would flow like water. The ripples of time would be harmonious.

This applied to every living creature on an individual scale. These numbers coincided with the DNA of every single atom on Earth. This unseen law was the way of the universe.

Everything was an equation.

Survival relied on solutions.

Chapter 17

The light around Sue had built to an electric storm of color. Bolts of energy shot in different directions and colors. This aura was one of rainbows and cosmic energy. To anyone looking on, it would look like galaxies and nebulas were spinning around the group. The electric rainbow became so intense, members of the international space station briefly saw it. At its peak, the radiance covered ten acres and was over ten million lumens of every color in the spectrum.

Sue's body felt like it would burst. Warmth from the radiance filled her like a balloon. She felt like she was floating above the ground; suspended in the light spectacle around her. She heard the gong, faintly in the distance, through ears distorted by haze. The smell of ozone accompanied the colors being emitted into the night. Energy, long dormant on the planet, was reborn with the storm emitting from Sue.

A bolt of lightning shot straight through her being and into the heavens. The burst shot her face skyward and made her body rigid. The laser, filled with color, came from the entire pod. For a moment, Sue knew what it felt like to see thirty-two spectrums of color. The sight was the most beautiful thing she'd ever seen. Her vision had turned into a kaleidoscope.

The intensity of the light flashed off. There was no transition, darkness just arrived. Sue was enveloped by it. Her senses were in shock from the sudden change. She tried to get her thoughts around what happened, but her brain wouldn't work one hundred percent. Her existence went from wide awake to foggy in a split second. The experience drained every bit of her strength. She needed to rest for a bit.

She knew she was safe here at home, with her family. Her men were nearby. When the light went dark, she held her position. Now, she completely let her muscles go and crumbled to the ground in a heap. She had a small smile on her face as she passed into the subconscious.

Sue re-lived hundreds of lives in her subconscious this night. Earlier in the day, the trip had taken her on a memory filled vision of these past lives. Now, however, she was reliving each one of them like they were all happening simultaneously.

The hallucinogen's effects long outlasted her conscious mind.

As it was in all trips, she wasn't out of her mind; it was the opposite. Sue was fully aware of what was happening. The drug, if anything, made her smarter by using more of her brain. She re-lived things ancient to her being. Things humans knew, before the mind-control started, came back to the woman. She was returning to the level she achieved in each of her lives. Wisdom, from each, combined to make her whole again.

In every existence she relived, her husband, Lisa and Jim were with her. What they said about her being part of their clan throughout time was accurate. She saw what they told her earlier; it was the truth. She was reborn countless times, always walking the same path with her true clan. This was the clan she shared dimensions with. She was offspring of the ancestors, just as every other human on the planet was.

At one point in her slumber, Sue thought she died. She saw a light in the distance. She seemed to be getting closer to its radiance with every life she relived. She thought this was how it was when you died. You would relive all your past lives until you were re-born. Maybe the light was the point of rebirth. Or maybe the light was where you went when you achieved the goals from your flesh lives. Maybe this place was the paradoxical 'Heaven'.

Secrets of the galaxy came to her as she whizzed through the open space of the universe. The past lives became super-imposed across the cosmos as her being raced through the time-space continuum. She understood her place in the order of things. The infinitesimal lives of living creatures, compared to that of stars and galaxies, was silly. She was just a piece of dust in the whole scheme of things. She realized, even a grain of dust had its purpose in the universe. Its grandeur was made up of an astronomical amount of dust, after all.

She ended up in a lush forest. Its climate was pleasant and there was ample water. Trees and bushes covered everything. Sue was in a clearing, absorbing her senses. Three beings approached her and made her feel welcome. They were a humanoid species that seemed very advanced. Sue knew instantly: this was Jack, Jim and Lisa. This was either a time in the very distant past, or the future. This forest was where her husband and his family originally came from. This place was once their home, in a previous existence.

The three beings took Sue into the forest. They stopped at a large stone monument that was inscribed with symbols. There was a pattern to these symbols which wasn't random. This block was a roadmap of the cosmos. The beings pointed to a place high up on the stone where three dots were pecked. Sue knew what they were telling her. This place they pointed to was the center of the entire universe. It is where the equations were formulated and distributed to the rest of the cosmos. This is where everything began and ended. It was the brain of existence.

The next moment, the woman was back on Earth. It wasn't the planet like she remembered it. It was an Earth which was untainted by the touch of human technology. Trees and plants were of proportions that dwarfed those of Sue's time. She saw a group of human-like creatures in a crude village. Its dwellings were made of adobe and the roofs of twigs and leaves. One of the creatures, who'd been on watch, spotted the newcomer with the golden locks. The others in the group raced to Sue and encircled the goddess. They fell to their knees and worshipped the being who was prophesized by their shaman.

Sue spent months with these primitive beings. It took them a few weeks to realize; she was just like them. She made it a point not to introduce the natives to any sort of technology. She was there to learn and to be a part of the clan. She wasn't a goddess. She was just a regular person who reconnected with her roots. These were some of her first relatives; the first of many generations in her bloodline.

Sue lived naked for the duration of her stay. Like the others in the village, there was no need for clothes. When she first disrobed, it was her fifth day. By this time, the natives were getting used to her and were not dropping to their knees whenever she was around. When she dropped her clothes, another round of fascination took over. Sue had an entire body-suit of tattoos. Jack tattooed it on her over the years of their marriage. Tattoos were unknown to these people and Sue's awed them. It was the one thing the woman brought back in time with her.

Their fascination with tattoos would spread to every culture throughout the world. Its artistic awe would be passed through every generation of human after this encounter.

In the end, she learned all the ways of the ancient humans in her clan. She learned where they came from and how they interacted with the planet and the stars. Humans were much more in sync before than after. At this time of evolution, humans saw themselves as equals to every living creature. Harmony was their way; war wasn't known.

She learned how the ancients killed only what they needed. She learned about the plants and other edible items the natives had full knowledge of. The plants spoke to them and told them of their nutritional, medicinal, and spiritual purposes. The plants also told them about the weather and when it would be time to migrate. When they listened to their surroundings, they could live amongst nature with relative ease. They knew the wisdom of the Earth and the stars. They respected its existence.

The clan knew how to propagate plants and breed animals. They bred amongst neighboring tribes to make the Earth a more diverse place. All the while, other species were inter-breeding and spreading DNA across the blue planet. These early creatures had many places, around the planet, they called home. They would travel from spot to spot as the weather and food provided. With these travels, their seeds were spread like a dandelion. The Earth had been a mixing pot for diversity, amongst all creatures.

Sue spotted Jack, Jim or Lisa a few times during the rejoining process, but they were always at a distance. None of the siblings interacted with Sue, once, in her months long expedition. Only the people who shared her DNA, the tribesman, had any contact with the woman from another time.

They taught her their early ways of language, arts and culture. When she first arrived, she thought of these people as primitive. When she left, she thought of them as the most intelligent humans she ever met. Their knowledge of everything was amazing. They were the children of the planet and they knew it. In this regard, they would never treat their parent, the Earth, like shit.

The most spectacular thing about them, though, was how they interacted in harmony with each other and their surroundings. They were a tight community who liked to play games. The art they created was inspired by the planet around them and participated in by all. They looked after their own people but also had empathy for the other clans.

These were all shaman. Direct offspring from the first humans to visit the planet. When these people wandered off, their blood-line would spread; becoming the shamanic people throughout the world. They would take their knowledge to the far-reaches of the planet, spreading wisdom.

When Sue left the village, the people had a celebration for her. A deer like creature, bigger than a horse, was hunted and cooked over the open fire. All the people, including Sue, painted their faces and danced around the fire all night. She had become an important part of the tribe. To her ancestors, she brought a glimpse into the future.

The elder brought out some magic buttons which were found in the forest. A tea, made of this peyote, was drunk by the entire tribe, even the children.

Sue didn't partake of this drink. She was already on a journey; she thought this might confuse her being, and her path. The elder told the others not to give any to the goddess. "This is for the mortal man, not the time-traveler," he told the others in their ancient language.

Sue's face and body, painted red with black handprints, was all the clothes she had on when she left the village. She walked about five hundred steps, into the green forest, along the path created by the villagers. The sunlight darkened the further she traversed. When she got to an extremely large tree, bathed in shadows, she stopped instinctively. The height of the behemoth was hundreds of feet. Its trunk was bigger than a house. At its large base, tucked amidst the roots, was a crevice that looked like a small cave. Dirt and needles were piled around its circumference, making a hill fifteen foot tall. The crevice was midway up this hill, into the side of the tree.

Sue climbed up the small slope to the opening with confidence. Her footing never once faltered as she scaled the mound. When she got to the opening, she could smell ozone being emitted. Cool, musty air hit her in the face with dampness. She didn't even falter as she slipped head-first into the crevice. The smell inside was one of organic mosses and dirt, mixed with ozone. It was one of the most beautiful things Sue ever sensed. The temperature was like a sauna inside the hole. It opened abruptly into a tunnel which seemed to go on a very long way. Tendrils of tree roots hung down from the ceiling of the tunnel, giving the passage an eerie feel. She saw a light that seemed much further than it should be. It illuminated the tunnel, guiding her way.

She still didn't hesitate. She was confident. There would be no going back; only forward.

Sue followed the light and within a dozen steps, realized she was going downhill. She turned briefly to look back; the path was unchanged. It looked like a straight shaft, but the decline was unmistakable. She didn't even think twice as she turned toward the light and trudged downward.

It took minutes before she got to the source of the luminosity. It was a large stone of a sort she'd never seen. Its greenish hue reminded her of a tektite Jim once showed her. This object was at least three feet tall and two feet across.

The glow coming off the stone was what led Sue into this chamber. Its luminosity was also the source of the heat she was feeling. This stone was emitting an energy Sue never felt before. It produced a nearly unbearable humidity in the enclosure.

The crystal sat in the middle of a stalagmite, which looked like an energy source. Her confidence didn't waver as she reached out to touch the stone. At first, she felt a warm vibration emitted from the object. Then it began to pull her into it, as if it were a magnet. When her hand encountered the crystal, it zapped her with an energy which threw her backward into the earthen wall. The force of the impact was extremely strong. It felt like her entire being was rattled. A second wave of energy hit her with a force greater than the first. The blow knocked Sue unconscious.

When she woke up, she was in her marital bed. She blinked her eyes into focus and groggily looked around the darkness. She tried to get her bearings, but it was difficult. She didn't know how she got to bed. She'd just been in a tunnel with some strange light and now she was here.

As she tried to figure out her situation, the trip began to mix with reality. She didn't know how she got to bed nor how long she was out for. She faintly recollected being with Jim and Jack, but they weren't present. She was never one to panic and now would be no different. Sue was a strong woman. Something just happened to her and she was going to get to the bottom of it.

She slowly got to her feet and unsteadily made it to the bathroom. It was a slow journey on wobbly legs to ensure the familiar trip wasn't deadly. After taking care of business, she felt much more alive and awake. She was still half asleep when she got into the shower. The warm water slowly brought her out of her stupor. As she was awakening, she could have sworn black and red dirt were running down the drain.

Her body seemed to be in better shape than ever. As she was soaping, she noticed the strength and tone in her muscles. She had little cuts and wounds over her entire body, but they were all healing. Her hands and feet were callused and rough, but extremely strong.

When she brushed her teeth, it seemed like she hadn't brushed them in months. It felt like there were organisms living in her normally hygienic mouth. Brushing her hair brought the same results. Napped in her normally soft locks were colonies of insects and tightly twisted hair balls. After combing her hair for minutes, she gave up on the hopeless situation.

After Sue put on clothes, she went in search of the others. She had to pass through the living room to go to any other part of the house; this is where she found Jim and Jack. She was expecting to find the worst and was prepared. After what she just went through, she was ready for whatever came her way.

There was no light in the room, but Sue could clearly see everything. Jack was lying on the couch and his brother was sitting in the recliner. Both men were smoking a joint. The faint glow from the cherry lit up each man's face slightly with its crimson glow. The sweet smell of weed told Sue what was up.

Jim looked to Sue when she entered and said, "it's about time you got up. We thought you were going to sleep forever." He didn't move any other part of his body but his head and arm to smoke the joint. His voice sounded strange to the woman. It sounded like Jim was much older.

"What are you guys doing in the dark?" Sue asked. "How long have I been asleep?"

"You've been asleep over twenty-eight hours," Jack said hoarsely from his sofa. His voice didn't sound healthy to Sue; like it wasn't even her husband.

"Sue, you went on a serious trip. It took a heavy toll on you," Jim said. His voice again sounded like that of an old man. Sue thought both Jim and Jack aged since she was asleep. She couldn't be sure in the dark, but their voices told the story. "You passed out when we were outside. I carried you inside and got you to bed. Sorry, I took off your clothes. I thought you would be more comfortable. I swear I didn't molester you. That was yesterday just after sunset. I have no idea what time it is, now." Jim's ragged voice trailed off into the darkness.

"Night-time," came Jack's gruffy voice from the background. Jim and Jack both broke out in laughter. Jim was like a loon in his wild

tirade. It sounded like a prospector from one of those old westerns the boys liked so much. Jack let go as much as possible in his sickened state. Whatever the joke had been, Sue didn't get it.

Just because she didn't get the joke, didn't mean she didn't see what was going on.

Jack hadn't looked at her once since she walked in the room. During the entire conversation and laughter, he kept his gaze pointed at the ceiling. Jim also kept his gaze mostly at the ceiling except when talking to Sue; then he looked her way.

"What's going on in here?" Sue asked with concern in her voice. "How did I sleep so long?"

"The answer is the same," Jack said with a monotone, worn-out voice. His cryptic message was not misunderstood by his wife. "You know what's happening here, Babe."

Sue broke down in tears. She could feel death permeating from her husband's being. She tried her best to remain strong, but in the face of her love's death, she doubted herself. The reaper had come knocking. There would be no thought of not answering.

She crossed the distance to her husband and embraced him. He had just enough strength to wrap one of his arms around her waist. Sue was perplexed. The last time she'd seen Jack, he seemed strong; like he was recovering. Now, one day later, he was just a portion of the man he was before. In the darkness, she could just make out his frail form. Holding him, he seemed to be over a hundred years old.

Sue was gentle as she laid her head on Jack's chest. A whisper escaped his lips that she couldn't understand. Just before she asked him to repeat himself, he said: "They've been here with us since you went to sleep. They're waiting for me, so they can be my guide. You have nothing to worry about. I'll be fine after I finally shed this flesh pod. It's my anchor that's holding me back. Our energy will always be together, Sue. It's always been together, throughout time. This isn't the end for us, Babe. It's the beginning."

"Who is here?" Sue asked rhetorically. She already knew the answer. She also knew these guys were tripping balls. They were on a level she couldn't understand in her sober state. She didn't even care. After yesterday, the last thing she wanted to do now was go on another journey. She was barely coming down from the last visit to the forest. Those visions would take her years to figure out. She didn't need more to convolute her conscious.

The brothers were indeed on the next journey. Day five began with five hits by each family member. The night before, when the gong summoned them, the family was reunited. After fifty-five years, they were once again whole. Jim, Jack, Lisa, their brothers and parents all went on a journey. After Sue passed out, the brothers stayed up all night long learning about these long-lost people. As they spoke, the brothers knew. It wasn't long before it all came to them. Their history was once again theirs.

After their minds were free of the equation, they could cut loose. This night, while Sue slept, the seven would go on a journey of laughter and madness. It was day five, there were seven of them and they each took five doses. These numbers, lined up this way, were magical. This day was meant to be. Solving the equation always made the numbers line up, like a grade.

They felt completely free after the restrictions were gone from their minds. Whatever they felt like doing, they would do. There was no hesitation on any individual with fear of looking like a fool. These were their original people. They performed and created for each other since the beginning. They would be continuing for eternity.

Now, it was the end for one of them. It was the way of things; they would all be united at this time of rebirth.

They had taken mescaline together at midnight. The brothers were still tripping hard when this new addition was added to their psyche. It blended their thoughts into this new hallucinogenic travel. By the time Sue woke up, exactly twenty-four hours later, they would be on the last leg of the journey. This was the one where their energy would fully combine, creating the box. Sue was the key to the box the seven had been waiting for.

"Our parents are here, and our brothers and sister," both men said in unison. "They are happy to spend time with us. They, like you, are early humans who we took into our inner circle. We trusted you five like no other human; our offspring we called you. The people we call our parents are named because they nurtured us throughout times. They fed us and made us things like parents would their children. They didn't do this because they were looking for favors from us. They did it because they truly liked us, and we liked them. Our brothers were the same. They were conjoined twins and ostracized by their clan. We readily accepted them into ours. They became companions who were always by our side. They naturally became our brothers. It was the same with you, Sue. You chose to be with us and now are chosen to be with us. We all complement each other. It's the way of the numbers."

"Our time has been stolen from us in this existence. We weren't with our true family." The words mixed in the air as it reached the woman's ears. Their voices became a duet, singing their melodious thoughts. What they said was beautiful and awakening. The early creatures tried to treat the three siblings as gods. The three stated over and over: they weren't gods and didn't want to be treated as such. The parents, brothers, and Sue were the only ancients who saw the siblings as equals. Equals was how they wanted to be seen. It was a natural friendship from the beginning.

Sue looked around the darkness and saw another cherry burning. From her angle before, she couldn't see this other presence. When the figure hit the joint again, the glow lit up the face. She wasn't surprised to see it was their sister, Lisa. Although she died a year before, she joined her brothers in the last moments to give her support. She'd been here all along, Sue knew it. Now, she knew the truth; there was no need for Lisa to remain hidden any longer.

Sue looked around the darkness but couldn't see anyone else. She did have an odd feeling there were many people in the room. Her head was disoriented though from the long sleep and the events going on. She couldn't be certain of anything. She was beginning to doubt she had woken up. Maybe she got to the light and now her existence was all dreams.

"I don't know what you guys have been doing for the past twenty-eight hours," Sue said with stress. She fought back tears as she finished, "I just hope you know what you're doing. I've been really worried about all this. You guys are pushing the envelope of sanity."

"We know exactly what we're doing," Jack said with confidence. "We've been planning this since we were children. Can't you see Sue, we're making history here. We're the ones who will cross over. Reality is ours."

"Yeah," Jim said, "I learned a lot from my travels. However, I've gained Wisdom since being with our parents. They're ancients who retain our knowledge throughout time. At times, we're reborn into new pods and aren't burdened with wisdom. Sometimes our existence is simple and others very complex. We realized long ago: if we were going to live as humans, it was best to get the full experience every time. Sometimes we would figure it out during our lives but other times it didn't come back to us until after our deaths. Every life was born to the same parents, our caregivers. Every time, our existence was completely different than any other. It was all part of the equation."

"Our parents have brought us into this journey," Jack said. "When the sun comes up, I will be entering into my final phase. It will be the eve of my death. I can now rest and prepare myself for the journeys to come. Jim, Lisa, my brothers, our parents and myself have been laughing all day and night about all kinds of nonsense. The wisdom has been passed back to me. My mind is now at ease. I'm ready to leave this flesh pod and move on to more cosmic ways. Trust me, Sue, I'll always be with you. We're connected for eternity. It was my choice from the beginning and it's still my choice now. You're for me and I'm for you."

The lights in the room came on but were only about twenty-five percent brightness. Sue wondered how this could have happened; nobody moved. The lamps magically lit at the end of Jack's speech.

She glanced to the clock above the fire place and saw it was a little past midnight. She also saw, standing on either side of the mantle, her husband's parents. Standing directly to the side of their father were Jack's brothers.

In a ghostly appearance, they were dressed in a ceremonial costume of some kind. The men's garments were entirely black with gold trim. The woman wore a long dress of black, only with red trim.

Between the parents, suspended by their hands, hung the gong. Its metal surface reverberated a soft hymn, but nobody struck it. The gong was playing itself.

Sue looked closely at the faces of her friends. Their weathered gaze was locked in return with hers. None of them spoke words. None were needed. The five human's thoughts were connected. They walked this Earth, together, repeatedly for millennium. Theirs was a friendship known by no other human on the planet.

Sue realized she no longer doubted herself nor her feelings. Her confidence returned with the reunion of her family. The wisdom was passed back to her upon the meeting with the clan. The dream from the night before came flooding back into her reality. Sue realized the parents and brothers arrived when she was sleeping and passed the wisdom back to her in her subconscious. The village she was part of in her sleep was really her original people on this planet. She'd gone back and relived a few months of her prehistoric existence. Now, she could fully understand the sibling's arrival and their interaction with the natives.

Sue sat with her husband throughout the early morning hours. After the long conversations before, there was no talk. Words weren't needed for the next six hours. The eight beings present in the room were connected, mentally. Communication through talk was something they didn't need. Their connection went back to the beginning of time.

Jack's pains spread to each of the individuals. All took a little bit of his anguish, alleviating the dying man's suffering. Each of them gave back some of their healthy aura to their family member. Together, their conscious was on the same level. All were sensing and experiencing the exact same thing as the others.

Jack and Jim were in their own world. Colors absorbed their beings. The cosmic serpents were rampant in this house. Their old friends came back in their time of need. As was always the case, the cycle repeated itself. It had always been the case. It always would be.

The brothers understood the serpents. They were the code of the universe which made life possible. These serpents inhabited the cosmos. Galaxies were their playgrounds. These creatures were the key to everything living. They traveled on the cosmic winds created by each star. Their time in the universe was since the beginning. They were true Gods of creation.

The only sound in the room was the ticking of the clock. Its rhythmic beat reminded Jim of a tune they used to sing as kids. Unity was what this night was all about. This journey was into the part of the brain that recollected old knowledge and tied it together with that of your family.

The connection with their people would give them time to rest and reconnect with what was truly important. It would give them a chance to recharge their batteries and get ready for the next two days. This was when the ultimate trip was planned. These other five days were a warm-up to what was coming in the next two.

They tapped into the other realm of their conscious this week. They had a mission and went on its crazy course. The adventure was progressing well. Enlightenment was filling their beings as they fulfilled their destiny.

They were almost at the end of their travels.

Everything was ready. The cycle was nearly complete. The participants were ready for the final adventures. They just had to wait until the right time. It was all part of the equation.

The moment wasn't rushed. Nobody wanted it to get here any sooner than necessary. The anticipation was high, though. Jim and Jack had been waiting for this moment their entire lives.

The beginning was upon them.

Chapter 18

The sunrise correlated with the light from the room until they became one. The moment the sun fully crested the mountains, Jim and Jack began a chant that was familiar to Sue. Throughout their lives, they spoke in tongues many times. Sue always thought they were talking gibberish. It always seemed like they were messing around. It was how she always perceived these ramblings, until now.

She could clearly hear her husband and brother-in-law speaking in forgotten language. What seemed like nonsense before was now perfectly intelligible. Now, this rhythm of voices conveyed a knowledge to Sue that had always been. Blocks in her mind melted in the last twenty-four hours. The truth was now clear. Now, she was ready for the reprogramming to begin. Wisdom, once again, was going to inhabit Sue's being.

The night was surreal to the woman. She saw strange, colorful shadows throughout the early hours. It felt like she was observing events through someone else' eyes. Her being had been split in two. The part implanted by the greed was eliminated. She was, for the first time in this existence, Sue.

As the light in the room brightened, Sue could see the fullness of the space. The parents were still standing by the fireplace, as were the brothers. They were transparent sentinels watching over the situation. They weren't the only entities in the room. Over fifty spirits were crammed into the small space. Each of them looked familiar to the woman. She wasn't scared, nor concerned. She knew this soul; they were part of the clan.

The chanting, started by the brothers, was harmonized by the other energies in the room. Each of them joined in the rhythm until the room was filled with just one voice. The sound was hypnotic to Sue. She was the only one not partaking in the strange melody. By not using her voice, her ears were able to absorb the true sounds. The melodious notes made her in-tune with her people. The cantillation made all the beings one.

The chanting grew in volume slowly. The tone and pitch remained the same; it just got louder. The sounds mingled and were intoned a bit faster. The ramblings took on a music that Sue hadn't heard for a very long time. She knew this song. Lisa played it at their wedding. It was the song of Jack's family. It was a family crest of sorts; a signature of their people.

The music intensified until it permeated Sue's being. Her bones felt like they were rattling inside her body. A strange euphoria overtook the woman. She felt like this was all that mattered. Life and reality as she knew it was a lie. Her perception of the world and her place in it was fabricated. Now, however, the blocks of this existence were fully gone. The truth had come back to her from ancients she once called her people.

The lighting got brighter with the increase in volume. It became so bright, Sue thought she could see through Jack. He and Jim's existence faded with the increase in the luminosity, while all the other beings present seemed to solidify at the same time. It looked like the parents and the rest of the clan drew mass from the brothers and used it to become flesh-pods again.

Sue shielded her eyes as the light intensified. It was blinding to her, like looking at the sun. The temperature in the room was sweltering as was the woman's skin. She was just on the brink of passing out when the sound came.

The strike of a gong is like no other sound. Its intensity will bridge the gap between dimensions. Its strength will make bad spirits cower in fear while the good spirits rejoice. Today its resonance calmed the situation.

Immediately, the luminosity went back to a soft level. Sue opened her eyes as the sound reverberated through the room. She saw the other beings were once again fading. Even the parents, brothers, and Lisa, were slowly disappearing from this realm. The large gong hung between the hands of the elders, echoing its spirituality.

Jim was again at normal density, but Jack was no longer present. Sue knew she should be shocked at this sight, but it didn't worry her in the least. Wherever Jack was, he was with his people.

Jim slowly extracted himself from the recliner he called home all night. He walked on steady legs to the spot where his parents were fading from existence. He stood directly in front of the gong. The position the three made was a perfect triangle.

Jim's father extended his hand and presented the younger man with the gong striker. Its wood handle, wrapped with gold wire, gave a glint in the soft light. The red, stuffed fabric looked like a heart, beating with all its might.

The mother too, extended her hand to Jim's and dropped something in it. Sue couldn't tell what the small object was, but she knew it was important. The three-stood silent for minutes. Their gaze was focused on each other.

Jim made a large sweeping circle with the striker. His shoulder came around two full rotations. On the third, the striker struck the gong right in its center. The sound shook the room with its reverberation.

Both parents, brothers, and Lisa vanished into thin air with the coming of the sound. The gong didn't drop; it hung in the air on its own, echoing its beautiful sound.

Sue surveyed the room and noticed Jack laying in his original spot on the couch. She raced to her husband's side. The sight was not a nice one. Jack looked like he'd just come home from war. His flesh-pod was done, losing its spark of survival.

"Where'd you go?" Sue asked in almost a whisper, as she approached Jack. The sight of her husband shocked and troubled her. The full reality of his death came rushing back to her mind.

Jack could barely speak. He rasped out a couple of tries, took a few minutes break and went for it. Through determination, he finally got the words out. "I went to a much better place. It's beautiful. You have nothing to worry about, Sue. I'm going back to paradise."

Sue hugged her husband with all her might. "I love you so much. I'm really going to miss you. I'm no longer afraid though. I know you'll be better off."

"I love you too," Jack garbled.

Jim was by their side. "Okay kids, you know it's time. I think it will be best if we get Jack back to bed for this next journey. Things are about to get really crazy."

Sue looked at the clock and saw it was already noon. She didn't know how all the time slipped away. She grabbed some linens and set about changing the sheets on the bed. Jim was in the living room scooping up his brother. The older sibling, in his weakened state, only

165

weighed one hundred pounds. It wasn't hard for Jim to carry his decrepit form to the bedroom

As she removed the filthy sheets, stained black and red, Sue wasn't surprised. After all the things happening this week, nothing was a shock to the woman now.

Sue was arranging the pillows on the fresh sheets when Jim entered the room. He gently laid his sibling on the deathbed, then stood aside as Sue made her husband comfortable.

"Can you get him some water?" Sue asked her brother-in-law.

Jim was out the door without a reply. He knew the next days were going to be spent with his brother. He also knew Sue would want some alone time with her husband. He decided to make a late lunch for the group. He hadn't even thought about food for the last two days, until he got to the kitchen. Now, it was all he could think of.

He took the water to his brother but swiftly departed. He had one thing on his mind. Nutrition. One of his and Jack's all-time favorites was eggs benedict. He did an inventory of the kitchen to see what was available. There wasn't much in the refrigerator. Some leftovers from Becky earlier in the week and some that were older. Expired milk, one egg and no bread meant Jim was going to the grocery store.

He knew of the small mom and pop place down the road from his brother's house. It was the only store of its kind in these parts. A small trek to the mountain market would bring a smile to his brothers and Sue's face. It was two miles away and would be worth the trouble.

He gathered up his wallet and threw on some flip-flops that were laying by the front door. During the ten steps it took to get to the car, something extraordinary happened. A large black crow swooped down and landed on the path in front of him. He knew this bird. He met it before on one of his many journeys.

The bird, too, knew Jim. They'd been on the same path for a very long time. The crow's ancestors traveled with this creature and its siblings since before history began. It, like other creatures, had been in-tune with the siblings and adopted as one.

The crow's shadow seemed to grow until it overtook Jim and even the car. It twisted in its darkness, creating a strange dance. Soon, the shadow turned into a whirlwind. Its blackness morphed into wings which became a strange, leathery material. Feathers held the blackness together.

Jim looked up into the face of the creature which emerged in front of him. Its shadowy form left an ugly feeling in Jim's being. The essence of the crow seemed to be gone. In its place was this darkness. It twisted and turned in the afternoon sun until Jim understood. This was the grim reaper. It came for the soul of his brother.

Jim laughed aloud at the absurdity of it all. The vision swiftly dissipated leaving only the crow. Jim knew the hallucinogens throughout the week were playing tricks on his imagination. He felt normal inside the house; when he got outside, however, he realized he was tripping balls. He was loving every minute of this awesome experience.

He whistled on the short walk to the car. This day, his step was a little snappier than normal. He opened the door of his car thinking maybe he shouldn't drive while tripping. The thought was interrupted by movement inside the vehicle. On the passenger seat was the same crow which was on the path before. It gave three loud caws and looked straight ahead.

Jim didn't know how the crow got in the car. It was a sign and the only answer he needed. He got in his car and drove the two miles to Spencer's market.

Chapter 19

The short drive to the market did wonders for Jim's head. The mountain air felt good on his skin. It felt like he'd been inside for months. One of his favorite songs came on the radio. He and his feathered friend sung along like the old pals they were.

They took a roundabout drive down Whiskey Slide road to a community fruit stand. The place had been there for years. The family preferred this stand for their produce. The price was good, the veggies were good, and the people who grew it were great. Their good energy was grown in every vegetable. They gave the family a life-long appreciation for buying produce from the small farmer.

Years passed since Jim last came to this spot. Nobody was around, as usual. The money box provided autonomous checkout. It was a great system by people who truly cared about their community. He dropped a twenty in the box without even weighing his veggies. He only got a few sad looking tomatoes, a couple of onions, and a nice-looking pumpkin. It was late in the season. He was happy with what he got but was also happy to hook up these cool people for seeds next year.

When Jim got back into the car, the crow was no longer in the seat. He looked briefly to the backseat, but it was the same. He looked to the trees for a trace of the bird but there were none. He began to think he imagined it all in his far-out state. Whatever it was, he didn't care; it was a cool experience either way.

He took a roundabout trip to get to the market. He wanted to give his brother and sister in law plenty of alone time. The sky was filled with clouds this day and Jim was happy to be in the elements. After the confinement all week, lurking about with death, this was the opportunity to let his soul run free.

When he pulled up to the store, many memories came back to him. More than ten years passed since he was in this small market. He lived up the hill farther and preferred going to Jackson or Pine Grove for his groceries. This was the place his brother and Sue came for their supplies.

As soon as he walked into the store, everybody inside stopped what they were doing. Every eye was on him. They all seemed to recognize him. The entire store looked shocked to see Jim. He immediately felt uncomfortable; like these people all held a dirty little secret, about him. He instantly regretted walking through the doors.

He quickly got his groceries. He was thankful there wasn't much on his list. Down every aisle and around every corner, somebody was there staring at him. Jim knew they were all looking at the wild man tripping on hallucinogens. Surely, he thought, they could all tell. He couldn't think of any other reason they'd be eyeing him.

He was happy there was no line. Even the guys at the meat department couldn't do their job while their eyes were focused on Jim. He was about to blurt out something to the entire store but held back at the last moment. He was already making enough of a spectacle just being here. There was a lot of stress in his life now; he didn't need to bring more upon himself or his family. Especially in his enlightened state of mind.

The middle-aged checker couldn't keep her stare away from Jim to scan his purchases. "Is everything okay with you people? You look like you saw a ghost," he asked with irritation.

The lady talked with uncertainty. "We just thought you had cancer and were dying. We haven't seen you in a month; but here you are now, healthy as ever."

"You're probably thinking about my brother Jack," Jim answered loud enough for the others in the store to hear. "He's the one with cancer."

The lady turned a bright shade of red and turned away from him. Everyone else in the store reacted the same. They all turned away, ashamed. Jim remembered why he stopped coming to this store, many years before. Some of the employees and patrons were very gossipy about the community. They liked to talk about people who they knew nothing about. Jim figured it was just the way of a small community but still didn't like it. People who talked about those they knew nothing about were the ones afraid of who they really were. They wore a false face.

There was no time in Jim's life for those who didn't know their identity. Or even worse, those who thought they were in a special club because of who they knew. Jim was an artist and creator, he had no time for small-talk people nor small-town cliques. He was his own club.

The cashier blurted out an apology that seemed sincere to Jim but unwelcome. The damage was already done. This community talked about his brother for the last month; not one of them helped Sue in the least. It was the same when Tommy died. The community talked about the family, extensively, and even held fundraisers. But none of them, nor their money, ever came to the help of the family. It was the opposite. The community looked at the grieving family as if they were outcasts; treating them as if they did something wrong. Jim never forgot this kind of treatment from a self-righteous boy's club.

"My god," the checker from the other register said. "You look exactly like your brother."

"Yeah, I've heard that my entire life," Jim said with sarcasm. "I guess I won't be hearing it much longer. Now, can you just ring up my items, so I can be on my way?" He was just about to bolt from the store, without the groceries, but knew it would make an even bigger scene. Plus, he was really looking forward to breakfast.

"I'm so very sorry," the cashier sobbed once again as she quickly scanned the six items. Jim bagged his own groceries, paid, and made a dash for the door. Just before he got away, the cashier called out, "Tell your brother we're all praying for him."

"Who are you praying to?" Jim asked. The words came out reflexively and he instantly regretted saying them. This was a religious community. He turned and looked blankly back into the store. Every customer and employee were standing there, looking at him with pity. It was as if the cashier spoke for all of them.

The clouds had parted; rays of sun fell on the market and parking lot. Its warmth was welcome after the frigid experience he just encountered.

A large shadow moved across the car as he opened the door. He looked up to see the crow flying overhead. The sun hit its wings just right, casting a long umbrage. Jim thought it odd anything could cast such a shadow in this part of the day. They usually occurred later in the day when the sun was lower.

With all the strange things happening this morning, Jim was ready to end his little outing. He was happy Jack lived close to the store. If he had a choice of being around strangers or being in the sanctuary of home, the decision was easy. He had no time for false empathy from people who didn't know him or his family. The people he cared for his entire life were home; it was where he was meant to be.

Breakfast didn't take long to make. Jim thought the others were probably not even aware he left. His trip to the store only took thirty minutes and cooking took the same. When he brought three trays of food and a pitcher of water into the room, Sue and Jack were pleasantly surprised.

Sue poured water for Jack and held it to his lips. His body was weak, but his mind knew it needed water. He drank the entire glass.

Sue fed her husband some hollandaise sauce Jim made. Eggs benedict were favorites of theirs. The sauce and eggs were at first the only parts he could get down. As he ate more, his appetite seemed to increase until he was eating solid pieces. She commended her husband after he got down one full piece of the benedict.

Jim and Sue ate everything that was left. Their hunger was created by mental exhaustion. They both thought to themselves: they could probably eat a lot more.

When it was done, Jim took the dishes into the kitchen to clean up. He wanted to give Sue one last time alone with her husband. He also needed to muster all his strength and courage for what was about to come. He and his brother were about to undertake an adventure no other humans had ever gone on. He needed to be fully prepared, rested and nourished.

He finished the dishes and went onto the front porch to have a smoke. Jim loved to smoke weed after breakfast. It would help him relax and maybe facilitate a nap. The crow was flying around the front yard, vying with the clouds to cast shadows on the hillside.

Jim saw a car approaching and wondered who would be coming. He thought maybe it was someone from the store to complain about how he acted. "So be it," he thought to himself. He was under a lot of stress. If they wanted this fight, it was with the wrong person.

He was relieved to see it wasn't a stranger at all. When the car turned into the drive, Jim instantly recognized it as Becky's. As it approached, he could see three people in the vehicle. He stood as the car came to a stop. Ronnie and Little Jack were the first out of the vehicle followed by Becky. The brothers raced to their uncle and embraced him in a three-way unification of energy. Becky joined the family hug and the circle was complete.

"What are you guys doing here?" Jim asked his nephews and niece. "I know your dad told you not to come around when he was almost done."

"We know Uncle Jim," Little Jack said. "We couldn't help ourselves. We had to come see our pops one last time."

"Yeah man," Ronnie said, "he wouldn't have listened if the roles were reversed."

"I agree, Guys," Jim said.

"How is he, Uncle Jim?" Little Jack asked with a weary voice.

"Why don't you go in and find out for yourself?" Jim said. "Keep an open mind guys. His soul is healthier than any other time since birth. Think of nothing else. It's just his flesh pod which is decayed."

The three passed by their uncle and filed into the house. Becky was the last and she stopped briefly to say to her uncle, "thank you for what you've been doing Uncle Jim. It means a lot to my mom and me. Not to mention what it means to my Dad. I will forever be in gratitude to you for this."

Jim smiled and waved his hand toward the door. His niece turned, gave him a knowing smile and disappeared into the house. The uncle's smile never receded as he thought of how much he respected these three youngsters.

The rest of the smoke didn't take much time. Jim enjoyed his time outdoors. He felt like god was in everything natural. If you were outside, god was all around you. Being inside was being confined by man-made control. Everything around you, inside, was a little bit of the pollution in your brain. It was all just to cloud your true senses.

The sun and smoke took its toll on the man. He couldn't seem to stay awake. The events this week were crazy; it was all catching up to him. He hadn't slept much, and his brain was working overtime. He was still feeling the effects of all the hallucinogens they took. After the journey they went on the night before, with their parents, the effects lingered. That one was a true celebration; a reunification of family.

Jim pulled himself from the chair and forced himself to the task at hand. There would be plenty of time to sleep later. Time was the only thing they had against them right now. Utilizing every bit of it would be helpful to the entire family.

He went into the house and made his way down the hall to his bedroom. He grabbed his bag and looked in for a moment. The next two doses were special. He acquired them from the most spiritual of all the shaman.

The dose they'd be taking tonight was from a young woman of about sixteen. Jim met her in Blythe, California. They stayed together for four days, exploring the region. They went to the intaglio glyphs in the desert and observed their symbols from a tall cliff. Some hallucinogens opened their minds and they could see the true meaning of the art.

This was a very ancient place, much older than archaeologists imagined. These pictures on the ground were made by an early race of human twelve thousand five hundred years before. They told of visitors who showed them things they didn't know possible. They taught them how to use their imaginations. During this era, the people of this region began dedicating their lives to creating.

The last dose was from the most special place. It wasn't even a human who gave this one to Jim. He went into Death Valley and followed his heart to a place called Wingate. This place sounded familiar to him, but he didn't know why. When he arrived, he knew the exact direction to go. There were fences all around, but Jim skirted them and snuck through the desert in the middle of the night; his only light being the full moon.

Some well-hidden caves were easily uncovered with Jim's visions. He entered the second cave. The opening emitted a green light which seemed to pulsate. The entire scene was surreal. There was no way he could have walked away from the oddness of it all.

Jim went deep into the fissure. It seemed like he walked for hours, all downhill. The light remained the same luminosity the entire time. It was as if the rocks, themselves, were giving off the soft glow.

The path ended at an underground lake. Its water was lit up with the same green glow that permeated the cave. Jim could see under the water for some distance; it was pure. He could see a network of caves, under the lake, waiting to be explored.

Jim was startled to feel a large hand on his shoulder. He turned swiftly and was standing face to face with a giant. The creature must have been nine feet tall. It was some form of humanoid species. Its smell was one of mold. The long hair covered its skin and face. The beast looked menacing, but Jim wasn't afraid. The bond was felt by both immediately. The two embraced.

This was a long-lost relative who survived a very long time in this underground world. The creature cared for a portal, deep under the water. The passage led to another dimension where beings would live forever. It was a paradise, where those who achieved spiritual enlightenment could spend eternity.

Jim hung out with this creature for five days. At first, communication was difficult. By the end of the first day, the two talked with their hands. By the end of the second day, the two spoke a language they invented together. They took hallucinogens daily and swam in the fresh, warm water of the cave.

Their food came from the creature's hair. A wealth of organisms grew on the behemoth. His entire body was a garden which in turn nourished the giant. The green from the lake was the fertilizer creating the rapid growth. Every time the creature was in the water, it would be mere hours before he was ready for harvest.

Jim wasn't skeptical in the least as the first feast took place. In this place, deep underground, one wasn't worried about taste. Here, away from everything, nourishment was what mattered.

On the fifth day, the creature tried to talk Jim into swimming to the other side. In the language they created together, the giant was very persuasive. "The portal is right there. It's an easy swim when you know the way. I know the way, it will be safe. You will answer all the questions you ask on the other side. Everything you seek will be found."

Jim told him he would pass. He didn't want a preview of the afterlife or another dimension. In his mind, they were the same thing. He preferred those experiences solely with his brother.

The recollections of these travels were soothing to his exhausted mind. As Jim lay back on the bed, these memories were his lullaby for sleep. He expected his dreams to be strange this day.

He wasn't disappointed.

Chapter 20

The house was silent when Jim awoke. He got some much-needed water and checked the time. The clock said 4:44, late afternoon. Jim's rest lasted a couple hours. His sleep had been very sporadic and scarce all week. The few times his mind couldn't take the exhaustion was the only time he rested. The dreams were vivid to the point of their own fatigue. Not only was Jim's conscious wearing thin, so was his subconscious.

He knew Jack hadn't slept much the last days, either. He doubted his older brother slept at all throughout this crazy journey. He figured he wouldn't sleep if he was in Jack's position. With only days left, every minute mattered. After all was done, there would be plenty of sleep for the dead. Until then, there was no need to get a head-start.

Jim went to his brother's room and knocked softly. Becky answered the door and slithered through the small opening. "We're saying our last goodbyes, Uncle Jim," she said. Her eyes were dry, but her voice betrayed her personification. "It's really hard."

"I know, Becky," Jim answered. He hugged his niece tightly before standing back. "Death is never easy to deal with. It's one big cycle though. You must understand. Your Dad is leaving this realm to enter the next. The end is truly the beginning."

"I'm just going to miss him," she said.

"Death is always hardest for the living. You're grieving your loss, but your Dad is rejoicing. He'll always be with you, Becky. His energy is part of you. Your memories and dreams will contain your dad for the rest of your life. We all live on in this existence until the last person forgets us. Then, our existence in this dimension ceases to exist."

"You always talked some trippy shit," she said sarcastically. "You definitely use your third eye."

"We all have it, most don't use it."

The door to the bedroom opened. Jack Junior and Ronnie came out with an exaggerated silence. Both men were sobbing as they hugged their uncle. Words weren't spoke, for moments, while Jim absorbed his nephews' pain. When they calmed a bit, Ronnie said, "I didn't know it would be this hard. It's difficult seeing him like this."

"What you're seeing is your Dads decaying flesh pod. His true self is healthier than ever. Just his body has given out on him; now is his time to move on. You're worried about yourselves and not thinking about the true well-being of your Father. You should only be concerned with his spirit at the moment. That will never die."

"You're right as usual, Uncle Jim," Little Jack said. "We're just thinking about our loss. The one who is truly losing something is our Dad. He's losing his flesh; the anchor. Now he can be whole and free again."

"That's right Jack," Jim said. "We've talked about this, many times, in the past. I know you guys understand. He's healthy and needs the assurance you'll be able to cope with this. Now, dry up them tears and get back in there and give your Dad a proper farewell. Let him know his kids are strong and can deal with this. It's what he truly needs."

All three siblings composed themselves and talked in hushed tones. Jim went into the bedroom to prepare the nights festivities. He wanted to give the family some time alone to sort this out. After moments of discussion, the three went back in their parent's bedroom.

Jack was happy to see his kids come back in. His eyes and face lit up with illumination at the sight of his beloved children. He saw the hurt in their eyes earlier; it wasn't the way he wanted to see them for the last time. He always wanted his children to be happy and now was no different. His heart felt like lead weights were lifted when he saw the change in his children's auras. When they left the room, their energy appeared dark and uncertain. It worried Jack. Now their auras were a multitude of colors, and confident.

The cosmic serpents hadn't ceased their presence since the last trip wore off. Jack was beginning to think he was on a permanent trip, since they did so much in a short time. He was confident the cancer had something to do with the way his brain was working. He saw the serpents all day long. He came to realize their purpose. They were god's real messengers. They watched over all and created all. God and the serpents were One.

It was getting harder for Jack to focus on what was reality and what was in his mind. His parents, brothers and sister were there sometimes and gone others. There were other visitors which he figured were relatives of some sort. When his kids came back in, he wasn't sure if it was real or his imagination.

Jack's body looked terrible. His face was sucked up and the whiskers were scraggly. He was never able to grow a beard, just a few tufts of hair here and there. His arms looked like bones with skin wrapped around them. Ronnie remembered pictures of starving people and thought their father looked the same. It appeared he had decayed in the short time they were outside the room.

Sue began a song the family sung when the kids were young. Little Jack didn't know the words to the tune but remembered its rhythm instantly. They never once sung it after Tommy disappeared, making the youngest not remember. The words came back to the older siblings like riding a bicycle. All three began the song softly but it grew louder by the minute.

After the first time around, Little Jack picked up the words and beat. He joined in, on the second time around. Even Jack mouthed the words and got out the little bit of sound that he could muster. The song repeated itself numerous times. A symphony of good energy filled the room.

In his mind, Jack was singing at full blast. He was carrying on the tune and dancing along with the others. Even though his body was broken, his mind was alive. Mentally, he felt healthier than ever in his life. He understood how dementia patients must feel. Fully awake inside their mind but unable to project their thoughts. This was exactly what he was going through. It felt like he was at the theater and everything happening was on the stage. Being the lone audience member, he was unable to interact with any of it.

At the beginning of each replay, one of the group would put their head next to Jack's mouth so they could hear the scant words forming. For all three children, this would be the last words they ever heard from their father. For the rest of their lives, they would remember the rush of energy they got from that fragile voice. For a moment in time, the family became one, just like old times. After all the years of happiness being robbed from them, they were finally healed.

Jack wrote this song many years before. It was after his first wife died. He and Tommy were going through tough times. Many nights were sleepless for the widower and motherless child. The tune was meant to cheer them both up and it worked. Whenever one of them were down, the other picked up the beat.

When they met Sue and her kids, the song came out one day. It was a natural part of life for the recovering Father and Son. They were healing with the help of each other. One night, Jack played it for Sue on his acoustic guitar; she instantly fell in love with him, and the tune. She too used the hymn to lullaby her kids to sleep. It quickly became her family's favorite, also:

> If you're walking down the street, crack a smile
> If you're feeling kind of down, run a mile
> If things aren't going right, turn the dial
> When in Africa, look out for crocodile

It was a silly tune, but they all loved it. Now, Jack was loving the moment; his family were once again singing this craziness to him. A tear welled up in his eye. They'd been so dry for the last weeks. The liquid was a welcome, soothing relief. His tears of joy were a sign of what was going on in his heart. He'd waited many years to see his family in this state again. On his death bed, his wait was over. It was the happiest moment of his life.

The kids didn't want to stop the song. They danced with each other, and Sue, as the tune played repeatedly. After an hour or more of the ruckus, Jack had enough. He raised his hand and made a sweeping motion as best he could. Sue was immediately by his side. The others slowed down in their revelry but didn't stop. Each took a dance step and hugged their father with length. The entire time, they never stopped their singing. After they all hugged Jack and sung one last verse to him, they slowly made their way out the door. Their dancing stopped but the song continued. Its rhythm slowed and quieted as they made their exit. After the door closed, the song didn't end until the verse was over.

Outside the room, the three siblings looked at each other and hugged in a triangle of solidarity. They'd always been close. Hardships coursed through their family repeatedly over this lifetime; they all stuck together to get through it. This would be no different. Just one more heartache the family would have to deal with. This time, death was different. They were prepared for it. When it happened, their state of mind was now going to be proper.

The rest of their lives, the three would never forget how each helped as a group. Together they were strong. These times of turmoil made lifetimes of bonding. Death and cataclysm always had a way of strengthening families. Every hardship thrown their way was met with the team. Together, they could get through any calamity while building their trust and confidence in each other.

Jim came out of his room when he heard the others in the living room. They included him in their group hug, but this time gave him back good energy. Only an hour passed since they last saw him, but so much changed in the span. Jim noticed the difference immediately. He commended his niece and nephews on their strength. "Leaving your Father with good energy is the greatest gift you've ever given him," Jim said.

They all three burst out with the song one last time. This time, their uncle chimed in for the last three lines. It would be the last time in their lives any of them would ever sing this magical song.

They said they had to get going. The sun was going down. Three cities were on the trip before they were all safely home. Jim told them about the shadows from the setting sun and trees. It was very bad at this time of year and at sunset. Becky said she knew of the dangers but there was no choice; they had to leave. Their mission here was complete. They wanted their dad and uncle to get back on with their business.

The group hugged once more and went to the porch. The three siblings turned one last time to wave goodbye to their Uncle Jim. It was a bittersweet goodbye. This would be the last time they looked at their parent's house with their Father inside. They each knew it was selfish, but they were sad never-the-less.

Jim could see it around the three. Colorful bursts of energy enveloped their beings. Their auras were alive and electric. Anyone who they encountered, on this night, would be forever changed by the cosmic energy they encountered.

The memory of the song formed a tear in the corner of Jim's eye. The three touched their uncle with their good energy; just as they'd done to their father. This was one of the nicest things anyone could do for another. He felt a warmth in his heart which was missing for a very long time.

Jim was amazed as the three got into the car. Light seemed to burst from the windows. The cosmic serpents were twisted all around the vehicle. Its multitude of colors slithered through parts it didn't feel like going around. When the car started, the serpents snaked their way into the inside and combined with the colors. Jim had never seen colors as beautiful in his life. He knew he would never forget what he just saw. Nor would he ever forget the song his family just sang for him.

Jim watched until the tail-lights were out of sight. He went back into the house, stopped by his room to pick up some things and headed to his brother's room. He knocked lightly and went in when invited. He saw the condition of Jack and Sue. She looked like she hadn't slept in days. They both looked like they aged many years in the last few days. It was sunset, and Jim knew the time was near. He sat on the corner of the bed and rubbed his brother's shoulder.

Their eyes met and lingered. Jack's eyes were vibrant blue. Jim didn't know how they changed from hazel to blue, but they had. Sue softly sung the song, just once. Jim looked over to the woman and smiled broadly when their eyes met. They were all together again. Jim knew she was going to be okay. He could see the look in her face and read it like his own. Her aura, in the last few hours, changed to one of brightness. It looked almost exactly like that of her kids.

Not just was Jack's soul healed, so was his family's.

Jim could see the relief in his brother's face, caused by his children's visit. The two brother's thoughts were connected; Jim knew exactly how he felt. He wanted to be treated the same if it were him. They weren't ones to have pity given them. They were strong and proud since birth. Pity was for the weak. Respect was for the strong.

Jack's aura was like nothing Jim saw before. The cosmic serpents, and his brother's energy, morphed into one. The serpents weren't only around Jack, they were in him too.

Jim learned much about the cosmic serpents in the last months. Now, however, they were ready to reveal their true secrets.

"Hey guys, I've got to go to my car and get some things," Jim said. "I'll be right back." He left and returned five different times with art supplies. First were the canvases and wood panels the brothers were notorious for painting on. Then came the brushes, paper and future shadow boxes. The last two trips were used to carry in the mediums and trinkets they acquired together, throughout the years.

After the second trip, Sue asked what he was doing. "You know what I'm doing, Sue. Same thing we've always done together. Create. This is our last time making things in this existence together. We're going to make some crazy ass shit tonight."

When Jim was done with his task, the room was cluttered with art material. Sue could see the spark in her husband's eye. He always loved to paint. This would be his night of liberation.

The exuberance in Jim rejuvenated Sue. She had a burst of energy but knew it was momentary. She wanted to give this time to her husband and his brother. She knew of their mutual respect and wanted them to create one last time. She secretly looked forward to what they would make this night. She could only imagine what kind of madness would ensue.

She told the men she was tired and going to lay down. She kissed Jack with a lingering smooch, bumped fists with Jim and was out the door. The brothers looked at each other with no emotion. They both knew this was serious business. Just because they were taking hallucinogens daily, they were not partying. They were learning; opening their minds like the beginning.

Jim began to set up the canvases and unpack the boxes of supplies. He laid everything on tables which he brought from the closet. It took over a half hour before the room was prepared. He talked to his brother the entire time; rambling on about all the stuff they'd be making and the creations they'd be creating.

"This whole room is going to be filled with art by morning, trust me," Jim said repeatedly. A few times he even made up a little ditty about his intentions for a night of creation. Jack took it all in. He watched his brother like he was watching a live play.

When the task was over, Jack waved Jim over with feeble hands. Jim got close enough, so he could hear the whisper that emerged: "How am I going to get to all that paint? I can barely move."

"Brother, you still doubt me after all these years," Jim said with bravado. "In ten minutes, you're going to be dancing around this room. We're the first modern humans ever to try this shit. It comes from another time. I met a young girl who guarded this sacred spot out by Blythe. We traded energies and knowledge. She made this hallucinogen from plants the winds told her about. The foliage spoke to her about their functions and purpose. She created this concoction out of eight different plants. The ancients knew all about these herbs, but the knowledge got lost with the onslaught. Just like so much else. It will make you feel alive, because you are. These herbs will repair your body, completely, for the next twelve hours." Jim was waving around his liquid as he talked and rummaged.

Jack crooked a finger, signaling his brother closer. His whisper was barely audible, but Jim heard it clear. "Did you fuck her?" Jim gave a good laugh at his brother's humor. He could see the true spirit through those piercing blue eyes.

"Nah Man, it wasn't like that. She was just a young flesh pod with a very ancient spirit." Jim spoke as he pulled his homemade beer bong out of a bag. It was obviously made from store bought items. Its length was only about one foot, with the funnel big enough for about two cups. The bottom had a baby pacifier with the nipple cut in half. In its place, the plastic tube protruded two inches. Its whole construction was for one purpose only. It would be a comfortable way for Jack to take the dose.

A jar of green liquid was the next to come out of the sack. Jim put it on the nightstand and removed the rustic looking cork. A small waft of greenish smoke billowed out of the handmade glass jar when oxygen hit its contents.

Jim put the bong to Jack's mouth, tilted his head back, and poured the brew straight down the hatch. The smooth liquid flowed down the older brother's throat and into his stomach. Jim turned the bottle and downed the remainder of its contents in one gulp. The taste was nutty, like walnuts. It was very pleasant.

Jim went to the window and opened it. The outside air was going to be necessary for their creativity. He fumbled around the table for a couple colors then turned around to see the new room. It was alive, as was Jack.

Green covered every inch of the space. Plants, mold, and trees were everywhere. Insects and animals Jim never saw before abounded. There was a smell in the room of purity. This place was good.

He looked to the bed to see Jack's condition, but his brother wasn't in it. Instead, he was climbing one of the trees which were growing before his eyes. Jack looked like a little kid in his pajamas. He was getting high up there; it didn't seem to end any time soon. Jim laughed to himself thinking his brother finally found the beanstalk.

Jim saw a multi-color banana slug, five feet long and big around as a fifty-five-gallon barrel. The creature looked over its shoulder and told the man to climb aboard. Its voice was mellow and inviting; Jim didn't have to think twice about what he was going to do. He climbed on the slimy creature and prepared for a slow ride.

It was the opposite. The slug took off at a speed like lightning. Things whirred past so fast, they were not intelligible. Jim knew they were traveling at the speed of light, but his body felt like it was standing still. The visuals going by were cosmic: the heart of creating.

It seemed like a very long time passed but Jim couldn't be sure. His sense of time didn't exist because time didn't exist while moving at this speed. He thought he might be traveling backwards in time. He had no clue of the direction of anything. All he was sure of was the streaks of stars as they sped by.

Some of the speeding lights flashed, while others were constant. Occasionally, they would become brighter or a burst would appear. Jim's mind was in awe of the sights. He could see it was a binary code he was observing. The entire universe, when moving at this speed, was a giant codex. This was the god who was god above the cosmic serpents. Somehow, some way, this code created and controlled the universe.

It's why numbers rule everything they created. The cosmic serpents are the bringers of life. The binary control that life and its destiny.

The moment he figured it out, the lights stopped, and he was back in the room. The green vegetation was gone and replaced by more than a hundred paintings. Jim shook his head in disbelief. Who painted on their canvases, he wondered.

He looked to the bed and saw Jack laying there, gasping for breath. He was covered in paint, answering the question of who painted the walls. Jim could see this was his brother's last day. The sun beam shining through the window knew it also. Its ray fell directly on Jack, laying lifeless on the bed. Jim could see his aura, so he knew his brother was still in his flesh pod. The aura was golden in the ray of the sun.

Jim couldn't take his eyes off the beauty engulfing his brother. He didn't believe in miracles, but this was a gift from the binary. He understood it all now. Seeing Jack lit up like that was truly incredible for Jim.

The sun-ray crept across the room with a shorter and shorter shadow until it was gone altogether. Jack was still lying lifeless; now resting in the shadow of the room. It gave Jim a chance to walk around the gallery and see what was hanging on the walls. There were mere inches in-between the artwork. Some were painted on the walls themselves, filling the spaces between canvas. The entire ceiling was covered in an oil mural.

Jim was beginning to take in the imagery and trying to understand it. They were the most beautiful paintings he'd ever seen. If Jack truly painted them throughout the night, he was a master. The gods were with them, and in them. This was all about the numbers. They could do anything, as long as they held the Wisdom.

Just as Jim crawled into the first painting, the door flung open and Sue came in with a pitcher of water and one of orange juice. As soon as she saw the condition of the room, it began to spin. She felt like she was in a tunnel and everything was getting smaller. It sounded like someone put cotton in her ears and sucked the moisture from her mouth.

Luckily, Jim was right there. He grabbed the tray, and Sue, just as the woman lost consciousness.

Chapter 21

Sue's visions in the subconscious were bizarre. Nothing was normal to her in this alternate reality. She was surrounded by scenes straight out of a renaissance painting. To the left were the gates of hell. Souls were marching to their eternal demise, prodded by demons, while angels flew above. The whole scene was animated like a blockbuster movie.

To the right were the humans being prepared for their fate. Judgement was being administered by a giant over ten feet tall. Its white robe was flowing in the smoke, created by the fire emanating from the pit below. The creatures black beard contrasted its sky-blue skin. Billows of smoke and turbulence filled the scene behind the creature.

Sue realized this was another dimension she crossed into. She was an invisible spectator to the carnage. She surveyed the entire scene and realized she was in the middle of a Luca Signorelli painting. He always was her favorite artist and now she was part of her favorite painting. 'The damned being taken to hell' surrounded her. The only exception: now it was animated and audible.

Demons abounded as the caretakers of souls. Their task was to herd the evil into their just reward. Sue could see familiar faces in the misery. Many politicians and movie stars were present for their reckoning. People she'd seen on television, magazines and news outlets were there, moaning their torment. Religious leaders were sprinkled in amongst the crowd. Even a few individuals from their own community, who let greed control their beings, were present.

Each of these sinners begged forgiveness, but none was granted.

Sue didn't have pity on these people. She saw the dirt humans could dish out on each other. She saw their evil ways of apathy. These were the worse of the worst. These humans never cared for anyone but themselves. They acquired riches at the cost of fellow humans and the planet. Now they were taking none of it with them. All they owned, now, was misery; an eternity of it.

Each of the souls was naked and beaten. Some of them were missing limbs. Those who couldn't walk were carried by the gigantic guards and thrown into the pit forcibly. Their screams of anguish were muted by the intensity of the situation. Sue's senses felt like she was inside an active volcano. Vibration, rumbling, heat, smells and tastes of damnation were abundant. The whole place was one of devastation and cleansing. A purging was happening while the woman stood and watched.

Sue could hear a voice in the distance, calling her name. It seemed like it was coming from above. She looked to the direction and was blinded by an intense light. She had to look away to shield her eyes. When she looked up again, she was looking straight into the eyes of a demon.

The creature was alerted to the woman when the outside light shone in its realm. Sue was illuminated by this light and made visible to the guardians of the portal. When they saw her, it was their job to see if she was evil or good. This place was for judgement, after all. It was what these demons existed for.

Once again, Sue wasn't scared. She'd always been a good person and lived her life being content with what she had. She felt like there was nothing to worry about. She never once went the path of greed.

The demon kept eye contact with her for a full minute. Its acrid breath burned the inside of Sue's nostrils. She sensed this creature for what it was. It was not evil in the least. It was doing a job just like every other living being did. This creature, like most, didn't have it in their thoughts to do their fellows dirty. They were happy to exist and put food on their family's table. They weren't into the politics of things; they were happy to merely get by.

The true evil were the beings meeting their destinies in this dimension. These were the greed.

The being with blue skin watched over the entire scenario. Its gaze followed every movement the woman, who came from the outside, made. The creature already knew this woman was good. Her aura was one of color and activity. She happened upon this realm because she was different than most humans. She came here because it was meant to be.

Sue looked to the blue creature and saw the warmth and empathy in its eyes. She felt a connection to the being that made her feel euphoric. This judge was kind to the souls it decided on. It wasn't here to perpetuate fear. Its job was to take out the trash; the torture and fear would come later.

Sue heard her name, again, and looked up instinctively. The light from above was diminishing. The portal was closing. The blue creature waved its large hand as if saying it was time to go. She looked back to the demon in front of her with need. The beast knew exactly what to do. He gingerly picked up the woman, put her foot in his large hand, and flung her toward the top of the cavern. The ease with his movement made Sue think the creature must have performed this escape before.

The wind was intense as she rocketed to freedom. Just before reaching the light, Sue worried about how she'd fit through the portal. The moment her head touched the light, she lost consciousness.

She woke up with Jim standing over her. It seemed so strange. Moments before, the demons face was eye to eye with her and now her brother-in-law was. She tried to focus her sight, but everything was blurry. The vision she just encountered weighed heavy on her thoughts. Her mind felt like it was ripped in two and her soul was pouring into the cosmos.

"Are you all right Sue," Jim asked with empathy. "You had us worried there for a minute."

"I think I'm okay. What happened?"

"You came in here with these pitchers, looked around and passed out. Luckily, I caught you and the juice. We were worried about you."

"How long was I out for? Some trippy shit happened." Sue's voice was shaky as she spoke. The ordeal she just went through, literally, took her breath away.

"You were knocked out for fifteen minutes. You were lying so still but your eyes were moving like crazy under the lids. It looked like you were in REM. It was intense. I tried to wake you up and even put a cold towel on your head. You didn't respond to any of it. I finally decided to wait it out and be here when you came to."

"Help me up," she said as she extended her hand. Jim helped his sister-in-law to her feet and saw the shock swiftly overtake her face. Her color went from pale to gray as she swayed on her feet. For a moment, Jim thought she might pass out again.

He held on to Sue until her legs got steady. After a few minutes, she raised her head and shrugged off her brother-in-law. She looked around the room not believing what she was seeing. The visions she just had were recreated on every inch of wall space. Scenes of hell and the rapture filled the bedroom. Where there were no canvases, the walls held the paint. The entire room was a seamless mural. Even the tiled part of the floor was painted. Her bedroom had been converted into a masterpiece.

She was breathless as she looked around. The large blue creature was painted in its glory, stretching from floor to ceiling. Its long black hair flowed out the window, caught on a breeze. The same souls she saw being taken into the pit were all represented. Even the background and flames matched that of her visions, spot on.

In the corner was her familiar demon which helped her come back to this realm. Its eyes looked so realistic she almost believed it to be real. Every bit of the painting was one of genius. Sue studied art in college and she absolutely believed this was the nicest painting she ever saw. It had hints of Signorelli mixed with Leonardo da Vinci, Michelangelo, and other Masters. Whatever it was, it was awesome.

She was impressed, and in awe: this masterpiece was created in one night. This was a project which would encompass a lifetime for a master painter.

This was the first time Jim fully looked at the creation which happened overnight. He was too busy tending to Sue to care about his surroundings. He pointed out many details to Sue as they both walked slowly around the room. The painting held so much hidden meanings and symbols, it would take months, or even years, to figure out. As Jim was pointing out things, Sue realized he didn't have paint on his hands. She painted with her brother-in-law many times and knew he was always the one to be covered in pigment. Looking at his clothes, she realized the same; no stains.

She looked to Jack, silently lying in bed. His breathing was so shallow, the others couldn't hear it, even in the silence of the room. She went to the bed and saw Jack's hands and arms covered in oil paint. It looked like every color of the palette was represented on his appendages. The tops of the blanket were smeared with the residue which had rubbed off Jack's arms. Even the smears on the bed formed a masterpiece, reminding Sue of Jackson Pollock.

"How could he have painted this in one night, by himself?" Sue asked with wonder. "Where were you when he was doing it?"

"We went to the other side last night, Sue. Jack was inspired by our true Gods and the painting flowed from his soul. As for me, I was much too busy speaking with God to be painting. My destiny to create my own masterpiece, is at a future time. For now, I needed Wisdom."

"I still don't understand how one man could paint something that took masters a lifetime to produce. This is art like I've never seen or imagined."

"I've been telling you for a long time, Sue. This reality isn't how we perceive it. Our existence is laid out for us. Every minute is mapped just as every cell is organized in our bodies. Our purpose is to get through this existence with the slightest imprint on the planet; then move on to the next. When we get to full enlightenment, then we go back home to be with our people."

"What if we never get to enlightenment?" Sue asked.

"Most never get to that point. Some decide to go faster than the speed limit and get more for themselves." Jim waved his hand around the room dramatically. "This is what those folks get. While the righteous live an eternity with their ancestors, the evil wallow in their own greed for eternity. Religions had it right in that one regard. There truly is a heaven and hell. It was portrayed well by the ancients."

"You're the least religious person I ever met, Jim," Sue said. "Now you're going to tell me about heaven and hell?"

"It's not about religion at all. Every one of those who took money from the humans, in the name of 'God', all went to hell. They were the greed, just like many others. They acquired a bit of knowledge. They kept this knowledge secret and used it for their own gain. Many humans died in the name of religion and their lies. Wars and destruction were, and are, synonymous with religion. It's a huge fuck-over."

"But you're talking about heaven and hell."

"There is heaven and hell. It was one of the only truths the church told the people. They used the Wisdom to create fear for their own profit. Wisdom that was meant to be shared by all humans was bastardized by those who called themselves the righteous. Hell is just how they portrayed it, but heaven is nothing like it. They didn't know the truth about heaven. Their kind never went there to know the slightest about paradise."

"If there is a heaven and hell, then surely there is a god and devil then, right?" Sue asked with doubt. This all seemed like too much for her to handle. Jim was talking about things that contradicted other things he was saying.

"You're not understanding, Sue. These were made up creatures for the religious purpose of taking money. God doesn't exist as humans think. I met God and the beings who bring about life. We humans are just a small number in the overall equation of things. You see, there is a binary system that controls the universe. This binary system dictates what happens every second of every day. It's been in place since the birth of the universe and will be until its demise. It's the brain that controls the entire cosmos. These numbers are like a fabric in space. Their only constant is change. It reflects in our existence."

Jim took a small pause and drank a glass of water. This talk of Gods dried his mouth out. "These binaries are inside each of us. Each cell we possess has these binary codes. They form together, making us whole. Existence is all through this God. The codes are wrapped up into a twisted bundle and it's what we call DNA. The cosmic serpents are the DNA. They are a byproduct of the binary codes. Without the binary, there would be nothing. Even our planet, moon, and sun are controlled by these binary codes."

"These codes also dictate the speed of light, sound, and every element known to man. They truly are the universe. Without the binary, our cosmos would be a blank void. With the binary, it's full of dynamic life."

"Wow," Sue said, "That's pretty intense. But I still don't understand about the heaven and hell thing."

"Well, the binary is not just in this dimension. It created multiple dimensions and multiple existences for its numbers and equations. When we die, we're reborn into this realm many times. Sometimes we're born again in the future and sometimes in the past. When we achieve the enlightenment, by solving the binary equations presented to us, we go to another dimension. This same cycle will happen in that dimension, as well, until we move on to another dimension. It's a cycle which has been going on for billions of years. In this regard, our existence is one of numbers; it will never cease to be unless we decide to destroy it. The only way to do that is with greed. They are the enemy to all in the universe. The destructive force who thinks they can take control. The souls of the greed are never given another chance to be reborn. They are sent to a dimension which is filled with anguish and despair. This is their eternal damnation."

"I think I'm starting to understand," Sue said. "The DNA code is what controls us. Its numbers make us who we are?"

"The DNA is just a small part of it. Like an appendage. The binary controls everything. Since we are numbers, we always have the same family over and again. Our kin have the same code as we do. Some other families, like you Sue, have a DNA that is complimentary to a family code. This person will sometimes travel through eternity with the same people. It's the case with you, Sister."

"I was aware the first time I met Jack that we knew each other, before. Even the way we met was predestined. There was no question with the familiarity we both shared. When I met you and Lisa, it was the same thing. I knew I traveled with you many lives in the past."

"Many lives, Sue," Jack said from his feeble position. Sue looked to him and saw a small smile creep up on his face. She knew that everything was going to be okay. Wisdom was returning to the family just when they needed it most. Jim came to visit and made everything good.

"I have to tell you one more thing Sue, before we get on with the day," Jim said. "These codes make a timeline for our lives. They can also manipulate our minds into believing anything they want us to believe. Some of the visions we've had this week were created by the binary. They gave us a gift of imagination and we used it fully. They have the power to make people think they're gods. It's up to you to believe what you will. They have used this, many times, throughout history. It swiftly weeds out any people who thought they could rule over others. In truth, the binary is constantly giving us tests to see what our reaction will be. If we react correctly, we get a star. Go toward greed, get a demotion. Our whole existence is a test administered by our hidden God. The binary is a scientist who collects as much data as possible. The binary watches and records everything. It uses this data for the future."

Jim walked over and pointed to a spot just above the door. A small wooden plaque with a painting of a void hung askew. Its red surface had great dimension. It looked like you were looking into a red tunnel. Sue took a step closer to get a better look. At first, she thought it was just a board with some red paint. Focusing, she noticed something very peculiar. As she got closer, she noticed the void wasn't empty at all. It held a strange spiral painted out of a darker shade of red dots. The red dots were of dashes and circles, tightly weaved together. The spiral went to the depths of the void and then seemed to flow back out. It seemed to be in motion. As sue watched, the movement inside the painting sped up until it began to make a shape.

The object in the painting became more defined until Sue could clearly see what was transpiring. The binary numbers on the painting formed into the shape of a human face.

The face looked blankly at Sue like it was an automaton waiting to be programmed.

The woman in the picture slowly and mechanically opened its eyes. Its sockets were eviscerated. Inside was the realm that originally pulled Sue into this picture.

It looked inviting in the void. Sue felt like she could crawl through those eyes into the blankness, where she longed to be. It wouldn't be difficult.

She knew this woman well. The face in the picture was that of her own.

Chapter 22

To know the date of your own death was a gift most folks would never have. Most people died suddenly without any prior knowledge. The only ones who may know the exact date were condemned people. Those who had illness could guess, but their waiting game was one of misery. To most, this knowledge wasn't a gift so much as a curse. It all depended on the person and how they perceived things.

As everyone was different, so was their last day.

Jack's last day was solemn, only in the fact that the dying man's strength left him. He didn't feel remorse, nor have regrets, for his life. He'd lived a good one. He lived his life with the truth. He was a good person who was happy with what he had. He worked hard, but with pride in mind; not greed. He helped many people in his life and showed countless humans the true path.

Mostly though, his legacy was the things he created. These were the things that would keep his memory alive for generations. His goal, constructively, was to create. There were never thoughts of money or glory. It wasn't a naïve way of thinking, just the way of spirituality which came from productivity. By using his imagination and creating in this existence, he was leaving a bit of himself behind.

Jim and Sue wandered around the room with amazement in their voices. They couldn't believe what they saw. Jack was proud, as he lay there, listening to their awestruck words. His eyes were barely functional as were his ears. He had to strain to hear and see his family in their proud moment in front of the 'Master'.

Jim had been inspired on his travels, and by the shaman. This, however, was the most inspirational thing he ever saw come from a single human being. He was awed and proud of his brother at the same moment. Jim, too, made paintings his whole life; they were amateur compared to this masterpiece.

Each of the unframed canvases had completely different styles and mediums. They looked like they were from a different era. Some were oils, acrylic, or watercolor, while others were charcoal, ink, or combinations of them all. Whichever medium, they flowed together like one single canvas.

In total, there were fifty-two paintings. Spaces in between were backgrounds of madness. Tortured souls and happy children splayed the background for the canvases which were like windows of sanity in a room of madness. Colors were so deep; Jim thought parts were real. If they looked at one spot for more than a minute or two, the image would come alive and suck them into its craziness.

The canvases ranged from twelve inches to six feet tall. Some were paper, canvas, or wood. A few objects, like the lamp-shade and dresser, provided an adequate receptacle for Jack's crazed imagination.

He was laughing to himself as he heard his wife wonder how he painted all this in one night. He was possessed with his own spirit. He'd been holding this energy inside for a very long time. This entire existence was a test and he just passed the final. He was off to the next level, with his re-found wisdom and his passing grade.

The next equation was coming his way.

"How did you get the energy to paint these things?" Sue asked her husband as she sat on the side of the bed. In the corner of the room, over-filling the garbage can, was the empty paint tubes and other supplies. Jack used every drop of every tube Jim brought. It was the exact amount to do the job in its entirety. The numbers, as usual, were exact. Nothing was a coincident.

"It's my last burst of energy," Jack said with the slightest whisper. It was painful, deep in the chest, to talk. Jack had things to say, though. "The drug brought me to the other side. Another dimension which was void of any other creature. I was there for fifty-two days. I was alone with my thoughts and my creativity. I painted one of these canvases each day I was there. When I came back here, they were already hanging on the walls. I don't remember painting the background. Maybe Jim did that part."

"I know that you know," Jim said. "They know that we know." He was making a sweeping motion around the room with his arm. "These paintings are your soul. Your existence here is a little part of who you truly are. It's a small grain in the hourglass of your being. This room is proof of that."

"I know that you know that I know," Jack said with as much of a chuckle he could muster. He began to choke a bit on his dryness. Sue held some water to his lips and Jack welcomed the cooling liquid. Since he'd been back in this reality, he longed to be back on the other side. He understood, though; there was his family to think about also. It might be many years before they saw each other again. Sometimes, centuries passed before bumping back into a family member if the life spans didn't line up properly. It was all in the binary code. It's how it was meant to be.

"It's amazing you painted something like this, Jack," Sue said with pride. There was radiance in her aura that made Jack confident and proud. He knew his painting helped her. "I will treasure this room forever," she added.

The cosmic serpents were slithering throughout the room. They were under the bed then around Jim. Their long tentacular shape covered every inch of organic matter. It was at home here. Even in this room, which was built by man, there was a lot of life.

The colors emitted from the serpents were like lightbulbs, further lighting the daytime room. The paintings completely came alive in the wake of God. Rainbows splashed a multitude of colors across the madness on the walls.

Scenes of hell and heaven weren't the only theme Jack painted. He painted one whole wall with an image of the other side. Where the ancestors lived. The place that was waiting for them all if they stayed true: Away from the greed. Against the greed.

The scene was one of beauty. A large white house surrounded by large trees. Green foliage was everywhere. The background looked like you were standing at the house looking into the backyard. If you got close to a window in the painting, you could see the lifelike features Jack painted inside the abode.

Through the large, open windows, one could see comfort in every room of the house. Not a false comfort, though. This house was furnished with crafts made from many different beings who carried the same DNA strand. Creativity was everywhere. It was what connected this strand of DNA. This clan held the numbers of imagination.

One room was an exact replica of the masterpiece Jack made in this realm.

As you walked around the room, the view of the white house changed with the angle you saw it. It was like you were looking in a doll house which was hand carved. Even the shadows, inside the house, corresponded with whatever angle you were viewing it from. Sue had never seen anything like it. The whole scene brought longing and tranquility from her. This was a place she wanted to go, with her husband, and spend eternity.

The other three walls of the bedroom were scenes of hell and the rapture. These walls were impressive. So many of the faces were recognized. Jack portrayed every one of them so well. When they looked in the pit of hell, hanging in the corner of the room, the scene gave off a feeling of pity. If they stood close to this spot, they would hear moans coming from the depths of the panting.

The ceiling was of angels and demons fighting in the clouds. In the middle of the room, right over the bed, was a break in the clouds. This break created open sky in a circle about ten feet across. The inside of the circle was of many tones of blue fading to black. There were stars that lined the circle and created a spiral as they went farther into its darkness. These stars spelled out a code that most would never recognize. Jim recognized these patterns. He'd seen them the night before on his cosmic ride.

Jack not only recognized them, he reproduced them.

The tiles on the floor were painted shades of green. When standing in the middle of it, it seemed like you were in a field of grass. The blades appeared to blow in the wind with the passing of time. In the middle of the field, emblazoned on the grass like a crop-circle, was a symbol. Its white lines were a stark contrast to the dark green beneath. The symbols meaning was unknown to anyone not sharing the family DNA.

The walls inside the bathroom were murals of Jack's life. From his birth, to this day, everything Jim or Sue could remember was represented. The likeness was of photographic quality. Others, made to be caricatures, were done with a precision that made them look real. Jim, Lisa, their brothers, and parents were all represented in a scene or more. Tommy and the other kids were all there, along with the grandkids. The canvases were an inspiration to Sue. They told her how much her husband loved his family; not that she had any doubts in the first place.

Jim told his brother how impressed he was for this accomplishment. Most painters dreamed of making a catalog of work like this in a lifetime. "You did it all in one night."

"It was actually fifty-two nights. That last shit really sent me there. It was great. Thanks Jim. I really needed it." Jim could hear his brother without a strain. Jack's lips barely moved, but in Jim's mind, he spoke normal.

"That's what I'm here for, Bro," Jim said.

"You've always been a great brother. Thanks," Jack said with pain. His voice was a rapture to use every time. The scenes of torture he painted throughout the room weren't far off from what he was feeling inside. He knew it was all part of the test. How he reacted was going to determine a lot. The solution was right there. He felt as if he were ready.

Pain wracked his body almost non-stop. He was unable to smoke any more pot, but he knew it wouldn't help anyhow. He didn't want to eat it because it made him tired. His time was limited; the last thing he needed now was sleep.

Jack's eyes felt like they dried up and went to heaven. Blinking felt like sawdust under his lids. The slightest movement of his flesh pod brought pain along with it. He painted the tormented souls on the wall with his own excruciation, keeping his screaming to himself. He was in anguish; it didn't mean he had to disgrace himself. These humans he portrayed would scream all the way to their judgement, and never stop for eternity.

Jim could see the pain his brother was in. It saddened him but at the same time he knew Jack was strong. Soon enough, the pain would go away.

The seventh trip was upon them. This would be the last journey Jack took in this existence. He would end up at the place in his painting: the white house. This was where his ancestors were. This was their clan; those who held the same equation.

Even death and the afterlife were part of the binary code.

Chapter 23

Jim held the most respect for his brother as humanly possible. He once again was considerate of the relationship the married couple had and went to do some chores. There was preparation still to be done for this day. This journey was going to be the most epic of their lives. Jim was dedicated to not fucking it up, now, after all they went through.

Both Jim and Sue knew Jack was exhausted. What Sue didn't realize was her husband was awake all week long. The LSD they'd been taking contained just enough speed to keep the trip going non-stop. That, mixed with his health, kept him in a hallucinogenic state all week. The little breaks they took weren't enough for the effects to wear off the dying man.

This interlude, away from Jim, would give the terminal man a small break. Maybe he could even get a ten-minute nap to prepare for the next journey. With Sue by his side, rest would be welcome. He didn't want too much, that would be soon enough. He just wanted to clear his head and make his own preparations. The lack of sleep had taken a toll on his mental well-being.

Jim went back to his bedroom. The dose this day was going to be different. Just acquiring it from the Sasquatch, in the middle of Death Valley, had been the trip of a lifetime. The creature kept the small seeds safely tucked away in its long hair. It pulled out exactly twelve of these seeds that looked like small acorns. Jim asked the creature, in its language, what they were. The beast would only say they came from the other side of the portal. It was forbidden to bring anything back from the parallel dimension. The important need for the brothers to have this medicine forced the Sasquatch to break the rules.

These seeds were easy to conceal with the long hair of the creature. The ancient shaman had visions of Jim coming for a visit, long before he arrived. He also foresaw the human wouldn't swim through the portal. There was only one choice left for the creature; he had to break the code to fulfill this destiny.

It was all part of the equation. Even the creature had to come up with the solution. There was always a right and a wrong answer. It was up to each creature to figure out the problem to the best of their ability. Nobody else knew if you made the right or wrong decision. Judgement was left to the binary who was grading papers.

This being took Jim places unknown to modern man. It was the first time in hundreds of years the beast had a visit from a humanoid creature. He was happy for the company; especially one from the same clan. From the moment they met, the two were brothers.

Parts of this valley had been turned into a bombing range by the Navy. The government heard stories from these parts. The stories were fantastical at first, but then their own scientists confirmed it.

Death Valley was home to an ancient people who lived here over fifty thousand years before. The caves were their homes. From this central point, they spread their DNA and wisdom throughout the Americas. The petroglyphs, which perplexed archaeologists for decades, had their origin in these people.

They had been a race of giants, over ten feet tall. Their sophisticated written language and art preceded other civilizations in Europe and Africa by thousands of years. The Native Americans saw these sites as sacred. They were the birth place of their ancestors. This is where all life came from. In their legends, these were the Gods.

The first white explorers were amazed at the artifacts they found. Gold statues, paying homage to unknown gods, were plentiful. Sophisticated weapons and tools made from obsidian, and a foreign metal, were left in the spot used last. The most amazing thing found, though, was the golden sarcophagus. It was over twenty feet tall and eight feet wide. They estimated it must weigh several tons. These explorers pilfered what they could take but their destiny was not one of riches. Most of them died in this inhospitable region penniless and destitute. The few that did survive its harshness, were the ones who spread the stories of riches.

The government soon heard about these strange artifacts coming out of the desert. They sent their people in and cleansed the entire situation. The first explorers came up missing and then forgotten as all recollection of their existence was erased. The few newspaper articles wrote about their discoveries were portrayed as hoaxes. Everything associated with Wingate Pass became a conspiracy theory.

The artifacts and cave systems were destroyed in a hail of bombs. For over sixty years, since its discovery by the government, the Navy bombed this historic site to dust.

There was one spot where the bombs hadn't landed. It was next to a small lake which the Navy decided not to destroy. The cave was situated in a rock formation on the bank of this lake. No other white man ever found the entrance to this portal until Jim came along. If not for the binary showing the way, its existence would never have been known to any man.

The Sasquatch showed Jim the ancient way of his people. He, too, was an offspring of the early settlers of this land. He retained most of the original DNA of these people. While the other creatures on the outside were evolving into humans, this creature remained hidden from the world. This place was its home since the beginning. He could easily pass to the other side with the portal. This passage is where its ancestors originally came from. The portal was created by the binary. The DNA used it to disperse life.

Jim fumbled around in his room and the kitchen for a while, thinking of his journey. The first guy in Colorado he met spelled out the whole scenario to him. Every one of the shamans, after the first, told him the same thing. He was to acquire a bit of hallucinogen from each of the medicine men he went to visit. Each of the shaman was connected in their visions. Their hallucinogen would be formulated to coincide with that of the others. When he was done collecting, it would be time for healing.

Each of the shaman was proud to send Jim off with their special brew. They all had the same visions and blended a special mix just for the brothers. Jim didn't understand when he met these distant relatives, but he did now. They were in his reality because of the numbers. The binary brought them all together. Their existence, and his, crossed at the exact moment it was equated. He wondered why he was drawn to each of the medicine men at the time, but now the truth was clear. This equation was written long before he was born.

Jim used a mortar and pestle he found in the kitchen to grind the seeds. He did six at a time to get the same exact dose. The medicine man told him it would be important for them to take the same amount. If not, their balance would be way off; it would have bad consequences.

The first smash of each nut created a purplish smoke which blew out the window. It looked like a dancer escaping a prison. Jim thought of a Genie in the bottle as each pod was cracked. After each was broke in two, the real work began. Each batch took thirty minutes. When he was done grinding the acorns into a flour type substance, it was time to mix it. The medicine man told him to mix it with salt water. On the other side, they drank salt water like we drank fresh water here.

There were important steps in concocting this visionary brew. Each of the shaman sent a warning not to take it lightly. These were powerful herbs. Nobody had ever used them in conjunction. Only a few people even heard of them. All the shaman knew about the last trip for the brothers. They all warned Jim about the dangers of this drug. It wasn't from this dimension, they told him. No human in this dimension had ever taken it.

After the powder was mixed with the salt water, there was one more thing to add. This was something the Sasquatch warned Jim about. He told him not to mix anything else with the seeds. They were all the hallucinogen one being could take. The last item in the mix, however, came from their parents. His father had handed him the strange object, passing on the knowledge. He told Jim it would help; and now it was the key element in their journey.

The medicine came in the form of a long seed pod. It looked like it came from a tree. When Jim held it, it felt like old leather in his hand. He knew, through his father's thoughts, this object had been in their family for generations. It originated in Latvia when the clan first arrived. When the pod was shaken, it sounded like a rattle with four or five large beans.

Jim used all his might to crack the pod in half. It didn't seem like it was going to break and then it just snapped. As soon as the object was broken, its contents came tumbling out. They were two small seeds which looked like dung beetles. Jim could swear they were moving on their own. He swept the first seed into the mortar. The seed pod cracked in pieces, depositing its ancient treasure in the concoction below. Jim mixed the watery mixture with the dry mix and stirred it with half the empty seed pod.

Jim knew exactly when the mix was finished. It started to smoke and make a strange hissing sound. It reminded him of a lobster boiling. He poured the concoction into a stone bowl he'd dug from the

Earth at Wingate Pass. He'd found the twin objects buried next to the lake. His inner eye told him exactly where they were located. The lids were highly decorated with a swastika in the shape of a spiral which gave off an aura. Jim had been able to spot this glow through two feet of dirt and rocks. The artifacts had revealed their location to the searcher.

Jim slapped the lid on the bowl and stopped the spread of its toxins. He didn't know what effect it could have on him and his brother let alone an unsuspecting bystander. At least the brothers knew what they were in for.

He repeated the ritual with the second seed. The second stone jar was almost identical to the first. When the lid was on the second, Jim's task was successful. He couldn't help but think about the warning from the Sasquatch, but he couldn't let it bother him.

He knew he shouldn't leave the mix alone but there was one more thing he had to do. He went to the shed out back and got the gong stand he and Jack made together years before. They made this wooden beauty in their youth. It was when Jack's first wife just died. Jim was there. He got his brother and nephew into woodworking. They inherited a badass gong from their parents and needed a place to hang it. The stand was their first woodworking project.

Then, it was also their twentieth project. As Jim pulled it from its confines, uncovering it in the process, he admired the beauty of the thing. It had hand turned dowels with wood endcaps. The side pieces were carved with intricate patterns of a tribal nature. The base was a crisscross of wood dowels forming a large spider web. The entire thing stood about six feet tall. They made it to fold and go into storage easy, but still be badass when set up.

The oak dowels were turned by both brothers and Tommy equally. The reinforcements were all of brass, which the three hand-crafted themselves. All the hardware, as well, was made by the three on a metal lathe. Even though Tommy was a little kid, he had worked like an adult on the family project.

The top of the stand was Jim's favorite. Each of them carved a skull and put it in its respective place on the rack. The top was where they ended the project.

They used the first stand many times in the past. After their skills got better, they built this one to replace their first attempt. It was cherished by the family and proudly shown off to all visitors. Unfortunately, in the last couple decades, it sat in garage solitude.

Jim finished cleaning any debris that accumulated under the wraps. He hadn't seen this stand come out for a very long time. The night they found Tommy's body was the last time Jim saw it. That night, Jack beat the gong all night long. His hands were bloody stumps when he finished his tirade at daybreak. The cops even came but, when they saw who it was, they left him alone. Every cop in Calaveras knew what the family just went through.

Even at an early age, the two understood the importance of the gong. The connection they felt with the object was cosmic in nature. Their adopted parents never told them how it was theirs. They just said it came from distant relatives as a gift. The rest of the story was a mystery until the brothers learned the truth.

They rang it at their adopted parent's funeral when they thought it was their real parents. It was rung at Jack's first and second wedding. It was also rung at his first wife's funeral. When Tommy came up missing, the brothers rang that fucker into the wee hours of the morning. They had hoped the energy put forth would bring their boy home.

After every devastation in the family, the gong would ring. The brothers would stay up all night long and speak of everything that came to mind. These talks, along with the vibrations, were therapy for the family. The instrument got them through some terrible times throughout the years.

When things got so bad and there was no hope in sight, the brothers occasionally dropped acid. The affects would be wonderful. The depression would be gone and replaced with dreams of the future. This is when the brothers understood the hardship on the living after death. It wasn't the person dying who had it the hardest. The dreams they had together, died along with that person. If they had no dreams, they couldn't see beyond the heartache.

Hallucinogens taught the brothers many things in the past. It's why they were prepared for death. They visited death and it wasn't something to fear. Unless, of course, you didn't pass the equation.

It was during one of these healing sessions the brothers came up with this idea. After all these years, they still remembered and were putting it into action. When they first talked about it, it was tripping talk amongst brothers. After a month, and the subject being on a nightly agenda, they both began to take it seriously.

These journeys were spiritual. The gong would beat while the brothers chanted all night long. Jack, long ago, found an instrument called an Okarina at a yard sale. It looked like a potato. He would play it in tune with the chanting from Jim. The sounds would resonate throughout the hillside. It was a thing of beauty to all those who could hear it.

This was the time of the brother's life when they blossomed spiritually. They became aware of the greed around them and wanted nothing to do with it. It was a hard time in the family's lives, but they got through it together. Some of the things that happened in this period opened their third eye. They woke up.

When they first came up with the plan, they just called it that: the end plan. After they talked about it for the next thirty years, they abbreviated it to: the plan. Their theory was about the cycle. The end was coming but it was going to be the beginning. Just like everything, life and death were the cycle. If life didn't end, life couldn't begin. It was all part of the equation.

It was the way of the universe. The cycles were test questions; once you got one right, you moved on to the next.

It was all in the numbers.

Chapter 24

It was 11:11 on the digital clock when Jim finished his tasks. The gong stand took some time to get set up just right. Its weight was heavy for one man. The gong, too, was heavy and awkward. In the end, Sue had to help lift the large bronze piece into place.

Jim's relentless pace had Jack worn out. He watched his brother hard at work and wondered where the man got his energy from. The excitement in the younger sibling was evident. His aura produced a large swath of light wherever he moved. The electricity in the room was so intense, Sue could hear its whine.

She stayed by her husband's side, except to hang the gong. She was staying positive, as best she could. The stress of the situation was almost too much for her fragile mind. She tried to stay strong the entire time, but sometimes, it was much more difficult than others. This life-changing event was not an easy one to deal with.

To many, this would be the worst day of their life. To Sue, that was exactly what it was. To Jack, however, it was a celebration. He was done with this existence. He long ago lost his tolerance for the stupidity of humans. In the last years, it became very difficult for him to even interact with other people.

Jack was ready to be with his ancestors, once again. He knew there would be a short stop in this realm, after he left his flesh pod. After that brief encounter, he would be moving on to the next existence.

This stopover was the heart of 'the plan' all along. It's what the brothers spoke of for so many years. It was always the same concept. Whichever sibling died first, his spirit would enter that of the other. The possession would be brief, only one day and night. At daybreak, the spirit would move into the realm of the ancients.

In the time they were one being, wisdom would be at the forefront. All Jack's knowledge would be passed to Jim and vice versa. There would be thoughts of two men inside one brain.

They told Sue about this once, in their younger days. She looked at them like they were crazy when they broached the subject. She'd gotten a bit angry at Jack and told him he was insane to always be thinking of these things. It was the last time they told Sue about 'the plan'.

When the possession happened, the brothers reasoned, both souls and minds would occupy the healthy flesh pod simultaneously. They would be equal pilots of one vessel.

It was all in theory, of course. The talk always came up during a hallucinogenic trip. They thought their minds were more efficient on these journeys. They thought it tore down barriers imposed by the greed. These drugs would enable them to use all their brain, for better or worse.

In the past week, all doubt had been erased in the brother's thoughts. The last few days were spent in a convergence of their minds. Sue slept while they figured out the secrets and stories they'd been given. The first three days were on a journey acquiring the knowledge. The last three were spent deciphering that information. They were given the equation, then they had to solve it.

With their minds working as one, the knowledge was swiftly turned into Wisdom. Their thoughts were pure and systematic. They now understood the binary as its numbers ran through their conscious. Puzzles which perplexed humans for millennium were solved like the mathematical equations they were. It was all so simple after you understood.

Jack looked very weak to Sue. His physical being was decayed to the point of death. The sickness had taken a toll on his body. Mentally, however, Jack was healthier than any other time in this existence. This was the transition. Energy was always the strongest at this juncture. Sue looked into his eyes and saw the inner strength. She could clearly see his soul was perfectly healthy.

Both men regained the Wisdom during the week. Wisdom was the true spirituality in every realm. It's why the greed kept it from the masses. If people were allowed the Wisdom, they would wake up. This would be the downfall of the control. When humans saw the truth, they would be pissed.

The shaman helped Jim because it was in their visions and their destiny. Each of them foresaw the man seeking knowledge of spiritual healing in their dreams. He came to each of them to get enlightenment, and in the process, left a little knowledge behind.

Each shaman told Jim his coming was prophesized by the numbers. It was a story told by generations of these people. The prediction was the Earth would begin to heal itself after this man came to visit. There was to be a purging of the planet which would bring about life. The cycle would start over again. Jim was a sign of the beginning.

The shaman took their job seriously. Each of them took a dose, which showed them the way for the brothers. In this state, their minds were open to make just the right concoction. On these journeys, the knowledge was traded. Every place Jim left behind, he felt much smarter because of the visit. It was a mutual feeling with each shaman after the tattooed man left.

Some of the shaman Jim contacted came and visited the brothers during their weeklong trip. Each time, the visit was one of spirits only. Jim spotted them throughout the week. They came to check on the patient. The visits were brief in nature. The shaman showed respect to a family in need of being alone. Their task was to pass the medicine along. Now they were simply observers.

Dark clouds began to block the sunlight. Jack got a small smile and the others knew why. His favorite weather was rain; thunder and lightning were a bonus. Jack felt comfort with the storm. Their coming brought an instant state of calm to the man. He figured his life was turbulent since birth; it was only appropriate to go out on a tempestuous day. Bad weather played such a big part in his chaotic existence.

Jack was ready to get rid of this flesh pod. It was old and decayed, like the shell of a dried-up nut. His mind was wonderful. He couldn't communicate to the others, but he knew they understood. He wasn't an invalid; his body no longer worked in conjunction with his mind.

Jim approached the bed as the shadows crossed the room. The clouds made the space into a cavern. The room was void of all beings but the three humans and the cosmic serpents. All the spirits, which were present for the past week, had moved on. This final journey was to be a secluded one amongst three old friends.

Death was always a private matter. The solitude made up for a lifetime of crowds.

Jim reached into his pocket and pulled out the small stone bowls he stashed there earlier. Sue knew without asking; this was some potent shit. She also realized there were only two bowls. She felt relief in this revelation. She wasn't prepared for a trip. It was bad enough she would have to see her husband pass this day; she wanted to have her head clear for her own journey.

The vessels weren't symmetrical. They were made of a green crystal that looked like Moldavite. Its unusual roundness was hollowed out. The objects were about one-inch deep and two inches in diameter. Being formed from a crystal, they were similar but not exact. Each vessel had its own character, which seemed to fit each brother's personality.

The lids were made of the same material with the swastika spiral pattern engraved on top. A metal ring around the rim was in the shape of a skeletal hand. Its lifelike rendition added an artistic beauty to the amazing objects.

Jim pulled the cap gently off the first bowl. One of the silver fingers swiveled to an upright position when it was uncapped. It was hollow at the fingertip. Jim pulled the silver object free and dipped the finger in the vile. He pulled it out and dropped a single drop in his brother's eye. He re-dipped the finger and placed a drop in the other eye. After six hits were dropped in his brother's eyes, Jim placed the small container to the lips of Jack. The chapped hunks of meat barely opened enough for Jim to get the liquid in. When it passed the lips, Jim turned the vessel upside down and administered the entire dosage to his brother.

He placed the empty on the nightstand and opened the second bowl. He instinctively reached his hand out, with the silver hand in it, and offered Sue a hit. "I think I'll sit this one out, Jim. I need all my senses today."

"Suit yourself Sue," Jim said. "I think you're making a mistake." He dipped the finger six different times and repeated the same ritual he performed on his brother. By the time he drank the remaining contents of the vial, Jim was tripping like no other time in his life.

Instantly he felt like his entire being was a helium balloon. His aura seemed to grow until it was bigger than the house. He could smell something in the air that wasn't there before. He knew what it was. It was ozone; the smell of lightning. Electricity ran through this room like high tension power lines. It was coming from him and his brother.

Jim looked toward Jack but could only see one thing. Cosmic serpents were exploding from the moribund man and slithered all over the room. Their girth was over two feet and they were filled with every color known.

Numbers were running along the wall like a flickering digital clock. Their blue and red hues coincided with their being a zero or a one. The room was lit up with life.

Jim had never seen anything so spiritual in his entire life.

God had come for a visit.

Chapter 25

This was a trip like Jack never felt before. He could see his brother and wife, but they were fading in and out of existence. The colors and numbers in the room obscured everything else. He saw digits flying in equations that would make the best mathematician scratch his head. In Jack's mind, the problems were clear and easy to solve. These were the numbers of his life.

The cosmic serpents were everywhere. Their movement was fluid and simple. These were ancient beings; bringers of life to dark planets. They were also bringers of death. The rebirth was near. The serpents were always more prevalent when death was near. They were also frequent visitors to the very young. They were guardians of sorts who ensured the children developed properly. By the time humans were five or six, they lost the ability to see the true gods. After that, their minds were clouded by society and false religions.

These beings were present to every creature on Earth. Some animals saw them naturally, but only a few. Some species of butterflies and sea anemone were the only species that could see them their entire lives, without drugs. These two creatures could see sixteen and thirty-two spectra, respectively. The cosmic serpents fell within that spectrum.

Some creatures could see them in a hallucinogenic state. Many animals ate mushrooms, fungus or other animals which sent them on visionary journeys. Humans weren't the only Earthlings to alter their reality.

Jack could smell something different in the air. It was so familiar but so lost to him at the same time. It smelled like ozone mixed with roses. It brought along with it a sense of purity in the room.

Jack's senses were alive as his body was dying.

The taste in his mouth became sweet, mimicking what he was smelling. Even his skin could feel the cleanness of the room. Everything, together, was cleansing Jack's soul for the next level. He'd always been a spiritual being, and now his spirit was being taken care of.

The speed of the serpents was so fast, their colors became a haze at times. At others, it was as if they were moving like snails. It seemed to Jack as if they were resting at these times; building up their strength for the next onslaught of energy.

The numbers, all the while, were mixed up with the melee. Their flickering beams of red and blue were like lightning crossing the path of a rainbow. The contrast was beautiful to the dying man. His mind was full of wonder and awe at what was truly there. The religions of the world and the non-believers each had it all wrong.

God was alive, well, and in the room with Jack.

He'd been right all along. God was inside all of us. We were all part of God. We were the numbers and the numbers were us. The numbers controlled everything. Therefore, everything was God. The cosmic serpents fell under the exact same definition. Their twisting numbers, controlled life.

He couldn't take his eyes off what he was seeing. It was moving in a way which made patterns. Jack could see these patterns and realized they too were equations. It made his mind open even more. This was the next level. When you figured this out, you were about to move on.

These patterns of the binary were created with the numbers. So, this was another realm beyond this existence. This outer pattern was becoming more and more visible in Jack's mind. The more he looked at it, the more he could see exactly what it was. It was like a wave flowing off reality. A ripple from what was happening here.

The more Jack looked, the more he understood. He felt as if he could truly see again. He felt as if he held this knowledge before but forgot it in this last equation of the life just lived.

His eyes focused further away from the ripple and saw more in the distance. As far as his eye could see, these warps of dimensions receded. It was like looking in two facing mirrors and seeing your reflection in both. They seemed to go on forever.

The first ripple was the only one Jack was able to clearly see. The rest blurred and were lost to the imagination. In the first, they were in a room, but it looked like a much older house. The craftmanship of the solid wood walls was impeccable. The window overlooked a large pasture peppered with oak trees.

In this room, Jack was looking at the mirror when something caught his attention. He saw a quick reflection of himself much older and dying. When he looked again, the face was gone. The vision changed.

In the next wave, he could clearly see himself as a strong young man in good health. He wore the clothes of a craftsman. Overalls and work-boots stained by years of use. He could also see Sue in the background. She was without a top and her youthful breasts were on display. Jack reveled in the sight. He loved his wife now and her body was perfect the way she was. However, this vision brought back wonderful memories of their youth and the time they spent together.

Jack could hear the family gong ringing in the background. He was faintly aware of Sue rubbing ointment on his skin. She kept dabbing a wet washcloth in his mouth to rehydrate him, but Jack didn't need it. He was done taking care of this pod. A couple of times, Sue's face appeared in the middle of his vision. He just figured it was another part of the ripples in time he was seeing.

He was faintly aware of his children and old friends coming for a visit but wasn't sure if it was just part of the vision. The colors and the numbers were everything. These people were all tied to him with the numbers. Their like numbers would come up again. Eternity was a very long time. There were a lot of ripples out there. Each of them held a shadow of this existence.

He didn't see his ancestors but understood that equation too. He would be seeing them soon enough. In the next ripple he settled in, he would be with his people once again. When he landed in that life, he would set off a series of ripples that would be just like this one. Each time a life ended, it began anew, with many dimensions running parallel to it.

Jack was excited to get moving on. He was done with this existence and had been for a long time. After the hardships his family went through, he was appalled how most others treated them. Their family had been shunned. Outcast for fears of an unknown nature. When you walked with death, people feared you.

It seemed like hours were passing as Jack stared at the cosmic display happening in his bedroom. He was alive inside, he just needed to get rid of this pod. He needed to shed it like a snake sheds its skin.

The gong continued its serenade the entire time. Jim was always dedicated to anything he did; today was no different. He would beat that gong in their family rhythm until Jack's last breath.

The melody flowed with the colors and numbers Jack was seeing. With the smell and taste, he realized this was how it was when you were first born. Everything smelled so clean and pure because you were. Every sound you heard was beauty because you never heard sound before. Not to mention, all your senses were brand new and working better than they ever would again.

Until your death, Jack thought.

He felt more tired than ever in his life. It seemed like the lack of sleep all week caught up with him at once. He'd been absorbed in the light and forgot about his own well-being. This exhaustion felt the same as going to an art museum all day. His body and mind were both tired on the same level.

His eyes fluttered but he fought the urge to close them. Sue was right there with her washcloth, this time rubbing it on her husband's forehead. She was saying something softly, but Jack could no longer hear her tone with his ears. All he could hear was the beautiful music coming from the gong.

He could fight it no longer; his eyes were just too heavy. He knew if he closed them for a few minutes, he would be good again. He still needed to say goodbye to Sue, once again. He needed to get his head straight before he took the long sleep.

Subconscious overtook Jack.

He knew the moment his eyes closed: Death took him.

Chapter 26

Sue stayed by Jack's side. She held her husband's left hand while Jim rhythmically beat the gong. This song was one long, continuous tune. Its melody played on all day long.

Shadows played across the room as the storm got stronger with each passing hour. The creatures formed by the darkness danced a beat to the melody Jim played. The entire scene was surreal to Sue. She never felt more like a spectator in her life.

The gravity in the room seemed to get denser. It felt like Sue was weighted down. It was difficult to move and even more difficult to speak. It didn't matter, though; she and Jack were communicating with their minds. She was telling him how much she loved him; he was telling her everything was going to be okay.

Sue glanced in the direction of her brother-in-law on occasion to see if there was any change in his behavior. Jim was behaving like a man possessed. His arms flung in a frenzy as the striker beat out his harmony. Sometimes when she looked, Jim was merely a blurred shadow. His movements became so intense, they were one. She wondered how her brother had the stamina to play this instrument, without break, for so long.

The music being created was hypnotic to the couple. It soothed their minds and took the stress of the situation away. The melody permeated their beings. They heard this song many times in the past, but this time it was played with perfection. With their minds, they spoke about the dedication Jim showed toward their family. They spoke about the role he'd be playing in the future of their family as well. While the two watched their brother perform, they silently praised him.

The first time Jack died, Sue felt his thoughts being ripped away from hers. It seemed like his energy rapidly disintegrated into blankness. She instantly felt empty inside. Half of her being was torn away. She instantly looked to her husband's eyes and saw exactly what she expected: the lifeless stare they held.

Jack didn't float above his room like the legends he'd heard. It was more like he was tethered to the Earth while being propelled into the cosmos. His energy was thrown backwards into a limitless abyss. All the while, he could see his bedroom, along with the three humans inside it. He could see his wife crying by his bedside while his brother beat the family gong.

The image got farther away until it was a pinpoint. Jack could barely make out the movements of the room as it faded into the distance. The farther he got away from the scene, the less he cared about the existence he was leaving behind.

Suddenly, he was rocketed back by the tether and slammed into his flesh pod. His death was replaced by a new breath of life.

His eyes fluttered weakly as they focused on his wife. She felt his energy return even before her husband took another breath. Sue was happy, for a moment, her husband had come back to her. The feeling was brief when she realized the truth: she would be going through the same thing again.

Jack tried to mouth some words but the only sound that came forth was a long sigh.

Sue could tell immediately their mental connection dissipated. She could no longer hear her husband's thoughts in her head. There was a faint whisper in the area of her brain where they communicated before, but it wasn't discernable. Her husband was too weak to communicate this way anymore. It was their last way of speaking and now it was lost.

Jack's grip tightened and loosened in that of his wife's repeatedly. He was going through a torrential flood of endorphins. DMT was being produced in his brain at a rapid pace, enhancing the effects of the drugs Jim gave him earlier.

After he died and came back, his people were there. Jack was seeing all his ancestors file through the room. One by one, his family made their presence known. His parents, brothers and sister were right by the bed. They stood as silent sentinels, preparing their boy for the next level. The cosmic serpents were like tour guides to the entities. They huddled them around and grouped them in certain areas. The serpents were in control here; the entities were mere numbers flowing through the equation.

Waves of people came and went. Ancestors Jack didn't know existed were everywhere. Some wore clothes from the past while others dressed from the future. The only thing in common was the familiar faces.

Jack was seeing other things too. The binary was giving him a full force of hallucination to carry him over to the next side. He was seeing creatures that didn't exist in this realm. There were moths in the room that were the size of dinner plates and had long tails. Some blue butterflies flew around that produced a light, making them look like flying lanterns.

There were cat-like creatures on the ground playfully chasing a round looking animal with no legs. It just rolled away every time one of the cats approached. Small humanoid beings were standing on objects throughout the room. They reminded Jack of yard gnomes with silvery clothes. A six-legged dog roamed in and out of the paintings. It chased a monkey with a human head who whistled show tunes.

Insects abounded in every color imaginable. Square serpents with long legs feasted on the bounty. Large birds with carpet texture wings flew in and ate the serpents. They, in turn, were consumed by a three headed, black lion.

Life was in full force inside the room. The ceiling was no longer visible. The sky was a strange color of purple and blue. Its calmness was soothing to Jack. It was all very inviting. There wasn't a single thing happening around the man which created fear in him. It was like he'd entered a magical emporium of fantastic reality.

The spirits began to multiply until it seemed like thousands occupied the room. Their presence was so close together, it made them appear as a shadow. As they merged, the beings began to take on the appearance of a single entity. This being didn't take on an identity at first. As it slowly merged, it started to become recognizable. It was a on a different level than the other beings. Its identity was itself.

When it did become something Jack could recognize, he became very happy. He waited all week and now the time was here. Jack's face broke into a painful smile. His swollen, cracked lips bled a bit as the movement broke them open.

Now, he could be truly complete. His son, Tommy, had come for him.

The boy materialized out of the shadows. As he emerged, he grew lighter and brighter until he was glowing like a lantern. His aura would have been blinding under normal conditions, but in Jack's state, it was just the right intensity. His son was the light; now, he'd be rejoining him. It was wonderful what he was seeing; it made his heart fill with elation. It had been too many years since he'd seen his boy. Their connection was one unlike any he ever shared with another human.

Jack realized the whole thing with Tommy was part of the equation. He saw it was a test on every member of the family. In the next life, Tommy may live to be over a hundred. It was all in the numbers you got for each existence. It was pre-written destiny concocted by the binary.

The entity was a combination of all the ancestors. When Jack died the first time, all his ancestors came to be a part of his transition to the next cycle. Now, they combined their energy into one being; the one who meant the most to Jack.

As Tommy approached the bed, the light bedazzled Jack. Sue, sitting on the bed next to her husband, didn't see the boy. She did see an orb of light hovering in the middle of the room. It was dim, but she could clearly see it. She felt its presence. She, too, had been close to Tommy. She'd met his father after his mother died. She never tried to replace his mother, but she was a damn good substitute. The two shared a very close relationship. Her bond with the boy, while not as tight as that of his father, had been solid.

The tight grasp of Jack's grip brought Sue's attention back to her husband. She could feel the cosmic energy in the room, but her husband was her priority. She looked to his eyes and saw an elation that made her smile. Jack's eyes were happy. He was looking directly at the orb of light. His grizzled lips showed the slightest, bloody smile.

Jack felt himself die again. He knew the moment he stopped breathing and thinking in the conscious. His thoughts were completely shifted into the subconscious. Sort of like a dream but one long continuous one. There was no need for physical form in the subconscious. Only pure thinking.

He once again was pulled outward but this time not so abruptly. He slowly ascended through the open roof, into the bluish, purple sky. He looked down at the room and saw Tommy hovering over his flesh pod. Sue was looking on in wonder at the sight she was seeing in front of her. The orb was like a special effect from the movies. It danced and moved three feet over the bed where the dying man was laying.

Jack could see and hear Jim, still beating the gong. His song was continuous since it began. It was a beautiful melody Jack could hear even as he ascended into the cosmos. It was a song the brothers heard in every existence they ever existed. This melody was tied to their DNA by the cosmic serpents who gifted the family with it.

Jack was again yanked back into his conscious like a bag of garbage thrown into the dump.

The serpents were in abundance as were the numbers flickering their codes. Jack could see it clearly as did his brother. The layers and ripples created by the numbers were still there. He could clearly see how they controlled everything; including his thoughts about the numbers.

Jim knew, that Jack knew, it was time. Tommy's light was so bright it took some of the colors away from the cosmic serpents. A few of them, closest to the boy, appeared white from the intensity.

Jim beat the gong a little louder and a bit faster. Both increased for about ten minutes while Jack clung to this existence.

For humans, it was always difficult to let go of the flesh pod. Even when they knew what awaited them, they still held on. It was all part of the equation. Gods way. It was their final solution to the equation which dominated this existence.

The room became a blur to the dying man as the colors and light mingled. This was so much for his brain. His thoughts were in overdrive. He wasn't stressed about the situation. It was like his existence was going two hundred miles an hour and he was buckled up for the ride.

The beating of the gong in the distance made the pace of reality faster. As the melody sped up, so did Jack's final minutes.

Jim could see it all. Music was an equation, just like everything. When you figured out the problem, you could make the music.

One last sense hit Jack. He smelled something burning and it was very close. He tried to look around but couldn't. His flesh pod no longer worked as he commanded. He could smell the smoke but the light in the room prevented him from seeing anything.

Suddenly, Jack's reflexes sat him bolt upright. He looked at his brother, who never stopped the tune for one beat. Their eyes locked and remained frozen for a moment. When the gaze was over, both men saw what was going on.

A fire had started at the foot of Jack's bed. It looked like the heating blanket malfunctioned. When they first smelled smoke, they would have been able to put it out swiftly. It wasn't the way it was meant to be, however. That wasn't the way the numbers added up. The gods had a completely different plan for this family.

Jack laughed inside when he saw the flames spreading. His entire bed was engulfed but he didn't feel a thing. It felt like he was in the middle of a movie and the end was coming up. He was more than ready. It was time to leave this pod, and this existence, behind.

His smoking flesh, accompanied by the banging gong, were the last things he sensed before Tommy took his hand.

Jack felt himself die, once again. He knew, this time, it was going to be final.

The moment Jack passed, the song ended.

It would be the last time Jim ever played the gong in his life.

Chapter 27

The smell of smoke was Sue's first warning. Somehow, she had been oblivious to the fire but now saw what was going on. Jack's bed was burning.

Sue was in a panic as the flames spread across her husband's bed. She frantically tried to smother the inferno with a blanket, but her efforts were futile. Within seconds, the flames licked their way up the drapes. The fire, having ignited the flammable bedding and drapes, was swiftly out of control.

She was happy when she heard the gong end but also knew what it meant. If Jack weren't already dead, the flames would surely have done him in.

Jim ran to the assistance of his sister. In his cosmic mind, a large creature, made of fire, was trying to drag his brother off. He was going to have no part of that. Jim grabbed the pitcher of water from the nightstand and threw it on the fire. It did little more than make a sizzling sound as it helplessly splashed the bed.

The angry phoenix turned its head and swooped a tail of fire toward Jim. He ducked just as the flames whipped a hole in the wall. This creature was strong. The shaman at Death Valley told him about it. This was the creature of rebirth. The brothers had cheated death this week: this creature wanted its share. Rebirth was the way; the path was clear. The end was over.

Sue grabbed the phone and called 911 as the room crackled with the spread of flames. The fire from the drapes spread to the ceiling. In mere minutes, the entire room was engulfed in the inferno. She saw her brother-in-law standing by the bed of her husband. Everything seemed surreal to the woman. Jim was staring at the flames while Jack's lifeless face looked to the same spot. The paintings enveloped the flames, adding to the insanity of their imagery.

Jim stopped his fight with the phoenix, immediately, when he realized what he was fighting against. This was the bringer of life. His brother's pod was empty now. This fire-god was taking Jack to the next round. He stood in awe as he watched the soul of his brother merge with that of the phoenix and pass through the window. The creature left an inferno in its fiery retreat, igniting the room further.

"Run!" Jim exclaimed. It was the loudest he ever yelled in his life. The house felt like it shook with the power of his voice. He knew he possessed superpowers right now. The drug, mixed with the intensity of the situation, made his entire being work at maximum potential. With this new strength and endurance, came fearlessness.

Sue didn't need to be told twice. It sounded like thunder in the room when Jim yelled. She ran straight through the open door into the small hallway. The entire house was fully engulfed with flames. She wondered briefly how this could have happened so fast and with such intensity. She hadn't even seen the fire start and now it was everywhere.

The thought didn't last long. She was on the brink of joining her husband in death. The idea didn't sound bad, but she wasn't a quitter. The thought of her kids and how much they would need her propelled her. Her grandchildren were amazing creatures to her; she wanted to see them grow up. If she let go now, she'd be letting down her entire family.

It was all the encouragement Sue needed. As she weaved her way through the cataclysm, she carefully counted her steps. A loud noise from behind made her turn around. She could see nothing in the rage that was once her house. Jim was briefly in her thoughts, but she couldn't think straight; the oxygen was getting sucked from her body, feeding the inferno. She turned back around but was disoriented. Breathing became painful as Sue fell to the floor.

Jim knew he had only one option. His family would never forgive him if he let his brother's body burn like this. Even though his soul was free, Jim still had respect for the pod of his brother. He reached through the flames, which encompassed Jack like a coffin, and ripped the burning blankets off the dead man. Beneath, Jack's skin was smoldering, but his pajamas were intact. Miraculously, the blanket absorbed all the fire. The flames hadn't yet reached his face so there was no sign that he'd been in a fire, except his extremely red skin.

Jim grabbed his brother in one swoop and raced out the door. The house was filled with fire. There was no sanctity nor time to pause. Jim hollered for Sue, to make sure she got outside, as he ran through the front door. He listened for a reply, but the storm of fire consumed his senses.

As soon as he was clear of the smoke, Jim lay the lifeless body of his brother in the driveway. He choked a few times, which felt like fire, and caught his breath. The clean air was the sweetest thing he ever took into his body. His mind was clearer than ever before. His thoughts were supercharged and ready for the next part of this adventure. He swiveled his head looking for Sue. When he didn't see her immediately, he became worried. This was the most feasible place for her to be. He ran around to the back of the house and was in awe at what he saw.

Smoke was billowing from the enclosure. Its thick black clouds were forming skulls which accumulated, forming one large skull. This skull was looking at the house as it burned to the ground. Jim got a very bad feeling in his gut when he saw this apparition. No matter how bad it was, he knew this was not the time for fear.

He became terrified about Sue; she should have been out here already, or in front of the house. He ran to the front one more time and looked to the lifeless body of his brother, laying on the driveway. Jim knew if she got out, she'd be here, by her husband's side. There was nothing Jim could do, now, but save his sister.

He raced back into the house, which was complete flames. He couldn't see much through the thick blanket of smoke and heat waves. The temperature was intense but somehow Jim didn't feel it. His mind was in a state that gave his senses extra strength. Between the drugs and the adrenaline, there was nothing that could stop him at this moment.

He ran toward the bedroom, but there was no way Sue could be in there and still alive. He started to head for the kitchen, but an outside thought came to his mind. She was in the laundry room. The idea was so strong he couldn't ignore it.

Jim knew these thoughts weren't his own. He was certain Jack was now a part of his conscious. It was why his mind was working so well. There were two brains working inside his one. His superpowers were doubled by the strength his brother was contributing to his being.

The laundry room, somehow, hadn't yet caught fire. It was located next to the pantry. The multitude of canned foods Jack and Sue put-up, over the years, acted as a buffer from the flames. The stored fruits and vegetables, they worked so hard canning, saved Sue's life.

The billowing black smoke told the tale: it was about to burst into flames at any moment. Jim dropped to the floor to escape the choking fumes. This is when he saw Sue. She was lying on the ground in a fetal position just three feet away. She was unconscious and lifeless.

Jim grabbed the woman by her shoulder and tugged. She moved a couple of feet and he tugged again. When he got her out of the room, the devastation of the house was fully upon them. The entire living room was now a pit of hell. Jim scanned for an exit but could find none that wouldn't put them right through the flames. He felt like his consciousness was becoming dimmer. He was beginning to focus on what was really happening, not his fantasy. The flames became hypnotic to him. They seemed to be dancing and singing a tune of destruction.

Suddenly, the phoenix reappeared. This time, it had two heads. It burst through what was once the ceiling and came face to face with Jim. Jim smelled the charred breath on the beast and tried to raise his hand. He felt like he was a prize-fighter with just one more round left in him. He was being cooked alive. The fire-god, ever so briefly, breathed a spark into Jim. For just a moment, his confidence came back to him.

A thought came to the man like it was kicked into his head. There was an access to the crawlspace in the closet just to his right. It was one of only two access points underneath the house. He considered that direction and indeed saw the door to the closet. It was closed and was burning but hadn't been completely engulfed by fire yet.

Jim kicked at the door and it flung open. It was littered on the inside with all those things that find their way into a closet. He started throwing all the closet stuff into the room. Each of the objects were smoking as he pulled them from their hiding spot. He was aware that he was fueling the fire but there was no option. When the vacuum came out, he saw what he was looking for. There, just as his mind told him, was a trapdoor.

Jim pulled the ring and the door reluctantly came free. A breath of fresh air hit the man in the face. It was refreshing and invigorating. The brief blast of oxygen was what his mind needed for the task at hand. He felt like he got shot with a dose of whatever he needed to activate his superpowers. The oxygen and the phoenix, together, revitalized him.

Jim poked his head into the opening to see what was happening. Again, the numbers were lining up for them. The floor was collapsed in the bedroom, but the rest was intact. He could see a foundation vent about ten feet away and knew it would be a good starting point.

He reached behind himself and grabbed Sue by the arm. He was worried he'd gotten to the woman too late. Her lifeless body felt like a rag-doll to the man. He shoved her into the four-square foot hole and pushed her away from the opening with his foot. When she was sufficiently out of the way, he slithered into the escape.

The crawl space was only three feet at its highest spot. Jim had never been under this house and didn't know his way. He scanned the darkness for a few seconds to get his bearing. He saw the living room floor was beginning to collapse: its fire was beginning to pour into the crawlspace.

He knew there wasn't much time. He grabbed Sue, under her arm, and dragged her to the nearest vent. At least there, they could get some fresh air as he looked for his escape. He put his face to the small opening and inhaled deeply. He looked to Sue but couldn't tell if she was breathing or not. He knew there was no time. More and more of the floor was collapsing into their exit. This was about to be their final resting place. If they were going to get out of this, it was going to take all his strength; mentally and physically.

Jim was wishing for a flashlight when another notion came to him. Just three feet to the left was a door leading out. He knew it must be Jack giving him these key bits of information. Wherever they were coming from, they were saving their lives.

The man found the door, instantly, but it was locked from the outside. He turned to get a good kick and noticed the flames. More than half the underneath of the house was now on fire. The inferno was swiftly moving in the direction of Jim and Sue.

He fell onto his back, raised his legs and kicked the door with all his might. The door didn't simply open, it flung away from the house by twenty yards. Anyone from the outside would have thought there was an explosion. Like his voice earlier, Jim rocked the house.

He popped out of the opening, turned back to the enclosure, and pulled Sue to safety. It was another five feet to drag her past the deck, which was about five feet high. The redwood of the patio just started to burn but wasn't yet fully engulfed.

As soon as they were clear of the deck and house, Jim picked Sue up and ran into the field, fifty feet away. When they were out of harm's way, he checked on his sister's condition. Her face was black from soot and she wasn't breathing. He checked her pulse and found none. Jim didn't panic in the least. He sensed everything happening was planned. All part of the numbers and the equation. How he reacted would be instrumental to their survival.

The rhythm of his CPR was the same as he hammered on the gong all day. With each breath he breathed into her lungs and each compression on her chest, Jim knew Sue was coming back to this existence.

He gave her CPR for nearly two minutes before the woman coughed loudly. She continued to cough until a large black ball of gack shot from her lungs. She gasped for breath before she could even focus her eyes. Tears and sweat streaked her face because of the coughing fit. She looked to Jim and choked out, "what happened?"

"The fucking house caught on fire. Jack's bed lit up and the rest of the house followed. I barely got you out. I swear man, I don't know what the fuck happened."

"Where's Jack?" Sue asked sheepishly. "Did he burn up in there?" The look on her face would have been comedy to Jim if he didn't know how important this was to his sister.

"Fuck no Sue, I got him out. He's in the front yard, man. After I dropped him, I saw you didn't get out. I went back in the house to get you. You were passed out in the laundry room. I thought you were a goner for sure."

"How long have I been out for?"

Jim was animated as he spoke: "I don't know man. You fucking died Sue! I don't know how long you were dead for; but you were dead. I brought you back to life right here where you're sitting right now. That crazy ass fire bird was right there. It came back for us; sensing our impending deaths. This time, it was not in our equation. It helped us escape. That shit was insane." His mind was racing trying to collect the thoughts he was having. As soon as Sue awoke, Jim looked to the house and saw the phoenix flying into the night sky. It seemed to look back to the immortal, promising a visit in the near future.

"That explains the dream I had," Sue said. "I was sitting in a rocking chair and Jack was sitting in one of his own. We were by this beautiful pond and we were fishing. We weren't talking or anything, we were just enjoying being next to each other. I felt like there were no worries in the world. I felt more at peace than any other time in my life. I shared a closeness with my husband as if we were one. I guess it wasn't a dream after all."

"We better go out front and check on him," Jim said.

He helped Sue to her feet. She was very unsteady, so Jim took one of her arms and draped it over his shoulder. It was then Sue notice the wound on Jim's body. Half his torso, the entire left side, was scorched. His clothes were melted to his skin and together they looked like a charred mess. Both his legs were burned to the knee and one of them was entirely melted into his torso wound. Sue knew Jim shouldn't be standing, he should be in shock. These were third degree burns. Wounds like this would require years of medical attention; if he survived this ordeal.

She tried to tell Jim about his wounds, but he shushed her. Sue was too weak and fragile to argue or complain about anything. She just wanted to be next to her husband. If she was going to die, it was going to be by his side.

The two hobbled into the front yard to see ten of the neighbors standing around Jack. The fire alerted them; they found the body in the drive when they came to investigate. One of the neighbors had a hose in his hand and was feebly trying to douse the inferno.

"Oh my God," one of them yelled when they saw Jim and Sue come around the corner. They all raced to the aid of their friends. The neighbors were shocked to see anyone emerging from this nightmare. Unfortunately, the two didn't look like they had a chance of survival. The neighbors took Sue from under Jim's care and led the weary woman to the side of her husband, at her insistence. Another group helped Jim to his brother's side. When they got him there, the younger brother collapsed in a heap of exhaustion. His adrenaline ran out. There was no more energy, nor resolve, left in him.

Jim heard the sirens coming from a distance. It reminded him of Sunday morning westerns when the cavalry came. They were coming to the rescue of the family. Just like in the movies, they were almost too late. Just in the nick of time to save the day, but not after a few casualties.

Sue became part of her husband's pod. She glued herself to her soul-mate and wouldn't let go. She had no strength left in her being. She barely survived this ordeal, which wasn't even close to being over.

The death of her husband was bad enough; now she had no place to live either. To top it all off, her and Jim were completely fucked up, physically.

The neighbors were trying to console Sue, but she heard not a single word they said. She was in her own world; one of grief and anger at the turn of events. She'd always been a good person to others. She didn't understand why bad shit always happened to her.

The fire department raced into action, but it was much too late. The fire consumed everything, leaving only the burning skeletal remains of the frame. Everything else was a pile of smoldering ash.

A few times, when the fire was raging, and even when it was going out, Sue could swear she heard that damn gong playing in the background. She thought it must be her imagination. She and Jack talked about this before. Whoever died first would send a signal to the other letting them know they were okay. Sue thought this ringing might just be that symbol.

Paramedics rushed to the aid of the three. Sue told them immediately; her husband was dead. He had cancer and it was over for him. "Please help my brother," she told them. "He saved my life and he needs a lot of care. Way more than me or my dead husband." Black-soot tears steaked down her face as she saw the condition Jim was in.

Sue pulled herself from her husband to take the hand of her brother-in-law. She saw the man was in shock. His face was pale and gray; he was sweating profusely and convulsing slightly. His blank gaze was held toward the heavens. As the paramedics readied him, all Jim could focus on was the full moon rising through a break in the swirling clouds.

She told her brother thank you just before the ambulance crew had him in their care. When they closed the door behind him, Sue burst into tears. It was bad enough losing her husband and house; she didn't know what she would do if she lost her brother too.

One of the neighbors came and soothed Sue. This had been her true companion in the area. Another ambulance arrived and attended to the woman. Her friend stayed by her side the entire time, giving words of spirituality. The things the neighbor told Sue made her calm down. She spoke of an inner strength and the need to use it. She talked about how we're all Gods and can do anything we put our minds and hearts to.

These were not new words to Sue. She believed this philosophy most of her life. She and this neighbor spoke of this spirituality many times in the past. She was just repeating their conversation but at a time the grieving woman really needed it. The bond with this neighbor tightened into one of family proportions with her empathy on this night.

The ambulance wanted to take Sue to the hospital, but she would have none of that, until she got Jack's situation in order. There was nobody else to take care of the devastation that just occurred. She would have to be tough and deal with it on her own.

Jack just died, and she was already having to take things on alone. She didn't like it, but knew it was now the way of her existence. She took hits off the oxygen bottle they gave her as she tried to keep control.

The fire chief asked Sue what happened. "I don't really know. We were in the room with Jack when he was dying and somehow his bed caught on fire. We were out of it, or something, and didn't realize until it was too late. We tried to battle the inferno, but it was no use. It spread so swiftly. I wouldn't have made it out if it weren't for my brother-in-law. He saved my life."

The chief seemed skeptical. Fires didn't start in occupied rooms and nobody noticed. Something seemed wrong to him here. He made a note to the investigators stating as such. This seemed like it could be insurance fraud or something else criminal. A guy dying of cancer was sure to rack up a good amount of bills. These people, with all their tattoos, couldn't be trusted. They were up to no good, he reasoned, the minute he saw the three.

The police arrived shortly after the fire was completely extinguished. Smoldering patches marked the spot where their home use to be. The first of two squad cars contained an officer who, once, tried to bully Jack. He didn't put up with this kind of behavior from a public agent and raised an issue with the department. It led to this officer being reprimanded. Now, this bully saw his chance for revenge.

The sergeant strode toward Sue and asked her in a very loud voice, "what the hell is going on here? It looks like a war zone."

His loud voice and uncaring demeanor made Sue angry. She was not going to let this asshole see her cry. "My husband is dead, that's what's going on here! My house just burned to the ground. That's what's going on here! My brother just got taken to the hospital because he burned over half his body, saving my life. That's what's going on here! So, Mister Bully man, I suggest you get the fuck away from me before you have serious problems!"

The cop went to say something but was interrupted by his lieutenant. The older man was in the other car and heard the entire exchange of words. He told his junior it would be best if he were to leave. "I have a handle on this," the lieutenant said. "You're just making the situation worst by being here."

"I will stay if I damn well want to," the officer shot back at his superior. "These people tried to ruin my life and now I want to know what they're up to."

The lieutenant lost his composure for the briefest of moments. "Listen here Daniels, get in your car and get the hell out of here before you lose your dignity. This lady is in pain and she doesn't want you around her. Now leave before I have you escorted away."

The sergeant threw his arms in the air and paced back to his cruiser. He got in, slammed the door and sped off in a cloud of dust and pebbles.

The lieutenant approached Sue to apologize. It was too late. She had passed out and was now lifeless on the driveway. She'd fallen, examinant, crumpled on top of her husband.

The lieutenant was saddened by the scene. It looked like two lovers who laid down for a much-needed rest. He saw the love the lady had for her husband. It made a tear form in his eye.

Suddenly, and a bit late, the sky opened like a faucet. Torrential rain fell, soaking the cop and washing away his tears. He stood momentarily, before walking back to his car.

He wondered if his wife would treat him like this in the same circumstance.

Chapter 28

Jack was aware of his surroundings the entire time, but it seemed like he was watching himself in an old movie. The colors weren't quite right, nor the lighting. Everything seemed to be happening slow. All the while, his existence was being pulled like taffy at an incredible pace.

He sensed he was again being pulled into the cosmos while his conscious was still tied to the Earthly existence. He knew he had a purpose. There was something he had to do before he could let go.

His focus was going in and out. It would be a fine point at one moment and then full screen the next. He was seeing things from a distance and then close. He knew there were forces pulling at him and he wanted to let go. He sensed the beauty of where he was going. At the same time, he knew he must get this done. His family needed him; if just for this one last moment.

A few times, he saw the doom in his wife and brother. They got themselves trapped and were sure to perish. Jack knew the house better than anyone. It was his thoughts that guided his brother and wife to safety.

He was in a place of numbers. Everything in front of him were numbers. He could clearly see a grid surrounding reality. This dimension was laid out in numerical squares. Jack realized this was what humans perceived as destiny. It wasn't destiny at all; life was mapped out, for every living creature, in the binary. Just like a video game.

It wasn't difficult for him to jump between these grids once he could see them. He simply jumped into the grid of his brother and gave him solutions to his equations. What they talked about since their youth was partly true. You did have the ability to pass to your loved ones, but only briefly. It was possible with combinations of the grid.

Few humans ever did this. It took strong willpower to stay behind when you knew what was next. The ones who did were truly dedicated to their families. They were ones who legitimately saw the way. Their actions would be noted by their grade on the equation of that life.

When Jim was being burned, Jack could clearly see the cosmic serpents getting a little crazy. Their movements intensified like they were the ones receiving the pain. Their writhing motions made Jack think maybe even Gods were vulnerable. He understood now; each of us had our own pair of cosmic serpents. They were tied to us, creators of our lives. Some would call them our aura or our energy, but they were the individual god in each of us. They were our eternal spirit, living outside the pod.

Jack knew Jim was still on the trip they'd taken. He was showing super-human strength. The flames didn't harm him in the least, while he was playing hero. He'd been strong and got Sue out of the inferno. Jack was proud of his brother. He was always there for the family and now, once again, he saved the day.

When Jim got Sue out of the house, the woman had been dead for six minutes. She succumbed to the toxic smoke even before Jim reached her. After getting lost in the smoke, she found her way to the laundry room with the guidance of Jack's thoughts.

He knew how to reach his wife just as his brother. While Jim was giving her CPR, Jack threw his whole energy into the lifeless woman. For him, it was jumping to another grid like hopscotch. Sue was hit with this jolt, making her pulse and breathing restart. Life was slammed back into her flesh pod. The first thing Sue thought when she awoke was Jack just passed through her. Their love was true. She knew her husband's energy. Although barely beating death, Sue felt a light in her heart from the experience.

When Jim half-carried his sister to the front yard, Jack was right there on the other side of her. His aura helped keep the woman upright. It kept Jim from falling at the same time. When they got out front, the vitality of the crowd was too much for Jack's spirit. The extra energy was like static from multiple radio stations. It polluted his thoughts and made it clear his purpose was almost over. He was here to help his people; nothing more.

With the onslaught of the others, Jack departed.

His spirit raced through the cosmos he recently became familiar with. Passing every galaxy and solar system, Jack remembered the information learned long ago. He knew the names of these constellations. It was part of his schooling since the beginning. His last life, as a human on Earth, was one where he held no memories of the past lives. It was an existence lived blindly in search of who you truly were.

He was happy to be back with the Wisdom. It was all around him. Wisdom was everything. It was the numbers and the DNA combined. It was the creator of everything that happened in the universe. It was life and it was lifelessness.

Jack wasn't alone in this space. There were other beings just like him who were an energy waiting for its next assignment. It was a small in-between period all beings who passed the equation got. Some could even go back to their last existence for a bit but not in the same capacity. If they returned, they would be a ghost of their former self. Their existence would be one of voyeurs who couldn't control anything. A voyeur content with what played in front of them until their energy would fade away, into the next existence.

Most of these beings, who returned, were humans. They were tied to their possessions and their wealth. Family members might return briefly, but greed and revenge are what truly keep ghosts hanging around.   Animals had no real reason for returning to their former lives. They saw the beauty in the cosmos and understood the cycle of life. A few did return; those pampered by their human "owners".

Before he was reassigned to his next existence, Jack would have some time getting caught up with the Wisdom. Sometimes it was days, years or centuries before the rebirth took place. None of it mattered. Time was a concept created by the binary. It didn't exist in this dimension.

Jack already knew what his next life would be. For the next thousands of years, he would be with his family, at the white house. Tommy would be there. Jack's real parents, brothers and sister all would be present. Many of their ancestors and offspring would join in the party. This was a special time for their clan. All the members who survived multiple levels were doing particularly good at solving equations. They were being rewarded with a reunion that would only cease when it ceased. In the meantime, the clan would be part of writing the equations. The binary had taken notice of them.

Before Jack went completely into the next, he felt there were some things to be done on Earth. He thought his mission was complete, but obviously something changed. It was all part of it. He knew it wasn't a good idea to return, but he also knew Jim and Sue needed him. Their children needed their mother now more than ever. It was important for him to help those who had always helped him.

Jack felt like he was in a strange tube. It was like two cheerleader horns were together on the big ends. He was in the middle of these two large openings considering the smaller openings at each end. The cosmos was still all around him; this was an alternate reality super-imposed on top of it.

The scene through both openings was ripping Jack apart. To one side was the white house. Everyone was on the porch. They were waving to him with smiles on their faces. On the other side was the house burned to the ground with Sue and Jim laying in the front yard. The paramedics were attending to them, but it wasn't looking good. Jim was badly burned while Sue was smoked from the inside. Both were going to need medical attention for a very long time to come.

The cylinder he was in pulsed in a wave-like manner. Ripples of time were coming from his being. It seemed to change reality just slightly with each ripple. Galaxies which were circular were now oval. Black holes would appear and then disappear with each wave. Jack knew he was in worm hole.

He was just torn on which way he wanted to go.

The cosmos was a beautiful thing to observe. Jack remembered its essence like a long-lost lover. When in the cosmos, you can truly feel the connection you have to it. You aren't an individual, just as the universe isn't either. It takes every grain of energy to make the universe. The universe is in each of us. Each of us is the universe.

The family is also a beautiful thing. Especially what Jack was seeing on the other end of his worm hole. He had eternity to be with family. His people who were alive now needed his help. The two scenes in front of him made up his mind. He would return to Earth until it was safe for his people. Then he could move on in peace.

He raced to the end of the tunnel with his thoughts. He realized he was now only thought. Pure energy. His true form.

Jim was in Stanford University burn unit. Jack was there his first day and saw the shock his brother was in. He entered his mind, having a nice talk with his younger brother. Jim was still tripping. He would be until his ordeal ended. His mind was in the hallucinogenic frenzy when he slipped into this coma. His mind wouldn't reset until he woke up. It would all be part of his healing process.

The brothers agreed it would be a good thing. They marveled at the fact 'the plan' worked. They merged their minds into one. Jack came back, and Jim opened his thoughts to him. Without their connection, it never would have been possible.

Jack gave his energy to his brother for the duration. The doctors put the patient in the American Medical Journal over his incredibly speedy healing. It took a fraction of the time they predicted for him to recover completely. Jim had third degree burns on sixty percent of his body. The doctors put him in a coma when, suddenly, Jim came out of it on his own. His burns were healed completely. The doctors, upon admission, opted not to do skin grafts. His recovery had been so good, even the first days, they thought it unnecessary. Even his tattoos remained intact and were clearly visible through the non-existent scarring.

Sue stayed by her brother-in-law's bed every day he was at the hospital. Healing for her wasn't as dramatic. It was difficult on her at first, but she too healed extremely fast. Her lungs were badly burned. It took a month of being on an oxygen tank, but she was salubrious again. She, too, had many dreams of her husband. While she was healing, his visits were nightly. As soon as subconscious came, so did the dreams. She was sad, over time, when they began to diminish. Jack's appearance in her subconscious was less frequent as time went by. The healthier she got, the less Jack appeared. He told her from the beginning: it would be the way.

The night before Jim awoke was the last time Sue ever dreamed of Jack. They were riding in a car. Sue was driving. Jack kept telling her it was time. They had to get there. He had to go. His time was up. The white house awaited, and he was ready.

The morning after the dream, when Sue touched her brother's hand, he woke up.

Chapter 29

Jim's coma was anything but ordinary. He was in a perpetual state of dreams the entire time. His brain provided entertainment while his body mended itself. He was aware of what was going on around him; he just couldn't interact with the others.

He was conscious and appreciative of Sue's daily visits. At least once a week, his nephews and niece would come. They would pour their hearts out to Jim about the death of their father and about their lives. The uncle would silently lay there, listening and thinking about every word they said.

Another visitor the entire time was Jack. Jim felt his older brother inside his pod. Both their spirits inhabited Jim's body at the same time. It's what made him heal so fast. Their combined energy supercharged the flesh pod. His body never worked this well when there was only one inhabitant. Jack's death brought life back into his brother.

Jack was a welcome addition to dampen the sorrow Jim was going through. With his family inside him and around him, he was far from being alone. He was in the place that was meant to be. The numbers, once again, lined up and he ended up here, severely burned. He fully accepted his fate; like he did his entire life.

Jim thought about the events leading up to his hospitalization often. The week he spent with his brother was awesome. They reconnected with the Wisdom and each other in the process. He remembered so much and learned even more.

He really didn't think about what he'd do when he got out. He'd always been a take care of business kind of guy and now would be no different. He didn't think of his life outside the hospital at all. His thoughts were here, at this moment. The time he spent here were in a self-absorbed inner meditation. He truly realized who he, and his family, was during this time.

If he weren't in this subconscious, his brother would have been gone long ago.

As it were, however, Jim did go into the coma and absorb all the knowledge. The things he and his brother learned throughout the week were too much for the conscious mind. It was the deepest meditations possible that allowed the knowledge to sink in to his being. When he would emerge from his deep sleep, he would know things humans lost knowledge of, millennium before. Wisdom of the Gods and the universe were once again his. When he awoke, the circumstances would determine what he did with that information.

Jim was tripping balls the entire time he was unconscious. The last dose was one that wouldn't wear off until consciousness returned. If it weren't for his history with hallucinogens, he would have thought he lost his mind. It wasn't the case, though. He knew he was tripping and using much more of his brain than ever before. It helped having Jack inside him. His partner on the long journey was still on board for the ride.

Jim knew, if he could just open his eyes, he'd be out of this coma and back on his feet. Something kept telling him not to do that, though. He sensed it was Jack who was trying to keep him bedridden. Whatever the reasoning was, Jim was in no hurry to get back out to the real world. He was more than happy to stay on this journey in the inner depths of his mind.

Every time he was ready to enter the conscious, Jack would stop him. He would explain how patience was going to be of the utmost importance. It was like when you made an oil painting and had to let the paint set. Jack explained to Jim: his mind needed to set, to let the knowledge soak in. If he awoke too early, knowledge and healing would be lost.

So, Jim became content to wait it all out. A couple of his nurses were attractive women in their fifties. Jim, in his thoughts, looked forward to the sponge baths these women provided. He even started to look at them as family of sorts. They were here to take care of him and it was obvious they cared.

Both nurses were amazed at the number of tattoos the burn victim had. His entire body was covered. They were washing him, daily, and felt it was okay to ogle the man. Neither had ever seen anyone with so many tattoos; especially in such good quality after the accident.

His routine never got boring because his mind was so active. His perception of things made him think he was in another dimension in his head. He didn't need to have his eyes open. He could see around the room and even around the hospital. Many times, while he was unconscious, he left his body and wandered around the empty spaces. Jim realized, at these times, that a burn unit was a very desolate place. Only nurses, doctors and patients were there. There were some visitors, but not many of them. Every patient was in a coma or coming out of one.

He tried to leave the hospital with his mind but couldn't get past the cement walls. There were forces that kept him from going too far. Like a radio signal, there were limitations.

Another man in his room was in the same predicament. He was burned more extensively than Jim. Eighty percent of this man's body was burned, including his face. Healing wouldn't be so easy for his roommate.

Jim went to this man mentally to try and help. At first, the man's mind was warped into an unintelligible mass of chaotic thought. Jim thought the fire must have scorched his body and mind. His thoughts were not sane. This man had lost his mind.

After three weeks, Jim was able to communicate with the other man one day. His name was Roy. He was in a steam explosion. His mind was still scrambled but Jim told him it would get better. He told his roommate that every day there would be improvement until the day he walked out of here. "Tomorrow you will progress, not regress," Jim told him, daily.

The words put Roy at ease. His family completely abandoned him after his accident. His only visitor was the comatose man in the bed next to him. He was the only person Roy could communicate with. During his stay, Jim saved this man's life with his kindness and respect.

When the day finally came, Jim knew it. He hadn't slept once during his recovery. Every moment wasn't awake nor asleep. He was in a kind of limbo between the conscious and the subconscious. That place you go right before you go to sleep. Jim realized this was the place that healed your mind.

Jack confirmed Jim's notion. Today was the day he would be waking up. He'd served his purpose. He passed the math test thrown his way; it was a difficult one, but Jim scored well. He, and Jack, could now move on.

It wasn't dramatic when it happened, it just did. Jim simply opened his eyes. His vision was a bit blurry without his glasses, but he could see the room looked just like he saw it in his mind. Unfortunately, it was two in the morning and nobody was around to see his awakening.

He was a bit disappointed by this turn of events. He would have liked to have one of his nurses there at the moment. He envisioned them being so happy he was awake, they would smother him in hugs and kisses.

He laughed at his silliness. Jim didn't care if he made a production or not. He was a guy who lived his life making things. Whatever he created, it was never for glory. Jim was a guy who could paint something, throw it away, and not care. The true spirituality came from the act of creating; not showing.

Jim's mind was clearer than ever before in his life. He felt like he'd just been born. The hallucinogen wore off the minute his eyes opened, shifting the warped senses into pinpoints. Wisdom permeated from his being.

Jack was gone from his brother's mind the moment consciousness returned. The older brother had a mission, and, upon awakening, it was accomplished. He had his own existence to get back to.

Jim laid there for another six hours until the shift change happened. He stayed awake the entire time. Sleep wasn't going to come to the man for a very long time. He tried to stand or even shift a bit, but his muscles didn't cooperate. He knew he wasn't going anywhere anytime soon. His body was in atrophy.

When a day shift nurse came in, she was shocked to see Jim awake. "Why didn't anyone notice you earlier?" she exclaimed. "How long you been awake for?"

Jim's voice was hoarse and dry. He was unable to speak immediately. He tried to lift his hand to point at the water pitcher but lacked muscle control. He could move his head, slightly; it was the only part of his body which cooperated. He tilted his head sideways, toward the pitcher of water on the nightstand.

The nurse understood and poured Jim a glass. She held the room-temperature liquid to his lips and poured it past the dryness. Jim felt the water course through his body. He felt like a tree watered for the first time in months. Its feeling in his parched body was euphoric. That one gulp of water made him feel alive.

"Where's my family?" Jim asked in a slight whisper. The water alleviated some of the dryness, but he had a very long way to go.

"Don't you worry about them, Sweetie. They've been coming here every day you've been here. You got more visitors in the last two months than all the other patients combined, all year."

Sue was walking into the room when she heard the nurse talking. Her heart raced a bit at the prospect. She was instantly excited. Her visit was early today. It was the first time she was here before ten in the morning. She promised her kids she'd go to lunch with them but wanted to still get in a full visit with Jim. She chuckled at the situation. She realized; there was no coincidence in this existence. Destiny was programmed numbers.

Sue all but pushed the nurse out of the way. She'd been waiting for this day a very long time. The joy was apparent on her face.

Jim came back from the dead; just like she had. He was going to be with his family, once again.

Everything was going to be alright.

Chapter 30

Within three days of waking, Jim was ready to leave the hospital. He was frustrated with two of the doctors and some nurses. They treated him like an invalid. He felt great, better than ever before. His skin was healed completely. The hair was beginning to grow back. There was no pain and the scarring non-existent.

He was most amazed with his tattoos. They withstood the ravages of fire and looked better than ever. The outer layers of skin regrew. It was fresh: the skin of a newborn. The new dermis enhanced the images. They were brighter now than before, even when first done. He finished his body-suit over twenty years before. As was the case with all tattoos, there had been fading, but now they were solid.

There were a couple images on his body Jim didn't remember having before. There was a dragon on one calf which once held a gypsy girl. His entire back was a Hannya before the fire, now it was a phoenix. He thought about it extensively but had no explanation; except he was losing his mind. He figured the fire must have done something to his memory, making him remember things the way they weren't. If the fire was anything like they told him, his brain most likely boiled in the inferno that consumed his body.

Jim had the run of the hospital. The two nurses who took a liking to the man were always by his side. They, for a moment, had someone to break up the monotony of their lonely job. They were friendly and flirtatious with their "miracle man". If it were only those two nurses working at the burn unit, Jim could have stayed much longer. Unfortunately, there were about ten other employees, too; some of them weren't so nice to the "disruptive man".

The final breaking point with the hospital came on the fourth day. Becky came for her daily visit and brought burgers from a spot down the road. When she entered the building, the head nurse tried to degrade the visitor in front of the other nurses. This was becoming ordinary for Becky on her daily pilgrimages to see her uncle. For whatever reason, the main nurse had a grudge against her since the first visit. Becky was a sane person who read people well. She was only here to see her Uncle Jim, nothing more.

The other nurses stood around, appalled, as the large woman reprimanded Becky by cracking jokes on her. The loud talking and cackle of laughter echoed through the hallway, alerting Jim to the situation. Becky had told him about the way the head nurse treated her. He confirmed the story, but from his own perspective. The nurse, obviously, didn't care about the patient who made the miraculous recovery. It was the opposite: she was filled with animosity for Jim and everything associated with him.

Upon hearing the ruckus, Jim knew one of the voices was Becky. He walked down the hallway, as fast as possible, with his hospital gown flowing behind him. The open back provided a draft, seeming to propel him even faster. His muscles were sore, but his niece needed him. The closer he got, the more he heard what was going on. The nurse was berating Becky for bringing food to her uncle.

He'd gone to investigate and found the argument heating up. The nurse was ripping into Becky while the others tried to talk reason into their co-worker. He burst into the area containing the nurse's station and cleared his throat noisily.

The nurse stopped her tirade, abruptly, while the others gawked with a look of relief. She looked to the noise which interrupted her, rudely, she thought with anger.

Becky wasn't one to lie down and take verbal abuse from anyone. Especially from a bully with no reason. She was standing a few feet away, holding her ground with her head high. Her fist was just about to bust the nurse's lip when her uncle cleared his throat. The distraction to the nurse gave pause to Becky's defense. Jim thought today might be the day his niece snapped. He got between the two women, trying to regain peace. There was no reprieve or calm; the head nurse verbally attacked Jim, instead.

She accused him of everything she could think of. From thinking he was better than everyone else to him always getting his way. She vented every frustration she had with the man. Jim saw the outrage in her face. He saw it wasn't so much about him and Becky; this lady hated her job and hated her life. She was angry with the world. He tried to explain to her; he had good insurance and was paying for this stay. He was the one in charge, not the nurse. If he wanted burgers, it was his choice. When she told him, he couldn't go outside to eat, he realized what the fight was about. This is when Jim spoke his mind, loudly. This lady was a control nut.

"You work for me! I'm a grown man! I don't know who you think you are to talk to me or my niece like this. There's no need to throw this hatred at us. Whatever you think you're doing here, you're wrong."

The nurse raised her hand as if to strike Jim. Her eyes were red as she glared at the man in front of her. Her swing was stopped short by a doctor interrupting, coarsely. "Nurse Tatum is there a problem here?"

"Yes sir," she replied with a stammer. "These two are trying to get smart with me."

"Come on, man," Jim exclaimed. "My niece was bringing me food and you started a big fight over it. I'm not in the wrong here. Neither of us wanted problems. We just wanted to eat.""

"You're in the wrong if I say you are, boy," the nurse growled.

Jim took a defensive stance at the words. This woman was much bigger than he was and now she entered intimidation mode. The doctor interjected his thought, "I'm sorry sir. We don't have many conscious patients here. Our rules were put in place long ago. They don't always reflect the times. Our staff doesn't always have the best people skills."

The nurse was nodding her head, dashboard style, with the doctor's words until the end. "What do you mean I have no people skills?" she blurted.

"It's not an insult Nurse Tatum," the doctor said bluntly. "Anyway Jim, we don't allow food in here. I'm sorry. You're welcome to go outside and eat if you like. You're not a prisoner here."

"Thank you doctor," Jim said. "I'll take you up on that offer." This was the younger of three doctors working at this facility. He and Jim formed a bit of a relationship in the last two days built on respect. The other doctor was older and had more of the Nurse Tatum style of bedside manner. He too was obviously a control freak. Luckily, he was the doctor on duty the day Jim awoke but hadn't been back since.

He wedged himself away from the position the nurse had him in. He didn't even look at the woman as he took Becky's hand and headed for the door. He had no time for this nonsense. His niece was here, and he really enjoyed her company. He was looking forward to this visit all day and wasn't going to let Nurse Tatum ruin it.

They made their way through the halls which led to an open entryway. A three-foot Christmas tree was sitting lonely in the corner. A week had passed since the holiday. Obviously, somebody here was trying to hold onto its festive atmosphere. Its fake branches hung sadly with the weight of a single strand of lights. Jim thought it was the loneliest thing he'd ever seen.

It was the third time Becky came for a visit in the last four days. The day Jim awoke, she came immediately upon hearing the news. Her brothers came that day, too, but she was the only one who returned since. Her uncle reminded Becky of their dad. The loss was still fresh after two months. She needed the connection which had been taken away. Being with her uncle was great therapy and even better company.

As they walked to the car, Jim dipped into the bag of food. It smelled so good and his appetite was enormous. The food here wasn't so nice. The cook was used to making nourishment that could be force fed to the comatose. He wasn't going to cook up a big ass burger for the only conscious patient.

There were no benches, grass, or anything else making this place nice. It was simply a flat fronted building with a parking lot out front.

Jim still didn't walk at full speed. His strength was eighty percent since the atrophy began to wear off. He'd been hard at work for the last days trying his best to get back into shape. He didn't want to spend his entire life here: not even a couple more days, or hours.

Becky's car was parked at the far side of the expanse. A large oak tree stood as a lone sentinel over the near empty parking lot. They sat in the front seat and dug into the food.

As they ate their burgers, the conversation flowed freely. These two were friends for a very long time. The day Becky came into the family, they were close. "What's happening with your recovery," she asked.

"It's kind of strange. I feel good. I don't have any scars even. The doctors are in awe. The last couple days, some specialists from other places have come in and taken pictures of me. They say I'm a miracle. The first person in written history who healed their burns like this. I feel like they don't want me to leave. It's like they have an agenda for me."

"I kind of get that idea too," Becky acknowledged. "That nurse seems to have it in for you. What's her issue?"

"I have no idea. She's nice to the other nurses. She just has a grudge against me. I think, maybe, she doesn't like tattoos. She's been treating me like crap since I woke up. I've been watching, and she holds apathy for these other people. She really thinks she's better than them. She's fucking mean to these people. What she doesn't realize is they're conscious of everything she's doing to them. Whatever her issue, I'm sick of it. I'm ready to get out of here today and get on with my life."

"I don't blame you for wanting to leave. It seems annoying. The vibes are definitely not good here."

The two talked for the next thirty minutes. They slowly ate the burgers and their fill of the fries. When they finished, the garbage went back into the bag and Jim crumpled it up for the trash. Becky brought a joint and to the merriment of her uncle, sparked it up. Two months passed since he smoked pot. He knew: not only did he really need it, it was going to be very potent.

The worries of earlier were forgotten as the smoke filled his lungs. It tasted so sweet to Jim, like a long-lost friend. He was instantly high after the second hit; something that hadn't happened to him in a very long time. He wasn't one to stop, however. Jim loved to smoke. After a couple of hits for Becky, Jim puffed the rest to his head.

When there was a quarter of the smoke left, a loud voice barked at Jim from the open window of the building. It was over eighty feet away, but the two could clearly hear what was being shrieked at them by the head nurse. "What the hell are you doing out there?" The window slammed shut with such force, the two thought it might break. About thirty seconds of silence followed, only to be interrupted by the head-nurse again.

The woman came out of the building, crossed the parking lot and stormed to the back of the car. The two watched her with a careful eye as she made her approach. Then, she was right by them; standing with her hands on her hips and staring at the man. "That is enough with you mister. You need to get your ass inside right now. What you are doing is illegal and I am a law-abiding citizen."

"Easy now Tatum," Jim said with a bit of mockery in his voice. "I'm an adult and I'll do what I want."

Jim had his arm resting on the windowsill. The nurse slapped it below the elbow, making him pull it away. The blow had enough pressure to hurt pretty good. Jim opened the door and stepped out. The joint was still in his hand and he didn't once stop smoking it. He stood defiantly in the face of Nurse Tatum, his gown billowing in the wind.

She went to slap the joint out of Jim's mouth, but he was much too fast for her. He ducked away from the blow and the next two the bully swung. When she struck out the fourth swing, Jim saw his opening. He hit her with all his strength right on the ball of her shoulder. He knew from experience what this blow would do. The nurse crumbled to her knees with the blinding pain. She cradled her useless arm while trying to regain a bit of control. Jim knew her mind was filled with stars. His strength hadn't been one hundred percent, but it was good enough.

Becky filmed the entire scene on her phone. Her uncle tried to avoid a conflict, but the woman pushed him too far. She had the evidence if anyone wanted to call the cops or start some bullshit.

Unfortunately, someone did call the police. One of the other nurses followed the head nurse to make sure there was no trouble. The two were friends. She didn't want anything happening that she may have been able to prevent. When Jim struck the head nurse, her coworker called 911. What she didn't know, was that Tatum called the cops when she saw Jim smoking pot outside. The second call in two minutes in this sleepy area was cause for major alarm.

The police arrived in minutes. Jim tossed the roach to prevent any more problems. He didn't see there being problems for him, anyhow. He was defending himself. However, he knew from his experience; the cops could be very prejudice people. Especially toward someone with multiple tattoos.

As soon as the cruiser pulled up, Jim knew there was going to be problems. Their family had issues with this guy, going way back. "What's going on here Deb?" the sergeant said to the head nurse.

"That son of a bitch just hit me bro," the nurse said. She was on her knees, still cradling the arm. Tears were running down her repugnant face.

Jim knew he was in trouble. The look on the cop's face confirmed it. "Did you really hit my sister asshole?"

"Hey man, she was attacking me. I was defending myself. You would have done the same."

"Why were you attacking this patient?" the cop asked his sister. "I can tell he's one of your residents." The sergeant waved his hand at Jim for emphasis. Jim, dressed in his hospital gown, looked very vulnerable.

"Because I came out here and he was smoking pot," replied the nurse. "I told him to stop and he just hit me. That devil weed made him crazy."

"That isn't true in the least," Becky jumped in. "I taped it all. I have proof you're lying."

"Well let me just see that, darling, and I'll decide for myself," the cop said with a note of flirtation. He reached out his hand and tried to take the device from Becky.

She was recording the entire time. "I'm not stupid. You can get my phone with a court order. Until that time, officer, fuck off."

The cop looked at Becky for a moment blankly. It was obvious he was trying to decide his next move. When it came, he said, "have it your way." The sergeant walked back to his vehicle and got in the driver's seat. He fiddled with something on the dash. Becky thought he was probably calling for help. Whatever it was, she had the proof on her phone.

The cop was in his cruiser for more than five minutes. Becky began to think he was getting a search warrant. She stopped taping for a minute to send the video to her mother and explain what was happening. She knew if there was a warrant, this video would disappear. This way, at least she had a copy of the scenario.

Another patrol car rolled up with lights and sirens blaring. Becky thought they were putting in good theatrics for her video, which she was now live-streaming. When they stopped, the two new cops got out with weapons drawn. Both nurses went back inside when the first cop retreated to his car. They were watching the drama from the safety of the building.

The first cop on the scene paced angrily to Becky and got in her face. He was so close she could smell the stench of donuts and cigarettes on his lips. "Fuck you, darling," he said with a sneer.

The officer spun around and grabbed Jim by his arm. The other two cops put their weapons away and ran to get Jim confined. They threw him onto the car and roughly handcuffed him. When he was restrained, they dragged him toward the first police cruiser. His sandaled feet scraped the ground, leaving a small skid mark behind.

The two cops roughly threw Jim into the backseat and slammed the door. Becky was looking on in horror. She still had the wits to keep taping but couldn't believe the scene in front of her. It was like a movie where nobody won.

The first cop spun on Becky and in one motion had her phone in his grip. "I'll be taking this. Court order, you fucking cunt." The cop dropped the phone onto the asphalt and smashed it with his boot. He looked at Becky with a crazed look that frightened her. She could see this man was not one to be trusted. He looked like a serial killer, she thought.

"Why are you taking my uncle?"

"We've been looking for him for months, girly. Your uncle killed four people and left the scene of the crime. I don't think you'll be seeing him any time soon." The cop laughed as he walked away. When he got to his car, he turned back and yelled across the distance: "One more thing. Fuck you." He laughed one last time as he got in his car. The cop sped off with Jim looking helplessly at his niece through the back window of the cruiser.

The other two cops looked at the woman briefly, got in their car, and drove away. Becky stood in the lot trying to figure out what just happened. She knew she needed to get things taken care of but first she needed to decipher it all. She reached into her purse to grab her phone but remembered immediately: it was no more. She really needed to talk to her mom and get some advice for this situation. Nothing like this ever happened to her before. It felt like a strange dream she couldn't wake-up from.

This time she saw the nurse coming at her. The large woman had murder in her face. "I told you to get the fuck out of here, you witch," she yelled at the stunned woman.

Becky had no time for this kind of anger. She wasn't one to have physical conflicts with people, unless necessary. She just wanted to live in harmony with her surroundings. She got in her car and drove off. When she looked in the rearview mirror, she saw nurse Tatum was still yelling after her, like a lunatic.

When she pulled out of the lot and back on the highway, Becky realized many things. First, their family just completely changed once again. A new ordeal was here just like the river of others before it. They would all have to pull together to get through this one, as they always did in the past.

She also realized: these were little equations to solve. Their solution would bring you to the next puzzle. Life was about this. Strife was not the only conundrum, either. Happiness, solitude and every other emotion or trait had an equation.

How you dealt with these equations, and retained its knowledge determined your level of wisdom. Everything was a mystery, waiting to be solved.

Life, itself, was a puzzle we spent a lifetime trying to figure out.

Chapter 31

Like the rest of his life, the numbers aligned for Jim. Sometimes it would be positive, others negative. The outcome was how you dealt with the situation. Today, he knew, there would be many equations to solve.

As they drove down the highway, Jim had nothing better to do than stare out the back window of the police cruiser. It was his first time being arrested since he was a young man. The situation felt alien to him. He'd gone through so much, now he had to deal with this.

He saw a news crew pass in their high-tech van. Unknown to Jim, the local news station was headed to the hospital for an interview with the man who miraculously healed. The same nurse who started the strife with Jim was the same one who tipped off the media. She had hopes of financial gain, but it turned out much different for her in the long run.

Becky also saw the KCRA van going in the opposite direction. She knew there was nothing else on this road, except the burn unit. The crew had to be going to the hospital. She decided to flip a bitch and go in search of what was going on. It was unusual, she thought, for a news crew to go to a burn unit. Especially with what just happened. Becky didn't believe in coincidence. Everything happened how it happened.

When the police car came to the main intersection, Officer Richardson drove straight instead of turning toward town. Jim noticed the miscue immediately. "Where are we going?"

The cop scowled at Jim in the rearview mirror. "You talk when asked a question boy! Until then, I suggest you shut the fuck up."

Jim almost laughed at the actions of the cop. The guy was maybe forty years old and calling his elder, 'boy'. He didn't want to make the situation worse for himself, so he held his laughter inside: However, he never was one to restrain his words. Now would be no different. "I don't know why you're treating me like this officer. I did nothing wrong. You can just let me go and we'll forget about it. I'm still in my hospital gown for god's sake." Jim spoke with sincerity and calmness. He wasn't angry at the situation but was swiftly becoming tired of the way he was being treated.

"You did plenty wrong, asshole. You killed four innocent boys behind a convenience store. We did our police work and know it was you. Now you're going to pay for what you've done."

"I didn't kill anyone," Jim said in defense. "I've been in a coma for two months and before that, I was traveling. I have people who will testify to that."

"I watched the tape personally. We couldn't see your face, but it was you. You were smoking a cigar, the cashier said, and we put the pieces together. You were the only one buying a cigar from that shop, which is across the street. She also told us about your tattoos, and your cancer. Not too many people with a body suit, asshole. I don't know how you took out four healthy young boys, but there's no doubt who the perpetrator was. Now shut the fuck up before I pull over and shut you up."

Jim knew he was in trouble with this cop. The tone of his voice told the prisoner everything he needed to know. The officer was insane. He thought he was above the law and was prepared to take justice into his own hands. Jim met plenty of cops like this one in his life. Some of these guys would put on a badge and their entire being became hard-ass. Their entire reasoning to become a cop was to harass and bully people. Whatever the reason for this guy's behavior, Jim knew his life was in danger.

Becky pulled up alongside the news van as its occupants were getting out. She rolled down the window and asked the lady holding a microphone if they were looking for Jim. The newsperson looked confused for a moment before checking her notes. "Yes, we are. Do you know him?"

"He's my Uncle. However, you're too late. The police were just here, and they arrested him. That head nurse lady in there tried to attack him and he struck her in self-defense. The cops arrived; it was the nurse's brother. The dude took my Uncle away."

"They came here and arrested him for that? At this hospital?"

"Yeah," Becky replied. "She wouldn't let him go outside at first but when the doctor got involved, she had no choice. We came out here and ate some burgers and smoked a joint; we both have our prescriptions. The nurse lady came storming out here and hit my Uncle. She tried to slap him four more times; finally, he socked her a good one. The cops were here in minutes and arrested him."

"Do you have any proof of this?" The cameras were set up now and the entire crew were listening to the crazy story unfolding.

"I videotaped the entire thing on my cell phone, but Officer Richardson took it and smashed it. It's right over there," Becky said while pointing to the wreckage five parking stalls away. "That stupid fuck didn't realize I sent my mother the first half of the tape and live-streamed the second part. He destroyed my phone but not the evidence. That guy just broke so many laws and I'm going to make sure he pays for everything he's done."

"We're going to help you do just that," the reporter said. "It sounds like there's something really strange going on here. Come on guys," she waved to her camera crew, "let's get this woman's story. This is going to be on the evening news for sure. First thing: get a clip of that broken phone over there." The reporter sprang into action. She was passionate about her job and realized she just came across a great story.

The road the cop drove on turned from asphalt, to gravel, then to dirt. Jim was aware they drove a long distance into the forest. They didn't pass a single car or house in miles. He knew he better start preparing now. He was going to have a fight for his life when arriving, wherever it was they were going. This cop had a death warrant for Jim and was going to be happy to serve it.

When the car finally stopped, it was in a small clearing. Jim saw there was a hole dug on one side of it. At this time of the year in this part of California, everything was green but only centimeters tall. It was a time when the roots got strong in preparation for the hot summers. It was also the only time when the ground was soft enough to dig a grave.

Richardson got out of the car and yanked Jim's door open. He grabbed the man by his arm and pulled him so hard out of the backseat, he fell to the ground. "Hey man, there's no need for this kind of behavior. I came with you peacefully. I'm sorry I hit your sister. She was going crazy on me. I had to defend myself."

"It has nothing to do with my sister, asshole. You see, those four boys you killed, they worked for me. One of them was my nephew.

He was the son of the nurse you just hit, dumb-ass. She knew all along that you killed her boy. She's been pissing in your food for months."

"I swear to you I didn't kill anyone. I wasn't even here when that happened. My brother confessed to me on his death-bed; it was him who killed the four. They were robbing him. One of them tried to harm him and he got the upper hand. My brother wasn't a violent man. He was just protecting himself."

The cop pulled his gun and pointed it at Jim's head. "Get on your feet, asshole. I'm tired of your shit. You can save all your excuses and tell them to the devil when you get to hell. You killed four good boys. They were hard workers. They sold my drugs and robbed people. We all shared the profits and I made sure they kept out of trouble: until you came along. Now, out of respect for their families, I'm going to give you the same treatment."

It was difficult for Jim to get on his feet with his hands behind his back. He rolled to the side a bit but was careful not to let the cop see his back. He'd broken his thumb, years ago, and it never healed right. He could easily pop the joint in and out of socket. He did this, while in the car, to relieve his wrist of the handcuff. Officer Richardson didn't know but Jim was free of his shackles. He gripped the open end of the torture device and held it ready, as a weapon.

After Becky was interviewed in the parking lot, the news crew headed to the burn unit. After the story they just heard, there was no way they were going to pass up on this opportunity. They walked in the front door and followed the sign to the nurse's station.

Nurse Tatum was the first to speak up when she saw the reporter. Her face lit up with the prospect of getting a bit of fame or money. She rushed to the camera and was fixing her hair when the reporter introduced herself.

Becky remained outside, at the request of the newswoman. She said she would get a much better interview if the nurse didn't know what was going on. Becky agreed. She didn't obey though. She didn't wait outside. She had a bad feeling her Uncle Jim really needed her right now. She was getting a premonition warning her: he was in serious trouble. She got in her car and again got on the road. This time, her pace wasn't so slow. She was almost frantic as she drove over a hundred miles an hour to the main road.

When she got there, she looked to both directions. Neither seemed like the right way to go. Something called her from the road straight ahead. An invisible force was pulling her in the direction. This was the way, she knew it in her heart.

Officer Richardson grew tired of waiting for the cuffed man to get up. He grabbed Jim by the shoulder and forcefully pulled him toward his awaiting grave. The cop had a few of these graves dug out in these parts, at the waiting. You never knew when you would need to bury someone, or something, he reasoned.

When they were about three feet from the hole, Jim made his move. He was planning it, all along, and saw his opportunity. The overweight cop was tired from dragging the man. He was complacent in his regard for the helpless prisoner. Jim came up on his bare knees in a swift move. In the same motion, he swung his hand as fast as possible right at the cop's neck. The real criminal didn't know what hit him. Jim caught him right in his jugular vein with the open end of the hand-cuff. A stream of blood poured from the puncture through the officer's clenching hands.

Jim kept eye contact as he saw the panic in the other man's face. The cop knew his fate. There was nothing he could do but accept his calling. Jim's face was emotionless as he watched the younger man dying. He was one to have empathy for other humans, but in this regard, there was only apathy.

The sound of a car broke Jim's gaze of the condemned. He looked to his left and saw Becky pulling into the clearing. Her car came to a sliding stop in the dirt. She had a look of emergency on her face. Jim understood. The two were connected. She felt his vibes and came to help. Luckily, she was too late. If she would have arrived seconds earlier, things may not have worked out the same.

Becky saw the scene in front of her the moment she pulled up. She saw the dying cop on the ground bleeding out. She saw her Uncle, covered in blood, but could tell he wasn't wounded. The look on his face told his niece; he just killed a man. Shock and disgust were written all over Uncle Jim's expression.

It wasn't until she got out of the car when she saw the danger.

The cop, with his last dying moment, pulled his gun from its holster. With unsteady arms, he took aim and shot. When Jim turned to look at what Becky was seeing, he got caught with the bullet at close range. The slug hit him square in the chest, instantly staining his hospital gown. He flew back about five feet and hit the ground with a thud.

Becky was by his side in an instant. She looked briefly to the cop but could see that he dropped the gun from the kick-back. His face was grey. He tried, unsuccessfully, to mouth a few final words. Becky knew he only had moments left. She didn't care what the man who shot her uncle had to say. She raced to Jim's side and grabbed his bloody hand.

She looked into her uncle's eyes and held his hand. The dying man was gasping for breath. Black blood was bubbling out of the chest wound with every intake. Becky knew her Uncle Jim only had moments himself. The look in his eye, however, told Becky everything was okay. He was going home now. Soon, her uncle would be back with his brother and other family. She was happy for him in a strange kind of way.

Becky saw the madness of this planet for a very long time. It wasn't the Earth which was the problem, it was the humans. She wanted to be with her people and nobody else. Just like the scene in front of her, humans had a knack of fucking everything up. This was the final straw she could deal with from this species. She'd always given people the benefit of the doubt but from this moment on, she would hold a distrust for everyone except her family.

Jim was mouthing something, but it was almost inaudible. Becky got as close to his ear as possible and listened to the dying words. "One," was what her uncle repeated. She knew the meaning of this. Their family, together, was one. Everything, together, was One. As she comforted her uncle's flesh pod in its last moments, Becky felt as if Wisdom were passing through him into her. She was feeling a rush of knowledge; knowing it was coming from her trusted friend.

When Jim died, he simply went away. Becky felt his energy leave the pod and dissipate into the crisp winter air. There were no bells or whistles, he just ceased to be there. Now, he was where he truly belonged.

Becky shed a single tear. She knew all was better. Jim was going to a better place. It was only sad for the living, knowing they would have to be without him in this existence. It was selfish, Becky thought, as she wiped her tear away.

The numbers lined up and took her uncle this day. Like every other event, the numbers made it happen. The binary, once again, had its way. It's what controlled the universe. Becky understood it all. With Jim's knowledge, everything was clear.

For Jim, it was awesome! He could finally take the trip he was ready for. His lifetime was a good one, now it was death's time.

This whole existence for him was a good one. He lived it to the fullest. He was with his people and used his time to create. However, like every life, once you remembered what was beyond, you would want to go back there. It's difficult to stay on an over-populated planet after you've been to paradise. He remembered everything with the assistance of the hallucinogens and the company of his brother. He saw what was beyond and was ready to shed this existence.

Everything worked out the way it was meant to be.

As Jim crossed through the cosmos, his existence was free. He left his pod completely behind, like garbage he no longer needed.

Jim died.

Now he could live.

The trip began.

ABOUT THE AUTHOR

Sol Gatos is a creator, writer, painter and tattooer. Hailing from Mountain Ranch California, this global citizen knows the value of the imagination. For more information, check-out: Solgatos.org